A CALL TO CHINA

A CALL TO CHINA

JEFFREY F. MEYER

IngramElliott

Published by IngramElliott, Inc.
www.ingramelliott.com
9815 J Sam Furr Road, Suite 271, Huntersville NC 28078

Book design by Maureen Cutajar, gopublished.com
Cover design by H.O. Charles

Publisher's Cataloging-In-Publication Data
(Prepared by The Donohue Group, Inc.)

Names: Meyer, Jeffrey F.
Title: A call to China / Jeffrey F. Meyer.

Description: [Huntersville, North Carolina] : IngramElliott, [2017]
Identifiers: LCCN 2016952475 | ISBN 978-0-9966864-7-1 (hardcover) | ISBN 0-9966864-7-9 (hardcover) | ISBN 978-0-9966864-8-8 (paperback) | ISBN 0-9966864-8-7 (paperback) | ISBN 978-0-9966864-9-5 (ebook) | ISBN 0-9966864-9-5 (ebook)
Subjects: LCSH: Sisters--Fiction. | Missing persons--China--History--20th century--Fiction. | Coming of age--Fiction. | Missionaries--China--History--20th century--Fiction. | Spiritual life--Fiction. | China--History--20th century--Fiction. | LCGFT: Domestic fiction. | Religious fiction.
Classification: LCC PS3613.E94 C35 2017 (print) | LCC PS3613.E94 (ebook) | DDC 813/.6--dc23

Published in the United States of America. Printed in the United States of America
First Edition: 2017, First International Edition: 2017

Acknowledgments

Many friends and colleagues had a hand in the making of this novel and I wish to thank them, principally Kim Wright and my Brinkers writing group, especially Ed McKeown, Jim Drew, and Melissa Cady, who worked with me for over a year to improve the book, chapter by chapter. I am grateful to many others who commented on earlier versions of the novel, and offered helpful suggestions, especially Susan Gardner, Janna Shedd, and Jonathan Meyer. Thanks to the artistic hand of Elizabeth Liu, who provided the beautiful calligraphy for the book. And finally, thanks to my brave publishers at IngramElliott, who took the risk and encouraged me to bring this novel to print.

Author's Note

In 1990, my wife and I adopted a daughter in China. That event, after many years of scholarly writing in the field, helped me realize that my connection to China was not just a matter of academic interest, but was a love affair that wanted expression. It was many years in coming, but this novel is the outcome of that realization.

This is a work of fiction, but I have tried to set the story in an accurate historical context—the tragedies and triumphs of twentieth-century China. The Boxer Rebellion, the May Fourth Movement, the Japanese occupation, the Communist Revolution, the Great Cultural Revolution, the opening under Deng Xiaoping—these are all key moments in China's history during the years between 1900 and 1985 when the novel ends. Deng, Mao Zedong, Chiang K'ai-shek, Chiang Ching-kuo, Yuan Shikai, and others are of course key figures in that tumultuous century. Except for such major historical figures, all the characters in the story, Chinese and American, are fictional. Major locations like Beijing, Weixian, Datong, Beijing Normal University, the White Cloud Temple, the caves at Yungang, the mountains and monasteries of Wutaishan, are real. The nunnery Yindong An, the towns of Old Stonebridge and Baita village, are fictional.

A word on Chinese words and names. I have used the Wade-Giles system to transliterate place names in Taiwan and in China before 1950, the Pinyin system for China thereafter. But to avoid confusion, I have used the current Pinyin name Beijing for the Chinese capital throughout the novel, though the city was called Peking and Pei-p'ing at different times earlier in the twentieth century.

For ease of transition, Chinese titles are provided for those chapters which are set in China and Taiwan.

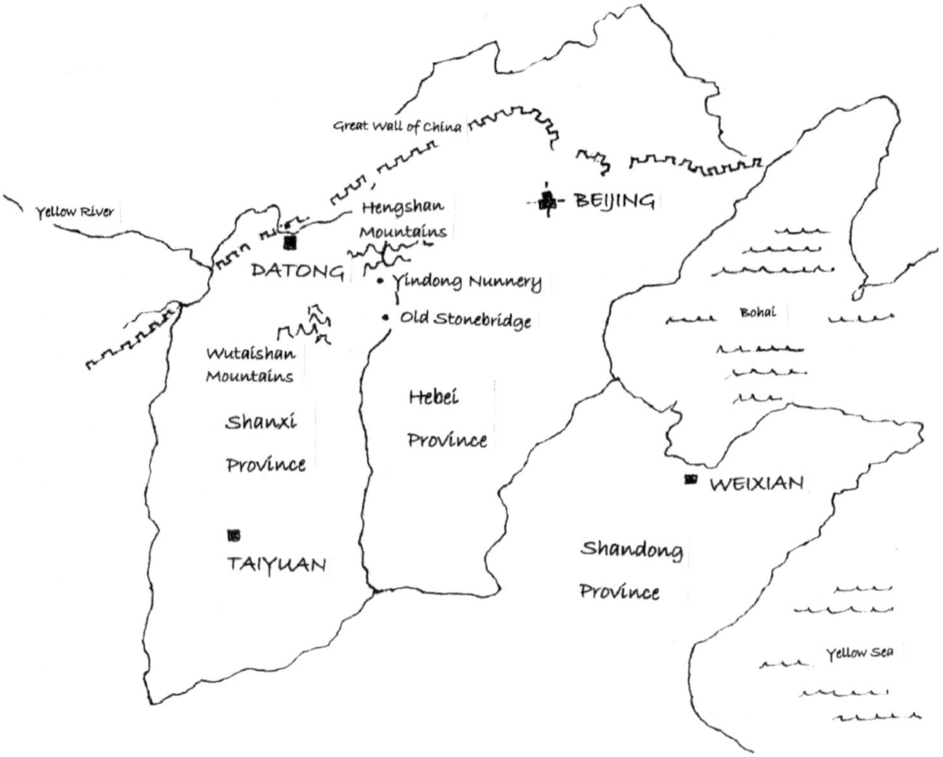
Great Wall of China
Yellow River
Hengshan
Mountains
BEIJING
DATONG
Yindong Nunnery
Old Stonebridge
Wutaishan
Mountains
Shanxi
Province
Hebei
Province
Bohai
WEIXIAN
TAIYUAN
Shandong
Province
Yellow Sea

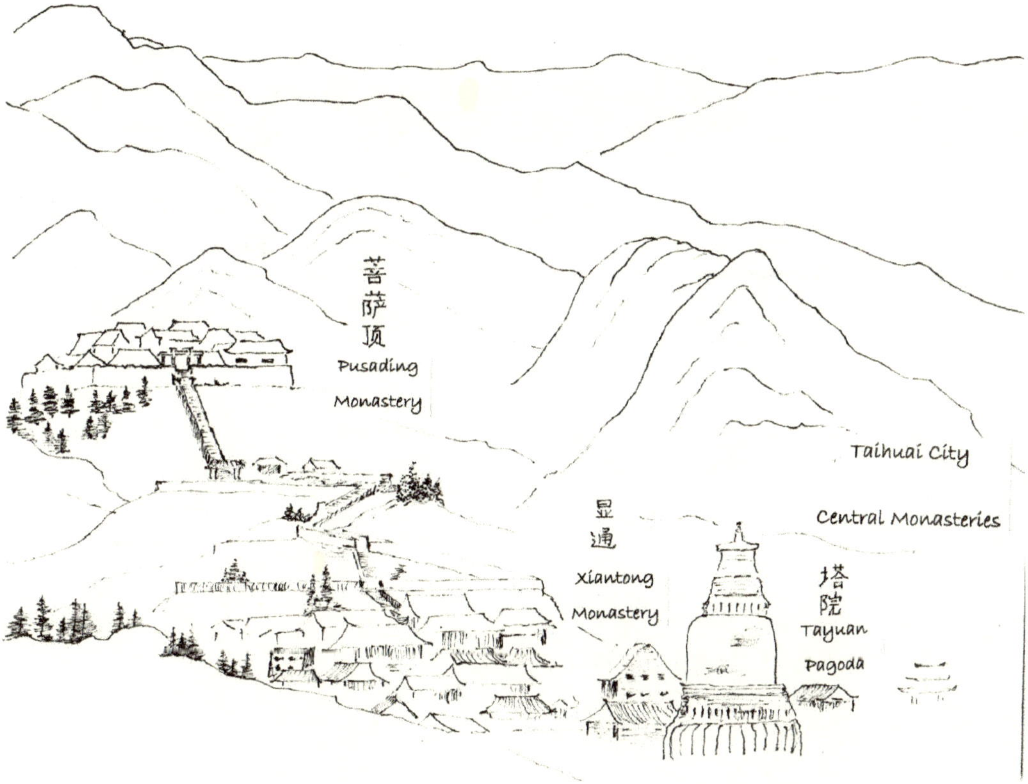
菩薩顶
Pusading
Monastery
Taihuai City
Central Monasteries
显通
Xiantong
Monastery
塔院
Tayuan
Pagoda

北台
Northern Terrace
中台
Central Terrace
西台
Western Terrace
東台
Eastern Terrace
Datong
Taihui City
Wenshu Cave
Huayen Cave
Guanyin Cave
五台山
Wutaishan
Five Terrace Mountains
Taiyuan
南台
Southern Terrace

事由天定

PARENTHESIS: 1940–1985

Things Determined by Heaven

Beijing. Winter 1940.

They were a secret sect, calling themselves the FourOne Society. Heiyen and Guzhi, their leaders, had summoned some members with special skills to meet at the Hundred Fragrances noodle shop, which stood in a row of dilapidated stores near the southwest corner of Beijing's massive city wall. Heiyen had chosen the location carefully, one close to the White Cloud Daoist Temple.

Outside, the cold had cut through their padded jackets like a sharp knife. Indoors, it was still warm from the evening's cooking, and scents of fried garlic, ginger, and star anise hung in the air, familiar and comforting. Under the counters and cabinets, hungry mice sniffed at bits of food dropped on the floor, and behind them, in the darkest corners of the kitchen, cockroaches waited for the human intruders to complete their business and leave.

The owner of the eatery bowed slightly to each member of the sect as they entered the shop, offering a tumbler of flower tea to warm their bellies. They took their places at a battered wood table, five men on one side, four women on the other, sipping their tea but not speaking.

Heiyen nodded to Guzhi, who recited the syllables of a mantra, the others repeating it three times. Then, after a brief pause, Heiyen said, "Brothers and sisters, the spirits have spoken to us clearly. Now we must put aside our fears and act."

The group stared at him, boggled. Finally, Guzhi spoke up, her voice trembling: "To seize the American child is madness!" She was coleader of the FourOnes, their trusted medium, who entered into deep trances and brought messages from the spirits. "Even if we can lay hands on her," she continued, "how are we to escape with the child? We will have to flee to the borderlands and hide with the Mongols."

Though she brought the words of the spirits, when her trances ended she was often troubled with doubts. "Did I say that? What could that mean?" The other members did not seem troubled by her outburst. They had witnessed this dance of yin and yang between their leaders many times, and trusted that through the interplay of the two, wisdom would emerge and all would be well.

"It is not without risk," admitted Heiyen mildly, "but when the spirits speak, we humans must obey—you yourself brought the message. Now we must do what they have commanded."

Guzhi tempered her objection. "But when and where? How shall we know? The spirits never concern themselves with such details, do they?"

"Our informers, by the Presbyterian mission, will report the family's comings and goings. When opportunity arises, we will act." The rest of the group nodded their heads gravely.

"The pastor, the girl's father," said Guzhi, "is a big and powerful man. What is your plan to handle him?"

Heiyen did not answer immediately but waited, as though allowing the others to think it through for themselves. Then he spoke. "As the Old Master has taught us: weakness over strength, yin over yang, female over male, soft over hard." He paused before continuing, the others expectant. "We will not match strength with strength, but with weakness."

The following week, on the opposite side of the city to the east of Chaoyang Gate, Old Zhang, the rickshaw man, came home at dusk with good news. "Binji," he said to his wife, "make me a nourishing meal tomorrow. These old bones will need all their strength. My nephew, Lin Kaiyuan, is driving the American missionaries to White Cloud Temple for the festival, and they need me to drive the other pedicab. My old legs will ache like a rotten tooth, but—ha!—the Americans are rich and will pay us well."

Binji fed Old Zhang his *miantang*. He slurped it eagerly until the last noodle disappeared between his lips. His stomach filled and body warmed, Zhang's chin fell to his chest, and he began to snore. Binji slipped out the door and went off to find matchmaker Gao.

"Auntie Gao," she said, "I have some news for you. Day after tomorrow, in the evening, the Americans are going to White Cloud Temple for the festival. My old man and Lin Kaiyuan will pick them up in the late afternoon."

The matchmaker, who knew everyone's business in the Flower Market Street neighborhood, smiled, nodded, and reached into her pocketbook. Her gnarled fingers pinched a yuan coin and pressed it into Binji's palm, knowing that Heiyen would reward her five for one. "Make your famous marrow soup. Your old man will need strong legs for the journey."

The spirits had spoken, and Heiyen felt assured of their help. Had they not guided the missionaries to White Cloud Temple? Yet he also knew he would have to design a shrewd plan if they were to succeed. They would need perfect coordination, when all around them was chaos. The success of his plan depended on the clever use of that chaos. He gathered the materials they required: a large wooden box with a tight-fitting lid, strings of firecrackers, a heavy blanket, wooden staves, a ball of soft cloth, and a donkey cart to haul the box.

Heiyen drilled everyone on their assignments. They knew that the Americans would have to cross the great square in front of the temple. They would plunge into a noisy crowd of worshipers, revelers, vendors, acrobats, puppeteers, touts, and pickpockets. Strategically placed, members would mingle in the crowds. And hidden among them, almost invisible, would be the key to their success, their most helpless member.

Wutaishan. Bodhisattva Hill. 1985.

The nun continued to finger the rosary as she spoke, one bead after another slipping between her thumb and forefinger. "When we first talked, you asked me what happened that night at White Cloud Temple. I was reluctant to talk about it, since the followers of the Dharma should not dwell on the past. But my progress in the Buddha's way is not as great as I had hoped. I will tell you what I remember.

"As you know, my name at that time was Chen Bailian. I was amah and cook at the mission. It was bitter cold that evening, right after the Lantern Festival, the nineteenth of the first month, the day when the Immortal comes down from Heaven and mingles with the people at White Cloud. We wrapped ourselves in padded jackets and scarves. Only our eyes and noses were exposed to the cold air. It was hard to breathe with the smoke from all the charcoal fires. Your father didn't want to go, and Meimei was in a terrible state, poor little thing. I had given her a talisman to wear around her neck for protection, and she had forgotten to bring it. Your mother—we called her Taitai in those days—tried to comfort her. I had told Taitai about the Immortal, and she was intrigued. We called your father by his Christian title, Wei Mushi, 'Pastor Wei'—his name, Harold Wayman, was too hard for us to say. I was so young then, and I gloried in my power to influence the family I worked for. But I have learned in my long life that you must be careful when you seek to bend events to your own advantage.

"Taitai had argued with Pastor Wei the night before. I heard their raised voices and crept under the paper window outside their bedroom to listen. I could not understand everything they said, but what I did understand struck my flesh like a pinprick. I did not like it. Pastor called the festival a ragbag of superstitions. I remember those words. Taitai wanted to go for the sake of your sister. Poor thing, a foreign girl, no one to play with except me, and no proper school to attend. Those were the years of the Japanese occupation of Beijing. Most of the Europeans and Americans were fleeing the city like vermin from a burning house, but Pastor Wei was determined to stay. I will say that your father was very courageous. And it was my fault they argued that night. I told Taitai how exciting the festival would be. I talked about the food and games, acrobats and mummers . . . and the chance to meet the Immortal.

"We rode across Beijing in two pedicabs, along Flower Market Street, Brass Street, Lantern Street, Liulichang, past Xuanwu Gate, east to west until we reached White Cloud, just outside the western wall. Old Zhang drove your father and little Meimei in one pedicab. Taitai and I rode in the other. It was driven by Lin Kaiyuan, Pastor Wei's number-one boy. He was handsome . . . well, not exactly, but he had a wonderful round face. When he smiled, the smile was in his eyes, not just his mouth, and you could tell he was sincere. Even in those days I knew I did not want to marry, but if my father forced me to do so, I thought that Kaiyuan would treat me kindly. But that was not to be."

The nun paused in her account, rubbing her eyes and massaging her temples as though to ease the discomfort in her mind. "I thought I had let go of these memories but I was deceiving myself. I remember even the Christian hymns Pastor taught us. Why is it that it is so much easier to remember songs than mere words? 'Praise God from whom all blessings flow . . .'" She sang the words in English, shyly, in a thin, faltering voice. "You know that one. I can still sing the whole hymn." The nun stopped for a moment and laughed ever so slightly. "Strange that a follower of the Dharma would have that hymn still lurking in her head! But to return to my story. What happened that night changed everything in my life, it changed everything for your family. Whether for good or ill, I cannot say. Only Heaven knows.

"As we came near White Cloud, you could hear the noise of the crowd getting louder. Kaiyuan and Old Zhang drove us to the great square in front of it, between the *pailou* and the temple's main gate. Crowds of people pressed up against the pedicabs. We could hardly dismount, the throng so dense you could hardly reach down and scratch your bottom. Someone knocked off Meimei's hat, and when people saw her copper-colored hair they reached out to touch it—they who had seen, for their whole lives, only black-haired children. They thought she was a miracle child, eyes green as Lake Tai, and her complexion so white you could see the blue veins pulsing behind the skin of her forehead. She looked delicate, but her spirit was very strong.

"Pastor Wei lifted her up and swung her onto his shoulders and headed toward the big gate. I knew he did not want to be there. Taitai and I followed as best we could, but he was pushing ahead so fast that we could barely keep up with him. He strode right past all the things people usually come to the fair to enjoy: the tea and fruit juices, sweets, roasted yams and sesame buns, candied crab apples, and roasted scorpions. Pastor was like a monk, immune to the cravings of the flesh. He ignored the food and drink, the jugglers and acrobats, actors and magicians. He was not frightened by the white-faced ghosts on stilts. Inside the main gate he lifted Meimei off his shoulders and placed her on the ground. She saw a crowd by the left side of the inner gate, waiting to rub the stone monkey's black belly, which gives you luck for the year. Meimei wanted to rub it, too, but Pastor Wei made an ugly face, shook his head, swung her up on his shoulders again, and continued on into the next courtyard. Taitai was upset with him. 'This is just harmless fun,' she said, shaking her head at him.

"We followed your father, walking from one courtyard to the next. But the deeper we went into the temple's inner courtyards, the fewer people we met, and those who were there had come for religious purposes. They burned incense before the Immortals and prayed for blessings. As the crowds thinned, Pastor Wei began to relax and put Meimei down again. I looked back to the gate and saw a man enter. I'd noticed him before, which frightened me, so I took hold of Meimei's hand.

"As we came to the main door of the Temple of the Eight Immortals, I bent down and whispered in her ear that this was the night when the Immortal Qiu Chuji comes to earth. If you recognize him, I said, you can become an immortal, too. I told her that he had built this temple almost a thousand years ago and was so famous that the Great Khan had summoned him to come teach in his court. Maybe Meimei didn't understand my words, but she asked me what the Immortal looked like. I pointed to a painting on the wall, of an old man with long white hair and beard. He stood at the side of a bald monk, before the throne of the emperor. There he is, I told her, but I warned her that he wouldn't look the same if he came that night. He would take on a different body. 'It might be that of an old woman, a beggar, a fat priest . . . or a cripple. Who knows? Someone unlikely. You must search earnestly for him,' I told her, 'beyond appearances.'

"'How will I know him?' Meimei asked. 'You will know,' I answered. Oh, I was foolish then, a stupid gourd. I regret the words I spoke that night, but I myself was only sixteen years old. Pastor Wei was looking at me suspiciously. He knew that I was whispering more 'superstitions' to his daughter.

"'We've come as far as we can. Beyond is the dormitory of the Daoist monks,' Pastor Wei said. He decided that we must return to the square and find the pedicabs. He promised to buy us all roasted yams to eat as we rode home, and Meimei clapped her hands happily. But that was not to be.

"When we got back to the square it was even more crowded than before. You could barely move. Strings of firecrackers were exploding all around us. Pastor shouted at me to hold on to Meimei's hand and once again he strode off, leading us toward the other side of the square. He was the sort who barged ahead and expected others to follow. I struggled to keep up with him but in my haste I tripped on something—I think it was someone's staff—and I fell to the ground. I was afraid of being trampled and as I struggled to get to my feet she yanked her hand from my grip. 'I see him,' she cried, 'I see him.' Then she was gone.

"At first I did not know what she meant, but then I knew. The Immortal . . . there was an explosion of firecrackers, right near us. I shouted to Pastor Wei and Taitai, 'Meimei's gone!' We screamed out her name. With his big preacher's voice Pastor Wei cried out her English name 'Victoria! Victoria!' His loud voice rolled out above the noise of the crowd but it was swallowed up in the explosions. We heard no answering cry. We pushed our way through a thicket of flailing arms and padded jackets. We could hardly move. Meimei must have scampered through the legs of those people like a wild creature running through the underbrush, but we adults could not follow.

"Suddenly a space opened in front of us. In the middle of the space, down low near the ground, I saw Genghis Khan, his Mongol face large and flat, his eyes shining like polished black stones, his expression fierce. His powerful chest thick as the flank of an ox. His presence frightened me . . . but he had no legs. His stumps were strapped to a board with swiveling wheels. With a contemptuous look on his face, he turned, and using his massive arms and chest, propelled himself away. The crowd recoiled and let him pass, as though making way for a god.

"Then I knew what had happened. Among this throng of people there were those who thought the legless man was the Immortal. And I knew I would never dare tell pastor what I had whispered to Meimei—that he could appear in the form of a cripple.

"Perhaps the legless man was Qiu Chuji. I do not know. I can only say that Meimei disappeared and we never saw her again. I learned something that night, sad but true. We humans must submit to the workings of karma and the dispensations of Heaven."

This event, recounted by the nun in 1985, took place in the year *gengchen*, on the nineteenth day of the first month of the lunar calendar, the year of the dragon. It was February 27, 1940, according to the Western calendar. The police came and questioned people all over the square, but no one had seen the child. The parents stood by helplessly as the police officers investigated in the din and confusion. It was hopeless.

Several hours later, the festive noises gradually diminished and the crowds began to disperse. Late in the night, darkness and quiet settled on the empty square before White Cloud Temple, and despair seeped into the parents' hearts. The police had left, promising to resume their search the next day.

"There is nothing more we can do," the pastor said, his voice dead with fatigue. He took his wife's hand, but she pulled away from him, running into one of the alleys that led off the square. He followed helplessly. "Victoria, Victoria," she croaked, her voice already weak and ragged from shouting her daughter's name so many times before, first to the noisy crowd then to the empty square. She tried other alleys, but all were empty, blank walls of brick, stone, and plaster, broken only by the wooden doors that were locked for the night. Her words echoed in the empty street, then died.

"Use that big voice of yours," she raged at Harold. "If you hadn't been in such a rush . . ." When he tried to take her hand again, she jerked it away. "I won't leave until we find her."

Still later, with a glimmer of light in the east, the two pedicabs began their journey back to the Presbyterian mission on Flower Market Street. Taitai sat hunched forward on the seat, her face in her hands, sobbing. The pastor, with his arm over her shoulder, sat upright, looking straight ahead. The amah rode alone in Old Zhang's pedicab, frightened by the thought of what she had done. Even with the lighter load, Old Zhang's legs ached as he struggled to keep pace with Kaiyuan. Cold and stiff from the hours of inactivity, he dreamed of a bowl of soup and the warm bed Binji would have ready for him.

As the pedicabs headed eastward, back toward the mission, another group of people proceeded in the opposite direction, toward the countryside west of Beijing. A donkey cart with iron-rimmed wheels bumped along in the potholes and over the ruts of frozen mud in the street, its progress slow but steady. The driver was a man. Four other men walked alongside, and riding in the cart, with a large wooden box, were four women and a man without legs.

PART

1

THE MISSION FAMILY

四海皆兄弟

CHAPTER 1

All Men Are Brothers

The Amah. Beijing. 1940.

Bailian awoke before dawn, but did not get up immediately, enjoying the warmth under her quilt. It was a month after the disaster at White Cloud Temple, the despair at the mission heightened by winter darkness and persistently cold weather. The old calendar called this two-week period the time of "stirring insects," when the first small signs of spring appeared, bringing hopes that it would soon get warm. Each year she looked for the swelling of tiny buds, the emergence of insects from their homes in the soil, the songs of returning birds, but she never found them this early. Here in Beijing, the earth remained frozen like a slab of stone. Maybe, she thought, the calendar was devised farther south in China, where the crickets chirped and frogs croaked earlier. She searched her heart for some trace of hope, but did not find it.

After a few more minutes under her quilt, she threw it off, swung her legs over the edge of the cot, and slipped her stocking feet into hemp sandals. She sat for a moment, perfectly still, breathing deeply ten times, as Nainai had taught her. "Do this every day and you will be a healthy child." Her grandmother was full of such instructions. As she was inhaling and saying to herself, "Nine," she was startled by a loud squawk from outside the wall. It was probably a magpie, a bird whose feathers were black and white in equal proportions. The magpie's call was unlucky so early in the morning before the dark had lifted. Nainai had said so. It was a warning, she thought, that her days here at the Presbyterian mission were coming to an end.

Sometimes her American employers were a complete mystery to her; at other times they were quite normal, just like Chinese people. She remembered the saying, "Within the four seas, all men are brothers," and thought hopefully: *We are all of one family.*

When Meimei disappeared, she was not surprised by the reactions of Pastor Wei and Taitai. They rushed around in the crowd, pushing and shoving bystanders, frantic with worry. But their words were eaten by the thunder of firecrackers. They angrily berated the police, just as her own parents would have done, especially if the child were a boy, "a great blessing." In Bailian's own family, she was the eldest of three "small blessings."

As the days passed, she heard Pastor Wei again and again complain about the incompetence of the Chinese police. But that was not fair—even her father said so. The Japanese army now occupied Beijing and did not like the Chinese constables questioning people all around, just to track down a foreign child. Their task was simply to keep order on the streets while the Japanese troops watched for any movements that might threaten their control of the city.

Bailian combed and pinned up her long black hair. She missed Meimei and the games they had devised together and played in the protected space of the mission courtyard. She missed teaching her Chinese, for the child was so quick to remember words. Bailian would point to the chrysanthemums in the pot by the side of the chapel door and say, "*Mudan.*" Meimei would repeat "mudan" and remember it from then on. She was so bright.

Bailian leaned forward and saw a fractured image of herself in the cracked mirror propped up on her chest of drawers. Meimei had been careless and broken that mirror. Taitai fussed at her, picking up the pieces and throwing them into the dusty garbage bin. When no one was looking, Bailian pulled out the largest piece of the shattered glass. Now she tilted her head so that she could see her whole face reflected in the shard. She was not beautiful, yet young and attractive enough, she thought, to draw the glance of a man. But that thought did not please her.

Bailian left the room and walked directly across the courtyard toward the kitchen. A dusting of snow had fallen during the night so she left tracks in the powdery white snowflakes that covered the ground. When she reached the kitchen and touched the ceramic tile of the *kang*, she found some warmth remaining from last night's fire. The kang was the largest object in a kitchen, a tile-covered stove about chest high and big enough to sleep on. A wonderful invention, yet the Americans refused to make use of it. You could put a quilt on it and sleep in comfort all night, even in the coldest winter, yet pastor and Taitai had insisted on staying in their private room at the back of the courtyard where it was always dark and cold. She couldn't understand it, but that was their way.

The kang's warmth made the kitchen a cozy place to begin her work on a winter's day. Bailian focused her thoughts on cooking, refusing to think about her former job as amah. She struck a match and lighted the gas boiler over in the corner, then took some glowing coals from the iron door at the bottom of the kang and placed them in the cooking stove. When she added some lumps of soft coal and fanned them, wisps of smoke rose from cracks in the stove. She would need it hot to make congee of last evening's rice. A plate of roasted peanuts and another of pickled vegetables, together with the congee, would make a good breakfast.

Bailian heard the boiler gurgle. She took a large kettle and filled it from the spigot at the bottom of the boiler tank, then placed it on the stove, hot from the coal fire. She thought of the kitchen as the center of the home, and the stove the center of the kitchen. The old folks believed that the kitchen god made a report every New Year to the Jade Emperor of Heaven, on household doings of the previous year. They left sweet foods as an offering for him on a small altar by the stove, so that the words in his report would be sweet ones, a little bribe. The kitchen god's name was Zaojun. He was handicapped in this home because they didn't use the kang for sleeping. How could he know what they were doing in the bedroom, closed and locked over on the north side of the house? How could Zaojun make an accurate report to the Jade Emperor? Pastor Wei would say that all of these beliefs were superstitious.

Bailian walked out from the kitchen. Now it was getting light, and, though the sky was gray, the snow covering brightened the courtyard. She could see the imprint of her footsteps where she had walked from her room to the kitchen. She walked on a tangent from that first path, south toward the main gate of the compound. She realized she was writing, with her feet, a huge character that covered the whole courtyard, the simple but important *ren*, which meant "a person." Was it by chance that her feet wrote *person* just as she herself was really becoming a person, distinct from her mother and father and her sisters? From the time when her blood began its monthly flow she had had strange thoughts like that.

She stopped before the large wooden gate, sliding the crossbar to the right and hooking one door to an iron ring in the stone wall. She left the other door closed. The wooden door was painted bright red, as custom required. No Chinese family would have left it open and unattended so early in the day. But Pastor Wei had a prayer service every morning and wanted it open so that any worshipers who came would feel welcome. The door to the chapel opened on the east side of the compound, just beyond her own room. The walls were whitewashed, the floor was made of gray tiles, and there were wooden benches for those who came to pray. She liked the quiet of the chapel, its simplicity and tidiness. It was her responsibility to keep it swept and clean, which she did happily. Sometimes, after she was finished sweeping, she would sit on one of the benches and enjoy the silence of the room. There was a fullness there, not a dead empty space, like the presence you felt when you visited a temple.

Bailian stepped outside the gate and looked up and down the street. She saw the indistinct form of a person coming up the street from the west. Her stomach clenched, knowing from the slight limp that it was her father. He walked with his shoulders hunched forward. Ever since the disappearance of Meimei, he had been so furious that he barely spoke to her. She knew he had always wanted the best for her, but now he seemed a different and almost frightening person. Although her heart was beating hard, she stood her ground, offering him the morning greeting—"*Zao!*"—as he passed. He did not lift his eyes, but limped past her, entering under the sign that said *Presbyterian Mission* in Chinese characters and, underneath, *42 Flower Market Street*. He stopped a few feet inside and turned around. "This is your last day here. And it is your own fault, not Heaven's decree." He turned and walked toward the chapel.

Inside, it felt like a vise was squeezing her lungs. She had lost Meimei and failed as an amah. They would get someone else to cook and clean for them, and her family would have to find her a husband, a thought that took her to the edge of a cliff above the yellow waters of the underworld, dizzy with fright. She had known from the time when she first learned what it meant that she did not want to be married. It was a woman's destiny to wear herself out serving her husband, and even more, her husband's parents, like a slave in their household. A lifetime of grueling servitude. Bailian couldn't bear the idea of being married to a rickshaw puller, a brick maker, or a pig farmer. In that instant of carelessness at the temple fair she had failed not only herself, Pastor Wei, Taitai, and Meimei, but, worst of all, her own parents.

She went back through the gate and over to the kitchen. There was nothing she could do now but wait for what would happen, as you do when the days shorten in the fall and you know winter is coming. She had to immerse herself in the simple daily chores, paying full attention to every detail of her tasks, letting her mind be so absorbed in them that there would be no room for her forebodings. She set the tea cups, bowls, peanuts, and vegetables on the long wooden table in the room adjoining the kitchen. Enough settings for six people. There were never more, and on a cold morning like this there might be only three or four. The most regular were Wang Taitai and Chun Taitai. Bailian thought they were trying to impress Pastor Wei, competing to see who could be the most faithful Christian.

After her preparations were complete, she sat down on a stool near the stove. Across the courtyard in the chapel, she could hear Pastor Wei intoning the first hymn, the one he used to begin the service every morning. She knew it well and liked it, but since Meimei's disappearance, some of its words seemed like a rebuke.

Awake, my soul, and with the sun
The daily stage of duty run;
Shake off dull sloth, and joyful rise,
To pay thy morning sacrifice.
Thy precious time, misspent, redeem . . .

She liked the music. It made her think of a group of people marching bravely toward an important destination. She sang the words to herself, but her momentary confidence fled quickly. How could she bend back time and redeem herself?

She completed breakfast preparations, knowing that she should go to the chapel and join the small group, but the thought of being in the cold room so close to her father and Pastor Wei made her uncomfortable. They would read a passage from the Bible, pray, and perhaps her father would give a short homily in Chinese. The god they prayed to now seemed to her so lordly and remote. Bailian was not sure she believed in the stories about the kitchen god, but still it felt better to think that the guardian spirit of this warm stove knew and understood her heart. It had not been her fault. Meimei had jerked her hand away so quickly, without warning. The crowd was dense. And yet . . . if she had not intrigued Taitai with stories of the Daoist temple and its immortals, they would never have gone to the celebration. Zaojun peers into the sincere soul, she tried to convince herself. He would make a favorable report and the Jade Emperor would have pity on her and give her a new life.

The service was concluding. She joined them, singing to herself the final stanza of the same hymn, the verse Pastor Wei used to close each morning service.

Praise God from whom all blessings flow.
Praise Him all peoples here below.
Praise Him above, ye heavenly hosts.
Praise Father, Son, and Holy Ghost. Amen.

As she heard the music stop, she got up to add hot water to the congee and ladle it into a large white bowl. She stirred it, adding a bit of salt, knowing the right amount without having to measure it. Taking a cloth to protect her hands from the heat, she carried the steaming bowl into the breakfast room. She lifted the kettle and poured boiling water over the flower tea and took the teapot also, placing it on a bamboo trivet in the middle of the rough table next to the congee.

Four of the worshipers, all women, came into the room with Pastor Wei and sat down to breakfast. Her father had not come, but both Wang and Chun were among the four, as always. She heard Wang, whose husband had been killed by the Japanese, and who was childless, bragging that her newly born nephew was "fat as an imperial prince."

Partly out of respect for Pastor's loss, and partly from agonized embarrassment, the four women ate in silence. It had been like this for over two weeks. It was a quiet that did not feel good. Bailian was numb inside, remembering days past when Taitai and Meimei had brought so much laughter to the table. Taitai always tried to turn breakfast into a language class and often had them laughing at her mistakes, like pronouncing the word *ma* wrong so that it meant horse instead of mother. Meimei chattered with the guests in simple Chinese. Pastor Wei usually said little, self-conscious because of his lack of fluency. These last weeks, Taitai had not been coming to breakfast, and it seemed uncomfortable and solemn as they ate their food. She knew that the loss of Meimei had brought feelings of discord into this family, like dark clouds hanging in the air above them.

After breakfast was finished, the four women left, saying no more than the routine *"Zaijian"* as they walked quietly out of the breakfast room. That left Bailian alone with Pastor Wei. He cleared his throat, and began speaking in Chinese. She felt something choke inside her. She realized that he must have practiced what he was going to say because the words came out more smoothly than usual. "Bailian, come with me to the office. I have something to say to you." She followed him across the courtyard to the church office. He closed the door behind her.

姐姐

CHAPTER 2

Victoria

Shanxi Province. Spring 1940.

The group of four, wearing the drab clothes of Chinese peasants, had come to a remote area in the eastern reaches of the Hengshan Mountains. The day was overcast. They climbed the path, making their way upward through a thick forest of wind-blown pines and lichen-covered boulders. The woman Guzhi held the young one's hand, for the path was hazardous, especially where it followed a narrow ledge along the cliff face. At the narrowest places, someone had chiseled rough indentations into the rock that served as hand grips. "Don't look down," advised Heiyen, glancing back at the two women.

The men walked ahead. It was cold, and all had pulled their collars snugly around their necks. They wore straw hats, even the little girl, their faces indistinct in the shadows under the wide brims. The path was dirt and gravel, with carefully placed flagstone steps at the steepest ascents. The nuns had chosen this refuge well. It was located high in the rugged mountains of Shanxi near the border of Hebei, about 150 miles west of Beijing. Few people were even aware of its existence, since it was not a pilgrimage destination, but a small nunnery where religious women sought to practice their Buddhist disciplines in peace, cloistered from the ordinary world of farms and villages below them.

The last steps, near the summit, were made of larger stones, arranged like a flight of stairs, rising to an archway that bore a sign reading:

Yindong An, Nunnery of the Hidden Cave. The men reached the top first. One of them knocked on the wooden door, which was quickly opened, as though they were expected. A young woman whose head was shaved and who wore a gray robe greeted them silently and motioned for the four of them to enter.

"Yes, she will be safe here. But if we are to keep her for you, we will need the stipend. Two hundred fifty yuan a year, as we agreed," said Abbess Gaoyun with authority. Buddhist women's institutions did not attract the large gifts often given by layfolk to monks at the more famous monasteries. The abbess may have been advanced on the Way, but she was also very practical, her mind one minute on profound teachings of the Buddha's Dharma, the next on fixing a leak in the roof or how to get enough rice to feed her nuns. Her community lived on the knife's edge between failure and bare survival. Her eyes narrowed as she examined the ragtag group that stood before her. Her sour expression made it clear to them that she detested this arrangement, agreeing to it only to save her nunnery. Why did these peasants have the little white girl? Suspecting that she did not want to know, she asked no questions. She balanced her worries with the thought that they would be able to train the child in the Buddha's path.

"We are able to give this to you now," said Heiyen, handing her a soiled brown envelope, "the rest in six months."

The abbess opened the envelope and counted the bills carefully. The side of her mouth twitched in irritation. "Yes, I shall be expecting it. The remaining 125 yuan in six months. You understand that we are not just feeding, housing, and teaching her. We are assuming a great risk. If the Japanese come here and find a foreign child among us we would be in deadly trouble."

"You will get your money. We are the FourOnes, and when we give our word, we keep it."

"So I have been told." She spoke the words tentatively, implying that their reputation for honesty was hearsay until proven with actions.

"We will return in six months." He removed a pencil and small scrap of paper from his vest pocket. He wrote on it, *Due 12th month, 1st day: 125 yuan. Heiyen.*

"I shall expect it."

"On the same day," continued Heiyen, "we will take her with us for a month or so, then bring her back to you. We believe the Dharma will be good training for her. The principles of *dao* and *de* are the same, in our community and yours."

"So I have been told," she conceded. "Otherwise we could not accept her."

"The other principles, particular to our path, we shall give her as she grows older and can understand them. The spirits have given us this child and we know that they will protect her. They will protect you and your sisters as well."

The interview was over. The young nun who greeted them at the gate entry now came and took the little girl's hand. "Come with me. I will show you where you will stay."

Neither Heiyen nor Guzhi made any attempt to hug the girl, nor even to say good-bye. But the man looked at her solemnly: "Remember, we are your family now. We will return for you."

Since the night of the festival, when she had felt the strong brown hands close over her mouth and the blanket thrown over her head, no one had called her Victoria. But that was her name, the one given to her by her mother and father. They told her that they were Americans and had come from a distant land across the ocean and that they would return there some day. Even Bailian and Kaiyuan, who were Chinese, knew her proper name and tried to pronounce it sometimes, but it was hard for them. So they generally called her *meimei*, "little sister."

Victoria was terrified that night when the strangers had seized her, forcing her to lie on a smelly blanket in the wooden box. She cried continuously as the cart rumbled and bounced along on the frozen roads. Finally, despite all the bumping and lurching, she had fallen asleep in utter exhaustion, awakening only when the cart came to a full stop. She heard no human voice, but suddenly a gust of cold air swept into the box as someone pulled open the lid. She rubbed her eyes, sore from crying, and saw that there were eight people standing around the cart. Not a single familiar face. Victoria screamed in fright. Where were her father and mother? Who were these people? She looked at them more carefully. They did not react much to her scream, and their faces did not look threatening. Only attentive.

Victoria glanced upward at the cold sky and saw that the stars were fading in the predawn light. She could tell that they were in a courtyard, not so different in size from the one at the mission where she had played games with Bailian but more cluttered. She saw some old bicycles under the overhanging eaves, a heap of limp cabbages, cloth bags, piles of charcoal, and bundles of cornstalks tied together, leaning against the brick wall. When she turned to look behind her, she was surprised to see the man without legs resting just behind the box, on the wooden bed of the donkey cart. If he was the Immortal, as she had thought the night before, the other people did not seem to be paying him any special attention. "Wutui," someone said to him, "do you want to get down?" He nodded and they helped him down.

Then a pang of fear overwhelmed her, and she began to cry again, the tears running down her face. Her head bobbed and her body jerked with sobbing. "Heiyen, tell her that she is one of us now," said an older woman.

"We are your new family," the man said, offering no other explanation. That made her feel even worse. She did not want a new family.

She was dead tired and very hungry. The women in the group came to her and began to fuss over her. They gave her a cloth to wipe her eyes, touched her hair, patted her shoulders, and stroked the backs of her hands. The oldest among them, the one they called Guzhi, took hold of her hand, helped her down from the cart and led her into a kitchen where the farmer's wife offered her a bowl of broth. It was almost as though she herself were the Immortal, the way they fussed over her. Somehow this thought comforted Victoria, because of course she was not the Immortal. These people would soon discover their mistake and take her back to her parents. Maybe it was the legless man, but it certainly was not her.

These people did not seem to be unkind, she thought, as she slowly sipped from her bowl. They wanted her to eat, and when she took her first spoonful of soup, she noticed that they were visibly relieved. It reminded her of that day last winter, when the frail orange kitten wandered into the mission, and how they all stood around watching the scrawny creature wobble over to the bowl of warm water that Bailian had placed on the floor. When her little pink tongue began lapping up the water, they all clapped. Surely these were not bad people, but why did they take her? Until she found out, she would be strong and not let them see her cry again.

The next few weeks were mostly filled with nighttime traveling and stopovers, for days at a time, usually at a farm house. They rested during the day, and she understood that they did not want to be seen. She thought about running away, but she had no idea where she was, and if she were caught, it might make these people angry at her.

They took good care of her, making sure she had warm clothes and food to eat and a place to sleep, not far from the stove. But they rarely spoke to her. They told her that her name was Bu'er. She shook her head. "No," she said firmly in English, "my name is Victoria." The man Heiyen, who was their leader, said that used to be her name, but the Old Master had spoken and revealed this new name for her. From now on her name would be Bu'er.

Victoria remembered that last night at White Cloud Temple, when Bailian showed her the statue of a strange old man with an enormous forehead and a long wispy beard. He was the oddest looking person she had ever seen. "That one," she said, "is Laozi, the Old Master." She was not sure that she liked the idea of such an odd-looking person giving her a new name. Guzhi told her that everyone in the FourOne group was given a special name. "Heiyen means Black Eye, and Guzhi means the Stubborn One," the kind old lady laughed softly, and Victoria saw that a few of her teeth were missing. "And Wutui means No Legs!"

Victoria wondered how the Old Master had spoken to them. She knew that a god was a powerful person that you could not see with your eyes. Her father had told her of a god who had created her, and another god whose name was Jesus. The Chinese called him Yesu. He loved her,

her father said. They prayed and sang hymns to him. She had a great memory and quickly learned them all, singing the hymns and saying the prayers, but she didn't know what the words meant.

Then one night, a few weeks later, when they had stopped in a small town in the mountains, she found out how they spoke with the spirits. Their group was in the back room of a small temple. Guzhi sat behind a table. In front of her was a wooden tray with sand in it. Guzhi was holding a tree branch in her hand, poised over the sand. The stick was forked like the wishbone of a chicken. Victoria was frightened to see that the old lady's eyes were closed and her body was shaking. Then the forked stick moved, making markings in the sand. Heiyen and a woman leaned over her shoulders, calling out words. Then a woman wrote them down in a ledger. Finally, Guzhi's hand stopped moving. She stopped shaking, opened her eyes and looked normal again. She had not said a word and had barely moved, but she looked exhausted. The writing woman then read out the words. Victoria could understand ordinary conversation, but she could not understand what these strange words meant.

After the reading, Heiyen came and sat down on a wooden stool, right in front of Victoria. "Bu'er," he said, "it wasn't the Old Master who spoke this time. It was Lord Guangong, the god of war. He has warned us that we are all in great danger, especially you. The Japanese are all around us here. The people do not have enough to eat and many have been killed. The god has advised us to put you in the care of some nuns who live in the mountains. You will be safe there until this war is over and the dwarf pirates are driven back to their island. Then we will come for you."

"Bai hua bing! Bai hua bing!" The little girl, wearing a black robe and looking like a miniature nun, stuck her tongue out and shouted at her again. "Bai hua bing!"

Victoria clamped her hands over her ears and shouted back at the girl who was about the same age as herself: "My name is Victoria! Victoria!"

"Bai hua bing!"

Victoria burst into tears of frustration. She had cried only once, that first night when they took her out of the box and she looked on eight strange faces instead of the familiar ones of her mother and father, of Bailian and Kaiyuan. As she fought for control of herself she decided she would not cry again. But now even those who had stolen her away were gone, just as she was beginning to get used to their ways and beginning to trust their kindness. They had led her to this mountain place today and left her.

"Bai hua bing!" taunted the small girl again. Victoria had no idea what those words meant, but knew the little one was making fun of her.

Just then an older girl rushed into the courtyard. She was taller and looked somehow more refined than the round-faced one who was taunting her. "Xihai, you must be quiet. It's against the rules to shout like that." The newcomer looked at Victoria very carefully, appraisingly. "And anyway, you are wrong, Xihai, she is not a bai hua bing. Her eyes are not pink." She looked at the short hair on Victoria's head. "And her hair is red, not white." Then she looked straight at Victoria's face. "Meimei, my name is Weizong. What is your name? I've never seen anyone with red hair."

"My name is Victoria."

"That is hard to say. I have never heard that name before."

"The people who brought me here call me Bu'er. That is my Chinese name. Or you can call me Meimei."

"We will call you Bu'er, won't we, Xihai?" The little girl thrust out her lower lip, but said nothing.

Weizong shook her head in disapproval and said to Victoria confidentially, "Xihai's family is from the countryside, not far from this mountain. They had no money and couldn't feed her, so they sent her here to live with the nuns. Her family can't read or write. She doesn't understand about manners. My family is the Gao clan from Taiyuan, a great city far from here. Have you ever heard of it?"

Victoria shook her head truthfully.

"It is famous. When you get older you will know about it. My family brought me here because I was so sick that they thought I would die, so they prayed to the Buddha and said if he would save my life they would let me serve him as a nun. And the Buddha saved my life. My family brought me here and gave a great gift to this place, a white statue of Buddha Omito. It is the very best one here at Yindong An. Come with me to the chapel and I will show it to you," said the girl, taking Victoria's hand. "Xihai, you can come, too."

"I've seen it before," said the younger girl, pouting and walking in the opposite direction, "a hundred times!"

父親

Chapter 3

Pastor Wayman and the Tofu Man

May 1940.

Yesterday he had come to the point of despair, to the place that the old pilgrim, in his day, had called the "slough of despond." It frightened him to find himself in such a state, overwhelmed by so many worries and doubts. The Beijing Presbyterian mission had been established in 1871, staffed by dedicated couples down through the years, and now it was in his hands—his and Adele's. They had been here the last five years and he had hoped to grow the congregation, but that had not happened. The numbers were pretty much the same as they had been when they arrived in 1935, twenty or thirty regulars who came on Sundays, and only a handful to worship on weekday mornings. Deacon Chen was a good man, but lacked warmth. And Mrs. Wang, head of the Altar Society, was, in his opinion, a little too impressed by her own position.

The stagnant situation at the mission had pushed him in a new direction. He'd become involved with the YMCA, which was working to develop native Chinese leaders for the church. Their push to support a labor movement in China had given him some hope of a significant accomplishment, but that work had withered quickly, like an unwatered vegetable. When the wealthiest American donors heard about the Y organizing labor in China, they stopped giving. Since they opposed the labor movement in the States, why would they support it overseas? The

Communists had some success organizing strikes and marches, enough to scare the factory bosses who paid thugs to beat up the strikers, leaving many wounded or dead on the streets. Now the Japanese occupiers would not tolerate labor organizing of any kind, whether Communist or Christian.

These were yesterday's black thoughts, but worse than the failures of his ministry was the loss of Victoria. It weighed down his mind and heart every day, after three months still poisoning the relationship between him and Adele. They had gone through their daily routines, each grieving in their hearts but unable to comfort each other. He had preached, more than once, on the theme of how tragedies, with God's help, could be transformed into opportunities of divine grace. But in their own case, it had not worked. He had heard the words "physician, heal thyself" and could not help but rebuke himself: "Preacher, save thyself."

In the morning he had made his weekly trip to the Office of Public Security, where he asked how the investigation was going.

"There is nothing to report," the man said, as he had been saying every week for the last two months.

"Look, we can solve this. All we need to do is to mount a full-scale search. Surely someone must have seen her that night."

"The people who attended the festival came from all over Beijing and dispersed the same night. We have done all we can. We have posted photos of your daughter in the newspaper. No one has responded."

"If it is a matter of money, I will get it for you. Pay more of your men to search for her. If you won't help, I will hire detectives myself."

"I've said this before. I will say it again. The Japanese authorities will not allow us to conduct the kind of citywide search you are talking about, and they won't allow you to do it, either. They don't want the public order disturbed by a mass investigation . . . If anyone responds to the newspaper photos, I will let you know. And now, if you will excuse me . . ."

Then came the crisis, yesterday, late in the afternoon, when Adele had come back from the Medical Union Hospital, and he had returned from the YMCA meeting. Both were tired and discouraged and he made the mistake of complaining about how the Japanese occupation interfered with their Christian work. Adele exploded. "How can you think about that?" she shouted at him. "We have lost our daughter! If you hadn't been so impatient and ugly that night . . . if you hadn't pushed ahead of us in the crowd . . . if we had stayed together . . . we would still have Victoria with us."

"And if you hadn't insisted on going to that stupid festival in the first place, it wouldn't have happened," he had countered. "It was a hodge-podge of paganism and ignorant superstitions—shooting off firecrackers to scare away the demons, burning fake paper money to trick the gods, and all the rest of it—we should never have gone there. That is exactly why we have come here, to save the Chinese from that sort of nonsense. Now we can't even save ourselves!"

But strangely, the outburst had helped, dissipating some of the anger that had been building up inside them, and later that night, just before they went to bed, Adele finally let him hold her. Not that everything was suddenly fine. In fact, as he held her, Adele had said, "It will never be the same again," and he had suspected that she meant not just their family situation but the marriage itself. At least, he consoled himself, in the opening of their hearts and getting out the long-repressed feelings, something positive had happened.

And then, this morning . . . astonishing. They had made love, for the first time since Victoria was taken from them. It wasn't like the exuberance of the first few years, but it was consoling, it was good. Their bodies touched, but also, he thought, their hearts. It wasn't a full healing by any means, but a coming together of two wounded beings who realized that they shared something very human: the realization that fallen and fallible as they were, they could still share a measure of consolation in their weakness. Was it not a moment of grace?

Adele had gone back to sleep, and he would soon have to get up for the morning service. But as he lay there, wide awake in the gathering light, he thought it a certainty. It was grace, the gift of God at their time of greatest need. But how strangely the grace had come. It was the call of the tofu man out in the *hutong* behind their house that waked them, much earlier than usual.

Just then he heard a different call, the night soil man who came to collect the slops up and down the alley, which he sold to nearby farmers for fertilizer. There was something endearing about this city and its strange customs. Someone should write a book about the string of peddlers and collectors that appeared every day in Beijing's hutongs. He couldn't understand the words, but the sounds were all distinctive and he had come to recognize them. Along with the calls and chants, each had their own bells and rattles that identified their business: charcoal vendors, fruit and syrup sellers, knife grinders, bead and trinket sellers. And the collectors, each with their unique drumming sounds, seeking everything from antiques, jewelry, jade, and stoneware, to dilapidated furniture, newspapers, and bottles.

But earlier than all of them this morning had come the tofu man, waking them in the dark. They had made love, touching affectionately for the first time in months. As he lay in bed, he thought about how in past ages God had used unlikely people as His messengers and prophets—the overconfident Isaiah, and the timorous Jeremiah. And this morning he was tempted to say that God had sent the tofu man. The old man came every other day, calling out, "Tofu, ah . . . blah, blah." Something or other. It reminded him of an auctioneer's call, meaningless but rhythmic. But when he came, out came the cooks and housewives with their bowls. The man was a mess, his ragged pants fraying at the cuffs, his bald head, the stubble of beard, his narrow eyes and wrinkled face, his dirty straw sandals. The old man lifted up a burlap cloth and underneath, resting on a wide board, was a white slab of the tofu about three inches thick. He sliced off a block of it with his thin cleaver, placed it deftly and gently in whatever container his customers brought with them. No one asked him to weigh it. They handed him some coins. He did the exchange with such artful motions and tender care you would think he was distributing gold ingots. Harold was convinced that the odd old beggar was an angel of God.

Three months later, Harold could only look back on that day and think that what they received was much better than a gold ingot. God bless the tofu man! More important than either he or Del could have imagined, waking them up in the dark with his strange yodel at just the right time and on the perfect day. They had come together and conceived their second child. When Adele's tummy grew large, Mrs. Wang said to Harold: "May the Lord bring you a 'great happiness.'" He knew that meant a boy, but neither he nor Adele cared about the child's gender, and when the "little happiness" came, they named her Olivia.

母親

CHAPTER 4

Adele

Beijing. Fall 1940.

A sea turtle swims the vast expanse of the sea as it migrates hundreds of miles to its summer destination. It is so intent on its goal that it does not pause to rest or eat. Finally, as it nears the end of its long journey, it comes to the surface. It happens that a wooden yoke is floating in the water, perhaps the only one in the entire ocean, and when the turtle lifts its head above the surface of the water it is in the circle of the yoke. How likely is such an event? Among the vast number of creatures in all the cycles of life, the good fortune of a human rebirth is even more rare.

—*Buddhist Parable*

Living halfway around the world from Raleigh, North Carolina, gave Adele a new vantage point on her own childhood. Some events and experiences blurred or faded from view while others came into clearer focus. She was surprised at how visual the memories of her parents had become.

When she thought of her father, Dr. Gerald Convey, he was sitting on the edge of her bed, in the circle of light cast by the small lamp on the night table, the book in his lap. She loved having him to herself for those last precious moments of the day. She knew he was often very tired, exhausted by his daily house calls to his patients, yet he always came home in time to read her to sleep. Once or twice she remembered him so tired that he fell asleep before she did. "I'll just rest my eyes for a moment," he said, and was soon fast asleep at her side. She saw the humor in it, enjoying the thought that she had put her father to sleep.

Grimm's Fairy Tales was their favorite bedtime reading. "These tales may give you a gloomy view of human life," he explained one night after they had read "Hansel and Gretel." "But it doesn't hurt to have a peek at the dark side of things. You'll run into it now and then and you should be prepared." Thinking of his heart attack and death a few years later, and now the loss of Victoria, Adele thought the words prophetic.

When she sees her mother Martha, she is sitting in regal composure in front of the mirror at her vanity table, applying the creams, lotions, powders, and lipsticks to make herself look youthful. Adele stands behind in the dim light watching her mother with fascination as she skillfully applies the beauty aids to her aging face. Her mother never turns around to look at her directly but peers at her shadowy image in the mirror. She brushes her white hair and says, "I call it the silver transformation. The Manigaults do not dye." Her lips contract into a tight smile, thinking that Adele has not caught the pun.

Her mother, Martha, is a Manigault, a card-carrying member of the DAR and the Daughters of the Confederacy. She believes passionately in three things: the righteousness of the "Lost Cause," the divinely sanctioned segregation of races and social classes, and a firm anti-Catholicism. These were the convictions Adele heard delivered from the vanity throne. As she grew up, Adele heard countless discourses on these subjects, and the more her mother talked, the more Adele felt inclined to think the opposite. But she had not inherited her mother's contentious nature, so she swallowed her objections with a grimace, like the cod liver oil she had to take every morning with her orange juice.

After her father died, the house where she and her mother lived on St. Mary's Street felt more like prison than home. Her mother had strict rules, unchangeable routines more like the discipline of a military academy. School, homework, supper, a bit of needlepoint or piano practice, then off to bed.

On Sunday they would go to the Episcopal church, and that was the full extent of religion's influence in the household. No discussion of the sermon, no prayers before meals, no Bible readings or private devotions of any kind. Only the single public appearance each Sabbath, wearing the clothes her mother deemed proper for a young lady of the better sort. "Wear something nice for dinner every evening, my dear," she would remind her. "Eat with moderation, not like a little piggy. Never underestimate the value of a trim figure for attracting the right kind of suitor when you come of age." But Adele knew that she was gangly and large boned and would never cut the petite figure so cherished by her mother.

Everything changed when Adele went off to Women's College at Greensboro. Success in her studies brought freedom and strengthened her resolve to be independent of Martha. Within a year, she had quit her education major, which her mother had chosen for her, and switched to nursing, to favor her father. She began to investigate employment in her senior year, at hospitals in all the major cities of North Carolina, excluding Raleigh. But about a month before graduation she went to a dance and met Harold Wayman, a recently ordained minister. He was tall, handsome, and very idealistic. They had been dating only three weeks when he began talking of marriage. "Come with me to China," he said. "It will be a great adventure, and we will save souls for Christ."

She laughed at his enthusiasm. "You will be very persuasive in the pulpit someday, Harold Wayman!" She was dazzled at the thought of exploring new worlds and exotic cultures. She barely heard the words about saving souls for Christ. Her visits to the Episcopal Sunday school had left her vague on the more somber aspects of the Christian message, so although she had heard the phrase "saving souls" many times before, she never stopped to think what it really meant.

She knew perfectly well that she did not love Harold. The words "until death do us part" frightened her, but Harold kept up the pressure and she finally said yes, knowing it meant a clean break with her mother. Surely, she thought, if her father was able to endure life with Martha, she would have a picnic with Harold, who was a kind and considerate man. Love would come later.

Martha immediately opposed the marriage. "Such haste is indecent. People will talk. And who are the Waymans? I've never heard of anyone of substance from Rocky Mount!"

"His father has a church there right now. Their family came from Lenoir, Mother."

"Lenoir, Rocky Mount . . . it makes no difference. Raleigh and Charleston are the only cities of culture in the Carolinas!" Harold Wayman, she went on, would follow in the humble footsteps of his father, destined to poverty and Low Church irrelevance. "He will preach at country churches, and preside over endless covered-dish suppers with shoofly pie for dessert. The ladies will gush over him. You will help the ladies clean up while he chats with the local Presbyterian grandees. The least you could do, if you are determined to wed a religious man, is to find an Episcopal priest." Her mother's disapproval made Harold's proposal seem all the more attractive.

The next year, 1934, was a windstorm of activity—their marriage, her pregnancy, preparations for the move to China, Victoria's birth, and, barely a month later, departure. Her mother was outraged. "How can you take a child, barely out of the womb, to that filthy and poverty-stricken country? You must think of your daughter's welfare!" Adele ignored her mother's objections.

They took the train to San Francisco and, after three weeks aboard a cargo ship that accommodated a few passengers at a reasonable cost, landed in Tianjin. There they finished their trip in "Elijah's chariot," an ancient truck owned by the United Christian Congregations, which took them to Beijing. Adele sat in the cab with the driver, Harold in the truck bed with the luggage. Since she couldn't speak Chinese she smiled a lot at the driver, who could speak little English. He did not smile back.

Once in Beijing they made the decision to live in the old traditional Chinese house on the mission grounds. Their first few weeks there gave her a fresh feeling of new beginnings: making a home in a new city and a strange culture, setting up a kitchen, buying furniture and cookware, hiring a houseboy, a cook, and an amah to help with the baby.

After a few months in the mission on Flower Market Street, the excitement wore off, and their lives became routine. At first, that was a relief from the previous year of frenetic activity, but as the months passed Adele felt a growing sense of constriction. Conquering the world was one thing; living in the walled mission compound day after day was something else. It wasn't that Harold was bossy. He was in fact very considerate and reasonable, a complete contrast to her mother, even though, in the end, he usually made the decisions. But after they had settled in, it was the claims of his calling more than his character that shaped their lives. She needed to get out, and when she found work at the Peking Union Medical Hospital, Harold approved. After all, Jesus himself was a healer.

But as the months passed, Harold became more vocal about the difference between Adele and the other missionary wives. She read his remarks on the topic as subtle ways of asking her why she couldn't be more like them. And most disturbing to him, she found herself fascinated by Chinese beliefs and customs. "I really don't understand the need for exclusivity," she told him one time. "Kaiyuan says he is a Christian and a Buddhist. Why can't we do the same? I think we have a lot to learn."

"Because there is only one truth, one way," Harold replied, thinking he would have to have a talk with Kaiyuan. "As Jesus said, 'Unless a man be born again of water and the spirit, he cannot enter the kingdom of Heaven.' And he also said 'Go forth, make disciples of all nations.' That is why we are here."

Three entries from the diary of Adele Convey Wayman:

August 15, 1940. We've been here in China for five years and this is the first night I have not slept at home. I am at a nunnery in the mountains west of Beijing. Arrived last night and was welcomed with a bath. What a surprise! I stood naked, alone in a dark room, lit by a single candle, the bathing room of the nunnery. The wooden ceiling is so blackened with ages of candle smoke that its beams were barely visible above me. I had placed my clothes in a pile on a wooden bench and pinned up my hair. I dipped ladles of cool water from the bucket onto my neck, front, and back, and let the water run over my whole body. I watched it splash on the stone floor where I stood, gathering in a small gutter that ran over toward the outside wall of the room. Where did the water go? I followed the gutter over to the wall where it flowed through a hole under a small window. I looked outside and saw that the washing room was built on the cliff side, and as I leaned out the window I could hear the water splashing on the rocks below. A light breeze entered the window and touched my body. I felt the smoothness of the cool stones under my bare feet. Was it sacrilegious to enjoy myself so much in a Buddhist nunnery? But it was a simple pleasure, not a sinful one. Just the feeling of refreshment and relief as I washed away the dirt and grime of the trip from Beijing. The porter nun showed me my room, then brought me here immediately, fetching me the bucket and a small cloth to dry myself with. She placed a candle on the wooden bench and slipped quietly from the room. It was the community's gesture of welcome, all done without words. But none were needed. No bath or shower I have ever taken has felt so good.

Harold was upset that I wanted to come here by myself. I couldn't explain my reasons to him with any clarity, but I know that the main thing was my grief at the loss of Victoria. My emotions have been like a poison inside me. Without my work at the hospital, I do not think I could have endured these past six months. Harold was embarrassed that we had to borrow Elijah's chariot from United Beijing Congregations and release our boy Kaiyuan for the day to get me here. Kaiyuan is a treasure. We passed three checkpoints along the way. The Japanese soldiers bent over and looked suspiciously at me, an American, and carefully scrutinized my papers. Kaiyuan told them I was just a taitai, a wife, going on pilgrimage to the sacred mountain. Chinese women come to a temple on this mountain to offer prayers to goddess Guanyin to become pregnant and bear a male child. But that's not why I'm here. I'm already pregnant, and I don't care if it is a boy or a girl. I watched the rivulets of water running over my breasts and down my belly, already beginning to swell a little.

It took four hours of travel along hot dusty roads to get here. Crossing the city to Fucheng Gate, passing through miles of flatland where the crops have to be watered by hand. It has been so long since we've had any rain. The roads were terrible, really just donkey tracks. Elijah's chariot bounced in and out of potholes that made our progress very slow. But Kaiyuan was glad to drive me here. He is a good driver, willing to go slowly and stop for donkey carts and herds of goats without losing his temper. As we began the ascent of the mountain, the air became cooler. At one point as we rounded a bend, I looked back and saw the city in the distance, gray in the haze.

My room here is a small cubicle. The walls are wooden, the floors also, with a bamboo mat by the bedside as a rug. The bed was made of wooden planks covered with a thin quilt, which is where I'm sitting now as I write these words. I must stop writing and see if I can sleep on this hard surface. Mother should see me now! I'm sure she would disapprove.

August 16, 1940. Late afternoon. Some rain clouds moving in. They seem to hover over the mountains and refuse to move out over the plains where they might relieve the drought. There is a nun here who can speak some English. Like the rest, her hair is shaved to the skull, and she wears the gray robes of the order. I think they must shave their eyebrows, too. Their faces look so naked. The nun seemed kindly, with remarkably bright young eyes in an old face. There were six round white scars on her head, about the size of peas. The Buddhists place cones of incense on the heads of the novices, light them and let them burn down to the flesh. Enduring pain to end suffering! The Buddhists like to compare this life of ours to what they call a *kuhai*, a sea of bitterness, and when I think of Victoria I can agree with them completely.

The nun showed me around the main temple, took me out behind the monastic compound to the graveyard where many generations of monks and nuns were buried. She gestured toward the wooded hills above the cemetery. A few monks and nuns live as recluses and hermits up there, she said, but most stay here in the monastery. We walked back to the main compound and sat on the stone steps that lead up to the large temple where the nuns gather to chant and prostrate themselves before the statue of Buddha. We were sitting there quietly when my guide pointed to a pot of yellow chrysanthemums at the bottom of the steps and said a single word: "Buddha." Where? I said, thinking that she was referring to something other than the mums. No, no, she said, indicating the flowers. She pointed to her heart, and said again, "Buddha." Then she pointed to my own heart, and said it again. At that moment it was like a dam broke inside me. I sobbed. I felt such a fool, but it was also an immense relief. I was thinking of Victoria, and I realized that the sorrow inside was destroying me. I had no one in Beijing I could talk to. Sadly, not Harold, who seems so disconnected from what happened, and so convinced it was my fault. I felt like I could confide in the nun if only my Chinese was good enough to find the right words. But for that moment, she just took my hands in hers and held them.

I tried to explain. Finally, using a combination of my bad Chinese and her limited English, we were able to communicate with each other. I was able to tell her about how we had lost our Victoria. Why? I asked. Why? She kept saying, "*Yeguo*," which refers to karma, an idea that didn't help me at all, even when I finally understood what she meant.

Harold has a low opinion of Buddism. He insists that the Buddhists are ignorant and dirty, the monks uneducated and the lay people superstitious. The old Chinese culture belonged to the Confucians, he said, and the future belongs to those who have been given a Western education. I don't know if he is right, but I find that the walls and buildings here are eloquent, speaking of ancient times and old ways lovingly preserved. The temples with their quiet dignity, the statues with their serene features, the banners and paintings, the arrangements of the courtyards—everything expresses a wonderful balance.

If Harold could experience this with an open mind, he could not say that they have no culture. How could anything be more cultural than courtesy and hospitality? They have shared their vegetarian food with me. They welcomed me with warm water and a bath. They have not asked for money, although I will leave some when I go. They have allowed me to come to their temple and hear the chants, to watch them bow and prostrate themselves with such grace. Some might find the chants boring, but I find them calming. I cannot understand the words except for the ones they repeat so often throughout their devotions. "*Namo Omitofo.*" It is calling on the Buddha who vows to save all sentient beings. I repeat the words with them and think of Victoria.

August 24, 1940. I am back in Beijing. I have mostly recovered from my injuries. I want to get these experiences written while they are fresh in my mind.

It happened the evening of the sixteenth, the day of my last entry above. After the vegetarian dinner, I decided to skip the night prayers and go for a walk. I thought I would follow the path that led to the hills up behind the monastery to the area where the recluses lived. The path was rocky, sometimes ascending sharply, sometimes making its way horizontally around boulders and stony outcroppings. Occasionally the path led close to a sheer drop, which took my breath away. I have always had a fear of heights. Some areas were completely exposed to the elements, some were protected by groves of stunted pine trees and oaks. I passed some stone and plaster huts but none seemed to be occupied.

The light was beginning to fade. I rounded a bend in the path and just then a mist blew in. I was almost blinded and feared losing my way. I could hardly see five feet in front of me. I stood there for perhaps six or seven minutes, listening to the dripping of water somewhere close by. Then, as suddenly as it had appeared, the mist blew away and I could see again. The first of the brightest stars were visible in the darkening sky. I walked on, noticing that there were smaller branching paths that led off in various directions. Since it was getting dark I thought it better to stay with the main path.

Just as I was thinking I should turn around and return to the monastery, I saw what looked like a roundish knoll ahead, rising off to my left. I wondered if I could see Beijing and its evening lights in the distance. At first it seemed like a path went up the knoll, but as I climbed it the path disappeared. Loose rocks and stones began to give way under my feet, and I felt very insecure as I reached the top. Then suddenly another mist blew over the ridge, and in a moment I could see nothing but the rocks and vegetation close to my feet, more dim now as night was falling. I waited, afraid to take a step. After what seemed a long time, the mist blew off. Then I made a mistake. I looked over the edge and down. A great abyss opened up beneath me in the semidarkness. I was suddenly frightened and lunged back toward the safety of the main path. But I moved too quickly, my feet skidded in the gravel and I felt myself falling. I thought of my baby, and I remember screaming in terror as I fell.

The scream is probably what saved me. One of the recluses must have heard it and found me, fallen unconscious in a heap at the base of the knoll. He (or she?) had somehow got me back to the monastery. I know the next thing I recall was waking up in my room, with three nuns, obviously very concerned, standing around my bed and looking down at me. My head ached and pain shot through my right arm when I tried to move it. "*Ni hao*," I mumbled weakly. And they laughed in relief. No murder investigation! The foreigner would not die at their monastery.

I won't say much about getting back to the city. Kaiyuan came as planned on the second day after my fall. I dreaded Harold's anger. What a foolish thing I had done. I had risked my life, risked the life of our child. Why couldn't I be like the other wives, going on group excursions to the Great Wall, the Ming tombs, and the Summer Palace? Have the house boys pack us picnics and bring us back in the evening. "Because I'm not like the other wives," I wanted to say, but I knew that would just heap coals on the fire. So I just ignored him, acting like I was too sick to reply.

I know the baby is all right. My arm is beginning to heal, but I can barely scribble these words. What have I learned from my trip to the mountain? I have learned I will not get over the loss of Victoria any time soon. And I learned something about myself. That all my religious experience up to now has been reactive. Reacting to Mother's ranting, reacting to Harold's fixed beliefs, reacting to other people's notions of what a minister's wife should be. I must find my own way.

隱洞庵：入佛田

CHAPTER 5

Yindong Nunnery

Victoria. Shanxi. 1940–1942.

The brass bell woke Victoria every morning before daybreak. She rose quickly and put on her black robe, walking to the chapel where all the nuns gathered to chant and meditate. It was difficult to make anything of the sounds they chanted, but she loved the feeling of warmth their music created inside her. "Namo Omitofo, namo Omitofo . . ." Over and over until it became like breathing, like her heartbeat. It was a calm feeling that you didn't have to force but happened of its own accord.

While they were all together in the chapel, Victoria took stock of the community she was living with. There were thirteen nuns, wearing gray robes, with their heads and eyebrows shaved so that you could not tell the exact color of their hair. At first they looked alike, but soon enough the faces became individualized. They were mostly very old, forty or fifty at least, two or three much older. Then there were the black-robed ones—herself, Xihai, and Weizong—and they were all very young. They also had their heads shaved but not their eyebrows. The gray-robed ones were their mothers, the grandmother was Gaoyun, the abbess. The three black-robed ones were the young sisters. This was the family in the nunnery.

But there was also another person that Victoria couldn't figure out at all. She wore black robes but was older. Sometimes she was there to chant or eat with the others, sometimes not. Her hair was short but not shaved off. Actually she would have looked better with her head shaved. Her scruffy hair was black with some gray mixed in, sticking this way and that. It looked like a nest constructed by an unskilled bird. Weizong said that her name was Zhu Mingling, and when Victoria asked about her, Weizong just shook her head and shrugged, saying that Mingling had grown up on a farm, as though that disqualified her from being a person of interest.

After chanting, they ate breakfast in a large room with long wooden tables. The nuns and Mingling sat around two of the tables, the young ones had their own smaller table. They almost always had congee with salty pickles in the morning, soup or vegetables and rice for the other meals. They were silent while they ate. After breakfast, the young black-robed ones had school. Their teacher was Bolai, who was the youngest of the nuns, but very stern. She taught them how to write, using small brushes and black ink. They learned by imitation. Bolai said to Victoria, "*Da, da, da*," over and over, writing the character that meant "large." Da, da, da, endlessly, until she was able to imitate her and Bolai was satisfied that she could write it perfectly. Then, "*xiao, xiao, xiao*," three brush strokes also, but arranged differently, that meant "small." Weizong and Xihai were more advanced at first, but Victoria caught up with them quickly.

Bolai also taught them how they were expected to behave. In simple things they followed the way of Confucius. They should study hard, obey their superiors, and remember to honor their families. "But we have left our families," said Weizong, who was always very contrary and didn't hesitate to ask impertinent questions. "We shall not get married and have children to carry on family worship."

"You must let your brothers and sisters support the physical family," said Bolai. As followers of the Dharma, she said, they must pray and acquire merits for their parents and grandparents, so that they will be reborn in a better situation in their next life. That was the best service they could offer to their families. At first Victoria did not always understand what Bolai said, but she repeated herself so often that finally she got it. Her Chinese improved rapidly.

They were training to be nuns. They must follow the rules the Buddha laid down for them, such as the five precepts: they should never lie, they should not steal, they must not drink intoxicating beverages, they must not harm any living thing. It meant humans, of course, but also animals, birds, and even insects. That was why they never ate any meat or fish, explained Bolai. And last of all, they were never supposed to be alone with a man.

"What about your father?" Weizong asked, who was sometimes visited by her parents. They were great benefactors of the nunnery, and as she never failed to remind Xihai and Victoria, very important people.

"Being alone with your father is fine. You will understand this rule better when you get older." In fact, the only man they ever saw close up was Weizong's father. So the rule was a puzzle to them, but even if they could not understand it, they could tell it was very serious.

Bolai explained the teachings by telling stories about the Buddha. For example, when she talked about having compassion for all living things, she told the story of the young prince who was walking in the forest one day. He came upon a mother tiger with three cubs. The tiger was a pitiful sight, so emaciated she could not provide milk for her babies. It made the prince so sad that he cut off a piece of his own flesh and offered it to the tiger to eat. But she was too weak even to chew the flesh, so he held his cut arm to her mouth so she could lick his blood. She kept doing that and gradually became strong enough to eat the prince's flesh, produce milk, and feed her cubs. The young prince died but came back in a later life as the Buddha. That was real compassion, said Bolai. In this way, the three young ones learned how to live in the Dharma.

"If I met a tiger in the forest," said Xihai after Bolai had left them alone to practice their characters, "I would rather meet a strong one and let him eat me right away. I could never cut my own arm."

"It's just a story," said Weizong. "No one would ever do that." Victoria said nothing, but in her heart she was touched by the courage of the young prince.

After lunch they were allowed to take a short nap, then sent to work, usually helping the older nuns working in the garden, or cleaning the nunnery, sweeping the courtyard, washing dishes and bowls, and other hard tasks. The worst job was cleaning the smelly latrine. The only older person they never helped was Mingling, the black-robed one. Victoria noticed that she often left the nunnery after breakfast, wearing old pants and a cloth jacket and with a cloth bag over her shoulder. She wondered what the old nun was doing. Or was she a nun at all? Without her black robe she looked like a farmer's wife.

Abbess Gaoyun was sitting at her desk reading the *Diamond Cutter Sutra* when she heard the knock. "*Jin lai*," she said, and Mingling entered her room, bowing slightly. The abbess found Mingling annoying to deal with, because she was different and didn't fit easily into the community. She had strange ways and an independent attitude. She was a lay sister who was considering whether she wanted to become a nun or not. Gaoyun knew that Mingling was educated somehow while she lived in Beijing, although she told the abbess that she had never attended a school. But she could read and write, and knew about the events of the twentieth century, in China and beyond. Gaoyun waited in silence until Mingling finally spoke up.

"My work is heavy. I ask you to provide me with some help. Perhaps one of the young ones would do."

The abbess did not reply immediately. She was bothered by this request and wished she could simply refuse permission. "You have been doing this work for a long time. Why do you need help now?"

"More and more people in the villages have heard that I am a healer, and the demand for my services has increased. There is the garden to tend, and the medicines to prepare. I cannot do all that alone any longer."

Gaoyun knew that she had to be careful in making her response. She knew some other things about the history of this strange creature. Her father was a Boxer, her mother a member of the Red Lanterns Shining, a group of female Boxers. Both had been killed when the European armies attacked Beijing and lifted the siege of the foreign legations, now almost fifty years ago. The infant Mingling had then been raised by her grandfather and her grandmother, who lived on a farm east of the city.

Mingling had lived at Yindong An for over two years, not a member of the order, yet she was one of the main reasons that the nunnery was able to survive. As donations dwindled during the Japanese occupation and hard times fell upon China's farmers because of the depredations of the soldiers, Mingling's work as a healer provided a small though steady source of income. The people in the villages and farms in the valleys below were able to pay a small amount for the medicines and healing herbs they received from her. When they could not pay, they often gave Mingling a small bag of wheat or millet, some vegetable or fruit that was in season. She brought these payments back, giving any coins to the abbess and food to the cook. It was not much, but it helped keep them going.

"I can't spare any of the nuns," said Gaoyun finally. "Most are too old to help you anyway. And as for the young ones, none of them is suitable. Weizong's parents would find such work demeaning, and I can't afford to anger them by assigning her to help you. They are one of the few families still helping to support us. Xihai is too young and silly. The new one, Bu'er . . . well, we cannot allow anyone outside the monastery to know that she is with us. If even one farmer found out . . . Gossip breeds in the village like mosquitoes. I wouldn't want the Japanese authorities poking around Yindong An."

Mingling spoke her mind. "I think Bu'er, though she is very young, would be best. She is serious and thoughtful. She has already tasted the sea of bitterness. I see that she has inner strength. I would use her here at the nunnery, and to share the burden of my herb-gathering trips. I would never take her with me down into the villages. I promise you that."

As Gaoyun mulled over the request, she had the feeling that if she refused, Mingling might simply leave them, walking right out the door without a backward glance. So she acquiesced, nodding her head once. "Yes, then, under the conditions you have described, she may help you. But she is never to go down to the villages or farms below." Mingling bowed as she left the room.

So began Victoria's apprenticeship with Mingling. While the other two young black robes worked in the nunnery's vegetable garden, Victoria worked in the herb garden. "Wick-to-li-ya," said Mingling, pronouncing her name with care and near accuracy. "I shall not use that English name. I will call you Bu'er. Do you know what it means?"

Victoria shook her head.

"It means 'not two.'"

The little girl was puzzled. "Heiyen never told me that. But what does 'not two' mean? It seems like a silly name."

"It is a profound name. I cannot explain it to you now, but one day, when you are ready, you will know what it means."

Within a few days, it became obvious that Mingling had special plans for her new helper. She wanted more than an energetic worker, she wanted to teach the little pale-skinned girl about medicines and healing, passing on what her grandmother had taught her. That was the one thing in this world of red dust that she had found worth doing. The young girl was only about eight or nine years old, but there was a quiet strength reflected in those large round eyes. She could learn the art of healing and something more.

Victoria's first task was to learn the names of the plants in the herb garden, how much water and sun they needed; whether to harvest the roots, the leaves, or berries; whether to dry or pickle them for preservation. Mingling taught her the nature of each herb, mushroom, or substance useful as medicine. Yarrow was not fussy at all, and all of the stems, leaves, and flowers could be taken together, chopped, and dried. You dug the roots of ginger and kept them in moist sand for months, during the winter, but as the warmth returned you had to dry them or they would sprout. With hairy agrimony you must dry the stems and leaves and then you could use it to treat dysentery. With wolfberry, which was a bush, you saved and dried the bright-red berries. Mingling kept a small sort of garlic which she said was a strong medicine, better than the larger garlic cloves cultivated in the nunnery's vegetable garden. With angelica, the roots were the important thing. You needed to slice and dry them. After a few weeks, Victoria had proudly mastered these and all the other herbs in Mingling's garden. She knew how to care for the clumps of mint, rhubarb, dandelions, peony, yams, and the trellis of honeysuckle. The knowledge excited her and gave her a sense of competence, a feeling of having accomplished something for the first time since she was kidnapped. Really, for the first time in her life, because, as far as she could remember, she had done nothing significant as a child.

One day they were working in the pharmacy room, sorting herbs and wrapping them in small paper cones. Mingling had made a short trip to the valley behind Yindong An and brought back with her a number of herbs. Mingling laid them out on the table and remarked to Victoria that she would teach the little girl how to use the new plants and medicines she had just collected.

"Well then, I think I will know everything in a couple more weeks," said the little girl innocently.

Mingling looked at her apprentice, an amused look on her face. "Have you ever seen an elephant?"

"Yes," said Victoria, recalling a memory. "My mother took Bailian and me to the Beijing Zoo one day, and I saw the elephant."

"Well then, did you notice they have toenails?"

"Yes," said Victoria.

"What you know now about healing is like the smallest toenail on the back foot of the elephant!" She pointed to a large cabinet with many small drawers. "You must learn all their names and how to use them, which ones can be taken together in harmony and which ones fight with each other if taken together. You must go with me to the mountains to learn where to gather the plants, leaves, roots, and mushrooms that do not grow in our garden. You must learn about others that grow only in the south part of China, far away from here, the ones we must get from the pharmacy in Datong or Taiyuan City. Besides the medicines, you must learn of the five directions, the five flavors, the five elements, and how they connect with the five feelings and the five organs of the body, how they generate each other and diminish one another, of diagnosing through the tongue and pulse, of the great forces of yin and yang and how they interact, of all the meridians and all the pressure points that mark the passage of qi through the human body . . . and all of this is just the beginning. There is much that I myself do not know. But that is all right," she said, noticing the crestfallen look of her apprentice, "you are a bright one. You will learn quickly."

"It is the season of white dew," said Mingling one day, a few weeks later. "The great heat of summer is over. We must go west to the higher mountains to gather herbs before the cold weather comes. It is a hard journey, and we will need to leave very early, before the brass bell rings to wake the others. We will walk to a far place and stay overnight, coming home the next day, after everyone else is asleep. Can you do that?"

Victoria could hardly contain her excitement. After all the weeks and months in the nunnery, here was an adventure beckoning. She told Weizong and Xihai about the plans, then watched their faces cloud with envy.

"I don't know why you get to go on a trip," said Weizong in frustration. But another thought crossed her mind and she immediately regained her composure. "Really, I wouldn't want to go. It will be awful, stumbling along on the rocky paths, sweating like a farmer, grubbing in the dirt. You will get blisters on your feet, and your hands will get scratched and cut by the thorns, and dirt will get in the cut, and you will get an infection and die."

Victoria thrust her jaw forward. "And if that happens, Mingling will put salve on my cuts and they will heal! I won't die."

Weizong adopted a scornful look. "People like Mingling are low class. Why would I want to be her slave? That's what you will be, a slave. When someone gets sick in my family, a physician comes and bows at our door and serves us. They are not like us."

"Who saved your life when you were so sick? Wasn't that a physician? You shouldn't be so ungrateful."

"The Buddha saved me, not the physician."

As this verbal duel continued, Xihai looked more and more pleased, sensing a realignment of the relationship among the three of them. She had got her friend back from this little white-faced stranger.

The knock came in the dark, before the morning bell had rung. Mingling said, "Bu'er, here, wear these," handing Victoria a small pair of trousers with a draw cord and a short padded jacket. "Meet me at the front gate. Don't forget your hat." She put on the clothes, took her hat from the peg on the wall, and hurried down the dark corridor of the dormitory to the gate. It was fun to be set loose from the folds of the robe, her legs free for a change. She wished she could have run at top speed as she used to do when she ran with Bailian on the quiet streets of the legation district.

Mingling was waiting for her at the gate, with a large cloth bag slung over her shoulder and holding two long bamboo sticks. "Bu'er, take one of these," she said, handing her one of the bamboo poles. Instead of walking down the stone steps, they followed the outer wall of the nunnery, then when they got to the rear of the building where the wall turned westward, continued along a barely discernible path through the trees.

"Stay right behind me. It will be easier as soon as the sun rises. We shouldn't encounter anyone on our trip, but if we do, keep your head down. I don't want anyone to see your face."

The two walked continuously until noon, stopping only when Mingling saw a plant she wanted to collect. It was early fall and the leaves of the deciduous plants had not yet fallen, but some were already coloring and showing ripe berries. Sometimes the nun collected leaves and stems, sometimes she dug up tubers from beneath the soil, or mushrooms, or sometimes gathered certain flowers, although those blooming in the fall were few. She wrapped each separately in a piece of old newspaper and placed it in her cloth bag. In each case, she told Victoria the name of the plant and what it was used for.

"I can't remember all these names and uses," said the young one in distress.

"I'll go over the names again when we return and prepare them for storage. I will write the name of each. That is when I expect you to remember them." The two travelers passed a tree with cinnamon-colored bark. Mingling took a knife and stripped away some of the bark for her collection bag. "You peel it vertically, you take only enough for our needs, but never so much as to injure the tree. Like a wound to our bodies, it will heal itself. By next year, when we return, you will see what I mean."

They stopped for lunch at a clearing where the water of a small creek gathered into a clear shallow pool before continuing its course down the hill. The terrain they had crossed was very arid and it was the first water they had seen. Victoria's throat was dry, and she quickly knelt at the edge of the water and drank, using her hands as scoops. Mingling had a small gourd dipper hanging around her waist, and she offered it to Bu'er. "Dip it carefully and it will stay clear." The water was cool and fresh. After Mingling had also drunk from the pool, they sat on a fallen log nearby and had lunch. Mingling had brought some steamed buns filled with chopped greens and mushrooms. "Six of these, two for us now, two for dinner, two for tomorrow lunch on our way back."

They ate quietly. It was almost a perfect silence. No bird songs, no insects buzzing. Mingling reached over and put her left hand on Victoria's shoulder, silently pointing with her right to a cluster of red ants milling around a mounded hive in the grass between the log and the pool of water. Advancing toward them was a column of smaller black ants. Soon the two groups were fighting. Victoria watched in fascination.

"Ants are like humans," said Mingling, "always fighting."

"Bolai taught us that we are not to harm any living thing."

"She is right. But the ants don't follow the Dharma, nor do most humans."

"I think the big red ones will win," said Victoria, watching the first skirmishes of the insects with interest.

"I don't think so. The little ones are angry and mean. They are better organized. They will win. Watch and you will see. When I am down in the villages, they tell me of how the Japanese have taken over most of the land east of us, all the way to Bohai and the Yellow Sea. They have even taken Taiyuan City. We still have Datong, but for how long?" Victoria knew that Weizong's family lived in Taiyuan, but she had never heard of Datong.

"Can we beat them?"

"In the end we will, but it might take a long time. The Old Master says, 'Yield to overcome.' Our troops will yield and eventually the Japanese will overextend themselves. They will not be able to hold the ground they have stolen in our vast nation. Then we will win. But he also says that even victory, when it comes, should be celebrated like a funeral."

"I don't understand."

Mingling thought for a while, then said, "Because of all the deaths that happen. The funeral is the ritual for the dead. Many die on both sides. You see some red ants dying and some black ones also . . . You will understand this when you are older. But while humans fight—and I see no evidence that they will ever stop—there are things we can do." She reached into her bag and pulled out a root. "There are people who speak against war. But we can do more than talk. We can heal," she said, removing a clump of roots from her bag. "This is called *canqi*, a root that stops bleeding. Yarrow works as well. That is what we can do, not with ants but with humans." In this way, Mingling began to teach Victoria how to observe nature closely and learn its virtues.

Late on the second day, they were on their way back home. Each had a bamboo pole on their shoulders, with a cloth bag on either end, filled with herbs and medicinal substances. As they turned onto a path that passed near a small village, they heard a sudden burst of words. Mingling frowned, at first unable to understand the harsh speech. "Japanese," she hissed. "Quick," said Mingling, "get behind those rocks." They scrambled up through a narrow fissure between two boulders, dropped their poles, and ducked low. Stock still, they peered from behind the stones, watching the two soldiers come around the bend to their left. They were pushing and shoving an old man, forcing him to walk in front of them, poking him with their rifles to drive him forward. On the path, just in front of them, they stopped. "Zuoxia," shouted one to the old man. He sat down. They took out cigarettes and smoked, squatting on the side of the path. Bu'er was panic stricken. Mingling placed her finger over her lips, and the two of them knelt immobile behind the stony barrier, hardly able to breathe, until finally the soldiers threw down their cigarette butts. They shouted, "Qilai," and when he had struggled to his feet, again prodded the old man with their guns as they continued up the path away from the village.

Bu'er wanted to ask more questions about the Japanese, but Mingling raised her hand and silenced her. "We must be quiet and hurry back to Yindong An," she whispered. A few minutes later they heard two shots ring out, and when Mingling saw the panic in Bu'er's eyes, she said: "I think the old man's days in the sea of bitterness are over." She took the little girl's hand and led her off the path to the hillside, which was harder to walk but safer as they began their steep climb toward the nunnery.

救自天來

CHAPTER 6

Salvation Comes from Heaven

Detention. Shandong Province. 1943–1945.

M*arch 25, 1943. We were a sad-looking trio,* wrote Harold in the final entry of his mission log. He brought it along, hoping eventually to get it back to Presbyterian headquarters in the States.

We trudged along Flower Market Street, Hatamen, and Legation Street, passing the French and Russian compounds and finally entering the gate of the abandoned consulate of the United States. I carried two large suitcases, Del two smaller ones. Little Olivia had a cloth bag slung over her shoulder. Thirty or forty people stood in the courtyard, fear on their faces, their voices diminished to the murmur of timid questions and uncertain answers. Their fright was contagious and Livia sensed it. "Daddy, why are all the people here? What are we doing here?"

The letter had come to the Presbyterian mission a week earlier, on February 27, 1943, signed by the Japanese authority.

Livia, Del, and I were commanded to report to the US consulate on March 5, bringing only what we could carry in our own hands. No "bearers," no number-one boys to help us. From the consulate, the letter said, we would be transported to a camp "somewhere." They were doing this for our safety and well-being. The authorities were pleased to announce that at that unnamed place "every comfort of Western culture would be ours."

Del had been right after all, he thought. We should have left with the diplomats, right after Pearl Harbor. "We have lost Victoria. Do you want to risk losing Livia?" she'd said. "And ourselves? How can we possibly be safe here in Beijing with the Japanese in charge?"

But I resisted, wondering how I could abandon a mission that had been here almost seventy years, the work of so many dedicated men of God. "Let's wait a while and see if there is something we can still accomplish." But then it was too late.

They brought us here to Shandong Province, near the town of Weixian. It is in the heartland of ancient China's history and culture, the location of China's sacred mountain, Taishan, and the home of Confucius and Mencius. But we might as well be in the Gobi Desert, locked up in this old missionary high school—Presbyterian, wouldn't you know—a rectangular compound about four hundred by six hundred feet. Over two thousand of us, enjoying "every comfort of Western culture," mostly Americans and Brits, though there are a number of Belgians and French as well. Packed in this small space like sardines in a can. The first few days were a nightmare of overcrowding, hunger, filth, the stink of clogged and broken toilets, sickness, and outbursts of anger. And the unspoken fear of death. We had heard rumors of the Nazi camps in Europe. What would happen to us? Most were accustomed to the luxury of maids and number-one boys to take care of us, drive our cars, cook our food, clean our rooms, and shop for us. Now I watched fine ladies peeling potatoes, and gentlemen speaking the King's English while they cleaned privies.

The Japanese have crammed all sorts of people into this camp. Along with ministers and businessmen there were bankers, lawyers, scholars and teachers, and that sort of expat who manages to make a living by teaching and translating. On the outer fringes, there were the "operators" who mastered the underground highways of their trades: drugs, alcohol, and prostitution. But not many. Most of this sort had sniffed danger in the air and bribed their way out of the country right after Pearl Harbor.

Once settled at Weixian, Harold quickly became involved in the administration of the camp. The Japanese authorities adopted a hands-off policy, sending food supplies regularly to the main gate of the camp. They were packed in boxes and carted in on ancient mule-drawn carts under the watchful eyes of a Japanese guard. The Chinese locals, who drove the carts and whose farms produced the food, were not allowed to enter the compound. They had to unload the boxes at the main gate where they were picked up twice a week by a troop of able-bodied men from inside the camp. These brief encounters allowed the emergence of a sort of black market. Camp leaders always sent someone who could speak Chinese to help unload the food. A few whispered words indicated their needs. There was a cluster of trees just across the east wall of the compound. One branch hung over the wall, and soon baskets of eggs, pork, cigarettes, and "white lightning" (Americans' term for *baijiu*, the local liquor available), were being hauled over the wall at night. And occasionally an underground newspaper. On its return, the basket contained dollars, pounds, and francs from detainees' pockets to repay the farmers for the risk they took.

Although outside contacts were strictly forbidden, the Japanese gave the prisoners nominal control of the major functions inside the internment camp. They were surprised to find that they were free to run the place, choose their own leaders, and appoint directors for all the tasks that had to be done: cooking, cleaning, medicine, child care, housing, waste disposal, education, entertainment. Harold took some part in the early organizational meetings, fascinated with the idea of turning a motley crew of two thousand into a real community. He spoke up and voiced his opinions. As a result, he was chosen as one of two assigned to direct the housing committee. The other was a young Englishman named Guildford. He was trained in theology and history at the University of St. Andrews in Scotland. He was tall, thin, and blond. The sparse hair on his chin was a fine and wispy yellow. Adele was busy as well, nursing in the makeshift medical clinic they had set up in the compound.

A general order did begin to emerge as they chose leaders for all the main tasks required. Those with practical experience became the true leaders in the camp. Their skills made daily living possible. Bankers, lawyers, business men, ministers, and industrialists frequently had to learn from people they had formerly given orders to. Men and women with everyday skills and a good sense of humor were most respected. Those who had neither had to learn or step aside.

One day after lunch, Harold and Guildford left the dining area together. At the end of the meal, they had been collared by three men from room B in block seven who had complained bitterly about their assigned spaces. "Those fellows were a bit tetchy, weren't they?"

Harold agreed. "But with good reason. I would have felt the same way. There are eleven people in room B. Only nine in room C. Rooms are the same size. But the solution is simple. We'll move one out of B and put him in C. I think they'll see the logic of that."

"One would hope so. I do think it is time to organize quarters in the fairest possible way. We've been here three weeks now and made do. But there are some real inequities. Of course we are all horribly crowded together. No one has enough room, but we can at least strive for equity in discomfort."

Harold smiled at this whiff of British humor. They really had it better than anyone had a right to expect. While the soldiers of Japan and the United States were slaughtering each other on the islands of the Pacific, the internees had enough to eat, a cot to sleep on, their basic needs met. Life began to take on an air of normalcy. Babies were born. They established a school for the children staffed by volunteers. There was a small chapel in the camp where ministers and priests led church services for their respective congregations, praying to God for a swift Allied victory, and glad their camp overlords were not listening. They organized sports, discussion clubs. Even drama and music groups formed to provide weekend entertainment. "Yes," Harold said, "I agree. It's time to draw up plans and rationalize the whole space-assignment system."

As they passed between blocks ten and nine, Harold saw a group of young children running around and playing games in the dusty courtyard. It looked so normal, like a scene from an elementary school playground in the United States, and he wished that Victoria were playing there as well. Among the shifting groups of children, he caught sight of Livia running in loopy circles with her arms flung out, her hand grasping streamers of green fabric that fluttered behind her. Four or five children ran after her as she shouted and repeated a jingle:

Wo wo shou, wo wo shou,
Wo shi Cixi Taihou
Wo pa shan, wo pa shan.

Livia and her minions were about to rush by when she saw her father. She stopped.

"You shouldn't talk such nonsense," he said.

Livia pouted. "Kaiyuan always told me I was Cixi Taihou. Anyway, no one else knows what it means."

"Kaiyuan was teasing you." Harold put his hand on the shoulder of one of the little acolytes following Livia. "What's your name, young man?"

"William Jackson," the boy said.

"Do you know who Cixi Taihou is?"

William thought about that. "Some kind of boss," he said finally. "And I'm Huang Di."

"Who is Huang Di?"

"I don't know, but she can boss him." Harold laughed, as the children ran off to continue their game.

"Our house boy used to call my daughter Cixi Taihou," Harold said by way of explanation. "The last empress dowager. Huang Di is the emperor, but he was a weak fellow and took his orders from his mother."

"Your daughter has ambitions," Guildford observed.

"So it seems," said Harold, smiling.

They reached block seven and knocked on the door of room C. A man wearing a greasy, mashed cap opened the door. "We're from the housing committee," Harold announced. The odor of sweaty bodies drifted out the door.

"I'm Baker," said the man with the cap, suspecting something official about the visit. Two other men came up behind him. "What's it about?"

"I know we're all in a tight spot," said Guildford. "Nobody has enough room. But the fellows next door, over there in B, have eleven men, you've got nine. B and C are the same size, twelve by fifteen. We're asking you to accept one of them . . . to even things out."

Behind Baker's shoulder one of the men said: "Like hell we will. Got no room here."

"Not enough space to cut a fart!" shouted someone from inside.

"Your pipes ain't clogged," shouted another.

"Ain't stoppin' you, is it?"

"Now look here," said Guildford in his best Oxbridge English, "we've been appointed to oversee camp living quarters. Hit and miss is understandable for the first few weeks. Now it's time to sort things out and set up a system of housing that's fair and just."

Baker moved forward until his face was just six inches from Guildford's. "Who gave you that job, chum? We didn't." The other men in the room, who by this time were crowding up to the door behind Baker, shook their heads in agreement. "We ain't takin' nobody else. You can't make us. You send that bloke over here and we'll throw him out. And if you come back here again about this, we'll throw you out, too!" Baker slammed the door in their face. Harold and his partner looked at each other.

"Not a promising start for the housing committee," said Harold as they walked away from the block.

Guildford was silent for a while. "Look, Wayman, we need to change our approach. Those boys came over to China with a team of railroad engineers from south London. This is not the place to start. We should begin with the leaders of the community. The bankers, doctors, ministers, businessmen, professors. That sort. They'll be able to see reason, and once they are aboard, the others will fall into line."

"Think you're right. Why don't you take the businessmen and other professionals? I'll take the ministers. They would be the first to see the need for justice here."

Harold had noticed that Guildford was reticent about his religious views, despite his theological education. The young man admitted to him that, as the son of a vicar in north Yorkshire, he had been sent to St. Andrews to prepare for ministry. "The longer I studied theology the more I had doubts. Not that I'm an unbeliever. It's just that I can't fancy myself being a rep for the church, answering questions, defending beliefs, explaining things unless I'm convinced of them myself. I sat in the pew with Mother all those years and saw their faces when Father delivered his sermons . . . I was in the community hall for all the bazaars, the clothing drives and bake sales, the art exhibits. I heard what people were saying. You can fool yourself as a preacher. You get to orate for an hour every Sunday. People rarely dispute what you say. But behind your back . . ." Harold wondered what people were saying behind his own back.

The two men spent the next week studying the available spaces, writing a report on the current status that they presented to the governing council. Then they drew up plans to make space allocations more equitable, including an idea they thought was brilliant, creating dorms for the older children. They would get respected ministers to take turns as chaperones for the boys, their wives for the girls. That would free up a good number of rooms. The children would be happy with companions their own age. Parents would have some privacy. Everyone would be satisfied. The council approved their plans. They called a general meeting one evening, explaining with great patience the need for fairness, order, the sharing of space. Everyone agreed in principle, convinced that they would be *given* extra space. But in fact, to give someone extra space meant someone else had to give it up. No one, without exception, was willing to do that. The housing committee had hit a stone wall.

Harold sat on the north steps of the chapel one evening. This was the only place in the detention camp where trees grew. It was now late fall and the leaves had a dusty-gray look about them. Here in North China, the leaves went quickly to a dull yellow, then to brown before falling to the ground. Harold thought wistfully of the red, orange, and yellow splendor of autumn in the Appalachians. He had never felt gloomier about the future of their camp, nor more depressed about human nature generally.

For all the reasonableness of their plans, they got nowhere with the community leaders, including the ministers. No one was willing to give in. Upper classes, lower classes, religious people, nonreligious people, English or Americans, Belgians or French. Almost to a man they clung to their miserable little spaces. One red-faced martinet actually shouted at Harold: "Get the hell off my property. I'll take you to court when this is all over!"

Harold walked into the dimly lit chapel and sat on a bench, discouraged. He tried to pray, but no words came to him. He knew what he wanted: delivery from this camp, the defeat of the Japanese. Biblical scenarios came to mind: the destruction of the Pharaoh's army, the liberation of the children of Israel. But something inside him said that the Red Sea was not going to part. Suddenly the fate of himself and his family and the poor souls in this detention camp seemed insignificant, hardly worth praying for. Harold shook his head in despair, rose, and left the chapel, feeling for the first time doubts about his calling.

He had KP duty that night, assigned to cutting up the vegetables for the soup. The potatoes were no problem, but when he tried to cut the carrots, some of the little orange wheels rolled across the table and fell into the dirt. "Damnation," he shouted in frustration. A Belgian priest who couldn't speak English came to his rescue, patiently showing him how to cut the carrots lengthwise first. Half wheels could not roll off the table.

At six o'clock, the camp began arriving for dinner. He saw Del and Livia walking hand in hand into the dining area. He waved but could not sit with them. After the work crew had eaten and cleanup was completed, he walked down to block twenty-one where they lived. Del and Livia were sitting on their bed. Livia was playing with her collections of rag dolls. Del was working on a new one.

"Hey, little sugar," he said, "you're getting quite a family there."

"I already got two brothers," said Livia, holding up two of the raggedy creatures. "Now I need a sister. That's what mommy's making." He cast a quick glance at Del. Her eyes were focused on the task, but he knew what she was thinking. When were they going to tell Olivia about her missing sister? Neither of them could bear to bring up the subject. "Marissa's mommy is making a real one in her tummy. That's the best way to do it."

"Is that so?" he said guardedly. "Well, it's up to the good Lord." He sat on the single stool provided for their room.

"Or the tofu man," Adele said, without looking up from her sewing, and before he could respond she asked: "How did your work go today?"

"Stymied. No one will listen to reason, no one cares about fairness. All they want to do is cling to their miserable spaces."

"I would have thought with all the men of God here, it would be easy to appeal to their Christian compassion. Isn't there a passage in the Gospels where Jesus says if a man asks you for your cloak, give him your tunic also?"

Harold made a disgusted sound. "Like 'turn the other cheek.' More honored in the breach than in the keeping. One good minister of the Gospel told me last week that he couldn't possibly accept a second child in their room because he was often asked to preach a sermon and he needed peace and quiet to prepare his thoughts. Bosh! And you remember Reverend and Mrs. Martin? Met them at the club on more than one occasion. Kindest, gentlest, most gracious couple you could ever want to meet. But when I asked this morning if they would allow their children to sleep in one of the proposed dormitories to free up an extra room, they refused. They wouldn't consider breaking up their family. 'God wants families to stay together.'" He shook his head mournfully. "Hanging on to their bourgeois values in this miserable situation. It's enough to make a communist out of you!"

Adele looked thoughtful. Finally, she said: "I hope you would defend our family. Just like Reverend Martin did his. Things are bad here, but they could be a lot worse. Why don't you just let everybody stay where they are?" Harold was speechless. How could she not see that their community had to be based on fairness and justice? "You're always grasping at big ideas. Just let people alone."

"Del, I've been chosen to be in charge of housing here. I've got to do my job."

"Well," she sighed, "what exactly is bothering you? Do you think the Christians here are worse than the others? Is that why you are so discouraged?"

Harold thought about that for a while. "No," he said finally, "it's not that they are worse. What bothers me is that they aren't any better."

A week later, he and Guildford admitted defeat. They went to the south gate and asked admittance to the Japanese section of the compound. The officers were living grandly in six large detached homes that had once belonged to the American minister, the administrators, and teachers of the school. They were shown to the home of the commandant. They explained their plans and admitted their failure. The commandant nodded.

Next day the commandant rounded up a group of the internees, one representative from each housing unit. He sat behind his desk in full kit and regalia, his arms crossed in front of his chest. Even though he spoke passable English, he barked his orders in a harsh Japanese. As the representative of the Japanese government, he commanded them, through an interpreter, to share their spaces, give up rooms, send their children to dormitories, and do whatever else was required to implement the proposed plans. "Follow these plans," he commanded, stabbing his index finger on the papers neatly stacked on his desk. It was as though the deity had spoken. They all meekly obeyed. Where the ideals of democracy and justice had failed in their camp community, imperial mandates worked very well.

The next day Harold ran into Del outside block twenty-one, as she was returning from her work at the clinic. A look of distress came over her face when she saw him. "Harold," she said, "how could you do it? Everyone is saying that you and Guildford sold us out to the Japanese! You actually let them take control of . . . of . . . everything, our living, our rooms, our space. They're calling you lackeys of the Japs. Oh my God." She held her face in her hands. "I can't face any more of this."

"Those were our plans, not the Japs'. We worked on them a long time, and the council approved them. All the commandant did was to tell everyone to follow the guidelines that we created. We didn't sell out to them at all!"

She looked at Harold for a long time, without speaking.

"Well?" he said.

Finally, she said, "All we have is our little spaces . . . You just don't get it, do you? You just don't get it."

On August 15, 1945, the Japanese formally surrendered to the Allies in the Pacific. Rumors of this great event reached the camp. Two days later, they heard the roar of a four-engine plane in the distance. Unbelievably, it was heading toward their compound. As the sound got louder, the haggard residents looked skyward and saw the most improbable sight: seven great foliate forms drifting downward, like leaves from a celestial tree, landing miraculously a short distance from the camp as the B-29 flew on. Like lunatics freed from a mental institution, hundreds of the prisoners broke down the camp gate, shouting and rushing out to greet their saviors. The Japanese guards stood aside, gape jawed, raising no gun to stop them. The leader of the saviors, a major in the US Air Force, marched with his six men toward the compound. He walked like a god into the office of the commandant, aimed a gun at him and demanded the surrender of the camp. For a long minute the commandant looked grimly at him, without blinking. Then he opened the drawer of his desk, took out his pistol and ceremonial sword, and surrendered them to the major. Weixian detention camp was liberated.

苦海無邊

CHAPTER 7

In the Sea of Bitterness

Bu'er. 1944–1949.

She no longer thought of herself as Victoria. After five years of separation from her birth parents, she was now Bu'er. Her mental images of Harold and Adele had become gradually less distinct, while the images of gray-robed nuns began to replace her parents in her thoughts and even her dreams. The sights and sounds and silences that had once seemed so strange to her were now familiar—the drift of incense smoke in the chapel, the smell of garlic hissing in the kitchen woks, and the wonderful odors of herbs in Mingling's workshop. But the texture of her days was colored even more by the perfect silence of the place, so different from the ceaseless noise of Beijing.

She, Xihai, and Weizong had become young women. Cloistered from the world and separated from the older nuns, the three of them had learned to become friends. Perhaps it was the gentle persuasion of the Dharma, perhaps they had simply grown up. Xihai had outgrown the pouts and jealousies of her earlier years. Bu'er and Weizong now found her occasional spontaneous remarks funny, lightening the normally serious mood of the nunnery. Weizong had lost some of her airs, rarely bragging about her family and its grand home of many courtyards.

Next year, Weizong would take her vows and become a nun, an official follower of the Buddha. She would wear the gray robes, and as she recited the three refuges—*I take refuge in the Buddha, the Dharma, and the Sangha*—they would shave her head and burn the incense cones right down to her scalp. The ability to endure pain would show her determination to follow the Buddha's way. Her parents would come and provide a big vegetarian feast for the nuns at Yindong An. Her school days with Bu'er and Xihai were over.

Bu'er now recognized most of the healing herbs Mingling used, but the more she learned, the more she realized she did not know. When Mingling went out to gather ingredients or visit the sick, Bu'er always went along to help, but sometimes now Mingling sent her alone to a few farm houses in the upper valley. She looked forward to these errands but always felt a bit uneasy, remembering how the two Japanese soldiers had almost discovered them on their first herb-gathering trip. From that time on, whenever they came into the vicinity of a village, they left the path and took the longer and more difficult route along the steeper ascents of the mountainside.

Mingling remained a mystery, though the young girl admired her greatly. She was never harsh but often seemed a little remote. She rarely touched Bu'er or showed her any explicit signs of affection, yet it was clear that the older woman had come to trust her completely. Bu'er wanted to go to the villages with her and learn how to treat the sick, but Mingling's promise to Abbess Gaoyun had made that impossible. "Perhaps someday, after the war is over."

Gaoyun made occasional trips to Taiyuan, staying at a large Buddhist nunnery there that was located in the middle of the city. She often brought back some newspapers for the other nuns to read, if they chose. The papers were not meant for the young ones, but Mingling would often bring an issue of the newspaper to the pharmacy. She would pick out an article and go over the words with Bu'er, discussing the events of China and the world. "Look at this article, Bu'er. If you read carefully you will know that the Japanese are not winning this war. Your nation is fighting with them on many of the islands of the Great Peace Ocean. The article does not say that America has won these battles, because the Japanese still control Taiyuan City, but you can be sure that the Japanese will soon be defeated."

"Bolai says that we should ignore what is going on in the world," said Bu'er, excited by the reports of events in the newspaper but bothered that Mingling was teaching her things forbidden.

"She is right. First we must all separate ourselves from the world," answered Mingling. "But eventually we must go back to it, because our world is one of the Buddha fields. You have been separated from the world for more than five years now. You have begun to find the Buddha within your heart. I think that it is time for you to know other Buddha fields." From that time on, Mingling would give her informal history lessons, about China and even about America and Europe.

Each of the first two years, Heiyen and Guzhi returned to the nunnery, gave Abbess Gaoyun some money, and took Bu'er away with them, walking south a full three days until they reached a market town named Jiushiqiao, Old Stonebridge, on a tributary of the Dasha River. It was located where the tributary emptied into the Dasha, and over the smaller stream was the beautiful moon bridge built in the Tang dynasty that had given the town its name.

They stayed in the river god's temple, a large compound near the bridge. It had once been a grand temple, but over the years Old Stonebridge had lost its importance and fewer pilgrims came to celebrate the river god's birthday. Parts of the compound were used as a warehouse, crammed with junk, old boards, tiles, and other building materials, iron pipes, pots and jugs, broken bicycles, corrugated metal sheets, and dilapidated furniture. The compound had an inner section cut off from public entry, offering a refuge for the band of Heiyen, Guzhi, Bu'er, and other members of the group who came and went freely. They were called the Siyishe, the FourOne Society. Most of the townspeople were very familiar with the society because Guzhi had originally come from this town and still had relatives there, including Mayor Ma Jin, who was her nephew. Many belonged to the group. The name FourOne came from a well-known saying, "The four rivers flow into one sea," which expressed one of their beliefs, that all religions had the same goal.

Most of the directors of the temple were also members of the FourOnes, so nothing stood in the way of their using it for their headquarters. There were no Japanese soldiers garrisoned in the town. It was likely that its poverty and small size made it uninteresting to the authorities, so as long as they met their food production quotas, the town was left in peace.

The days at Old Stonebridge brought Bu'er a new sort of education. "Take her to the room behind the kitchen and teach her," said Heiyen, "if you can. You won't be disturbed there." The kitchen was used only a few times each year, to prepare food for the feast day of the river god and at the New Year.

Guzhi beckoned Bu'er to follow her. She sat her down on a wooden stool behind a small table. "Hold your head straight up as though it were suspended by a string," said Guzhi. "The string holds your head erect. Then imagine that someone loosens the string. Let your head bob down, your chin fall to your chest. Now lift it again. In a circular motion. Now drop it. Now lift it. Stay loose. Do not be tense." Guzhi continued in this fashion until Bu'er was dazed and confused. "All right, now you rest a while, and then we'll try it again. After much practice you will be able to go to the place where you meet the spirits. And after you have mastered that, you will eventually be able to do it without bobbing your head. You will know that place and be able to get there more easily." Guzhi took Bu'er's hands between her own calloused ones. "The spirits have told us you would be our leader. We must always know their will. I do not know the number of years remaining to me so I am teaching you how to do this."

Bu'er was dizzy from the head bobbing, and found herself taking deep breaths to balance herself. She had no idea what Guzhi was talking about, but the woman was unfailingly kind to her and she wanted to please her. At the same time Mingling wanted her to learn the healing arts, so the child felt burdened by her responsibilities. "What if I can't learn to go to meet the spirits?" she said to Guzhi. "Then what?"

"You will learn."

It was about a month after the Japanese surrendered that Bu'er first went to the place where the spirits spoke to her. Just when she had almost lost hope, her inner spirit woke up. She went into full trance in the river god's temple at Old Stonebridge village. Guzhi called out to

Heiyen to come and write down her words as she spoke them in a strange new voice they had never heard before. Heiyen rushed into the room with paper and pencil, elated, then sat stunned as the words tumbled out of her mouth. He strained to hear and make sense of them but couldn't. He and Guzhi looked at each other dumbfounded. Bu'er was speaking in another language. Heiyen crumpled the soiled piece of paper he had brought and threw it into the incense burner. They later found out that it was English.

The next years were chaotic as civil war ravaged North China. It was even worse than the Japanese occupation. Like the ants, armies advanced and retreated, leaving thousands of dead soldiers in their wake. Bu'er did not spend any time with the FourOne Society during those years. Fearing for her safety, they left her in the care of the nuns at Yindong An. The Communist troops were gaining ground, and soon the Guomindang armies of the national government began to withdraw toward the south and east. With the warfare ended in the north, Bu'er was able to accompany Mingling as she made her rounds to the villages in the valleys below Yindong nunnery, and that allowed her to teach Bu'er the practice of diagnosis. One day, after they had examined an old woman called Widow Li, she took Bu'er aside and asked her to diagnose the patient. What was the illness? What herbs or treatments might alleviate it?

Bu'er had mastered most of the herbal medicines and was beginning to learn how to examine a person's tongue for clues to their illness, whether it was pale red, as a healthy person's would be, or coated with white, or yellow, or too wet, or too dry, or any of the other manifestations of sickness. She began to learn how to analyze a person's pulse at the three different positions on the wrist as each related to the main organs of the body, to test the rate, the strength, quality, and rhythm of qi and blood flow. Both would do the tests, then Mingling would take her pupil aside and quiz her. Bu'er was not always correct, especially at first, but as the months passed she became ever more skilled in her analysis. Her small fingers were able to recognize the strong pulse, the weak pulse, the thready pulse, and so forth.

"You are so young," said Mingling one day, "but your karma has already made you a healer."

"My grandfather was a doctor," said Bu'er, remembering the stories her mother had told her about him, a man who had died long before she was born. "And my mother was a nurse." Mingling nodded, as though she were not surprised.

The villagers were aware that there was something strange about the young apprentice, but had so little experience of the world beyond their rural district that they were unable to articulate much beyond the fact that she was different. Her eyes were strange to them, "too pale," "too round." They asked Mingling if her odd appearance was the result of a sickness. "Her karma," said Mingling. And she had already learned how to darken the little girl's face and hands with a mixture of herbs boiled in flax oil and rubbed into her skin. Her ghostly complexion became light brown. She dyed her hair brown too and insisted that she always wear a headcloth. Thus disguised, she escaped most of the countryside gossip.

Some weeks later, Mingling was working in her pharmacy, preparing medicines for their next extended trip to the north villages. Against her better judgment, she had sent Bu'er on a brief errand to Baita village in the valley. She told her to visit Grandmother Ai at the tea house first, then go to see Lao Du, the farmer with chronic dysentery whom they had treated many times. She gave her the proper medicine to carry in her shoulder bag and made her promise to return as quickly as possible.

Bu'er had left early, but it was now midafternoon and she had not yet returned. Mingling began to worry. She waited another half hour, then walked out to the front gate and peered down the hill. Her eyes followed the path as it disappeared among the mountain pines. Some premonition drew her on, and she continued down toward Baita village. She came to the level area just before the narrow cliffside passage. It was then that she saw what looked like a twisted heap of clothes thrown on the ground. As she drew near, it became a human figure. Mingling cried out, "Bu'er," and rushed down toward the prostrate form. She saw that the little girl's pants were bunched around her knees. Her thighs were smeared with blood. Mingling saw that the place between her legs was still bleeding. She bent down and grasped the girl's shoulders. Bu'er screamed out, "Don't touch me!" Her little fists flailing and smashing against the older woman's face and chest. The blood spurted from Mingling's nose and ran down into her mouth. Without stopping to staunch her bleeding nose, she picked up the child and staggered up the hill toward the nunnery.

"This is all my fault," she told Gaoyun later, when she had got Bu'er back to the safety of the nunnery. "I should never have let her go alone to Baita. She is too young."

"How is she?"

"She is better now. I have applied canqi root to stop the bleeding, but she is still hallucinating. She is unable or unwilling to speak. I hope that she knows now that she is safe," said Mingling to the Abbess. "When I first found her she beat her fists against me. She must have thought I was the brute who raped her."

"Who do you think it was? Surely no one from the villages would have dared to attack someone that belongs to our nunnery."

"She had a torn piece of material clutched in her right hand. I pried her fingers loose. It was wool, that gray color they use for army uniforms."

Bu'er became dimly conscious, aware that she was in her own room. She felt the pain between her legs and immediately remembered what had happened. She felt the man attacking her, pushing violently into her again and again. She could not stop the sobs that racked her body, like waves of severe chills, every time she thought of the man's cruelty. She remembered first seeing him in the village when she arrived, sitting on a low wall outside the tea shop, smoking a cigarette. She felt his eyes on her as she passed by. Ai Taitai, who owned the shop, said to stay away from him. He was a soldier, a deserter from the Guomindang army. No one in the village knew him. Unshaven for weeks, his face looked dirty with its patchy growth of beard. On her way back to the nunnery, Bu'er saw him again, sitting in the same place, and again his eyes followed her. It was about halfway up the mountain path that she heard a sound behind her and saw that he was coming after her.

She began to run. But soon she came to the place of the narrow ledges and that slowed her down. She hoped that they would slow him down as well. But he was agile, and when she reached the end of the narrow ledge he was only a few paces behind her. He took the last of the ledge in a single leap, grunting as he lunged toward her. He caught hold of her shirt and pulled her into his arms, rubbing his face against hers. Then he pushed her to the ground and fell on her. He ripped off her headcloth. "Fucking nun," he growled when he saw her shaved head. Then he grinned crookedly. "Pretty face. *Aiya*, but you have a pretty face," he said, marveling at the round green eyes that stared at him in horror and fright. He pulled down her pants and unhitched his belt. "Very white. Very pretty," he said, excited by this exotic creature he had seized. She screamed as she felt the pain between her legs.

Mingling sat by the side of Bu'er's bed. It was the third day after her attack. She looked down at the darkened face that saved her from gossip; it had not been enough to save her from the beast who violated her. Mingling had once lived in the great city, Beijing, when it was the capital of China, and people from all over the world came there. She knew about violence and cruelty. She knew of the greater world beyond the borders of the Middle Kingdom, beyond the four seas where the powers of Japan, Europe, and America were located, always poised to send their armies to penetrate China if they chose. It was they who had killed her mother and father forty-seven years ago. This young white girl was one of their kind, yet Heaven had sent her here, she believed, to be her assistant, to learn her craft, to carry on the tradition Mingling had received so long ago from her grandmother. And yet Mingling had failed to protect her from the cruelty that existed among humans wherever they gathered, even here in the remote countryside.

A thought crossed her mind, a way to expiate her feelings of guilt. She could return to Beijing, look for her American parents and return the girl to them. That would infuriate Gaoyun and the FourOnes, but she was not afraid of them. She knew from Gaoyun that Bu'er had lived with her parents in Beijing before the FourOne Society had taken her. The parents might no longer be there, but she could go to the police and find out if the incident of kidnapping had been recorded. But was this the right thing to do? Could Bu'er now, so much later, go back to her own culture? Or was it too late?

While she was thinking these thoughts, Mingling cleaned the wounds again and applied a salve. She wiped her face with a soft cloth dipped in hot water, and tried to reassure her that the pain would go away. But she did not know if Bu'er understood her words. The girl looked at her with open but unseeing eyes, finally drifting off to sleep in the late afternoon.

Mingling was in her workshop when she heard Bu'er awaken and begin to talk. She rushed to the room and heard her repeating aloud, over and over again, "Pretty face, pretty face, pretty face." Then she suddenly sat up in bed, her eyes wide open, her hands pressed against her cheeks. "Not alone, with a man . . ." Bu'er leaped from her bed and raced to the kitchen where the cook was preparing dinner. She grabbed a scoop of water, walked to the wok where the cook was frying tofu. In a single motion she thrust her face over the wok and threw the cup of water onto the bubbling oil. In an explosive hiss of steam, she lost her pretty face.

明零小姐

CHAPTER 8

Miss Know-Nothing

It was the fourth day after the attack, and Bu'er was still feverish and sleeping fitfully. Her face was blotched with red sores. Mingling sat on a stool at the head of her bed, Abbess Gaoyun stood at the foot.

"It was a mistake to allow her to go there alone," said Mingling, with remorse. "I will never forgive myself for sending her. We had gone to Baita village so many times, and as she learned the healing process she was gaining a confidence—"

Gaoyun interrupted her. "My fault as well. I should not have allowed it."

"It was a horrifying experience and perhaps the blame is to be shared, but I do not understand why she has acted with such violence to herself. How could the teachings of the gentle Buddha lead to such madness?"

"That part, I think, was Bolai's fault," Gaoyun said, her arms crossed over her chest. "Not deliberate, of course, but she likes to tell the students dramatic stories to illustrate the Dharma teachings. She had told the little ones the story of the young woman, Bu'er's namesake, who was seeking to be an immortal. Perhaps you know the tale?"

"I am not familiar with it."

"The Bu'er in the story was attacked by two men, who attempted to rape her. She escaped but when she realized that it was her pretty face that had inflamed their passions, she held her face over a wok and threw water into the boiling oil to disfigure herself. I have warned Bolai that she must use her common sense when sharing these stories with the young ones. Such stories have their purposes, but one must know how to interpret them. I shall speak with her . . . This child has a fierce determination hidden under her gentle exterior."The Abbess stopped, letting her words sink in. "Tend her carefully," she said as she left the room. "This one is truly named Bu'er, for there is none like her."

Mingling applied a salve to her facial wounds and to the torn and bruised areas between her legs. Her body would recover, she knew, but what of her young and innocent spirit? As Gaoyun had said, "We will not have to struggle to convince this little one of the Dharma's first noble truth, that *the life of every sentient being is marked by suffering*."

Gaoyun left, and as Mingling watched over her young patient, she thought about her own early life. She was born just before the gengzi year in the reign of Emperor Guangxu. It was 1900 AD by the Western calendar, the year the Boxers rose up against the European powers and the Christian missionaries. The Boxers were zealots, her own parents among their ranks. They believed that their body-mind disciplines would protect them from the bullets of the British and the French. Both her parents had been cut down by those bullets when she was just an infant.

Her father's parents, Yeye and Nainai, took her into their home and raised her as their own daughter. Yeye worked hard as a tenant farmer on the estate of a wealthy landholder, but it was Nainai whose industry raised the family above the level of mere survival. Besides her chores in the house and garden, which she did with energy and determination, she knew how to use herbs and other healing techniques, using her skills to help neighbors. They paid what they could afford for her services.

The lives of Yeye and Nainai had been marked by times of flooding and drought, failing crops and civil strife, more than a taste of the sea of bitterness. Two of their children had died in their infancy, a breech-born daughter who strangled on her umbilical cord, and a little boy who had died of typhoid fever when he was about two years old. The other three grew to adulthood. Then Mingling's father died in the Boxer troubles, and his brother died in battle many years later, after being conscripted into Yuan Shikai's army. Their eldest daughter married early and moved with her husband to Tianjin, rarely visiting them except at New Year.

Despite these sorrows, Yeye and Nainai counted themselves blessed by their ancestors. They placed regular food offerings on their home altar, cleaned and decorated their graves at the Qingming festival every spring. And Nainai always gave thanks that the ancestors had sent them Mingling, who had become like their own child. She could not replace the great happiness of having a son, but she brought good humor, energy, and extra hands to help in their daily labors. Mingling learned from Nainai the names and uses of herbs, and the old lady was pleased that her knowledge of healing would not die with her, as she had feared, but live on in the skills of her granddaughter.

Mingling continued to watch Bu'er sleeping fitfully. The little girl's body jerked and twitched. *Bad dreams,* she thought, and she had no medicines to cure them. The healing of the heart and mind took time. She must wait as Bu'er went through her own struggles to cope with the violence she had suffered.

She closed her eyes, remembering the day she left Yeye and Nainai and went to live in Beijing. A cousin had offered her a job as a sort of janitor for a building that he owned. "Come to the capital," he had said. "I will pay you what is fair, and you may meet the foreigners. An opportunity might open for you. You could be an amah for a rich family." His building was located southwest of Qian Gate, in a run-down part of the city. The year was 1920, just after the end of the Great War in Europe, when the Allies cheated China out of Shandong Province. It had been the German sphere of influence, and instead of returning it to China, they gave it to Japan. The Chinese youth went crazy with anger, seething with rebellious thoughts against their ineffective government. That was the beginning of the revolutionary May Fourth movement, named for the day when students demonstrated in the streets of Beijing and other large cities.

Mingling's first taste of the May Fourth movement came when she met the wild ones and learned of possibilities she had never dreamed of.

They had an office on the second floor of her building. They were brash and brilliant, youth her own age who attended the finest universities in China. They came from a different and privileged world unknown to Mingling where servants cleaned up their messes. They left empty cups of spent tea leaves on the table where they had their meetings. They argued, made speeches. They criticized writers and politicians. They thoughtlessly crumpled up sheets of paper and threw them on the floor along with their stubbed-out cigarettes. Mingling straightened and smoothed the papers and gathered the cigarette stubs to take home to her cousin.

Mingling was dazed by their frantic discussions and offended by their careless waste, so different from her home where nothing was thrown away. Yeye almost never had enough money to buy cigarettes, and when he did splurge on a pack, he smoked each down to the very end until his fingers were singed and turned brown like smoked herrings. Nainai poured hot water over the same tea leaves many times, until the infusion lost all its color and looked as clear as rain water.

The crazy ones were the editors of a new magazine called *Xin Shijie*, the *New World*. Its bold editorials were the talk of Beijing. Mingling floated around the magazine office like a ghost, dusting and sweeping, working always silently and quietly in the background. Had they been attentive, the young editors might have wondered why she was always nearby when they met. But why would they be aware of a janitor? She was functionally invisible, like an unused piece of furniture.

From the back of the room or from out in the corridor, she listened to them debate their revolutionary ideas. They argued their positions ferociously, freely criticizing all the venerable ideas of traditional Chinese society. Confucius was the symbol of everything they hated. Sometimes they shouted their disagreements at one another, sometimes they reveled in the comradeship of shared hopes for a future new society.

Mingling was caught up in the excitement, but she could not read the *New World*. Like her grandparents, she was illiterate. But she was a quick study and as the weeks passed, she felt she knew the contents of the magazine better than most of its loyal readers, just from listening to the editors' discussions. Mingling agreed with many things she heard them say, while rejecting others. But nearly all their ideas conflicted with the things Yeye and Nainai had taught her to believe. They were against what they called the old patriarchal family system, against the oppression of the poor by the rich, although all four of the editors came from wealthy families. They opposed arranged marriages and the superstitious beliefs they felt made China a backward nation. They were in favor of the equality of the sexes, women's suffrage, and science-based education for all. One or two of them even advocated free love. Sometimes Mingling became physically dizzy listening to the mad outpouring of their ideas.

One evening, as she listened to them scornfully discussing peasant superstitions, she could stand it no longer. "I do not see what is wrong with people worshiping their ancestors. In any case, they will never stop doing it." Her words were spoken in a barely audible voice, but they came during a lull in the debate, and she knew that the four youths sitting around the table had heard her because of the unnatural silence that followed. All eyes shifted to look at her, as though seeing her for the first time. Finally, Lang Dechun, the rising star of the group, said: "We cannot accept that. The common people must be educated." He held a dog-eared manuscript in his hand which he threw on the table near where she stood, holding her broom. "Here, read it."

His words felt like a kick in the stomach. She had longed to participate in a discussion with them, but knew that because of her lack of education they would ridicule her. They were the golden children who had gone to famous universities like Beida and Shida, the future elites of Chinese society. Why would they listen to an illiterate peasant? "I can't," she said weakly. "I don't know how to read." Again, the silence.

"What is your name?" one of them asked finally.

"My surname is Zhu, my given name Mingling," she answered. *Mingling* meant the "bright sound of jade pendants." The only girl among the four editors, Li Baocun, then gleefully twisted the meaning of *Mingling*, for the same two sounds could mean something altogether different. Miss Li laughed out loud and said, "Perfect."

"What do you mean?" Lang said, always eager for a play on words.

"I say Mingling is the perfect name for her," Miss Li said. "Because she is the one 'who understands nothing.'" Li continued: "I don't believe it. She argues against education, but can't read. Now that we know she can talk, we should affirm her name: Mingling Xiaojie, Miss Know-Nothing!" The others laughed. Mingling would gladly have killed Miss Li on the spot.

"She isn't arguing against education, she's arguing for ancestor worship," Lang said, trying to be fair.

"No, what she's really saying is that the common people will offer resistance to our ideas, which is true. She should be commended for her insight, a dose of reality to cure some of your ridiculous idealism," Chen said. Mingling felt like running away. Her eyes were on the floor. They went on talking about her as if she were not there.

"Lang," Chen went on, "you're always touting the great ideal of educating the people. Why don't you take her on as a project? She is obviously smart. She can think for herself. Teach her to read and write and we will have an enlightened peasant, a future leader in our new society. That article you wrote is full of that shit about educating the masses. Let's see if you are just farting in the wind. Here is a real person who needs to be taught. Educate her!"

Mingling hated being called "a project." She wanted to tell them they were spoiled brats, strutting little emperors and empresses, but the lure of learning overcame her anger and embarrassment. When Lang agreed to the challenge, she swallowed her shame and accepted. She would learn how to read and to think, and when she was ready, would argue with them if she chose. And they would have to listen.

At that time, Mingling had considered herself moderately attractive, her best feature her thick, lustrous hair. Most Chinese women had either dark brown or raven black hair, and hers was of the latter type. She typically wore it in a braid and was proud of its lovely blue highlights. Mingling remembered the day she woke up to that small vanity. She was alone tidying up the editorial room one evening a few weeks after Lang began to teach her and feeling pleased with her life. She was glad for her work, sweeping, mopping, and dusting. It paid for her basic needs and allowed her to send home a few yuan every month for Nainai and Yeye. On a night like this, with the cold wind blowing through the hutong, she could stay here and sleep in the building instead of returning home to her cousin's drafty shack.

Li Baocun, her nemesis, was the first staff member to enter the room that night. Her remarks about "Miss Know-Nothing" set the course of their relationship. It did not help that Li had feelings for Lang, who now spent an enormous amount of time educating Mingling. Mingling looked up as Miss Li walked over to the table and stubbed out her cigarette in the glass ashtray that Mingling had just cleaned.

"Miss Know-Nothing," she said, lighting another cigarette, "I've noticed that you have become an advocate of gender equality." Mingling said nothing, continuing to sweep the worn wooden floor. "Yet you continue to primp yourself, using all the usual feminine tricks to attract a man's glance. One man's glance in particular."

"I use no makeup," she said, choosing to ignore the reference to her relationship to Lang. They were no longer just teacher and student. She felt that they were becoming friends, and maybe something more.

"Yes, but you wear your hair in a style fit for one of the emperor's concubines." Miss Li's brown hair was somewhat thin and without body. But she made the most of what she had, wearing it cut short in the bobbed style she had seen in photos of American flappers. "Confess, Miss Know-Nothing! How much time does it take you to get your hair right every day? Two hours or so? Washing, drying, combing, braiding! Time that could be better spent working for a new society!"

"That's crazy talk," Mingling said. "Not even ten minutes. I have to work for a living. Your rich parents pay your bills. You are the one who has all the free time to work for a new society!"

Before Miss Li could answer, two more editors, Fan and Chen, entered the room. Mingling thought that Miss Li would drop the subject, but she merely changed the tone, shifting to a more generalized argument. "If you are really for gender equality, you would cut your hair short. If a man and a woman's hair were about the same length, that would remove one more element of discrimination between them. Fan, isn't that so?"

"Yes," Fan agreed, "we should all shave our heads like the Buddhists! Did you ever notice? Sometimes you can't tell the difference between the monks and the nuns. They are all bald and covered by those heavy robes. Why don't you two go shave your heads. Then I'll shave mine." He laughed, knowing his carefully pomaded, parted, and combed locks were perfectly safe.

"Hair is very important," persisted Miss Li. "Look at how the pigtail signified our Han men's subservience to the Manchus of the Qing dynasty. I say we should adopt the short Western hairstyles to show that we are now the vanguard of a new society." The argument went on until Lang arrived and their meeting began.

Recalling the argument about hair brought Mingling momentarily back to the present. She looked down at the sleeping Bu'er, thinking about the young woman's red hair that her dyes had turned dark brown. She ran her hand through her own bristly short hair and remembered. Hair, yes. They say that your enemies can teach you more than your friends. She had thought about it carefully, and the detestable Miss Li had been right. Hair was important, she had to admit to herself. Or really, unimportant, but we in our ignorance have made it the opposite. So it must be dealt with.

One night, a week or two after her encounter with Miss Li, Mingling came to a decision. While the editorial meeting went on, she slipped out of the room and went to the copy room where the staff snipped and cut the columns of the articles and arranged them on pages, formatting them for the printer. She found a large pair of scissors and went to the bathroom. She took a deep breath and cut off her braid. She knew the best way to anger Miss Li was to agree with her, but take the argument in a different direction. She had done that with the "Miss Know-Nothing" name, announcing mysteriously that she accepted it but "in the Buddhist sense." Miss Li, fearful of showing her ignorance, did not respond, only mumbling something about superstitious nonsense. Mingling would use the same trick with her hair.

She returned to the meeting, carrying the beautiful braid in her hand. The editors looked aghast at Mingling as she entered the room.

"Miss Li is correct," she announced. "We women should reject all the traditional vanities," she said, throwing her braid onto the table. "I'm told hair can be sold at a good profit, to help the cause of our magazine."

Miss Li's jaw dropped. And if the Chinese flapper had hoped Mingling's new frowsy appearance would repulse Lang Dechun, she was sadly mistaken. "Mingling is truly a revolutionary," said Lang, a tinge of awe in his voice. From that moment on, Mingling never paid the slightest bit of attention to her hair, except that, when it got too long, she took a pair of scissors and cut it.

In the year that followed, she and Lang became closer. Unless a *New World* deadline was looming, they had time to explore Beijing together, Lang speaking of the history of each place they visited, connecting it with the general history of China. They went to the Palace Museum and Lang explained about the Shang dynasty bronzes, the Song porcelains, the Ming and Qing landscape paintings. She remembered the day they went to see the astronomical observatory. This tower was near the southeast corner of the old city wall, displaying the armillaries, the celestial globe, and other instruments set up by the French priests three hundred years ago to observe the heavens. Lang used the visit to lecture Mingling about the many times the Europeans had humiliated their great country.

"But if the priests brought science to China, that was a good thing, was it not?"

"No," he said impatiently, "it was merely a trick to convert the imperial court to Christianity!"

Mingling had noticed a slight strain in their relationship. The more her education advanced, the more fluently she was able to express her own ideas and opinions. At the same time, Lang became increasingly determined to shape her thinking to mirror his own. He seemed both amused and attracted by her short, careless hairstyle, yet as time went on, something in his manner began to change, the lessons becoming increasingly pedantic. Still the experience was very exciting to Mingling, her mind expanding so fast she felt it might burst. During that year she saw very little of Yeye and Nainai, though she continued to send them a bit of money each month.

Then the atmosphere in Beijing began to change. Chiang K'ai-shek's army defeated one warlord after another, and in 1926 his Guomindang party took over the city. The generalissimo's power base was in the south, so he stripped Beijing of its status and created a new Chinese capital at Nanjing. The excitement of the May Fourth movement began to subside, and with it the passion for new ideas that had driven the success of the *New World* magazine. They had proposed all the shocking ideas they could, but none had yet been implemented. Where to go from there? Lang became increasingly surly as he saw the circulation of the magazine shrink and realized that their hopes for a new future would not be realized anytime soon. Chiang K'ai-shek also called for a new society, but anchored it in traditional Confucian principles.

One of their weekend trips of exploration took them to the eastern edge of the city, and after a morning visit to the Altar of the Sun, Mingling decided that it was time to introduce Lang to Yeye and Nainai. She had some misgivings, but she felt that if she and Lang were ever to become more than just friends, she would have to show him who she really was and where she had come from. "They are old," she said to Lang, "two generations before us. But they are dear to me. They have raised me, the only family I have ever known. Please be patient with them."

"Even among those whose parents are alive, the bonds of family are not as rigid as before. Our first duty is to ourselves and to the new society," he said, parroting *New World* orthodoxy.

They took the train east, getting off at the town of Gaojing. A misty rain was falling as they walked north from there along a muddy road to Pingfang, the village where she had grown up. Lang was fastidious about his new Western-style shoes, and as they walked along he paused occasionally to wipe off the mud on tufts of grass at the edge of the road.

Pingfang was a small farming village, really just a cluster of small homes built between two ponds. As they approached it, a sudden ray of sunshine flickered on the duckweed-covered surface, turning it a glowing chartreuse against the dark purple of the rainy sky. Mingling remembered the simple beauty of the place where she had grown up. On the north side of the ponds there were fields of corn, cabbage, wheat, and millet. A few dusky alders were scattered among the low brick houses.

It was late afternoon. Mingling knew that the workday would soon be over and Nainai would be preparing dinner. Their home was a small brick structure with two rooms. It stood alongside the path to the ponds, the last dwelling in a cluster of similar homes. In front of the house was a concrete courtyard, surrounded by a knee-high brick wall. It was late spring now, and the concrete pad was swept clean. In the fall, after the harvest, when it almost never rained, the courtyard would be covered with millet seed for drying and winnowing. Dry bundles of cornstalks would be jammed into a small shed attached to the left side of the house, which now stood empty.

"Xiao Ming," cried Nainai, on seeing them, and Mingling realized how much she had aged. Her hair was now completely white, and her skin lined and wrinkled like a walnut. She looked quizzically at Mingling's companion.

"This is Teacher Lang. I have told you about him. He has taught me so much."

"Yes, of course." A few months ago, when Mingling came to visit, Nainai had been astonished to see her new "hairstyle." She did not understand it but knew obscurely that it had something to do with this Teacher Lang and her granddaughter's new friends. Bad companions, she thought. Still she was able to say the words, "We welcome you, Lang Laoshi. Have you eaten?" It was the traditional polite talk, but in this instance it meant that Nainai was inviting the two of them to eat supper. "Our food is plain and tasteless. I am embarrassed to offer such miserable stuff to such an honored guest," said Nainai, bowing stiffly toward Lang. More polite talk. Mingling noticed Lang's irritation. He obviously didn't want to go through the empty phrases he should have used, begging Nainai's pardon for intruding, not wishing to put her to any trouble on his account and assuring her that he knew that her food would be delicious. So he said nothing.

"You are a good cook, Nainai," Mingling said finally, filling the awkward silence. "Otherwise I would not be so fat and healthy. We will be happy to eat with you."

Nainai smiled and bade them sit down at the rough wooden table, where she brewed them a pot of flower tea. The woks and stove were just outside the back door under a lean-to, since the small room where they sat had to serve all other domestic needs—a place to eat, to receive guests, to worship their ancestors. When she returned to the room, she and Mingling began to chat easily about relatives and neighbors.

Through all of the small talk, Lang sat quietly, saying nothing. Mingling saw him looking at the family altar that stood on a narrow table at the back of the room. On it was a small statue of Guanyin, two candles, a small pot of wild flowers, and a sand-filled brass urn with three or four spent joss sticks in the sand. On the wall behind the altar was a cheap colorful scroll, also depicting Guanyin, and flanking it were smaller framed and yellowed photographs of Yeye's father and mother, her own great-grandfather and great-grandmother. Mingling looked at Lang's stiff posture and knew that he was inwardly fuming over this display of "peasant superstition."

Soon Yeye came in from the fields, and after the appropriate introductions, they sat down to eat. Mingling began to see Yeye as she knew Lang must have seen him, a weather-beaten old man, with dirty clothes, mud under his fingernails, and a few days' growth of beard. Nainai served them. Mingling tried to help her, but she wouldn't allow it. They ate mostly in silence, as was their custom. Nainai's apologies for the plain food got no response from Lang. After Nainai took the uneaten food from the table, Lang got the bottle of baijiu from his leather bag and insisted on pouring everyone a drink. Mingling knew this was wrong. He should just present the baijiu to Yeye and Nainai as a gift. But now there was no stopping him. He raised his cup and said, "*Ganbei!*" toasting them all. They all swallowed their drink, and he poured another. "I see," he said, "that you have an altar to your ancestors. Do you observe their anniversaries? Do you honor their graves on the Qingming festival?" Lang hardly noticed their humble nods as he continued his observations. "Even I have felt the need to 'hurry to clasp the feet of the Buddha,' as they say, when I faced a test at Beida. But I resisted. That sort of thing is superstitious. If you examine the practice scientifically, you will see that praying does no good. Buddha could not help me pass my test. Guanyin cannot help you with your problems."

Mingling winced at this, knowing that Lang was "educating the peasants." He continued his lecture, swallowing a second cup of baijiu. Mingling and Nainai had not touched theirs, but Yeye took another sip of his, and she could see the rising color in his face. Yeye and Nainai were looking at Lang as though he were insane.

"Your ancestors are gone," continued Lang, more emphatically, "decomposing in the yellow earth. How can they help you? You owe them nothing! Ancestor worship is a waste of resources." Mingling felt sick at this turn in the conversation, thinking her poor grandparents helpless to defend their beliefs. But they surprised her.

"You are wrong," said Nainai quietly. "I have had five children. I have prayed to Guanyin each time and each time she gave me a child. Yes, four of them have died, but three of the five lived many good years in this home. And Guanyin has sent Mingling to help us in our old age."

"Our ancestors have always saved us," said Yeye. "After the drought years they sent us years of plenty. When the demands of the landlord were unreasonable, we were able to talk sense to him. We have been blessed. We have survived. If we did not worship our ancestors, how could we show our gratitude?"

Lang seemed surprised at how stubbornly they resisted the logic of his arguments. "Mere survival is nothing! All of those things you described would have happened anyway—the children, those who lived, those who died, your survival—all those things would have happened whether you prayed or not." The two old people shook their heads, sorry for this sad man and his perverse views.

Lang downed another glass of baijiu. The more he drank the haughtier he became. Nainai and Yeye were hurt, Lang angry at their obstinate refusal to accept his views. And Mingling was angry at Lang for lecturing her grandparents. His fine words soon faltered, as he realized that they were having no effect on the old peasants. He cast a pointed glance in Mingling's direction and said it was time for them to be going.

"The last local train to Beijing has already passed Gaojing," said Nainai. "We invite you to stay here for the night." Mingling could see that she was making an enormous effort to be courteous.

"If we walk back in the dark, your nice leather shoes will get muddy," said Mingling, taunting him. Lang looked at her, and she could see the anger in his eyes. They glared at each other. He finally nodded reluctantly. Nainai showed them to their cots, one in the cornstalk room for Lang, one under the kitchen lean-to for Mingling, where the heat of the stove would keep her warm for the night. Nainai dropped the canvas awning, to better preserve the heat.

It happened an hour later. Mingling had almost gone to sleep when she felt the warm, boozy breath on her face. Lang slid his hand under her shift and began roughly squeezing her breasts.

"Lang, stop it. This is their home. They will hear us."

"I can hear them snoring in there. We are for free love," he growled. "We must stand up for our convictions."

"You are for free love," she said. "I am not. Especially not in my grandparents' house!"

"We will show them," he said, ignoring her protest, "that we live in a new world." Lang pulled himself on top of her, pressing on her shoulder with his left forearm and tugging awkwardly at her pants with his free hand. Mingling thought: *He's never done this before.* He had talked a lot about free love, but like everything else he advocated, it was all theory. As he slid his hand between her legs, she cried out. He slapped her face and covered her mouth. "Shut up, you stupid bitch," he whispered fiercely. "You must honor your teacher. You owe this to me. Without me you would be nothing but an ignorant peasant like your Nainai!"

He covered her, leaning on his elbows. She fought against him. "You hypocrite!" she hissed at him fiercely. Holding her arms pinned to the cot, he struggled to push his hardness between her legs. She caught the distended look of his eyes. Then, up above his head, she saw a movement in the darkness as a clay pot crashed down on the back of Lang's head and broke into pieces. Lang went limp as his body collapsed on top of her. Mingling saw Nainai looming above them, the broken neck-ring of her pot still clutched in her right hand. Her grandmother looked down at her with unreadable eyes.

"Nainai, I need to get out from under him." The old woman nodded.

"And can you get him some tea and fix him up? I'll need to get him back to Beijing at first light. And quietly. Don't wake Yeye."

"Ha! Have you forgotten? Nothing wakes Yeye but the roosters."

Mingling's thoughts returned to the present. She looked down at Bu'er. *I am almost fifty years old now,* she thought, *and these memories that would take so long to tell in words flashed through my mind in minutes. One day, I will share these memories with Bu'er.* She only wished she could share Yeye and Nainai with her as well, but they had gone to join their ancestors years ago.

An hour later, Bu'er sat up in bed, the wildness and fear gone from her eyes. She looked at Mingling and said in a small voice: "I'm hungry."

PART

II

TWO SISTERS, TWO WORLDS

CHAPTER 9

Hillesum-on-Hudson

May 1961.

Olivia was preparing for final exams, unconsciously biting her fingernails. She had placed her desk by the window so that when she tired of reading or writing, she could glance out at the lovely campus. She found something calming about the big trees shading a well-cut expanse of lawn. She looked down at the bitten nails with disgust. The nuns who taught her had all praised her work. What was there to worry about? Sometimes she couldn't figure out herself, much less anyone else.

Hillesum was located north of New York City, a cluster of limestone Gothic buildings on a sedate campus of tree lined roads, woods, meadows, and ponds. The nuns who taught there were members of a unique group of religious women, called the Order of the Handmaidens of the Mother of God, Ordo Dei Matris Ancillarum (ODMA). They were to be addressed as *Mother,* not *Sister*. Livia's more irreverent classmates called them "odd ma's." But in the adult world they were intellectual leaders among the many orders of Catholic nuns, very selective about whom they accepted as a postulant in their order.

Students at Hillesum were not evaluated by letter grades as in most schools but by individual critiques written by their teachers at the end of each academic term. They called these things "summative" statements, a word Livia could not find in her dictionary. Livia's recommendations would be strong, and her adviser had urged her to apply to some of the most prestigious schools in the country. The offer of a full scholarship came from the University of Chicago, and since her father and mother were not able to offer her much financial help, she immediately accepted it.

Then there was another possibility. Early in her senior year, Mother Mary Seraphim called her to the academic counseling office. "Kudos, Olivia! We are all proud of your success here, and your acceptance at a fine university. I've talked with Mother Superior, however, and we would like you to consider becoming a member of our order. Don't answer now, but think it over and give it your prayerful consideration."

Livia felt flattered at the invitation and tried to picture herself as a nun. The intellectual life attracted her, and she was excited at the thought of engaging the great thinkers in human history. She wanted to shape young minds, as hers had been shaped. She thought of the security of the life in a religious order, with all her material needs taken care of. She thought of the beauty of the chanting and ceremonies of the liturgy, marking the annual cycle of the church year. And most appealing was the idea of being a part of a sisterhood, a family.

Livia's four years at Hillesum Academy had been a life-changing experience. She had fallen under the spell of the intellectual nuns, and at the end of her sophomore year had asked to be baptized into the Catholic Church. She was dazzled by the pageant of Catholic history—the grand cathedrals of Europe, the *Confessions* of St. Augustine, the *Divine Comedy*, the *Summa* of Aquinas, the simple beauty of Gregorian chant. Without hiding the blemishes in Catholic history, the nuns told the story with enthusiasm. They had reconciled faith and reason themselves, and encouraged their students to do the same.

She found she was eager to join a group that would connect her to a centuries-old community found all over the world, one that spoke the same Latin everywhere its majestic rituals were performed. She had learned that language at Hillesum. Some of the Catholic doctrines spoke to a deep need in her, like the idea of original sin. It was a favorite of the nuns, perhaps because it justified the strict discipline with which they attempted to hold in check the "fallen natures" of their students. What it meant to Livia was a sort of distortion that affected every person, a part of the sad inheritance of what it meant to be human. Even the church and its leaders were not exempt. She felt its reality in the brokenness of her own family and in the loss of a sister she had never known. Livia knew, as most teenagers did not, that it was foolish to expect perfection in a fallen world.

When she announced to her parents that she was going to become a Catholic, both were stunned. Her mother rarely spoke about religion, although she occasionally took her daughter to hear gurus expounding their Hindu and Buddhist inspired philosophies at various centers in Manhattan. But she never talked of their teachings at home.

During her annual two weeks with her father, there was at first a resounding silence on the subject of religion. But as her knowledge of Christianity deepened at Hillesum, she and Harold began to argue about it, and those arguments became a regular feature of summer with Dad. "I respect your decision to become a Catholic," Harold said when she informed him of her upcoming baptism, "but don't expect me to come and celebrate ... At least it's Christianity and better than your mother's loony oriental experiments."

Adele did come to Hillesum for her baptism, but with a man in tow. "This is my friend Eugene. He and I met at the yoga center, but Eugene used to be a Catholic, so I thought he might like to come and meet you." She kissed her mom, wondering why in the world she thought bringing an ex-Catholic to the baptism of a convert was appropriate. She extended her hand to Eugene, whose long, delicate fingers grasped her short, nail-bitten ones. With his free hand he patted the back of her right hand, holding on to it a little too long.

"I've heard so much about you. Thank you for allowing me to participate in the ceremony. It brought back many memories, of things that were meaningful to me at one time. At an earlier stage in my life." Eugene finally let go of her hand. His words oozed forbearance, a serene understanding of her youthful enthusiasm. He was infuriating.

They took her out to a good restaurant for lunch. The conversation was awkward. Eugene quoted bits of Asian wisdom that he thought she might find meaningful. "You can stay within the confines of your Catholic theology," he conceded graciously, "and still appreciate the wisdom of the East." He advocated a careful reading of the Vedic scriptures, especially the Upanishads, as a key to life's meaning. Or the teaching of the Buddha, if she found that more agreeable. "Truth is one," he said. She found herself hating him.

"Do you remember anything of Buddhism from your time in China?" he asked. "Your mom has told me of its influence on her."

What a stupid question, she thought. "I was only five years old. And the last two years we were in a detention camp."

"Oh yes, of course," Eugene said, seemingly unflappable. He turned toward Adele. "Why didn't you stay on in China after the war?"

"We stayed for a while, but it was too dangerous. When we left the detention camp we found the country half destroyed by the war and the people starving. It was too dangerous." She shook her head sadly. "It was so impossible! I wanted a normal life for Livia . . . and for myself . . . I don't want to think about that time again. Let's talk about something else." But there was nothing much to talk about, so as soon as they finished eating and she paid the check, Adele rose to leave.

Late that afternoon, when Adele and Eugene had gone, Livia pulled on her blue sweats and headed out for a run. She jerked open the front door of her dorm and almost collided with Jean, one of her classmates.

"You are going to run into a lot of rain out there." Some catty classmates called Jean "the apostle of the obvious."

"I'll go when it lightens up a bit." Jean snapped the raindrops off her umbrella and went inside while Livia sat down under the cover of the porch and waited. She thought about the invitation to join the ODMAs. It seemed good, except for one thing—that old feeling that had haunted her since childhood, that it was somehow her destiny to go to China. That was hard enough in itself to imagine, but as a nun?

Livia thought about her own memories of China, some of them quite vivid, though there were long blank periods, and of the earliest years she could remember nothing at all. The places she recalled were the Presbyterian mission in Beijing, the walled area and lovely trees of the foreign legations, and the detention camp at Weixian. She remembered her parents arguing after the war was over, and the final decision that she and her mother would return "home."

But America was not home to her. Unlike her parents, she had enjoyed life in the camp. There were so many friends to play with. There were games, sports, music, and plays. She felt no sense of being cut off from a greater world. And although the food was sometimes scarce, they never starved. On the ship, Livia was bored and irritable, alone with her mother as they slowly crossed the Pacific. She had memories of sitting on the floor in their tiny interior cabin, with its white metal walls and dirty green carpet. Nothing to do. She wanted a friend, a brother or sister to play with. And without understanding the mechanics of it, she knew that without a father there would not be a baby. She fussed at her mother: "Now I'll never have a brother or sister."

Then an indelible memory: She and Adele were sitting on deck, talking with a shipboard friend, a woman who chattered incessantly. Livia disliked her because she monopolized her mother's attention without saying anything that made sense to a six-year-old child. The woman began: "Having lost your daughter, I can't imagine . . ." She stopped, clamping her hand to her mouth in a silly gesture of remorse. "Oh, I'm so sorry . . ." Adele glared at her, the woman looked embarrassed. But her mother's unspoken emotion startled Livia.

When they were alone, Adele sat her down and explained what happened in her matter-of-fact way. "Your father and I should have told you this a long time ago . . . You have a sister." She told Livia of Victoria's disappearance at the temple festival, a brief account that must have filtered out the heartbreak of the event, and the anger that followed. When her mother finished the brief story there was a silence.

Finally, Livia asked: "Where is my sister now?"

"I wish I knew."

"Did you and Daddy look for her?"

"Yes, we looked for a long time. And the police looked. But we never found her."

"Is she dead?"

"We don't know," Adele said, "but I don't think so. It is just a feeling I have . . ."

"Let's go back to China and find her."

So simple. Livia smiled at the childhood memory, but for many years she had retained the idea of returning to China. She remembered the language better than either of her parents. Chinese words and phrases still popped into her mind, usually as she was engaged in some mindless task. She would be setting tables in the Hillesum refectory, for example, glance at a bowl of fruit, and suddenly the word *xiangjiao* would pop into her mind. Banana!

But now it was 1961, and the United States and China were declared enemies, having slaughtered each other's troops in the Korean War. How could she go to a place where Americans were so hated? Should she forget it and become a nun? Although the tranquility of academic study and teaching appealed to her, the requirements of religious life seemed too restrictive. There was something more exciting out there in the great world that she looked for, and China was in some obscure way a part of it. She envied some of her classmates who had mapped out their futures so clearly from the time they were in kindergarten. A doctor, a veterinarian, a nurse, a lawyer, a teacher. Or a beautician, as one class comedian announced, hoping to irritate the nuns.

The heavy rain had stopped. She hopped down the dorm steps, jogged across campus, and up the path to the ridge overlooking the Hudson. She could feel the drops of mist gathering on her face and hair as she moved through the moist air. She ran hard, almost cherishing the pain in her chest.

At the top, she collapsed on a wet rock. It was flat and offered a vantage point to appreciate the pewter ribbon of the Hudson River below and the dark palisades on the other side. Then the tears came, running down her face, already wet from the rain. When she had gotten the cry out of her system, Livia solemnly reached for three rounded granite stones among those that lay around the base of the rock on which she had been sitting. She made a sort of cairn, placing first the large stone on the flat surface. Then she placed the second, slightly smaller stone, next to it, touching it. Finally, the smallest stone, nestled between them. Last of all, remembering Victoria, she added a fourth stone, just off to the side.

A week later, when she and her mother spoke on the phone, Livia asked politely, "How is Eugene?"

"Oh, I don't know. I haven't seen him since that day. He's such a prick!"

"What did you say?"

"You heard me."

"Yeah, Mom!"

Livia's high grades and her inklings of some unique destiny meant that she was not terribly popular. There was something too intense about her for her more easygoing classmates. She wasn't disliked, but she could call only a few of them real friends. She wasn't inclined toward team sports, so she often ran alone for exercise, using the lovely campus trails that led up to the ridge along the Hudson River. She often watched the sun set from there, above the Jersey palisades. *Wo pa shan, wo pa shan.* The rhyme played monotonously in her head as she ran. She *would* climb the mountain, but she had yet to find out what that meant.

Livia needed to prepare for her final test in the class on the Greek lyric poets. The last poet they'd studied, the subject of the test, was Sappho. Mother Mary Canisius had introduced her work by saying, "Some people would raise an eyebrow at studying a lesbian poet in a religious academy like ours. But her poems, as you will see, are really about love, not sex. That is an important distinction that I will expect you to be able to discuss intelligently." She paused, then added mysteriously, "And as St. Augustine says, 'Love and do what thou wilt.'" She laughed merrily.

Livia was glad to have the opportunity to study Sappho. But Mother's lectures on the poet created a lot of knowing looks and snickering among her sex-obsessed classmates. And some speculation about the sexual orientation of their teacher. Because there were only nine students in the class, Mother Canisius had arranged to give each of them a private exam for their final grade, insisting that each girl memorize three of Sappho's poems in Greek and be able to explain and interpret all six of her poems that they had studied. Most of the girls picked the three shortest poems to memorize. Livia, typically, chose the three longest.

At 7:00 p.m., Livia knocked on Mother's door. Since there was no answer, she sat down to wait for the nun's return, her back pressed against a section of the dark pine wainscoting that lined the walls of the corridor. It was bone cold sitting on the linoleum floor, but she figured that Mother Canisius would soon return. The blue wool of her winter uniform helped. While she waited she recited the three poems to herself. No problem. She could discuss them and the other poems. She would pass with ease.

Sitting idly on the floor, her thoughts drifted back to her childhood. When her father and mother had separated in 1945, she and Adele had returned to Raleigh, her mother's home. They managed to live with grandmother Martha there for two years, but it wasn't easy for Adele, as the old lady did not hesitate to tell her mother how to live her life. Livia sensed the tension between them, dimly aware of her mother's irritation as Livia was being spoiled by Granny. When Harold finally returned to the States in 1951—"booted by the Commies," he said—he visited them in Raleigh. Livia wondered what her father and mother talked about in private, but after the visit neither parent ever made a move to live together again.

As the months passed, tensions increased. One night she heard her mother and grandmother arguing, and Livia tiptoed silently just outside her mother's door and listened.

". . .have standards. I will not have this obscene deity displayed in my house. We are Christians, not Hindus!" Livia figured that Granny was referring to a white porcelain statue of Guanyin her mother kept on the chest of drawers next to her bed.

"Buddhist, Mother, not Hindu."

"That's beside the point. It's pagan superstition, and I will not have it in my house."

"This is my room. I need my own space, and no one is going to see the statue."

"Malvina will see it when she cleans house, and will be gossiping about it to the neighbors."

"That is ridiculous." Livia heard the tone of finality in her mother's words, then the sound of her footsteps moving toward the door. She dashed across the hall and slid into the bathroom. She heard her mother hurry downstairs and the front door slam as she left the house.

It was not long before they left Raleigh for New York. They found an apartment in a Brooklyn neighborhood, and there Livia grew up as an only child, with no family and few friends in the city. Her life in Brooklyn passed rather uneventfully, their routines interrupted by occasional trips to Manhattan and an annual trip to Raleigh to visit Granny at Christmas. In the summers, Harold would drive up from Richmond and take Livia off with him for a two-week vacation, one week at his bachelor's apartment and the second at Rehoboth Beach on the Delaware coast. Watching TV in the apartment was a bore, but Livia loved the week at the beach, the long walks looking for shells, crab claws, shark teeth, and other debris thrown up by the sea. The summers seemed so routine, yet in a way reassuring to her, natural and predictable, like the rise and fall of the tides.

Livia moved through the local school system and planned on going to the neighborhood high school. It was all her mother could afford. But everything changed when a phone call came from a Raleigh neighbor saying that Martha had died of a sudden stroke. As the only child, Adele had to make arrangements for the funeral, so she and Livia rushed back to Raleigh. After Martha was properly buried in the graveyard of St. Bartholomew Episcopal Church, Adele looked into the will. She naturally assumed that, other than some possible charitable bequest, she would be the only beneficiary. Instead, it provided the house and a fair sum of money, both held in trust and earmarked "solely for my granddaughter's education." Martha Manigault was in command, even from beyond the grave. She had left Adele with a small fund "to lessen the burdensome responsibility of raising a daughter as a single parent." The lawyer would act as trustee. Martha had disapproved of her daughter's choices in life—first for marrying Harold, "the poor preacher," then for leaving him, then for moving to New York instead of staying in North Carolina, and finally for her "occult pursuits," by which she meant her interests in "Asiatic religions." Some of her criticism of Adele made it into the will, and she cringed at being forced to listen to the reading of the document. "I am sorry, Mrs. Wayman," said the lawyer when he finished, carefully sliding the will into a manila envelope. He looked thoroughly embarrassed. "I urged her not to include such personal remarks in her will. But you know your mother."

"Yes, Mr. Porter, I'm afraid I do." Both spoke of her as if she was still alive.

But Livia had to give her mother credit for carrying out Martha's wishes. With the funds now at her disposal, Adele paid close attention to where her daughter might go to high school. Hillesum Academy, on the river north of the city, was expensive but boasted a stellar record for getting its students into the best colleges and universities. With careful management, the funds should last until Livia was graduated. As Granny Manigault had been a staunch anti-Papist, Livia assumed that her mother's choice of a Catholic school was not an accident.

Livia was beginning to feel the cold and decided to sit on the Lyric Poets textbook, insulating herself from the cold floor. She wondered why Mother Canisius was so late. She tore a blank page out of her notebook and was about to leave a note, saying that she would wait in her room, when she heard the nun's energetic steps in the stairwell.

"Sorry I'm so late, my dear," she said breathlessly. "I had some errands to do in the city. The traffic was terrible."

"I could wait for you downstairs. Do you want me to return in a half hour?"

"No, no. Not at all. Come in, Olivia," said the nun, beckoning her to follow. "Just take that chair, over there. Make yourself comfortable. I'll be with you in a moment." Mother walked over to the bed, removed her long black overcoat and laid it across the foot of the bed. She reached under her coif, unclasped some pins and removed the head covering. She shook her chestnut-colored hair as if to free it from the constraints of the religious clothing. She wore a gray suit and underneath the jacket a pink blouse with an open collar, revealing a delicate golden chain and cross. Ageless and genderless in her black robes, she now seemed almost young to Livia, maybe no more than forty, and definitely a woman.

"You're the last of the nine to take the exam," she said as she walked directly to the fireplace. Livia watched with great fascination. She was unaccustomed to being able to observe these small everyday actions, although she knew that nuns, like everyone else, had to take off their habits at night, wash themselves, and do the other things required by normal life. She tried, without success, to imagine Mother sitting on the toilet.

The nun opened a box of matches, struck one, and leaned down to light the gas logs. Livia noticed the gray skirt pull tight around her hips as she bent over. She heard the click, then a whoosh of flame as the fire leaped above the logs. "I'll leave it on high for a while. It will take the chill off the room. We will be able to concentrate on Sappho and not have to worry about chafing our hands." Chafing. The "rubbish bin" instead of the waste basket. Mother Canisius had spent three years at Oxford getting her MA in the Classics, coming back to the order and her assignment at Hillesum Academy with the hint of a British accent and vocabulary. That was the talk among the students, at any rate. Still, Livia liked her. Without ever saying anything directly subversive, Mother Canisius managed to project a kind of rebellious and youthful air to her students.

Mother Canisius walked over to the small table by Livia's chair, leaned down, and switched on the small table lamp. "You may put your books and notes here, if you need to refer to them." She stroked Livia's hair affectionately as she spoke. The gesture surprised her, but Mother was already walking back to her own chair on the other side of the desk. Livia looked at the table lamp. A warm orange light glowed behind its shade, which was covered with a smooth opaque material pulled tautly over the ribs. It was the color of vellum, and Livia felt impelled to reach up and run her fingers over the strange lampshade. It felt soft and yielding, like human skin.

The exam went well. Livia parsed sentences, explained concepts, interpreted metaphors. She recited her three poems flawlessly. She argued for ideas she knew Mother favored and expected to hear. She felt some slight guilt for doing that, but that is what everyone did to get a good grade. When it was all over, the nun came over to her, took both of her hands in her own, and held them warmly. "That was brilliant, Olivia, a pass with honors. Now you sit here for a moment and relax while I get something. I think your success merits a little celebration."

Mother walked over to an oak highboy placed against the wall to the left of the fireplace. She opened a cabinet door. Livia watched her remove a bottle and two wine glasses. She brought them to her desk and filled the two glasses. "This is a fine port, a Christmas gift from a cousin of mine. I save it for special occasions. Cheers!" she said, lifting her glass in a toast.

The port tasted thick and fruity. Sweet. Not unpleasant. A gentle flame spread in her throat. After three or four sips she felt the warmth spreading from her chest to the top of her skull. The tension of the test had begun to fade, and she sank, relaxed and happy, into the soft fabric of the easy chair. She pressed against the chair back and let out a little sigh of pleasure. "That's a lovely chair, isn't it? I curl up in it when I read at night," the nun said, evoking a cozy scene of contentment before a blazing fire.

Mother posed a question: "Of course the test is over, but I would like for you to tell me which of Sappho's poems you like best, and why?" As she asked the question, she poured more wine into each of the glasses. "It is a bit too warm in here for me." She removed her gray jacket, placed it on top of her overcoat, and went to the fire. She turned down the gas jets until the flames were just tiny orange tongues gently licking above the top of the gas logs. Mother turned from the fire and arched her back as though stretching. Livia could see the outlines of her breasts pressing against the silken fabric of her blouse. "Take off your blazer, my dear, it is far too warm now for that."

Livia did as she was told. "Well, to answer your question," said Livia, "I like it when Sappho directly addresses Aphrodite in her poems. Her words seem so honest. My favorite line is, 'In my wild heart, what did I most wish to happen to me?' She seems to be groping toward some great goal in life, as I suppose I am. I find it both delicate and ambiguous, more about love than sex." As soon as she said the cribbed words, Livia was disgusted with herself.

Mother seemed not to notice and came around from behind her desk, standing in front of Livia. She took her two hands in her own and drew her up from the chair. The two of them stood facing each other, one side of their faces glowing with the reflected light from the fire, the other side shaded in darkness. Mother kissed her lightly on the cheek then found her lips. "Livia, which do you think this is?" she said, touching her neck above the collar of her white blouse.

Livia's memories of the minutes that followed were not clear, whether because of the wine or her growing excitement and panic. She remembered more kisses and the feeling of Mother's cool, dry hands gliding over her body, creating currents of electricity wherever the fingers touched. Livia felt herself respond.

How long was it until she pulled away? Two minutes, five, ten? She grabbed her blazer and fled from the room. She stumbled down the steps, crossed the lobby and rushed toward her room in the student wing, hoping desperately that none of her school mates would see her. She burst into her room, fell into her chair, and buried her face in her hands. She was not innocent, and when she thought about her own part in what had happened, a sense of guilt overwhelmed her. She felt the sticky sweetness of the port rising into her throat and ran toward her bathroom, throwing herself to her knees in front of the toilet. She stuck her fingers as deep into her throat as she dared, gagging and heaving, as though this physical act could cleanse her soul. The water in the basin turned red.

The next morning, she sat with classmates at a refectory table poking at the bowl of oatmeal in front of her, completely unaware of the conversations around her. She was thinking that it would be her duty to report last evening's events to Mother Superior. It was so disgusting. How could she admit her own part in it? What words of confession could she utter that would not sound completely sordid? Then, out of the corner of her eye, she saw a nun heading rapidly toward her table. It was Mother Canisius, her arms cradling books and a folder. The woman was energized, her eyes lively. "My dear! You left the test in such a rush last night," she said with a gay smile, "that you forgot your books! That's the price of being an intellectual, I suppose . . . a little forgetfulness." She placed the materials next to Livia and fluttered away. Knowing looks around the table as Livia felt the heat rise to her face.

At that moment, in the face of the nun's performance, Livia knew that she could say nothing to Mother Superior. Mother Canisius would deny everything, and Livia would be suspected as the hysterical liar. Mother Superior would judge her charitably, blaming the whole thing on end-of-semester tensions. There would be no blot on her record.

Livia could not bear that kind of charade. She would say nothing, quietly graduating with all the other students.

CHAPTER 10

Graduation Day

June 1961.

Livia sat between Adele and Harold along one side of a long table in the refectory, listening to a famous bishop deliver the commencement address at Hillesum. He was quite a catch for a small boarding school. The grooming of his black hair, highlighted with silver accents, was impeccable, his words had a sonorous quality, his eyes flashed with passion as he spoke. But her mother, obviously bored with the talk, was doing some kind of breathing exercises she'd learned in her meditation class. She was inhaling silently, through her nose. Her exhalations, through the mouth, sounded like air moving through a wind chamber. Her father fidgeted, clearly irritated both by Adele and the bishop. Livia was disgusted with both of them.

The bishop, known as one of the finest orators in the American church, rumbled on in his rich baritone. Graduation should have been a joyous occasion, but Livia was moody. For one thing, her parents were being perfect asses. Together again after so many years, her parents were acting like feuding teenagers. And she herself felt soiled and confused since the sexual encounter with Mother Canisius. Sickening images still ran through her mind. Again and again, she repeated to herself words that were, at least, a small comfort to her: "All have sinned in Adam, all have fallen short of the glory of God."

For two weeks she had felt an unspeakable guilt. She was too ashamed to go to the sacrament of penance. The chaplain for the girls was a Jesuit named Father Miles, who came every week to hear confessions. The nuns had chosen him because he was a youthful man with a sharp intellect. He would be able to communicate with their bright young students. Though handsome in a dark, Mediterranean sort of way, he had a tendency to be severe. Livia felt it would be impossible to confess her sexual encounter to the man.

Then, just a week before graduation, Miles had gotten sick. Mother Superior quickly called the local parish of St. Bonaventure and obtained the services of Father Jacob to hear confessions, just in case one of the girls might have fallen into mortal sin and wished to confess before communion service the morning of graduation. Father Jacob was retired and quite old, but much loved as a confessor.

Mother Superior introduced the old priest at assembly the Thursday night before graduation. He had a bald head partly covered by wispy strands of white hair, was portly, and had a long and pointed nose with a wart on it. Livia's friend Heidi leaned over and whispered: "Wasn't he in *Oliver Twist*?"

"I will be available for confessions in the chapel tomorrow afternoon and evening," said the priest. Then he joked with the girls, pointing to his nose. "The older I get," he laughed, "the closer it comes to my chin. I hope to go to my eternal reward before they meet." His belly shook, Santa Claus fashion. Instead of edifying the young students, he told funny stories about his life as a priest, some of them slightly off color. He had once made a faux pas at a parish affair, he told them, as he was reading out the prizes for the church raffle. He saw the word *brazier* and read it as *brassiere*! Second prize was a charcoal brassiere. The girls giggled. Mother Superior rolled her eyes, praying that their dignified Jesuit chaplain would get well soon.

Father Jacob's cheerful attitude was encouraging, but Livia was still reluctant to confess. The next day, as she stood outside the building that housed the chapel, trying to stir up the courage to enter, her friend Heidi popped out of the front door. "Livia, I just went to confession. You wouldn't believe what an old dear he is. You feel like you could tell him anything at all and he would understand. You should go to him, even if you've got nothing to confess. I know you're Miss Perfect. Just make up something. Like, you got angry at one of the nuns or something." She laughed, strolling off as though walking on air.

Livia climbed the stairs to the chapel, dipped her hand into the holy water and crossed herself. She walked up the side aisle to the area by the confessional, genuflected, and knelt in a pew. There were three other girls ahead of her. She intended to confess, but if she decided she couldn't bring herself to do it, she could easily slip out and no one would know the difference.

Then it was her turn, and she was relieved to be the last to approach the sacrament. She got up and walked into the dark booth. She heard the wood panel slide open. The old priest coughed lightly, as if to assure her he was there and ready to listen. She could see him obscurely through the white cloth that hung over the small window. She recited the formula she had memorized two years earlier, when she was received into the church. "Bless me, Father, for I have sinned. A month ago was my last confession." She wished she could go back that month, when all she could think of to confess was envy of a classmate. Now she was speechless, as the words she planned to use slipped from her mind. She tried to think of how to begin. The silence hung uncomfortably over the confessional. Finally, the priest said. "Don't be afraid, dear girl. Tell me what is troubling you. God is merciful. He wants to forgive you . . . place your sins before him. There is no sin so terrible that I haven't heard it hundreds of times before." He chuckled gently.

"I've been impure, Father," she stammered.

"With yourself?" asked the priest routinely, as though he had encountered this sin many times before.

"No."

"With some young fellow, then?"

"No."

"With an older man?" he asked, a note of apprehension in his voice.

"No." Livia hesitated, then blurted out: "With another woman. With a nun, one of my teachers."

"Oh my God," she heard him say softly. There was a pause, during which the priest cleared his throat but said nothing. Livia was horribly embarrassed and on the point of bolting the confessional when he finally spoke again. "Did she kiss you, something of that nature?"

"No, it was more than that. She touched me . . . in a sexual way."

"Did you take deliberate pleasure in that? Venereal pleasure? Knowing it was wrong, did you give deliberate consent to it?"

"I don't know for sure. I think I did. It was all so confusing. She gave me some wine to drink and I wasn't thinking very clearly."

"She gave you wine!" He seemed to be struck speechless again, then muttered something about a "den of vipers." Finally, after a long pause, he gave his judgment. "From what you've told me, I would say that an older woman, who should have known better, took advantage of you. It was not your fault, or at least, if there was some guilt on your part it did not rise to the level of a mortal sin." She could see him shaking his head behind the white screen. He gave her the rosary as a penance, just in case perhaps, then raised his hand to bless her and said the words "I absolve you of all your sins," he said in Latin, "*in nomine Patris, et Filii et Spiritus Sancti . . .*"

A different Latin blessing brought Livia back to the present. *"Benedic nos, Domine,"* intoned the bishop, raising his hand to bless them, *"et omnes familias nostras, qui vivat et regnat per omnia secula seculorum."*

"Amen," murmured the girls with relief.

Livia, Adele, and Harold rose as the crowd began to disperse. Her father muttered, "What a pompous ass! Why in God's name does he have to do that Latin mumbo jumbo?"

"Because we've learned Latin. It's a part of the curriculum," Livia said.

"It's like the Reformation never happened," Harold continued, as though he had not heard her answer. "I'm not impressed. I still can't see what induced you," he said, turning to Adele, "to send her to a Catholic school."

Adele waved her hand airily. "I'd have sent her to a Buddhist school, but there aren't any around here. Anyway, Hillesum is a good school. It got her a scholarship, didn't it?"

Harold did not reply. Livia thought that it was curious that he would not argue with Adele. As Livia had grown up and begun to have her own opinions, she and her father argued about religion, especially since her baptism. The nuns had taught her to be logical. Mother Adelbert, their philosophy professor, had one day projected a large photo on the blank rear wall of their classroom. It was the window of a Gothic cathedral. "This is an architectural statement of how your mind should work," she said. "See that circular window at the apex? Like a small rose window, is it not? That is the principle, the subject to be analyzed. Below it you see a division occurs. There are two windows, and below them three small windows under each. And finally, below those six are twelve windows. That is the beauty of precise thinking, of seeing the relationships between things, whether temporal or causal." *I wish the real world was that neat and tidy,* thought Livia, *instead of the messy affair it is.*

As they walked toward the parking lot after the graduation ceremony, Livia thought how her parents were the proverbial ships passing in the night. Her mother was, religiously, the exact opposite of her father, never arguing about religion or politics. She seemed to float above contention, waving her hand and saying, "These arguments never get anywhere." Her path was Asian, where the search for truth led beyond human words.

红星红尘

CHAPTER 11

Red Star, Red Dust

Shanxi. 1962.

"Scavengers! Dogs! Parasites!" shouted Lieutenant Jun Hao, standing outside the door of the Yindong An chapel. "Living off the labor of the people! Sucking the peasants dry! By order of the Shanxi Provincial Authority, this degenerate nunnery, this relic of ignorant superstition, is hereby closed." He clearly considered himself eloquent and bellowed his message as though a large crowd were listening, but he was talking to a group of seven old women in a small courtyard of the convent. Abbess Gaoyun, now feeble in body, but still mentally tough, listened to this rant, thinking how wrong, how completely wrong were the words of Comrade Jun Hao. Gaoyun was among the best educated of Buddhist nuns and found it hard to put up with such ignorant cant.

As Jun raved on, parroting the slogans of the regime, Gaoyun remembered their years of near starvation after Chairman Mao's Great Leap Forward. She thought of the hungry peasants, desperate enough to climb the long path to Yindong An. They shared their watery soup with all who came. None were turned away, though their own rice bag was almost empty. She thought about the healing work of Mingling and Bu'er, but kept her silence. She knew that arguments with cadres like this Jun were futile. Any hint of opposition would only provoke greater outrage and violence. He had already sent his men to destroy the statues in their chapel, and she could hear the sound of sledgehammers smashing their Buddhas. Even though most of them were not works of art, still they were the vehicles of many blessings, and their destruction was like the killing of members of her family, like the murder of her teachers.

"Where are the rest of the nuns?" demanded Comrade Jun.

Gaoyun gestured toward the six standing behind her and then included herself. "We seven are all that remain. Some years ago there were twelve to fifteen of us, including postulants. Some have died, some left during the years of starvation . . ." Gaoyun thought with relief that Mingling was away on a medical errand and Bu'er was currently with the FourOnes at Old Stonebridge.

"Shut up about starvation. The years of famine were caused by the stinginess and hoarding of the wealthy classes. If they had shared their wealth with the proletariat, there would have been enough food for everyone. Now it is too late. You must take your place, shoulder to shoulder with the peasants and working masses and advance our glorious society to its great socialist destiny. This nunnery is a relic of superstition that must be destroyed."

"Shoulder to shoulder with the peasants . . ." Gaoyun almost laughed out loud. "Look at us, comrade! What do you see? We are so old that we count ourselves lucky to be able to totter from our cells to the chapel. If we leave here, the state will have to take care of us . . . or watch us die in the streets."

"We are happy to arrange the latter," said Jun with a grim smile. "You must now leave and come join the revolutionary society, working to support yourselves and advancing our glorious socialist future. You are *capitalist roaders*, and the days are past when rich landowners like yourselves can steal bread from the mouths of the poor!"

Gaoyun knew it was the end of Yindong An, but had not the Buddha himself predicted the waning of the Dharma in the final age of the world cycle? Perhaps that time had come. And she also knew that death and rebirth were both part of a single process, the law of life in this world of red dust. A monastery or nunnery can die, just like a person. When Comrade Jun and his gang of thugs had left, Gaoyun began to talk with her sisters about where they might go for refuge when they left the nunnery.

"Things have not worked out as we had expected." Guzhi said, "The brothers are right. We risked everything and have nothing to show for it." She and Heiyen sat together on a stone wall in the courtyard of the river god's temple in Old Stonebridge village. They had just concluded a meeting with some dissatisfied members of the FourOnes.

"Do not say that! Our numbers have increased. Think of how many of us there are now, in Shanxi and Hebei provinces."

"But we cannot practice our beliefs in public. And I cannot forget that we tore the fabric of a family. Yes, they were Americans, but the family is sacred everywhere, its bonds created by Heaven. Where did we go wrong?"

"We did not go wrong," Heiyen whispered fiercely. "We had to do it. If we disregard the commands of the spirits, what is there left to guide us? Without their guidance we would truly have nothing!"

"If we hope to succeed, we must create communities in which our ideals may be practiced openly."

"We cannot do that now. And if we continue to practice secretly and are discovered, they will crush us even more fiercely."

"What path is left for us?" Heiyen could think of nothing new to say, so he kept silent. Guzhi knew she would get nothing more from him, so she rose from the wall and walked away, leaving their leader to his somber thoughts.

He believed that the two of them were chosen by the spirits to be *qian* and *kun*, the man and the woman, the universal principles, father and mother to the FourOnes. Bu'er, their "daughter," had grown to adulthood, and the three of them were the Way in its earthly manifestation as a family. He shook his head as he thought about it. How could he, an ordinary man, and Guzhi, an ordinary woman, or Bu'er, a child from across the sea . . . how could they aspire to such grandiose roles? Surely it was possible only through the power of the spirits.

His own life was a case in point. Twenty-seven years ago, he was Li Bingxian, in his early thirties, working as a clerk in the Beijing office of the municipal water supply. He was completely ordinary in appearance, not tall, not short, not handsome or ugly, neither intelligent nor stupid. Due to the support of his parents, he had graduated from Hebei

University in Tianjin, though without distinction. His parents had urged him many times to get married, but he ignored their admonitions.

It was on a night in the year 1935 when everything changed. Generalissimo Chiang K'ai-shek had launched the New Life movement, which advocated clean bodies and minds. There were campaigns against hawking, spitting, and urinating in the streets. The leaders advocated exterminating cockroaches and killing rats, poisoners traveling the streets, pushing carts loaded with the dead vermin. The New Lifers had also blundered into the field of women's apparel, seeking to eliminate the scandal of provocative clothing. Hemlines must be four inches below the knees, the slit in the traditional *qipao* dress no longer than three inches. It was all about as exciting as watching the leaves turn brown in the autumn.

One day Heiyen's boss, a New Life enthusiast, had urged all his workers to attend a rally at the Big Bell Temple in the northwest corner of the city. Heiyen got off the bus that night at the nearest stop and wandered toward the temple, but he had apparently taken a wrong turn, straying into a different temple in the same vicinity. He had heard loud voices calling out single words that he could not hear clearly. He assumed it was the rally with Guomindang leaders shouting out slogans to support Chiang's movement. But once inside, he realized he was in the wrong place and had stumbled upon some sort of religious ritual. He was about to leave when a voice shouted out what sounded like his deceased father's name: Li Caihong. He stood frozen in place. It was as though his father had come from the world of the spirits and was calling him. He listened very carefully to the words which followed: "Can you be as flexible as a child, can you play the role of a woman? Leading but not taking credit? This is the highest virtue, the way of Heaven." Heiyen was speechless. He had heard his father mumble some of those very words on his death bed! He did not know what they meant, but because of their strangeness he could not forget them. They were like poetry. Then he saw the woman writing, as though in a trance, and he saw men who leaned over her shoulders and called out her scribbled words. His mind was spinning, but he clung to the words he had just heard, like a drowning man holds on to anything that floats by him in dangerous waters. He kept repeating to himself: "This is the highest virtue, the way of Heaven."

Soon the ritual was over and a man summarized the message by calling out all the words that had been transcribed. Heiyen stood straining to hear. At the conclusion of the reading, the other attenders began to leave the temple, the crowd thinning until there were only five people left in the hall, three men and two women. One of these was the medium, to whom he introduced himself. She was Guzhi. He looked at her carefully. Like himself, she looked quite ordinary, even common, a little older than he, perhaps in her late forties.

"Why did you say my father's name, Auntie?" he said, implying respect for her greater age.

"I don't know what I said. You will have to talk with them," she said, indicating the three men who had called out and written the characters. He walked over to them and said: "Li Caihong." They looked at him, puzzled. "Li Caihong. Why did you call out that name?" he persisted. "He is my . . . he was my father, dead now nine years."

"We did not know the spirit who came. It was your father? We are the instruments of the spirits. They speak through her," said one of them, indicating Guzhi. "We call out what she writes in the sand."

"The words which followed?"

"The same."

"But what do they mean?"

"They are words from the Old Master. He teaches us the way to live. Have you never read the *Daodejing*?"

Heiyen shook his head, introducing himself as Li Bingxian. The three men looked at one another. One said that his name was auspicious, for Li was the surname of the Old Master when he lived on this earth over two thousand years ago. They invited him to join their sect, and when he readily agreed, they gave him, as they gave everyone in the group, a special name. They called him Heiyen, meaning "black eye," because one of his eyes was darker than the other. And so his transformation began, from an ordinary man, too irresolute even to look for a marriage partner, to a committed member of a new sect, called the FourOne Society.

Leadership did not come naturally to him. But Heiyen, the office clerk, came to understand that he had a higher destiny than working as a petty bureaucrat in the municipal government. With the encouragement of his new friends he began to realize that there was a different sort of leadership that he might aspire to, not one based on his physical stature or a loud voice that commanded attention, but a quiet authority based on the promptings from the other world—perhaps that is what the Old Master meant by "the role of a woman." Without that confirmation from above, he was just Mr. Li, a minor clerk of no account. But with it, he could be decisive. Years later, when the message had come to kidnap the foreign child, he did not hesitate to carry out the spirits' command.

Now the child had grown into a young woman, and things had become complicated. She had learned to contact the spirits, but only on rare occasions. Beyond that it was hard for Heiyen to see what her leadership role might be. She was, after all, a foreigner. At the same time, the government was out to destroy the "Four Olds," and among the olds was religion. The Communist mayor of Stonebridge, Ma Jin, who had been tolerating their presence in the town, had summoned them to his office. "Your practices conflict with the goals of socialist society. Our plans for the future must be based on science, not superstition."

"Jin," said Guzhi, who was the mayor's aunt, "we have harmed no one." Ma Jin had tolerated the FourOnes because of his aunt, who had spoiled him as a child with sesame buns and other sweets and charmed him with her kindly nature, a welcome relief from his mother, who daily hurled biting criticisms at him.

"The national government is going to crack down on religion and all the other remnants of the old society. You stupid turtle heads will get your lazy asses out of this temple or the comrades will drive you out." Ma Jin noted the sullen looks on the faces of Guzhi, Heiyen, and the others. "We are going to tear down this temple anyway. Worship of the river god is a blot on Old Stonebridge's reputation as a model socialist town."

One trouble after another. Heiyen felt overwhelmed with all the difficulties facing them, finally losing his temper at a meeting of the FourOnes where many had expressed frustration at their inability to establish their community publically. "Bring her in to me," he snapped at Guzhi, referring to Bu'er. Knowing of his anger, Bu'er entered the shrine room hesitantly, her eyes on the floor.

"You have spent too much time with Mingling. I know that healing is important work, but when will you take your position of leadership with the FourOnes? It is the intention of the spirits. We have cared for you now for over thirty years, waiting for you to rise to a position of leadership in our sect."

Stunned by the unfairness of Heiyen's words, Bu'er answered with an anger equal to his. "I . . . did . . . not . . . choose this path. You chose it for me when you took me from my parents." Her words came out as adamant as characters incised on a rock, and Heiyen, when he heard them, took a step backward. He was a simple man, and when he met resistance, his anger diminished quickly.

He said only: "It was the will of the spirits."

Bu'er turned away and left the room, deciding to leave the FourOnes for a while. She would go join Mingling at Baita village, below Yindong An.

Bu'er began her journey an hour after dark, feeling a bit guilty for leaving, but still angry at Heiyen's unfair criticism. Early the next morning, she had reached a familiar cave in the hills not far from the town of Shagua. It was a place she often visited on her trips between Old Stonebridge and Baita village, and her only hesitation was its closeness to Shagua. She was exhausted from the nightlong walk and looked forward to some hours of rest. The sky had gone from black to gray as dawn approached, though the inside of the cave was still dark. She stooped slightly and went inside, almost immediately catching the odor of sweat and of an unwashed body. But before she could retreat, she felt viselike hands pinning her arms to her side, then throwing her on the dusty ground. The man knelt down beside her and pulled off her headcloth so that he could better see her face.

Bu'er's mind flashed back to the rape, years ago when she was a defenseless child, and rage welled up in her. Before her attacker could touch her again, she sat up and stared at him. Controlling her anger with difficulty, she turned her face to the side and pointed at her cheek. "See. It is white." A frown crossed his face, and she hissed fiercely at him again. "It is white."

Expecting screams and a struggle, her response took him by surprise. White? He hesitated, looking more closely at her face. He noted the large round eyes, the marred complexion, and the pale skin of her cheeks. "What is wrong with you?"

She smiled at him, wickedly. "*Mafeng, mafeng*," she said slowly, with menace in her voice. "Do you know what that means?" He did recognize the word for "numb skin," the Chinese term for leprosy.

His eyes widened, but then they narrowed. She could see that he was not convinced. He wore some sort of threadbare uniform, so she assumed that he was a local constable, not an illiterate peasant.

"I have warned you," she said, "but if you are willing . . . Life is short. Why shouldn't we just enjoy ourselves." She forced herself to smile at him, her left hand unloosing the drawstring of her pants. She stretched her right hand toward him invitingly.

He pulled back quickly and stumbled to his feet, then ran from the cave as fast as he could.

She hurried to the cave entrance. "If you tell anyone in Shagua about me," she shouted after him, "I will say that we had intercourse. Then you are a dead man!"

Just before dawn, two days later, she reached Baita village early in the morning and found Mingling at Auntie Ai's place, standing at a sort of workbench with a bloody rag in her hand. "Mingling, what's wrong?"

"It's nothing. I pulled out my last three teeth." Bu'er frowned. "Bad tooth-karma," added Mingling. "All three on top. Useless." Mingling rinsed her mouth, walked over to the door and shot the bloody water out into the street.

"*Jiejie*, no one could accuse you of being timid!"

“Except when I eat.”

Bu’er sat down with Mingling, who told her that Abbess Gaoyun and all the nuns had left Yindong An. Bu’er told her mentor of the disagreement with Heiyen and the FourOnes, and of her encounter with the ruffian. Mingling made a wry face. “You used just the right words to frighten off the rapist—there is a superstition among the farmers that a leper woman can cure her disease by coupling with a healthy man to whom she transfers the sickness.”

“I remembered. You told me about that belief years ago, and I used it.”

“You remember everything, I think, and if a good memory was the most desired quality of leadership, your future with the FourOnes would be assured. As things are, I cannot help you. Your path in life is for you to decide. But little sister, why don’t you stay here while you are thinking about it, and help me with my practice. There are many people around here who need a doctor’s help. The two of us could be useful to the people.”

CHAPTER 12

Chicago

The 1960s.

For the first time in her life, Livia had a close friend. Her name was Naomi, and she was one of the brightest in their cohort. Her hair was black, parted severely in the middle, each side clinched with an ordinary rubber band into a pony tail. No fancy barrettes. The rubber band proclaimed her solidarity with the proletariat. She felt that Chairman Mao and Che Guevara were the only true revolutionaries left in the world, though the new guy in Vietnam, Ho Chi Minh, was showing promise. Naomi wore classic owl glasses that she constantly pushed up her nose with an index finger. The two girls were hunched over a table at Fifty-Seventh Street Café and Delicatessen, for them the heart of Hyde Park and university life. They spent more time here than in the library.

"You ought to do something with your hair, Naomi. For God's sake, something more your age. I mean, please. Those pigtails will bring out all the child molesters in Hyde Park."

"I'm not worried about the creeps. Among my other accomplishments, I've learned jujitsu. My hand's a lethal weapon." She whacked the table top with a moderately hard chop. "If I hadn't pulled my punch, this table would have been a pile of kindling." The few remaining customers glanced uneasily at the two girls. It was nine at night, an hour from closing time.

"Hey, owl face, take it easy on the furniture," Lenny yelled from behind the glass deli counter. His name was James McCorkle, but for some reason that no one knew, the regulars took to calling him Lenny, and the name stuck. Something right about a guy named Lenny working a deli.

"This table is crap," Naomi shouted back. "Buy some decent furniture and people won't feel an uncontrollable urge to destroy the shit. We deserve better." Two oldsters got up to leave.

"Deserve nothin'. You two are here so much I should charge you rent. You're driving off my paying customers."

"This place is a dump. New chairs and tables or we quit coming. Nonnegotiable."

"That a promise?"

Naomi looked like a kid about to play hopscotch, but was fierce as a female badger. She was Jewish, from Cincinnati, where her father taught political science at the university, and her mother was a public defender for Hamilton County. They taught their daughter to fear no one. *With one half of her chutzpah,* Livia thought enviously, *I could march through the world like Joan of Arc.* Livia realized that for all she had gained from the education at Hillesum, she had lost something, too. The brash little girl who wanted to get off the steamer and return to China was no more.

Lenny took the salami tray from his wooden work counter and replaced it in the glass case. "Can't do new chairs and tables. The furniture stays, just as it is. This is a historic site. Saul Bellow comes here once in a while. He used to sit at that exact table that you almost destroyed. He was working on a novel."

"Bullshit! That's what they say in every shop up and down this street. Every one of 'em is Saul Bellow's favorite place. How come I've never seen him, not even once?"

"Not here at the right time," Lenny mused, scraping crumbs off the work surface.

"When was the great man last here? Exactly."

He seemed to be reflecting on her question while wiping the counter with a wet rag. "A while ago. He hangs around here a lot, y'know, pickin' up atmosphere for his fiction. Read his next book. I think it's about a Jewish guy. I might be in it."

"A bit part, no doubt. You're Irish, remember?"

"Lots of other big names have been here too: Eliot Ness, Red Granger, Amos Alonzo Stagg. Nat King Cole, Benny Goodman. And Frank Lloyd Wright, while he was working on the Robie House. The good and the bad. Al Capone, John Dillinger. Mother Cabrini came once for a cup of tea, before they named that housing project after her. Kinda like the mecca of midwestern history."

Naomi rolled her eyes. "You're so full of shit. And tell Mr. Stagg, next time you see him, that I think football's a game for barbarians."

"I'll do that," Lenny said.

"Gotcha. He's been dead for fifty years, moron." She turned back to Livia, but continued in full voice: "It's a miracle anyone would want to come to this dump. But I guess there are some warped individuals who actually enjoy hearing flat-out lies as the normal form of discourse."

What drew Livia to Naomi was her brash talking and take-no-hostage approach to life. Livia tried to imagine her at Hillesum. The nuns would have expelled her fifteen minutes after she walked in the door. Whatever idea came into Naomi's head, she blurted out, usually with style. A drama queen. Sometimes her outbursts were annoying, but at least you always knew exactly where you stood with her.

"Naomi, are you ever sorry you came to Chicago? I mean, all the studying, the competition, the grim struggle for grades?"

"Grim struggle? This is a picnic, an'I'm sampling everything in the basket. Who's struggling for grades! This is my platform, my launching pad."

"Platform?"

"My stage. The supporting cast is the grinds and drudges. People like you. I'm the petunia in the onion patch. You guys are the onions. Onions are the ones who are always cautious, protecting their asses. You know how an onion is covered with layers of skin"—Naomi was beginning to appreciate the brilliance of the image she'd conjured up—"petunias are delicate, vulnerable, but they don't give a damn. If the rain hits them . . ."

"OK, OK." Livia interrupted her. "Enough. You're overworking your metaphor. What are you getting at?"

"Onions won't talk in class," she continued, as though Livia had said nothing, "they can't stand being laughed at, afraid of being wrong. Bor-ing.

I say what I think. Could be wrong, could be right, but usually interesting. I love it here, and have from the first time I got here, a year and a half ago."

"I've heard the dean of the college would like you to finish a few classes, instead of dropping out because they don't measure up to your standards. Even though they are taught by the brightest profs in the country, PhDs from the best grad schools in the world!"

"I'm not impressed," her friend said, gazing out the window.

"Then why did you come here in the first place?"

"I remember my first week here," mused Naomi, again ignoring Livia's question, as though focused on the greater task of bringing down words from Mount Sinai. "I walked over to the point at Fifty-Fifth Street to see the lake. Before school started. It was midmorning, early October. I went through the underpass beneath Lake Shore Drive, and when I came out the other side, in the park, I heard beautiful flute music. This man had set up a music stand and was playing this gorgeous piece. Maybe Vivaldi. All by himself, not a soul listening but me, and I don't think he even knew I was there. I sat down on the wall. I felt like Moses at the burning bush. It was like the thing I was waiting for my whole life. I knew this was the place I wanted to be. A place where that could happen. I stayed until he stopped, put his flute into a case, closed up the music stand, and walked away. Paid no attention to me. Totally unconscious of the beauty he had made. That's my ideal, sashay through life strewing beauty left and right, totally oblivious to the great things I'm doing."

"It sounds to me like you are very aware of the 'great things' you're doing," observed Livia.

"Don't interrupt my train of thought! A second thing happened, the same day, just a few minutes later. Kinda miraculous, when you think about it. What are the chances of two awesome events happening in your life, one right after the other? I walked over to the beach, you know, that runs between Fifty-Fifth and Fifty-Ninth? I was walking a foot off the ground. I looked out toward the horizon and saw something moving, way out off in the distance. At first I had the crazy thought that it was some weird sea creature. I squinted my eyes. As it got closer, I realized it was someone swimming. I couldn't believe it. It was about thirty-five degrees, for God's sake! I was wearing my heavy suede jacket and I was still cold! Who was this crazy person swimming? I sat down on a rock and watched him moving slowly across to the point. He got out of the water, red as a cooked lobster. He climbed up on the rock ledge. I watched him bend over and pick up a towel. He buffed himself all over. Then he reached down, picked up a plastic bag, took something out of it which turned out to be a matchbox. He struck a match and lit some dry leaves caught in the angles of the stones. Then he stood in the smoke and warmed himself.

"I didn't stop to watch him dress. I walked away happier than I've ever been in my whole life. Freedom! I was kin to the lobster man and the flute player. The weirdos. My people. I felt at home, like I've never felt before. I grew up in a huge house in Cincinnati. The neighborhood was called Hyde Park, too, just like here, but what a difference! Say 'shit' there and people, you know, like my grandma and her friends, get nervous, cough into their white gloves. I think I'll stay here for the rest of my life, the eternal student, going to poetry readings at coffee houses, browsing the used book stores, going to jazz events—important stuff like that."

"And when your parents finally wise up and cut off your money?"

"I'll just get a job, maybe serving tables here with Lenny."

"Well, I never thought I'd hear you witnessing to divine providence."

"I'm not. I'm an atheist. Well, maybe an agnostic. At least I don't believe in that Big Wise Guy in the sky they taught us about in Shabbat classes."

"Then you think those two happenings were just . . . dumb luck, chance?"

"Let's just say the universe gave me signs . . . oh hell, that sounds stupid, too. But you know what I mean. One of those life-changing moments. Don't know where it came from, but it gave me a jolt of energy, and I've been living off it since the day it happened."

"I'd call it a God-moment. You call it what you want."

It was getting late. They decided to split a Reuben and get another coffee before they were kicked out. Lenny groaned in protest. "We close in thirty minutes, you know." He put the Reuben together, grumbling all the way.

"You know, Lenny, this sandwich is named after one of my ancestors," said Naomi, placing a five-dollar bill on the counter. "Bet you wish you were Jewish."

Lenny rolled his eyes as he counted out a fistful of coins. "Sorry, I got no ones."

"Well, enough about me," said Naomi as she got back to the Saul Bellow table. "Now it's time to dissect you, Livia."

"You didn't dissect yourself. Just bragged about your love affair with the universe."

"Miss Muffet, you . . ."

"Oh for God's sake, don't call me that."

"Well, along came the spider and sat down beside her, and scared poor Miss Muffet away. Right? That's just my point. Fear. I can spot it a mile away. What are you afraid of?" Naomi pressed the glasses up against the bridge of her nose, looking owly and wise. "You need to let go, let the music in your life flow, like the flute man. Do whatever you want to do, no matter how crazy, like the lobster man. Stop being so uptight."

"Oh, sure, 'uptight' is the big sin now. Stop being uptight, and you can walk on water."

"Well, it's a start."

"Easy enough for you to say. Remember, I was educated by the nuns. Emphasis on decorum and discipline. Being ladylike."

"Yeah, a top-notch education for the nineteenth century!"

"It wasn't all bad. Plato was more of a revolutionary than anyone in the nineteenth century, except Darwin maybe, and I'm glad I know about him. Anyway, knowing something in your head and doing something about it are two different things."

She mulled over that thought and Livia realized that knowing and doing were all the same to Naomi. "You need some kind of transforming experience, Livia, something to jolt you . . . Like sex, maybe. It works for some people. You had any recently?"

Lenny began whistling as he cleaned up again, pretending disinterest.

"Where'd you come up with that idea?" Livia asked. "Did the universe feed you that notion too?"

"I don't need the universe to tell me. You're so repressed. You're a sophomore in college. Nice hair. Eyes are good. Figure's not that bad, either. I think. But you don't let anybody see it. You dress like a sanitation worker with your stupid overalls. You never go out with anyone. I'll bet you've never been fucked." As she spoke, Naomi adjusted the straps on her own overalls.

"You're talking crap. And keep your voice down. Three quarters of the world has been fucked," said Livia quietly, "and what good has it done? Is the world any better for it?"

"Probably. Better off than if they hadn't. But, we're not talking about the world. We're talking about you. It's an experience. Might change your life. And everybody does it, people, kangaroos, guppies, rabbits, everything. Why should we be different?"

"Such crap! Do you know that guppy moms eat their babies? Think we should try that too? Why are we talking about animals? Sex is not some world-changing experience! Rabbits. Why aren't we talking about something that's important to people? Like love? You got any bright ideas about that?"

"Oh, Miss Muffet of the lofty ideals. You thought you left the nuns two years ago, but they're still all over you, rapping your knuckles with a ruler. Lovely love!" she giggled.

"I'll deal with my past, you deal with yours," said Livia, feeling almost giddy at the wildness of the conversation. "You could start by getting a decent pair of glasses."

"Café's closed. You perverts keep coming here, I won't have a single customer left!" Lenny complained. "If this joint goes broke, it'll be your fault."

They rose from the Saul Bellow table, picked up their book bags and ambled toward the door.

"Hey Miss Muffet, if you need any help with that little project of yours, just give me a call. In the interests of science. You know, the rabbits and guppies, et cetera?"

"Fuck off, Lenny," said Naomi, with obvious affection.

It was cold and raining outside. They pulled up their hoods and leaned into the wind. "Naomi, I know you were talking about yourself back there," said Livia as they headed down South Woodlawn toward the Midway, "not me." Naomi didn't respond. But Livia didn't need an admission. They walked past Rockefeller Chapel and turned left on Fifty-Ninth, heading toward International House where they had rooms on the second floor of the old Gothic building, across the hall from each other.

"I was talking about both of us. Maybe we could use some kind of a twelve-step program."

A monstrous green-and-red dragon glided back and forth across the wet asphalt of Wentworth Avenue, undulating like a snake crossing a black river. Crowds of screaming children ran after it, surrounded it, then gave way, pretending fright, yelling as it swerved in a new direction. Firecrackers, linked together in a circlet, like a lei of flowers, popped and exploded, filling the air with staccato bursts of light, bangs, and clouds of smoke, adding a festive atmosphere to the gloomy winter weather.

"Jimmy, have you seen Livia?" Naomi yelled in his ear.

"I saw her back at Wing Fat's. Not since then. She might have come out with the Apostle."

"Shit," muttered Naomi to herself as she began looking for Livia in the crowds. She had gone to the bathroom as they left, and when she joined the group out in the streets, she did not see Livia. She was worried. Livia had organized the evening, convincing Naomi and some of their classmates to come to the Chinese New Year celebration in Chinatown. The plan was to have dinner and drinks together at Wing Fat's, then go out to watch the dragon dance and street celebrations, returning to I House for the party.

But word got around, and a few students they hardly knew showed up at the restaurant, including the Apostle and some of his followers. Wing Fat put together some tables and made room for sixteen. Naomi was on her left, but Livia spent most of the meal talking to the Apostle, who was seated to her right. He was tall and pale, with a gaunt Teutonic face and a stringy beard. Naomi leaned over, trying to get Livia's attention. "I thought you were going to say something about Chinese New Year. Most of us don't know what this dragon stuff is all about."

"Sure, I'll do that," Livia said. But she didn't, continuing instead her conversation with the Apostle. Naomi couldn't hear Livia's words above the din of the restaurant, but she picked up some snippets from the Apostle who leaned toward her as he spoke: "Altered states of consciousness . . . thin film between"—something, she'd not caught the word—"and everyday reality." He also talked about Timothy Leary, and what worried her the most, he used the phrase "spiritual freedom like you've never known." Naomi knew that Livia would be a sucker for "spiritual freedom."

Now Livia had disappeared, and Naomi scanned the crowds for her, slipping between the onlookers and the row of shops and storefronts behind them. She barely noticed the roasted ducks hanging from iron hooks in the shop windows, the curios, the cheap souvenirs, and other tourist paraphernalia. Livia could be so totally infuriating. One minute hesitant to do anything unconventional, the next wanting to explore the world of mind-altering drugs.

Then she saw her, off to the side of the group, waving to the Apostle: "See you soon."

"How soon? You could get yourself in real trouble, Livia," she said, sticking her finger in her friend's face.

"Stop it. You're the one always telling me to let go, stop being so uptight, do the outrageous, suck the marrow out of life! What about the lobster man?"

"It's not the same. You don't get it. You can get seriously hurt by this stuff. I've been reading up on it. When I talk about freedom, I mean freedom of the spirit, not the half-conscious hallucinations of an acidhead! You could kill yourself. You're always talking about China in your future—you're not ever going to China if you dope yourself on drugs."

"Reading up on it . . . how bookish. You draw these little boxes around your experience—that's not freedom. Remember the flute player and the lobster man. What's wrong with a little of the weed?" Livia smiled, looking mellow. "Puff the magic dragon, lived by the sea . . ." She sang the new song dreamily. Naomi stomped off, disgusted, went back to Wing Fat's to find her book bag.

When she returned, Livia was gone. When she found the rest of their group again, near the corner of Wentworth and Cermak, they were making noises about going back to the university. The crowds were beginning to thin out. "Who is this Apostle?" Naomi asked one of the unfamiliar students. "I think my friend might have gone off with him."

The student was hatless in the cold. He had beautiful long blond hair and a red beard. "A guy who pushes pot, et cetera. With stress on the *et cetera*. He's a true believer. He thinks if everyone smoked hash and zoned out, we'd all be mellow and loving. No more crime, no more war. I think I saw your friend go off with him, and Cady and Reese."

"Where'd they go?"

"Don't know. Might have gone to his apartment. It's somewhere around here."

"He lives way down here?"

"Yeah. Just a bus ride from the university and the rents here are much cheaper than Hyde Park."

"Where is his pad?"

"Don't know. Somewhere off Cermak."

"Come on, Naomi," Jimmy said. "Let's get out of here. There's the Chinese New Year party at I House tonight. Be a lot better than this."

"I can't find Livia. We came together and I don't want to just leave her here."

"She's of age. I think she went off with the Apostle. They're probably having their own party right now."

The streets emptied. Reluctantly, Naomi left with the group.

The next morning, first thing, she marched across the corridor and knocked on Livia's door. No answer. It was about three hours later when she finally heard the door open and close. She was there immediately. "Where were you last night? I looked everywhere."

Livia smiled. "Went with the Apostle and a couple of friends. I egged him on, told him I'd tried pot a few times but felt nothing except dizzy. He got out some of his best stuff. It's funny, he's so serious about it. Like he's bringing the world a new gospel. Thus his name. Made me inhale deeply, hold it in."

"What happened?"

"Weird, like they claim. I felt like I had the most amazing insights, experiences like I'd never had before." She laughed. "But when I tried to tell the others, I got out a few words, you know, like half a sentence, and then I couldn't remember how to finish the sentence. And then I couldn't remember how I started the sentence! Blazing insights, but if you ask me now, I can't recall a single one of them. Gone. The Apostle and the others just smiled at me, like that was supposed to happen."

"Well, you shouldn't do stuff like that. You could get hurt."

"Hey, quit it," said Livia, offended. "You're not my mother!" She turned around to signal the conversation over, and started singing, "In a land called Honalee . . ."

符咒

CHAPTER 13

Talisman

Taiwan. Spring 1964.

Livia had purchased third class, the cheapest ticket. Unity with the proletariat! From Taipei Central to Hsinchu, her destination, was only about fifty miles. How long could the trip take? So why spend a fortune on a thirty-minute train ride?

She had come to Taiwan for her junior year abroad, and was excited that the simple Chinese of her childhood was still somewhere in her head and, with a little prodding, was still usable. Miracles seemed to be happening every day. She'd say those strange-sounding words from the past, sometimes without thinking, and people here actually understood her.

The rail car had wooden benches running along both sides under the grimy windows, leaving a large central area for standing passengers and their luggage when the train was crowded. But *luggage* was too grand a term for the collection of cardboard boxes, worn bags, and frayed plastic sacks that she saw on the floor. It was Tuesday, midafternoon. Most of the passengers were country folk returning home. The seats were full, but no one had to stand. Livia felt the other passengers looking at her, perplexed and suspicious. What was a rich American doing on a third class train? From the perspective of the Taiwan farmer, Americans were by definition rich, although she didn't think of herself that way.

Progress was slow. The train pulled off the tracks to allow every other train on the line to pass. They had left Taipei an hour and a half earlier and had barely gone twenty-five miles. The passengers were snacking, dropping orange peelings, cracked sunflower-seed hulls, and wet tea leaves on the floor. Livia began thinking she should have upgraded to second class.

Just to Livia's right was a large, round, loosely woven basket full of chickens. Bamboo strips crisscrossed the surface, leaving large holes for the air to circulate; a crude basket made to hold small livestock. She could smell the birdy stink of the fresh chicken droppings. There were maybe eight or nine of the creatures crowded inside, clucking nervously. The man sitting by them must have taken them to market in Taipei and was bringing back the ones he could not sell.

A woman sitting to Livia's right said something to the owner of the chickens. He shook his head vigorously, waving his hand back and forth. The woman pointed at the basket of birds, and lifting her voice a notch or two, came back at the man. He got louder in denial. She answered forcibly, louder still. Soon the two of them were shouting back and forth in a full-fledged argument. They were speaking in the Taiwanese dialect. Livia could not understand a word of it. Something to do with the chickens. She leaned toward the woman on her left, a young mother with a small boy, asking her in Mandarin: "What's going on?"

"She says that one of the chickens is dead. She wants to buy it cheap. He is angry. Says they are all alive. He wants full price."

The woman suddenly plunged her hand into the basket, groped around, then drew out the limp body of a dead chicken. She smiled triumphantly at the man, reached into her bag, and pulled out a small change purse, offering some coins to him. He waved them away scornfully, and soon the shouting broke out again. In the end, the woman added a coin to those already in her hand, and the man accepted them.

Now the owner of the bird, the woman took from her purse a pocket knife, a plastic bag, and a rubber band. Livia watched with fascination as she opened the knife and quickly slit the chicken's throat, holding the bird upside down and bleeding it into the plastic bag. When the blood flow slowed, she snugged the bag around the bird's throat with the rubber band, then slung it under her seat. She settled back with a contented look on her face, tonight's dinner secured. At the next stop the man and woman left the train together, laughing and talking. Livia wondered if this sort of thing happened in second class.

The train again pulled off onto a secondary track and stopped, allowing a faster one to pass. Livia thought back to her first two years of college, marveling at the changes they had brought to her life. Under the prodding of Naomi, she had tried a lot of stuff—smoking, drinking, protests, watching blinky black-and-white pornography, a couple of "boyfriends." Then she tried drugs and things got weird. Naomi went berserk. "Livia, for God's sake, you're so naïve!" Livia couldn't figure her out. And then, without warning, just before the end of their second year, Naomi had dropped out of school with almost no explanation—something about education's implicit bondage to the establishment, and that her goal in life didn't require a diploma.

"What is your goal in life?" But Naomi never answered that question. Livia figured she'd return at the beginning of their third year, but she didn't. Livia trucked on, deciding she hated smoking and didn't need drugs. Life was exciting enough without them. Then the semester in Taiwan loomed and her total attention was given to preparing for it.

The train jerked forward. The little boy to Livia's left, about three or four years old, began to grab at his crotch. He wore shorts and a soiled pink T-shirt that said *Baby Punting*. His mother reached over and pulled down his pants. Livia couldn't believe her eyes. The little boy's penis let fly a healthy stream of urine, the pee gathering into a puddle on the train floor at his feet. As the train gathered speed, the pee began to move in the direction of her feet, and without thinking she lifted her sandaled feet to let the pee run by. A titter spread through the car. A weathered old man across from her grinned, showing his tobacco-stained teeth. Then he laughed like a crow, the sound edged with the raspiness of the chain smoker. Immediately the whole car erupted into full-bellied laughter. *Baby punting*. She'd love to give it a try. Smiling tightly, she swore to upgrade her ticket to second class on the return trip. Or maybe first class. Enough of the proletariat.

It was raining as the train jerked to a stop in Hsinchu station. From here the main line continued on to T'aichung, T'ainan, Chia I, and Kaohsiung, at the southern end of the island. Hsinchu was a medium-sized city of about seventy-five thousand, with few tourist attractions. She stood under the marquee, sheltered from the rain while she looked for a nearby hotel. She saw a small one across the square, with neon flashing *San Hua*, "Three Flowers." It was a narrow building, five stories high. She ran through the rain, carrying her rucksack, dodging carts, bicycles, and small trucks in the open square. The lobby wasn't much. Other than the reception desk, the only furnishings were two plastic chairs on either side of a high narrow table. On the table was a fake cloisonné vase with three dust-covered plastic peonies in it. There was a single attendant behind the desk. He had greasy black hair and a wild cowlick untamed by the heavy lube job. He demanded to see her passport before assigning her a room on the fourth floor.

Livia, feeling like she was covered with molecules of chicken shit and human pee, took a long shower in a dingy bathroom down the hall. Thank God it wasn't a tub. She wouldn't have tried a bath for all the tea in China, as they say. As she dressed, she began to think about eating. The rain had stopped. Her room was in the back of the hotel looking away from the train station. From her window, she could see a lively street that ran alongside a park. Crowds filled the street, both sides of it lined by vendors' booths. She saw a man wiping the rainwater off his chairs and tables, wringing out the towel, and moving on to the next table. Colored lights decorated the fence along the park and the eaves of the stores on the other side of the street. Festive. As she passed through the lobby, on her way out, Livia waved gaily to the unsmiling man with the cowlick. She was excited by the feeling that her Chinese was good enough to negotiate all these adventures on her own.

She loved the excitement of Taiwan streets at night. Life happened on the streets. Most of the people lived in cramped apartments or half-story warrens above their businesses. They played cards, Ping-Pong, and billiards on the street, cooked, ate, and chatted with neighbors on the street. Their small shops sold dresses, shirts, trousers, shoes, belts, socks, and other items of clothing. There were food booths of all kinds, selling their grilled breads, roasted skewers of meat, candied fruits, and fruit drinks made with papaya, pineapples, mangoes, guava, bananas, and watermelon, all fresh from the tree or vine. Livia longed for a pineapple-and-condensed-milk blend. No way. The fruit was probably OK, but the ice was likely made with unboiled water full of amoebas, and those little buggers could survive freezing. *Bu zhu jiu si* was the joke at her language school and the first principle for survival in Taiwan. "Boil it or perish."

She passed by a small temple, separated from the street by a waist-high wall and a metal fence. Through the main door she saw that some kind of ritual was going on, performed by a small corps of Daoist priests wearing gorgeous red vestments embroidered with gold, as elaborate as any she had seen for High Mass at Hillesum. And even more incense floated in the air. She thought of how the nuns would have called these rituals "pagan," offerings to the Jade Emperor and the Queen Mother of the West. But painted on the temple walls were scenes of flowery heavens and frightening hells where tormented souls were burning in fiery pits, flayed alive by lumpy-headed demons—not all that different from the hell in the *Divine Comedy*. Worshipers were standing in front of a table covered with offerings with joss sticks pressed between their folded hands. There were bowls of fruit, canned goods, and bottles of liquor on the table. She must have arrived the day before a temple festival.

Livia settled on an outdoor noodle stand, the cheapest and safest meal. The proprietor dropped a generous portion of noodles in her bowl, added a ladle of steaming broth, and sprinkled on top some grilled bits of meat and chopped green onion tops. Chili and soy sauce were set out on each table.

As she ate the comfort food, she thought about the day ahead. Henry Bishop would meet her at the bus station in Ta Lou village. Four years ago he had been a student at the language center in Taipei where she was studying. Now he was back in Taiwan doing research for his PhD, and the director of the school had asked him to give a talk to the current students about his work. Livia found it fascinating, close to her own interests. Henry was tall and lanky, not handsome exactly, but he had pleasant features and a boyish look about him. His brown hair was thick, parted on the left side, and it flopped down on his forehead. He was an anthropologist studying religion in rural northern Taiwan. Livia spoke with him after his talk, telling him of her own studies and interest in female spirit mediums.

"You should come visit me at Ta Lou. There is a woman who comes to the village on a pretty regular schedule, usually about once a month. She goes into a trance, contacts the spirits, and relays their advice to the people who come to consult her."

Livia was thrilled. "I'll do it. Let me know next time she comes."

She got off at the Ta Lou bus station, which was no more than a sundries store that sold soft drinks, candy, cigarettes, magazines, and pan. Pan was popular in Taiwan, chewed and spit on the sidewalks in scary looking red globs. Had she not known better, she might have thought that most of the Taiwanese were dying of lung disease.

No Henry.

Then she looked down the street and saw him running up the road. "Sorry I'm late, but Deng Taitai—that's the medium—came early and has already started her work." They hurried outside the village to the clan temple. It stood on a slight promontory overlooking the village on one side and a green valley on the other, the hillside carved into narrow rice paddies. The vista was really quite beautiful, like green meandering patterns in a textile. "We can enjoy the view later. Let's get on down so you don't miss anything. Deng speaks Taiwanese, but I can translate for you."

Deng Taitai had set herself up in a shrine to the right of the welcome hall. There were two women sitting on a bench just outside the main door. "We'll wait here for a minute," Henry said. They stood to the left of the entry door, leaning against the wall to catch their breath. Soon an old man emerged. "I'll be right back," said Henry, going inside before either of the women had a chance to rise. He was back in a few minutes. "She says we can listen . . . if we sit just inside the door." They both entered the shrine room and sat on a bench by the door, perhaps ten or twelve feet from the medium. Deng Taitai was tiny, but there was something arresting about her lined face. It was not stern exactly, but dignified and focused. She did not smile nor show any awareness of their presence.

The woman sat at a small table, her eyes closed. Small bits of paper were scattered on the tabletop in front of her. They bore Chinese characters, too small for Livia to read at a distance. Behind the medium, and just to her right, was an altar, with an image of the bodhisattva Guanyin. There was an empty chair on the side of the table opposite her.

A minute or two later, Deng Taitai rapped her knuckles loudly on the table. One of the women stepped in and sat down in the empty chair, facing her. The woman spoke first, in a plaintive voice. "She's telling Deng that she wants to speak to her son," Henry whispered, translating; his mouth very close to her ear. "He died four years ago. She's got financial problems and wants to know if she should sell their farm. It sounds like her daughter-in-law has gone to get a job in Taipei and now she's left alone and feels she can't manage by herself."

The medium said nothing for a few minutes, then her head began to bob up and down in a rhythmic way.

"What's happening?"

"She's going into a trance," Henry said softly.

After a few more minutes, her head stopped bobbing and she spoke. Livia was astonished at the low, gravelly voice that came out of the tiny woman. As she spoke, Henry translated. "The woman's son is speaking through her. He says do not sell the farm. The grandson will run the farm when he grows up. She should hold on until then."

"I'm impressed. How could she know about the son?"

"Well, that's not so impressive. Deng Taitai has been coming to Ta Lou for years. She knows everyone's affairs."

While they were talking, the medium had scribbled two lines of vertical script on a blank sheet of paper, then she tore it in half. She gave half to the petitioner and kept the other half herself, throwing her part on the table.

"What's the writing?"

"It's not regular writing. It's a talisman. The lady is supposed to chant it, like a mantra, to align herself with the will of the spirit."

In the next two hours, four more supplicants came and laid out problems of every sort: money, family, land disputes, infidelity. The final person was a deeply agitated woman who recited a laundry list of family woes that Henry summarized, "A husband and a brother had lost their jobs, there was a divorce, fighting among the cousins, a battle over an inheritance." The medium, as before, went into a trance and spoke again in a low voice.

"She says the woman's father is unhappy. She must dig up his grave and move it to a place that has better fêng shui."

"Oh my God. That's hard . . . and expensive."

Henry nodded. "Who are we to argue with the spirits?"

As before, the medium ended the session by giving the petitioner a talisman.

They waited for a while for Deng to come out of the trance. But there was some delay, and her eyes remained closed for what seemed to be a long time. Finally, she looked up and said something to Henry, in her normal voice, indicating the empty chair. Henry looked puzzled, and asked her a question, which she answered rather curtly. He turned to Livia. "I think she's confused. She thinks you are here to contact someone."

"Tell her thank you, but I didn't come for that purpose." Henry did so, and Deng responded. Livia could not understand what she said but could feel a certain impatience in her answer.

Henry turned to Livia. "Do you have an older sister? She is asking if you came here to contact her."

Livia was stunned. She felt the sudden sting of tears in her eyes. How in the hell could this woman know she had a sister? She swallowed, and all sorts of scenarios raced through her head. Finally, feeling in the grip of something beyond herself, she said, "Yes. Ask her if she can contact my sister."

Henry looked skeptical but relayed the message. "She says she will try. Are you sure you want to do this?" Livia nodded.

Henry spoke to the medium. "She wants you to sit in the chair," he said to Livia.

Livia did so. She watched the medium's face closely. No change of expression, but then Livia had a strange feeling as she looked carefully at the impassive mask, as though the woman was no longer Asian, just old. Finally, in a low whisper, she spoke three or four words. Livia looked at Henry, who was kneeling at her side. He seemed hesitant.

"What did she say, Henry?"

"I know what she said but am not sure what it means. In Mandarin it would be '*mei you, bu zai*.'" Among the commonest words in the language, but what did they mean? Deng Taitai had come out of the trance and was beginning to pick up her things. Livia thanked her, handed her ten *kuai*, and left the shrine, walking up the hill to the road as though in a daze. Henry caught up with her, and the two of them strolled back toward Ta Lou together, saying nothing. She felt that something important had happened, as though the spirit of her sister had approached her and then passed by.

They got back to the town and found a place that specialized in pot stickers and beer.

"I want to know what happened back there."

"It's odd," said Henry, "that simple words can be so ambiguous. The first part could be 'no' or 'there is none' or 'she doesn't exist.'"

"Meaning my sister is dead? Unreachable?"

"Her job is contacting the dead, so I think it's the opposite. When you add *bu zai*, I think it's got to mean that Deng Taitai couldn't contact her. She's 'not there.'"

"That means my sister is in our world. She's alive."

"Is that possible?"

"I don't know. I've always figured she was dead, although my mother didn't think so. She and Dad would never say much about her disappearance. I think her loss was the beginning of the end of their marriage, so neither would talk about it. And even if Victoria—that was my sister's name—was alive, there's no chance to go to China to look for her, is there? And even if the political situation changes and I get there someday, how to go about finding her in a land of seven hundred million people!"

"But it's possible," Henry said. Livia nodded. Henry snatched another dumpling with his chopsticks, dipping it in the soy sauce, chili, and vinegar. "Of course maybe Deng got it wrong."

"I don't think I believe you can contact the dead anyway," said Livia, taking a drink from her glass of beer, "when you think of all the imposters who have tricked gullible people into believing that they could do it. But I'll have to admit that when you asked if I had an older sister, I felt caught up in something powerful, something almost supernatural . . . Hey, this stuff is really good, isn't it? I love Taiwan beer . . . what I think is that Deng Taitai is a mind reader. There are people like that, you know. Somehow she picked up the idea that I had an older sister."

"So you're saying she picked up something from your unconscious that you weren't thinking about at the time? Seems unlikely. Oh, I almost forgot. You left the shrine so quickly. You forgot your talisman. I've got it here," he said, fishing a crumpled piece of paper from his pocket. "It's not like the other talisman with their weird markings. I can read this one."

The old woman had drawn on the paper a sort of oval shape. Something that looked like an eggplant, but along the bottom were five hairlike appendages. Inside the oval were two Chinese characters: *bei yue*, the northern peaks. "It means Hengshan, the god of the northern mountains," Henry said. "Not here in Taiwan. In China."

In every way she could think of, Livia's months in Taiwan were a success. She had collected enough materials on female mediums and religious leaders that she felt able to tackle her undergraduate thesis when she returned to Chicago for her final year of college. And maybe the most important thing—living in Taiwan felt like coming home. It was not China, but there was some sense of belonging that developed as she immersed herself in the culture and began to speak the language she first learned in childhood.

Over the year, Henry Bishop had become her friend. They had had some great adventures exploring the city and nearby sites, like Wu Lai, Jade Green Lake, and Milky Way Cave. They saw every corner of old Taipei and Pan Ch'iao, across the Tan Shui River. They went to an occasional American movie when they felt homesick for the States. You had to pick out the right one, or it made no sense. The government censors cut out all the "sex" scenes, even kissing, so American movies being what they were, the plots were often hard to follow. The films were always preceded by what the foreign students called the "Peanut and Froggy Show." It featured the Republic of China flag rippling over the presidential palace and American-made jets roaring overhead as the president and his heir apparent stood stiffly saluting, a look of noble determination on their faces. Peanut was Chiang K'ai-shek with his shiny bald head, and Froggy was his jowly son, Chiang Ching-kuo.

One late winter evening, Henry had proposed going to see "Snake Street." It was located in the oldest part of Taipei, lined with some of the usual small shops, but the area's specialties were seafood and snake meat. They saw a crowd had gathered out in the middle of the street around a fat man who was shouting enthusiastically and pointing at a small brown bottle in his left hand. Livia noticed that the crowd was mostly young men. She looked more carefully and realized it was all young men. "I can guess what he's selling."

"Yeah, an aphrodisiac. Mysterious herbs with some scrapings of rhino horn mixed in. They're all hoping to become big studs . . . I'll show you what they're working themselves up to a little later." Livia looked at him doubtfully.

The snake stores kept their own supply of live snakes in wire cages. They stopped in front of one shop where four or five dead ones hung by their jaws from metal hooks in the ceiling. A well-dressed man walked into the shop and nodded toward the owner, who showed him with flourishes to an empty table.

The proprietor then walked over to one of the cages, reached into the writhing mass, and pulled out a snake about five feet long. He held the snake tightly behind its head so that it could not strike him, but it wrapped itself around his forearm like a strangler vine. He impaled the snake's head on one of the sharp hooks hanging from the ceiling, pulling down hard to release his arm. He made a six-inch slit in the snake's middle section with a small knife. He stuck his index finger in the cavity and pulled out the guts, sorting through them and isolating a small white bladder. A waitress appeared, holding a glass of clear liquid under the organ, whatever it was. The owner stabbed it gently with the sharp point of his knife, and blood spurted out into the glass of clear liquid, turning it red. A Snake Street Bloody Mary.

Livia had never thought of herself as bothered by blood, but now she was feeling queasy. "Henry, I'm going to freak out. Could we take a break from this?"

"Sure." He thought for a minute. "Let's go see Lung Shan Temple. It's close, very quiet and peaceful in the evening. The oldest temple in Taipei City."

To get to the temple they passed through a narrow alley illuminated with red light bulbs. "I wanted you to see this place, too." Young girls sat under the lurid lights along one side of the street. Some were on chairs and others on steps, just outside the doors of the clubs, trying to catch a puff of fresh air. Groups of young men stood in groups, clustered along the other side. They were pointing and hurling insults across the street: fat, ugly, black skinned, big nose! The girls tried to look bored, ignoring the abuse. The buildings were dingy, and Livia saw a heap of wilted flowers and drying orange peels on the street, just to the left of where the girls sat waiting.

"They're working up their courage," said Henry. One boy was being goaded and pushed by his friends. He finally walked over and stood above a girl, handing her a crumpled bill. She took him by the hand and led him inside. His friends cheered.

"Let's go, Henry. This is disgusting."

"The worst of it is how young the girls are, some of them fresh off the farm. It's really child abuse."

"Then why did you bring me here?"

"It's the way it is. I thought you should see it."

They reached the gate of Lung Shan Temple and entered a candlelit and quiet world. *Too much reality out there,* she thought, snakes and aphrodisiacs, randy boys and child prostitutes parading before her mind. "I'll leave you to your thoughts," Henry said, seeming to sense her need to be alone.

Livia found a small chapel, entered and sat on the floor, yoga-style, with her back against a stone pillar. She looked up at the unreadable, starring eyes of the icon on the altar, identified by the embroidered banner above it as *Tianshang Shengmu*, the Sacred Heavenly Mother. It was a title for Matsu, a goddess worshipped all over Taiwan. She thought of that other divine woman she had first met at Hillesum, the Virgin Mary, and of the sordid life of the girls on Snake Street, her own age and even younger. She said an Ave Maria. *Ora pro nobis, peccatoribus.*

Just then, as her mind slowed down and settled, she heard the faint and lilting notes of an *erhu* coming from elsewhere in the temple. The notes floated by like sounds of a river, calming her spirit and blending all the conflicting thoughts in her mind into a single something that she could not put a name to. *Yes,* she thought, *snakes and prostitutes; heat and cold; good and bad; garbage and flowers; Matsu and the Virgin Mary; Buddhism and Christianity.* All the disparate things in her mind were harmonized in the sound of the music, and everything had its rightful place. Despite appearances to the contrary, there was goodness in the great scheme of things. "Thank you, thank you, thank you," she whispered, and didn't know whom she spoke to. It did not matter. Livia felt her spirit lifted and airborne on the notes of the erhu, not going anywhere in particular but wheeling in the night sky like a joyful swallow.

The next moments seemed outside of ordinary time. When she heard Henry's footsteps approaching, she had no idea how long she had sat there on the chapel floor, and she knew she would have no words to tell him what had happened.

"What?" he said, looking at her searchingly.

"I'd like to stay here forever." Livia smiled and wondered how foolish the look on her face must be. "Did you hear the music?"

"No," he said, a tinge of regret in his voice, "but I can see you did."

They decided to go to a Japanese restaurant. It was the right choice. A woman in a kimono led them into a private room with a sunken table and tatami mats. She got them seated on the floor, then bowed and left the room, closing the sliding door behind her. They could hear the hum of conversations in nearby rooms, not clear enough to understand, but soft and somehow soothing.

The rest of the evening was like a ritual, the scent of the steaming green tea; the warmth of the sake; the mathematical beauty of the plates of sushi, simple rice bowls, and meat skewers; the quiet coming and going of the woman in the kimono. They talked about their plans for the future. Henry's hopes were simple. He wanted to get his PhD and find a job at a small liberal arts college where he could work with good students, exploring the great questions of human life. "A place where you know people in town too, and you get a cup of coffee with friends in the morning."

Livia admitted that her plans were not so clear. "I've never told this to anybody . . ." She hesitated before continuing, "I've always had the sense that China was in my future, like there's some grand plan out there," she said, laughing at herself. "I know it sounds pretentious, but that's what I've always felt."

"Even now?"

"Especially now. And it feels almost like a vocation."

They ordered one more bottle of sake, the server placing it in a shallow bath of warm water. Henry refilled their tiny porcelain cups. It made her slightly giddy and relaxed at the same time. The bowing server had removed everything else, but had not brought their check. They were sitting along two adjacent sides of the low table, rather than opposite one another. Livia touched Henry's arm. "Thanks for dinner."

"Mmm," he said, flexing his back. "The food was great but sitting on the floor like this is giving me a backache." Other than holding his hand, she had never touched Henry before, but without thinking she reached up to massage the back of his neck. He flinched.

"Livia, I'm not good at this."

She was stricken. "What's wrong?"

"Can we just be friends? I mean, I like you a lot, Livia. Just not that way. I've never liked girls in that way . . . I'm so sorry."

Livia was stunned, and a little hurt. "Are you a . . ." Livia hesitated to say the word. "A homosexual?"

"That's what Mom and Dad think, but the truth is I don't feel that way about guys, either." He looked utterly miserable.

Livia's thoughts were a jumble, but one thing that came through the chaos of feelings was a deep regard for Henry. His confession meant that he trusted her, and that was something.

He filled her cup with the last drops of plum wine, and she proposed a toast: "Let's drink to our new friendship."

文化大革命

CHAPTER 14

Cultural Revolution

China. The 1960s.

Heiyen and Guzhi sat on each side of Bu'er, as though protecting her. They had convened a meeting of the FourOne leadership in the river god's temple to discuss her place in the organization. Four men and three women sat opposite them. One of the men, whose white hair marked him as the oldest person in the group, spoke his piece. "There are many FourOnes here in Old Stonebridge," he said rubbing the stubble on his chin with his knuckle. "They are puzzled about Daughter Bu'er, and what role she will play in our community. A neighbor asked me directly about it, and I did not have an answer. People see that she rarely brings us messages from the spirits. Auntie Guzhi is getting old. How can Bu'er replace her?"

"We leave that to the spirits to determine," Heiyen said.

"If you had been with us in Beijing, over twenty years ago, you would understand," Guzhi added. "The spirits chose Bu'er to be our leader and helped us to take her from the foreigners. It was a miracle that we were able to succeed."

"But Bu'er is different, she is a big nose from across the sea. We are Chinese. How can she lead us?"

"That was the very message we received," Heiyen said. "It seemed impossible, yet the spirits made it happen. Could Guzhi and I have conceived of such a brazen thing?" Before he could finish his thought

Heiyen was interrupted by a loud noise as the main door of the temple banged open, swung on its hinges, and clattered against the stone wall. Mayor Ma Jin strode into the temple followed by two cadres from the Shanxi provincial government.

"This building is hereby closed to public use," thundered Comrade Ma, handing Heiyen an official-looking document with a red stamp on it. "The temple of the river god is a relic of old superstitions. From here on it will not be used for any religious purpose whatsoever. As this document states, this temple will be confiscated by the municipal authority and utilized as a warehouse for the storage of important materials for the welfare of the people of this city, under the direct control of my office."

The seven members of the FourOnes bowed their heads.

"The approved religions—Buddhism, Daoism, Islam, Protestant, and Catholic Christianity," continued Comrade Ma more mildly, "are protected by our sacred constitution and may be practiced. But superstitious acts and secret cults are strictly forbidden. They are illegal, subversive, and dangerous to our socialist society." The Shanxi cadres, who had remained stone-faced up to this point, now looked pleased. "They will be hunted down and pulled up, root and branch," Ma said, mixing his metaphors, but showing great conviction. "We will destroy them. Any person caught practicing or spreading their poisonous superstitions among the people will be arrested, imprisoned, and punished by the tribunals of the people."

The leadership of the FourOnes waited a few days after the cadres left town, then went to Ma Jin's office to talk sense to him.

"Do you not understand what *no* means?" said Ma Jin to Heiyen and the others. "I will not turn a blind eye to your activities. I've been doing that for years. Not anymore. The government is serious about this. They are determined to eliminate all secret sects and cults, which are a threat to social harmony and Party rule. Even stupid cabbage heads like you," he said, thrusting his index finger at them, "should be able to figure that out."

"Jin," said Guzhi. "You know that we are no threat to social harmony. What harm have we ever done?"

"Listen Auntie, I'm doing this for your own good. It's not what you've done, it's what you plan to do. Your group is growing. Your people are not just here in the town, but out in the countryside as well, like a plague of grasshoppers eating the produce of the land. Your beliefs and practices conflict with our socialist society, and I'm telling you that the government is not going to tolerate it anymore. Do you know that the Red Guards are now fanning out over the countryside? Sooner or later they will come even to Old Stonebridge. They are destroying everything of the old culture they can get their hands on. They are denouncing anyone suspected of counterrevolutionary thoughts. If they discover the FourOnes' practices, they will either beat you up or kill you."

"We are here by the favor of the river god and the other spirits who have —"

"Shut up about the damn river god!" erupted Ma Jin before Heiyen could finish. "You are here by *my* favor. The river god is a . . . a . . . a . . . fucking superstition! Listen to what I'm saying. They're going to throw you in prison, they're going to kill you. Fuck the river god. The real problem is your damn secrecy. You think you know better than the government. I'm warning you. Auntie, you and this . . . this . . . stupid gourd here," he said, pointing at Heiyen, "and all your followers need to get out of the temple right now. Disappear! Blend into the families and towns and farms where you came from. Practice whatever religion you want to practice, but do it in your own home. Not in the river god's temple! And not in any public place in Old Stonebridge!"

"Comrade Ma," Heiyen said as he and Guzhi got up to leave the mayor's office, "we will consult with the river god."

"Dog farts! Your pious talk stinks! Get the hell out of here!" shouted Ma as they stood up and walked quickly toward the door. "And your mother is a whore," he added, glaring at Heiyen.

"He's really a good boy," said Guzhi to Heiyen and Bu'er, as the FourOnes walked up the street back toward the temple. "He just has a bad temper."

It was clear to the FourOnes that even though he railed at them in public, Comrade Ma had not given them up to the authorities. In fact, by haranguing them so savagely, he had saved them from investigation. The cadres had been impressed by his aggressive words and returned to Taiyuan satisfied that Old Stonebridge was in good hands. The FourOnes would be safe in the town as long as they stayed hidden among the people, carrying on their worship and trance-writing in private. Guzhi was grateful to her nephew, but she knew better than to say anything about her gratitude. Better to keep up the deception that he maintained his fierce opposition to sectarian groups and knew nothing about what was going on.

During this period of reduced activity, Bu'er thought about going to spend a month with Mingling. As Heiyen had said: "We have been lucky so far. No Red Guards yet. But they are roaming around the countryside and there is no telling when they might come. Go to Mingling at Baita village for a while. I will send word when it is safe to return."

Bu'er left Old Stonebridge, heading north toward the mountains and villages near the ruins of Yindong An where she found Mingling, still living in the back of the teahouse in Baita. She was treating the sick in the village and the countryside around it, sleeping in a kind of half-story loft above a small rear room that Mrs. Ai had set aside for her use as a pharmacy and dispensary.

Auntie Ai was a crippled old lady whose saving grace was the ability to laugh at her own misfortune. She was born before the May Fourth movement, when they still bound the feet of young girls so that they would be desirable as wives. "I was groomed for an age that no longer existed," she said. "When I was an infant my mother started binding my feet. It hurt like hell, twisting my big toe and rotting off the others. All that misery so the best families would want their sons to marry me. Ha! By the time I had endured years of torture and had these lovely little lotus feet, the young men all wanted women with big feet who could lug buckets to water the cabbages and slop the hogs." The bound feet gave her more pain as she aged, but she got around her tea house and sundry store with a cane and willpower. Mrs. Ai provided the two women with a pot of tea, and as they drank it Bu'er told Mingling what had happened at Old Stonebridge and how they waited in fear of the Red Guards.

"Those Guards are just children," Mingling said, shaking her head sadly. "There are gangs of them everywhere. They come down from the cities, claiming to be inspired by the words of Chairman Mao. But I think the real reason for their destructiveness is the repression. Our society is like a teapot," she said, pointing at Mrs. Ai's battered kettle on the stove, "whose escape valve is stuck. The pressure builds up and there must be an explosion. The Red Guards are that explosion. I do wish your FourOne group could set up communities to follow your ideals . . . It would be a heavenly dream compared to this nightmare with its spying, denunciations, and senseless striving for absolute purity. But now you must protect yourselves."

"Yes," said Bu'er. "We know that. Heiyen has sent us into another period of being hidden among the people, and asked me to come here to join you for a while."

"We can't hide you for long. The Red Guards will come even here, to Baita village. But I have an idea that might save both of us, and allow us to do some good at the same time. I have heard of a new movement that has begun to bring new medical personnel to the countryside. They are called Barefoot Doctors. Chairman Mao gave a speech a few years ago calling for better medical service to the peasants in the countryside. My idea is that you and I could go to the county headquarters, or to one of the large people's communes, and volunteer to be trained as Barefoot Doctors. Then we would be useful as they implement the new program and you would have a clear purpose and identity. The Red Guards could hardly bother people who are intent on carrying out Chairman Mao's medical directives."

"Volunteer to be trained? Jiejie, you already know much more about healing than the people who would be teaching you."

"Yes, in traditional medicine, but these Barefoot Doctors are going to bring many of the techniques of Western medicine to the countryside, things that are beyond my abilities. They will bring inoculations, antibiotics, new medicines. They bring the knowledge of hygiene, purifying water supplies, sanitation, and things like that. I saw some of these techniques promoted when I lived in Beijing. They are effective. Yes, there are things you and I can learn. And we will evade the wrath of the Red Guards." So Bu'er and Mingling became Barefoot Doctors.

It was six months later when word from Heiyen reached Bu'er. He judged that it was safe for her to return, so she left immediately, walking by night, hiding by day as always. But he was wrong. She had been back just two days when there were rumors of a new contingent of Red Guards that had moved out into the towns of eastern Shanxi from Datong, getting close to Old Stonebridge. The rumors described savage attacks on religious institutions, shrines and temples. The Guards burnt books, paintings, and other cultural artifacts, and maimed or killed those who owned them as enemies of the Great Proletarian Cultural Revolution. They looked at any attempt to make one's home attractive inside or outside—such as planting flowers or having art works—as an example of bourgeois decadence, a falling away from the Spartan ideals of Mao Zedong's thought.

They came into Old Stonebridge a week later, riding in two battered trucks, sporting their red armbands as badges of courage, terrifying everyone. "Down with old superstitions," they shouted, marching down the main road through the town, on the alert for signs of decadence. The FourOnes stood with the other townsfolk, watching dumbly from the roadside. The only building that caught the Red Guards' interest in Old Stonebridge was the dilapidated temple of the river god, giving them an "old" to destroy, a dark obscenity that cast its shadow over the shining purity of the revolution. They slashed at the faded wall paintings with their axes, smashed and set fire to the wooden altar. They took the small, waist-high image of the river god off his perch on the altar, tore off his clothes, hacked him into kindling, and threw the chunks of his body into a fire on the stone floor.

Besides the temple there was nothing much in Old Stonebridge worth destroying, so they went to Mayor Ma Jin's house to purge the town's corrupt leadership. They vandalized his few possessions, finding in an old box under his bed an antique scroll inscribed with literary characters and a few books in the classical language, including the *Analects* of Confucius. Comrade Ma, usually a tower of strength, was terrified, and that frightened the people of Old Stonebridge as much as the ravings of the Guards. Bu'er, Heiyen, and Guzhi listened as the Guards denounced Ma in the small town square, placed a dunce hat on his head, and hung signs around his neck. The one on his chest said *bourgeois rightist*, the one on his back said *landlord class*. Then they rolled up his pants and marched him through the town, beating his pale spindly legs with bamboo sticks until the blood ran down into his shoes.

"This is horrible," said Guzhi, standing in the crowd of observers. "I can't watch them beat Jin like this." As the procession reached the bridge, the Guards began to call him a dirty revisionist, accusing him of promoting the cult of the river god. That did it.

"You dog farts," he shouted at his tormentors. "I heaped curses on the river god. You ignorant bastards weren't even born when I became mayor of this city. Hypocrites! If you hate the old culture so much, why are you walking over this Tang dynasty bridge to cross the river? Get down and slog through the People's Republic of Shitty Water underneath it." Outraged, they surged around him and beat him senseless, and when he fell to the ground, they kicked at his limp body.

Guzhi could not stand it. She began to fight her way through the crowd toward Ma Jin's unconscious body. Heiyen followed, pulling at her arm. "Mother, you can't help him. They will do the same to you. They do not spare women. I'll go."

But before he could make a move, Bu'er, who was following as well, seized and locked her hands with theirs. They stood there, staring at one another, connected at the center where their hands joined, like three links of a chain. Bu'er spoke calmly but forcefully. "I am a Barefoot Doctor. Let me do this." She let go of their hands, then approached the place where Ma's body lay, curled into a fetal position.

"Stop," she shouted at those who were kicking him, pulling off her customary headcloth and allowing them to see her pocked and alien face. Stunned by her strange appearance and surprised by the strength of her voice, they stopped kicking Ma. "I am one of Chairman Mao's Barefoot Doctors. You have done your work. Now go! Following the beloved Chairman's directives, I will take care of him now—even if that means burying him." She stood there with her hands on her hips. The Guards, who were mostly teenagers, looked confused, maybe hearing in her words the authority of the god-like Chairman Mao. For a few moments, no one moved.

Then one of their adolescent voices rose to say, "On to Zhongduzhuang!" They marched out of Old Stonebridge, climbed aboard their trucks, and left to purge the next town.

CHAPTER 15

Ordeal

Chicago. 1969.

"Are you Naomi?" she said, incredulous.

"Livia?"

"Oh my God. I can't believe it. It's great to see you," she said, hugging her old friend but a little hesitant—Naomi had never answered her letters. They were standing in the Co-op Used Book Exchange, where Livia had come to sell back some course books. She backed up and looked at her more carefully. The woman standing before her bore little resemblance to "owl eyes" of six years ago. She had long black hair falling in soft curls and wore no glasses. "I almost didn't recognize you."

"I know you must be pissed at me for not writing, but my life changed so much. You would have accused me of betraying my principles. I started to write three or four times, to explain, but I could never finish the letters . . . It was, well, embarrassing. It was too hard to put into words."

It seemed a lame excuse, but Livia decided to let it go. "Well, that's water over the dam . . . D'you have time to get a sandwich at the Fifty-Seventh Street Deli? Lenny's gone, but it's the same old wreck of a place as before. Maybe we can sit at the Saul Bellow table and wallow in a little nostalgia."

"You still the champion of the proletariat?" Livia asked as they found a table at the deli. "I used to think of you when I felt uncaring thoughts about the proles during my year in Taiwan. Made me feel guilty."

"Yeah, I've had that effect on a lot of people. Hell of an accomplishment, when you think about it, your one claim to fame is making lots of good people feel guilty for the lives they're living . . . Livia, I'm married," Naomi said, flashing a modest diamond on her left hand that Livia had failed to notice. "Everything's different now—well, not everything, but a lot."

"Whoa! That is a change." They spent the next fifteen or twenty minutes in a rush of catching up. Naomi described falling in love with a guy named Charlie Byrd, marriage, two children—

"You have children? Oh my God."

"It all happened so fast. And yes, and I'm still the champ of the proletariat, but the new oppressed classes I worry about are women, mothers—not the old faceless masses working the satanic mills and choking on the smoggy air of Manchester and Birmingham. Have you read Betty Friedan's book? That lays it out. No? You've got to read it . . . I'm just 'a little mother' now, I can't get a job because the companies where I've applied are afraid I'll care more about my husband and kids than the firm. It's such garbage!"

"What are you doing in Chicago?"

"I live here now. Hard to believe, but it's because of Charlie. He is tops, the brass ring on the merry-go-round. I'm just so damn lucky. We moved here from Cincinnati so I could finish my BA, which I did, and now I'm into the nursing program. Something practical. But what about you? You must have run into a lot of prejudice at school."

"I'm only the fifth woman to be admitted into the graduate program in the Divinity School. So yeah, there are a few skeptics on the faculty who don't think women can handle serious scholarship, but my advisor and most of the faculty I've had for classes are very supportive . . . Oh God," she said, looking at her watch. "I've got a meeting. The fact is, I'm just coming up for oral exams in three days, and I expect to be admitted to the PhD program. Remember how I used to talk vaguely about getting to China somehow? Well, it's going to happen, and this is my ticket. I want to study women's leadership roles in Chinese religions, and get that approved for my dissertation."

"Great topic! Good luck with it," said Naomi, rising from her chair. "Sorry I've got to split, but I need to relieve Charlie. He's on the late shift at work tonight." Livia was actually happy to move on. She felt like she had a lot more work to do getting ready for the big exam. They exchanged phone numbers, promising to get to together again soon, after Livia's orals were over.

Livia's oral exam proved to be an exquisite torture. Of course she would pass, but she wanted more than that, to be invited to enter the PhD program in Chinese religion. Professor Chang, her advisor, and two of the other three examiners seemed satisfied with her answers. But a fourth man, Professor Eric Stegner, was not. She hardly knew him, and the few times she had run into him at school social events she sensed some disinterest or even antagonism, which was puzzling, since they had never even had a serious conversation.

"I'm not a China expert, so I will stick to more general questions," he said when it was his turn to question her, stroking his wispy goatee with his thumb and forefinger. "Please explain for me why you have this preoccupation with women's issues? When, as your bibliography makes clear, there is so little material available on that subject."

"That is just why I want to pursue the issue in my research. It is a huge gap in our knowledge. There is a fair amount of written material on male shamanism in China. I want to supplement what we know. Searching for the roles of women mediums in China will not just fill a lacuna in our knowledge of the religious lives of Chinese women but in our understanding of religion in general." Livia went on to lay out her plan for research in some detail, feeling when she finished that she had done it clearly and well.

"There is a lot of wishful thinking in what you propose," Stegner replied, "resources that will miraculously appear—"

But before he could complete his thought Livia blurted out, "So the sooner we get started the better."

He looked at her coldly. "I think you misunderstand my question," he said. "I am not objecting to the issue of women's leadership as a subject of research. What bothers me is the lack of texts to support your ideas." He said no more, and she thought that, after all, one unsympathetic person on the committee was not a death sentence.

There was a second round of questions, revolving around methodology. Her answers seemed to satisfy Chang and the other two professors. Then, again, it was Stegner's turn.

"I would like you to respond to a serious concern I have about your method. I have read your paper on Chinese shamanistic practices. I understand that is also what you propose to take as your subject of research if you are admitted to the PhD program, in particular the role of women in Chinese shamanism."

"That is what I plan to do. I realize that it is an ambitious project, but I believe I have the language skills that will allow me to carry it out."

"In the first part of this exam, I did not press my point about your methodology, but in this section it takes on a greater urgency. In my opinion there are simply not enough texts available for you to make a credible thesis about women's leadership."

"The problem is," Livia answered, "that nearly all of the existing books and articles on the subject were written by men. There are almost no women scholars in the field of religious studies."

"Does that tell you something?"

"Yes, it tells me that we need women in the field. I have seen women practicing as shamans, or mediums, in Taiwan. As a woman I will have an entrée into the religious world of women that is closed to men."

"Without good textual material, you will be unable to write your dissertation."

Livia pushed back: "Are you saying that the reality of religion is found only in texts?"

"Don't be ridiculous. I am only saying that it is the only material we can deal with using the methods respected in this school."

"I didn't think we were so narrow!"

Stegner made a dismissive sound. "So once again we will have to accept your assurances that you can do this research? And that the resources will be there. Miss Wayman, this is not a school of anthropology, yet you are proposing an anthropological study. What do you know about field work? What I want to see is texts. That, after all, is what we are about in this divinity school, the study of texts. Without texts we cannot be scientific, we cannot produce real scholarship." He crossed his arms in front of his chest in a gesture that said that the issue was closed.

Livia had a sudden realization. While she was in the clear with the women's issue, she had not thought much about the textual issue—every one of her inquisitors was a textual scholar. Stegner had pushed her, she had dug in her heels, and now she was faced with the consequences. A silence settled over the seminar room, and she felt the heat rising in her face. She hated the smug Stegner. The arrogant bastard. Her fingers shook. She dropped the pencil she was holding and disdained to bend down and pick it up. Just as she had become convinced that China was an important piece in the puzzle of her future, Stegner was picking apart her life plans and destroying that future. *You can kill someone with a stockyard sledgehammer,* she thought, *or dismember them with the scholar's stiletto. But the result was the same, a dead body.*

Chang said: "We have been at it for two and a half hours. I think it is time to wind it up. Professor Stegner, do you have any more questions?" Stegner waved his right hand dismissively. "No? Anyone else? All right then, Miss Wayman, you may leave. We will continue our deliberations. As you know, the results of all the oral exams will be available in the school office tomorrow."

When Chang did not call her that evening, she knew she was in trouble. She barely slept that night and hurried to school the next morning with fear pounding in her heart. Her future had to be China, and to clear the way for that she would need a PhD. She walked up to the second-floor office and checked her mailbox. The envelope, addressed to Olivia Wayman, contained a terse letter written on Divinity School stationery, signed by the Dean, stating that she had passed and been awarded a terminal MA degree. She had NOT been invited to enter the PhD program.

She stood there in shock, feeling defeated and physically sick from her lack of sleep. She glanced at the secretaries clicking away on their typewriters and realized that they were completely indifferent to her fate. Why would they care? She barely knew them. She felt completely alone, and this grand Gothic building suddenly seemed a ruins, representing an academic tradition that was dead to her. Three years of study wasted here.

She could not wait to leave the building. As she turned around to go, she saw him standing at the door. Stegner. How long had he stood there watching her? She did not know, but he must have seen her reading the letter.

"Congratulations on passing, Miss Wayman."

Instantly she felt a wave of anger rising in her chest. "I don't appreciate your irony," she said curtly. "You know I wanted the PhD program." She took a step toward the office door, but he also moved slightly to block her way.

"May I ask you to come to my office," he said softly. "There is something I want to tell you."

"No," she said flatly, finding everything about the man irritating, including his goatee and slightly stilted English.

"Of course you need not . . . but . . . please," he said, almost humbly.

She pondered for a moment, and curiosity got the best of her anger. "All right, I will." They walked down the corridor in silence, she following a few feet behind him. He opened the door to his office and motioned for her to enter first. Every inch of the man's office walls was covered by books, thousands of them. Endless texts. She sat down, anticipating disappointment. What good could come from this bookworm?

"Miss Wayman," he said after taking his seat behind his desk, "I do understand how you must feel. You are a person of determination and spirit." He paused. "And intelligence. I wish to help you move forward."

She shook her head in disbelief. "Move forward? You are the one who blocked my way!"

"Doors close, yes. But another way might open. I will not rehearse my points made yesterday at your oral exam. I firmly believe I am correct." Livia felt the distaste rising in her throat as the man spoke, like some lump of undigested food. "We in this school are strong in textual studies," he continued, "analysis, criticism. We must stick to those strengths if we hope to maintain the fine reputation this school enjoys. But," he continued, "we do not do field work, which is what you want to do. To invite you into the PhD program would not be fair either to you or to us. You must get your PhD in the department of anthropology. You were one of their stars as an undergraduate, and I have some influence there. I will help you."

CHAPTER 16

Coming Clean

Richmond. Summer 1971.

She had watched his downward spiral with a growing sense of helplessness. He ate terrible food, his clothes looked like they came from the Salvation Army, and he often went two or three days without shaving. He was a mess, with no real interests or hobbies. It had become painful to come and spend even two weeks with him in the summer.

"Is this a four star or a five star?"

"We're talking about a kosher all-beef hot dog, not stars."

Livia and Harold were having a pickup meal at Irving's Grill, on North Boulevard near the Richmond Braves ballpark, before going to the game. It was evening and the heat and humidity had abated a little, promising a comfortable night game under the lights. She would be away for a year, doing her anthropological field work, so she made a point of visiting him before flying to Taiwan.

"Let's sit outside," Livia said. "Maybe we'll catch a little breeze." The tables were metal, round, and white with rust spots and scratches, but the umbrellas were cheerful, offering a bit of shade on the warm evening.

"Atlanta hasn't siphoned off our best players, so Richmond is doing OK this season. But the Mud Hens are always tough."

"Mmm, yeah," was all Livia could say, completely clueless about baseball. Still, she thought, coming out for a ball game was better than their usual evening slumped in front of the boob tube enduring *Jeopardy!* or the *Dating Game*. They'd also had their usual conversations about religion, covering all the points of contention—sacraments, hierarchy, relics, indulgences, Marian worship, the Inquisition, saints, pilgrimage—an endless litany of things to argue about. These discussions carried on an annual tradition that began after she had become a Catholic and were by now depressingly predictable, with the same punches and counterpunches.

"These all-beef dogs are great!" Harold said, waving away her offer of relish. "The Jews really know how to cook."

She looked at him disapprovingly. "So do the Gentiles."

"But you don't want to put too much stuff on them," he said, ignoring her criticism. "Ruins the special hot-dog taste." He had prepared his the usual way, with a single clean swipe of yellow mustard as condiment. He looked suspiciously at the mess on hers—lots of mustard, catsup, pickle relish, and chopped onion. "Byzantine! But it figures," he added, needling her, "just like your taste in religion."

"I am grateful for your advice on the proper way to dress my hot dog. With all due respect, I'll do it my own way. Same goes for religion."

They picked up their Cokes from the counter and headed out the door to enjoy the evening sunlight flickering through the willow oaks across the boulevard.

"Some of those medieval popes had lots of bastard children running around the Vatican," said Harold, dragging out one of his favorite anti-Catholic chestnuts.

Livia was about to make the usual counterargument, but changed her mind. "Dad, why ruin a perfectly lovely evening talking about bastards in the Vatican!"

"We could do corrupt bishops instead," Harold said, "and how they led their troops into—" Before he could finish the sentence she raised her hand toward his face, palm outward, like a traffic cop. She felt a sudden and unexpected anger erupt inside her, and she didn't want to hear about bishops as military leaders.

"Stop, Dad, just stop. I'm tired of this charade." He looked at her, puzzled. She shook her head. "Your heart's not in this. You're going through the motions, rehearsing the same old arguments you probably heard in the seminary forty years ago—and we've thrown back and forth for the last ten years. This isn't a real discussion. It's phony and I'm sick of it."

He didn't respond to the attack, but looked surprised and crestfallen. He would not look her in the eyes.

"It seems like we've been doing this forever," she continued. "I mean arguing about religion. In case you haven't noticed, I've grown up, and I'd like to know what you really think. These endless arguments are just walls to hide behind. Have you lost your faith completely? Do you believe in God? Or grace? Do you believe in anything? And I'd like to know why you bother to take me to church? You probably haven't even noticed, but do you realize what you've been doing? We used to sit right in front of the pulpit. And now . . . we've been moving back farther every year. Think about last Sunday. We sat in the last pew! Next year, I guess, we'll be out on the front steps!"

She waited but he did not answer, so she went on. "Something happened in that Japanese detention camp, didn't it? And in those years after Mom and I came back to the States . . . I am tired of all the secrecy about that. You've never told me anything about my sister, or how she disappeared. I don't know why you and Mom broke up. That's one of the few things you two agree about. Don't tell Livia. Don't tell her anything."

He ran his fingers through his graying hair but said nothing.

"Oh, go eat your damn hot dog!" she said finally. The Catholic and Protestant hot dogs rested on their flimsy white paper plates, his shining with a yellow streak of mustard, half eaten, hers untouched, covered and surrounded by an overflow of colorful condiments.

He turned his head to the right, and she saw something in his eyes. Could that be a bit of tearing up?

"OK, Livia," he said finally. "You're right. Years ago it was easy to tell myself you were too young to understand. And now the years have passed . . . it's hard to say what could have been said more easily back then. These are such personal things . . . If it makes you feel any better, I've never shared them with anyone."

He stopped, and Livia waited, feeling like an angel had passed by. She did not want to ruin the moment with the wrong words.

Harold also waited. Finally, he choked out the words: "I'm sorry, Livia . . . tell me what you want to know."

Choosing her words carefully, she said: "Let's start with what happened to you? What changed you from a leader in the church, to a . . . a . . ." She could not come up with the right words, and was suddenly embarrassed. *A shell of your former self, a has-been, a feckless hobo.* She couldn't say what she really thought.

"Some kind of wreck," he volunteered, "like an old battleship that's gone aground." Harold pushed away the half-eaten hot dog. Finally, he began: "Yes, it started at the detention camp . . . The man who went in and the one who came out were two different people . . ." His words were halting, but he kept on talking, and Livia knew that his words were, finally, the truth. "At first, when they asked me to lead the Sunday worship, I preached what I thought was the Lord's Gospel. We were in a terrible situation and I tried to give them hope. We were all crammed together there, fighting for space, sometimes not enough to eat. I wanted the people to put the message of Jesus into practice: If a man asks for your shirt, give him your coat, too. Visit the sick, clothe the naked, feed the hungry, comfort the oppressed. Turn the other cheek. Despite the hardships, let's build a beautiful community here. Jesus is with you everywhere, even here. You only have to turn to your neighbor and you will find him."

Harold shook his head dejectedly at the memory, but Livia found herself moved by his words. "I still believe in those things," she said sadly, as she observed the way the lines of his mouth turned down at the corners, like permanent scars.

"As the months went by I saw that nothing changed. The Christians, who professed to believe the words of Jesus were no different than anyone else, no worse perhaps, but no better . . . I asked myself why I had come from halfway around the world to preach a gospel to the Chinese if it would make them no better than anyone else. There were loving atheists in that camp, and some damn mean and selfish Christians."

"You must have felt like giving up . . . Why didn't you just come back to the States with Mom and me when it was over?"

"I guess it was my last-ditch attempt to save my faith—I know, I know, you can't do that. It's a gift. But I wanted to try, anyway, to see if I could get back my conviction . . . But it didn't work. And then the Communists took over, and they finally drove out all foreign missionaries. That was the last nail in the coffin. I came back to the States feeling a complete failure. The words I had preached all those years meant nothing."

"But you still work at the Presbyterian office."

Harold shook his head sadly. "That's not conviction. It's just a living. I had to support myself, and they were kind enough to offer me a desk job at headquarters. I needed to send something to Adele and you every month . . . I wish I had a happy ending to tack on this story, but I don't."

"But you didn't give up. You still go to church."

"Going to church on Sunday and being a Christian are not the same thing." He looked down at their uneaten hot dogs. "So I'll just say that I'm sorry. I should have shared these things with you years ago. But there's one other thing I want to say . . . about our arguments over the years since you became a Catholic. I loved it that you cared enough to argue with me. Because of that I never felt that the arguments were phony. I think they were my way of staying in the game, maybe not a very good way, especially as you grew up and had your own convictions, but it was all I could manage."

Livia stood up, wanting to hug him. He was seated though, and as she came around he started to get up but hadn't quite made it to his feet when she put her arms around his neck. It was awkward.

"Thanks, Dad," was all she could say. "I've got a lot more questions, but I think I'll save them till tomorrow. And speaking of staying in the game, we better get going or we'll miss the Braves and the Mud Hens." They threw their uneaten food in a trash container, and began to walk toward the ball park. Neither spoke.

Finally, after two blocks of silence, he said, "Did you know, Livia, that there were three popes at once back in the fifteenth century?"

She laughed in spite of herself. "Dad, you're incorrigible . . . But I am glad you're still in the game."

"I guess what I'm trying to say is that my retreat to the back of the church you were talking about before has gone as far as it is going to go. I may be sitting in the last pew but I won't be going out the door."

CHAPTER 17

Chinese Curse

Summer 1972.

Livia drove south on I-95 in her rusty Falcon, feeling like a fool. Not because of the Falcon—"rusty but trusty"—but because she was the courier for her parents' divorce papers, of all things. Minutes after her mother had picked her up at JFK, she dropped a bomb. "Livia, your father and I are getting a divorce."

After a moment of stunned silence, she said, "Oh my God. After all these years? Why?"

"He says he has fallen in love and wants to marry the woman."

"What woman? Who is she?"

"I don't know anything about her except the little he told me. Her name is Matilda Grace Weaver. He calls her Tillie. An administrative assistant at the Presbyterian office where he works."

Livia shook her head in disbelief. "I hope she's not my age. Jesus, Mom, you could have waited with this until I got over jet lag!"

"Sorry, this is all I've been thinking about for the last couple of weeks. The divorce papers came three days after he phoned me."

Slowed by gridlock around Washington, Livia thought about her own affairs. The year of fieldwork in Taiwan had been productive, with reams of notes in her folders, mostly interviews with Buddhist nuns and female mediums. And best of all, she'd discovered a small religious society that made regular contact with the spirits through a female medium. The medium's followers compiled her messages into a sort of bible, a collection of sacred writings that gave them directions on how to live their lives. They called themselves the Sacred Truth Society, and her study of their sect would form the core of her dissertation. She planned to live with her mother while she wrote it, close to all the great libraries of New York City.

As she neared Richmond, the air conditioner began to make funny sounds, and when she put her hand over the air vent, it blew lukewarm. Thoughts about her father kept intruding. How had the hobo of a year ago managed to find a partner?

Minutes later she was driving slowly on Cutshaw Avenue, a few blocks south of US 33, in a neighborhood of one-story bungalows with large lots and plenty of grass to cut. The house was small, a clay-red brick veneer with white trim paint, peeling in places. *Must be Tillie's house. Good.* Anything was better than the dismal, cluttered apartment she had been visiting the past few summers. There was an old Chevrolet Impala to the right, where the gravel of the driveway petered out into the unkempt grass. *Also hers,* she thought as she parked behind it. She followed a path of cement-block stepping stones toward the front door, some of them cracked and almost hidden under the creeping crabgrass. She found herself attempting to land on the stepping stones as she walked, but they were placed a little too far apart for her stride and it threw her off balance. She felt ridiculous, like an obsessive who won't walk on cracks in the sidewalk. What was wrong with her?

Last year Livia felt that she and her father had had their first adult conversations, and she thought she had begun to understand him. But now? As she stepped up to the front door, she noted a piece of weathered masking tape covering the doorbell, so she knocked timidly. Almost immediately she heard heavy steps coming to the door. He threw the door open and drew her into a big bear hug, almost lifting her off her feet. Clamped in the embrace, her eyes closed, and when she opened them she spotted a movement in the dim light inside the house. A slight woman with red hair.

He held her at arm's length. "Let me look at you. You look great, Livia. Taiwan must have agreed with you."

Livia laughed. "Lots of sweat, lots of bike riding, and regular bouts with diarrhea will do wonders for your figure."

"Maybe I ought to try that myself . . . Here, let me introduce you to my fiancée, Tillie Grace." Livia suddenly felt an odd reversal, as though they were the children and she the critical parent that had to be pleased. The small figure moved out of the shadows and into a shaft of sunlight, the hair color not at all timid. For a fleeting moment she thought she was looking at a portrait she had seen in Raleigh—Granny Manigault before her hair had turned from red to silver.

She stepped back to look at her father and saw, not the half-defeated man of the year before, but a clean-shaven gent with black hair, combed carefully. Something like an aging Cary Grant. He'd lost weight, wore an open-collar dress shirt, khaki pants, and cordovan loafers. The little redhead had transformed him.

"Hello, Livia. I've heard so much about you." Tillie extended a small hand, but when they shook hands, the grip was firm. "Let's get a little more light in here," she said, tugging at the cord of the drapes. Livia could see her more clearly now as she moved into the bright light coming through the picture window. The woman was in her fifties maybe, but had the body of a much younger woman. The snug dress she wore didn't hide it. "Come in. You two sit down here," she said, pointing to the couch. "You'll have so much to talk about. I'll go make us some tea."

They looked at each other, neither knowing where to begin. After the usual "how was the trip," "the weather's been hot," and so forth, Harold got right to the point.

"I know this is out of the blue. You leave for Asia worrying about your old deadbeat dad . . . No, no," he said, seeing that she was about to offer a protest, "you must have felt something like that. And the thing is, you would have been right. You come back a year later and I'm a different person. Like the old hymn says, 'I once was lost, and now am found.'" Livia heard the whistle of the teakettle, the clink of cups and saucers, reminding her that it was not just the Lord who found him.

"You asked me once if I believed in the possibility of grace anymore," he said in a lower voice. "Now I've experienced it. Literally. Her name is Tillie Grace. Isn't that amazing?" Livia felt almost embarrassed and couldn't think of how to respond. Other than his words the night of the ball game, and some ensuing conversations, it was the most personal religious thing he had ever said to her.

"And you'd be proud of me," he added, laughing. "Tillie Grace and I are sitting right under the pulpit. You know," he continued, "it just struck me. The two of you have a lot in common—you can both speak Chinese, something I never really mastered. I'll admit it. I was envious even of you, a little five-year-old who could speak much better Chinese than I could . . . Tillie Grace was raised in a missionary family too, has two brothers and a sister. Good fellows. Her parents worked in Taiwan from the late '40s. Reverend Weaver is dead now, but her mother's still alive. Lives here in Richmond. You know, Livia, Tillie's the reason I got my life back, and my . . . well, let's just say that our life together is wonderful . . . In every way." Livia figured she could fill in the blanks.

Tillie came in with a red-lacquer tray holding a teapot, cups, shortbread cookies. "I thought you might like this Taiwan oolong. I've enjoyed reading of your experiences there. Brought back some wonderful memories." Somehow the thought of this stranger reading her letters to Harold bothered her.

Tillie placed the tray on the coffee table, then looked at the two of them as if to see whether there was enough space for three on the settee. There wasn't, so Livia obligingly moved over to the leather recliner, allowing Tillie to sit next to Harold, and again she felt a slight irritation.

Harold listened as each of the two talked about their experiences in Taiwan, Livia of her research and Tillie of the work of the Presbyterians there. "I don't know much about it," Livia admitted, "but my impression is that the Presbyterian Church is the most vital Christian church on the island. I think they have generally taken the side of the Taiwanese against the Nationalists. The Chiangs don't like them, and for me that is a mark in their favor."

"You're right about that," Tillie said. "We were there, working with the Taiwanese before the Nationalists came." She placed her hand on

Harold's shoulder. At one point, as they chatted easily, Livia saw her index finger move slightly, gently stroking her father's neck. The tiny gesture said a lot. She tried to remember some display of affection between Adele and Harold, but couldn't.

"Hi Mom. I've seen him," she said, making the call that same evening.

"Well, tell me all about it."

"You wouldn't believe the change. He looks one hundred percent better. He's not the same man that we've been worried about for the last few years. He's dyed his hair black. Can you beat it? The Reverend Wayman is using Grecian Formula 9! He's lost some weight. He's off Twinkies and onto carrots. He seems very happy. He and Tillie are even talking about going back to Taiwan, maybe some sort of missionary work." Adele remained silent, and Livia groped for a way to describe Tillie. "I think . . . I think . . ." Livia choked up, imagining the pain her words might be causing her mother.

Finally, Adele spoke. "I think you're taking this harder than I am, Livia. I haven't seen him for so long, and I suppose at some level I continued to worry about him . . . but it sounds like he may have found what he wanted all along, a partner to help him in the missions . . . what I could never be . . . Tell me what she looks like. She's not your age, is she?"

"No, thank God for that. Maybe somewhere in her fifties. She reminds me of what Granny must have looked like when she was young, a pert little redhead, only prettier, and not so bossy."

She heard a chuckle at the other end of the line.

"Mom, he talks like this relationship is a miracle of grace. He was lost and now is found. You know the hymn." Livia blew her nose into her handkerchief. "But how can they be living together and planning to become missionaries at the same time? Isn't that against Presbyterian morals?"

"Who knows? Maybe there's been some shift in theology we don't know about. But for me, this is closure, and that's a good thing. I guess I was lulled into imagining the future in a certain way . . . not that we'd ever get back together but that we'd probably die, gently estranged but still officially married. But that's not important now. To tell the truth, what I feel mostly is relief. I don't have to listen to that little voice telling me I should do something to help the bum of a year ago. Life is interesting, isn't it?"

"Careful there. That's the famous Chinese curse: May you live in interesting times!"

"Heard that one when we lived there. Did you give him the papers?"

"I'll give them to him tomorrow morning. We're having breakfast and then I'm leaving. See you around seven or eight. I'm calling from a Days Inn, by the way. Kind of burns me—Tillie apologizing for how small their house was—but God, I'd have been glad to sleep on the couch."

Adele laughed. "You know why you're in the motel, don't you?"

"Why?"

"They don't want you to hear the bed squeak!"

CHAPTER 18

Teaching

Athena, Ohio.

Athena College: Liberal arts. Named after the Greek goddess of learning and wisdom. Founded 1923, as a women's college. Opened to men in 1966. Seal: In Sapientia Virtus. *Nestled in the Appalachian foothills of southeastern Ohio. 2,642 students. Cost: midrange. Aspires to remain accessible to regional applicants. Emphasis on faculty collaboration and close contact between students and faculty.*

—Park & Stearns, *How to Pick a College*, 11th edition, page 27.

The headlights sliced through the venetian blinds, sending parallel bars of light diagonally across the blank wall of her bedroom as the car slid past on the wet street outside. It was a Sunday evening in early March, rainy and cold. It wasn't nirvana exactly, but for the first time in her life Livia was having a normal relationship. Damian was snoozing next to her, a warm presence under the quilt. He had long brown hair with gray accents, clinched in a ponytail. Pale skinned, not the outdoor sort. Livia was thinking about how ordinary it seemed—enjoying the warmth of his body next to hers, the periodic play of light traveling across the wall as a car passed, Coltrane's *A Love Supreme* playing softly on the stereo.

But, OK, there was a grain of sand in her shoe. Making love today somehow felt a bit different, like something was missing. A little too fast? Or absent-minded? Could sex get routine so soon? After two months? Was something wrong with her . . . or with Damian? She thought of Henry, with some feelings of guilt. Then exasperation. Why should she feel guilty, when she and Henry had never even kissed each other? As much as she cared for him, they were just friends. Just friends, she repeated to herself.

She was now teaching at Athena, and the road here had been surprisingly easy. Returning from a year's research in southern Taiwan, she had moved in with her mother, single-minded in her determination to complete her dissertation. Livia created her own space in the apartment. She set up two card tables in the living room, loaded them down with her field notes, a typewriter, pens and notebooks, 3 x 5 cards, chapter drafts, and stacks of books which she got from the Columbia library. She slept on the couch, woke early, pulled on her sweats, and ran a route through the streets, figuring out how best to avoid traffic on a two- or three-mile loop. It worked well enough if she got an early start. By the time she returned, Adele had left for the hospital, and she had the place to herself for the rest of the day. A shower and a cup of black coffee, no sugar or cream. Then she went to work, as disciplined as a nun in vows. A sandwich and Coke for lunch and back to work until late afternoon.

It was an ascetic life. Livia focused her mind on the work, deferring even simple pleasures until the evening. A late afternoon walk for a torte and espresso at the French bakery where she read the *New York Times*. A grim sort of existence, some would think, but she thrived on it. Sometimes she shopped at one of the small markets, or made an occasional trip to Chinatown for staples: soy, hoisin and oyster sauce, rice noodles, Japanese rice, tofu. Then she fixed dinner for herself and Adele, and, for the first time in her life, got to know her mother as an adult. Their conversations became more and more intimate and unguarded as the weeks went by and the spontaneous sharing made them realize something both felt but didn't have to say in words: they liked each other.

One night, as they were eating a dish of fried tofu, garlic, and eggplant, she heard a snicker. "You exist because of the tofu man." Livia raised her eyes and looked at her mother over the top of her glasses, waiting for an explanation of this bizarre statement. "And I can tell you the exact day and time you were conceived, almost down to the exact minute. You're an astrologist's dream! Your father thought God had sent him—the tofu man, not the astrologist—early, so that he would wake us up and we would . . . et cetera." Adele told her the story and they both laughed. Crazy, but it made her happy to think there might have been something unusual about her conception. And that her mother had chosen to share this intimate detail of her history, from a time when she was nothing more than a few dividing cells.

One night, while they were washing the dishes, Adele began to talk about herself. "I think I am going to spend the rest of my life alone. I'm not complaining—being alone doesn't seem a bad thing to me just now." No one had ever taken care of her, she said, even during her occasional love affairs over the years. She seemed to attract takers, not givers, and that can get old, she admitted, especially when you're giving all day at work. "You remember Eugene. What he needed was an appreciative audience, and I gave it to him for a while. But then I couldn't. He was such a pedantic creep . . . I've gotten used to having the last part of the day to myself, without the need for more giving. I'm just saying this because I don't want you to think I'm unhappy.

"It was a few months ago that they asked me to head up emergency nursing. I was flattered and pleased by the offer, and the pay was good, but at fifty-eight I wondered how long I could do it. Right now it's not so bad, Livia, because you're here. For the first time in my life—except for the years in China when we had a cook and a houseboy—I've had a caretaker, someone to keep house and make dinner for me. I know it's just temporary, but for now, what a luxury. You're going to spoil me!"

Adele's sandy hair was now streaked with gray that she made no effort to hide. She kept it cut short, waved and parted. No makeup. Bundled in her winter coat and scarf, and walking along the Brooklyn streets with her sensible shoes, she might have been mistaken for a man. She had stayed trim and Livia thought she was attractive. Or maybe *distinguished* was the word. Her features were too strong to count as pretty. The lines of definition around her eyes and mouth were set too deep. In the bathroom, Livia could find none of the usual lotions, creams, emulsions, and other products with French and Swedish names that promise eternal youth and unfading beauty. Her mother simply accepted the process of aging. And she seemed content with her uneventful life.

"Hardly uneventful," Adele said when Livia made the mistake of using those words one evening. "Let me tell you about today. It was worse than usual, I'll admit, but I'm not exaggerating. I had six rooms to tend in Emergency. There were two old gentlemen on vents. There was a young boy brought in screaming with pain, a burn victim. I ran to the code room for morphine. I couldn't get the lock opened. While I was fumbling with the keys, I got a page. MI victim wheeled into one of my rooms. I rushed back. He sat there on the bed holding his chest, swaying back and forth, babbling. His face was turning gray as ashes, right in front of my eyes. Frightened to death, probably thinking every word might be his last. I buzzed a supervisor and ran back to the code room. Need morphine for the boy, stuff to open the veins of the guy with the heart attack . . . yeah, I could use an uneventful life." Adele took a deep breath and threw her head against the back of the chair. "And the last thing. Late this afternoon. A family of children and grandchildren brought in their granny. You could see that they all loved her. Ninety-four years old. She stopped breathing on the gurney. They started yelling at me. 'Don't let her die! Respirate her, bring her back!' I was sure I couldn't do anything for her, but they kept screaming at me. Finally, I did it. I put my hands on her chest and pushed. Once. Oh my God. I could feel the ribs crack." Adele squeezed her eyes shut.

"Did she recover?"

"No. She was gone. . . but the guy with the heart attack survived, if you're looking for a happy ending."

Livia's thoughts were interrupted as Damian stirred in the bed next to her. He was awake. Another set of headlights threw sliding strips of darkness and light across the wall. "Damian, are you feeling OK today?" He mumbled something incomprehensible into the pillow, as though he were still asleep. He was faking and she knew it, probably as busily engaged in his own thoughts as she was in hers. She turned away from him and concentrated on enjoying the warmth under the quilt. They would get up in a few minutes and have dinner at the Crescent Moon.

The new dean wanted to see her tomorrow, after her 10:00 a.m. class. If there was a problem, it would be the first of any consequence. It had gone so easily, the journey from fieldwork in Taiwan, to the PhD at Chicago, to a job at Athena. And she was, for the first time in her life, earning a decent salary, and having some fun. But, she had an uneasy feeling. Why did the dean want to see her?

Daniel Webber, Dean of Humanities. Hired by Athena the previous year, now in his second semester at the college. Slender, tall, a head of wavy hair so silver it looked fake. Maybe it was. But a young face. Over all, a poster child for the word *distinguished*.

"Dr. Wayman, I note that your contract is up for renewal next year. Commended for your work in the classroom. Teaching evaluations quite good." He glanced down at the notes on his desk. "But you have only one published article, and I want you to be aware that for me to support you for tenure in three years I will need to see more evidence of research and publications. Hopefully a book with a good scholarly press. Or at least a couple of articles in top-ranking journals."

"Dr. Webber, with all due respect, those expectations were not part of the deal when I was first interviewed for this job. In fact, all the stress was on teaching, collaboration with colleagues, close contact with the students."

"Yes, I get it. Those were the guidelines under the former dean. But I was hired to raise Athena to a new level, to compete with the other fine liberal arts colleges here in Ohio, such as Oberlin, Kenyon, Denison. To reach that goal we have to create here at Athena a new culture of rigorous research and publication, and a salary structure that rewards it." He paused. "Am I making myself clear?"

"Clear, yes. But I would just say that I, and lots of others on the faculty, were hired under a different set of expectations. I don't feel that it is fair to change the rules in the middle of the game."

The dean, a lefty, held a pen between his third and index fingers. He tapped on the clip end of the pen. The tip made a soft staccato drumming on the notebook under his hand. With his right hand he raked his fingers through the silver hair. The waves parted, then fell back into place, like the wake of a departing ship. "As long as we are clear about what I'm asking," he said, making fussy tidying motions with a stack of papers that signaled the interview was over. "Perhaps, Dr. Wayman, you would feel more comfortable at an institution with lower expectations," he said as she rose and turned to leave.

Late that afternoon, she met Damian at the Crescent Moon. The front door of the restaurant was made of reclaimed barnwood, with a quarter-moon cutout, giving the place the look of a supersized outhouse. It was a favorite hangout for faculty and students. Livia was fuming, ready to unload on her friend. Damian waved as he entered and walked over toward her booth. "I'll grab a cup of coffee. Can I get you a refill?"

He came back with two Styrofoam cups of what she was sure was the worst coffee in southeastern Ohio and slipped into the booth. "What a dump! This vinyl is so badly cracked I'm always thinking I'll tear the buttons off my back pocket."

Livia started right in. "I just got out of my conference with Webber. What a jerk! As much as told me to leave and go find a job somewhere else. An institution with lower standards. I don't have enough publications to meet his expectations."

Livia expected immediate support, some kind of indignant retort, since Damian had never been much of a publisher himself. He liked to work with students, and he wrote poetry which was good enough to be published in a few small college literary journals. But he had tenure and wouldn't have to worry about Webber's "higher standards." His face merely fell. "I'm sorry," he said, and she found that response lame. But then he surprised her. "I may be leaving, too."

Her eyes focused on her Styrofoam cup as she realized, with sudden clarity, that their relationship was not very important to him—a distant second to the horse of his future career. She struggled to keep the emotion out of her voice. "Why? I thought you liked it here."

Damian turned his coffee cup absently. "I do. It's complicated. And I really don't want to talk about it."

Now she was really irritated. "Then why did you bring it up? Yesterday already, I could tell something was wrong . . . Look, I know we've just been going out for a couple of months and we don't have any commitments, but I still think you owe me an explanation."

He paused a while, then nodded. "Yes. I suppose I do. But you won't like it."

"Let's hear it," she said.

He sighed and rubbed the bridge of his nose. "It started in late January. In fact, I can tell you the exact time and date. You remember that big ice storm we had? I taught that evening. Went back to my office, thinking I'd work a bit until it let up. I was looking at my class list. I noticed that four students had apparently dropped out, three guys—Bass, Becker, and Del Vecchio—and a girl. You know how it goes—came a time or two and then didn't show up after that."

"I'm surprised you still remember their names."

"You'll see why in a minute. Anyway, I was about to mark *withdraw* on the preliminary list when someone knocked at the door. It was the girl. Name was Gina Visconti—a name I'll never forget either. I invited her to come in and sit down. She was wearing this improbable outfit. A calf-length fur coat, maybe muskrat. I could see tiny beads of ice stuck to the tips of the hairs. They were beginning to melt and dribble on the floor. Looked like she was wearing some kind of red stockings and high heels. Can you imagine that? In all the slush and ice? I can remember thinking what the hell brought her out on a night like this, dressed for a nightclub. But you know we have these student poseurs, twenties gangsters, floozies, Russian generals, flower children. So I didn't think too much about it. Just another weirdo. But a pretty one.

"I pointed out that she'd missed a lot of classes. Said she was very sorry, that's what she wanted to talk about. So she proceeded to give me this story about a death in her family, a dear grandmother. She had to go home, which is in Idaho somewhere. You know, it was the usual bullshit. Said she wanted to do whatever it takes to catch up, extra work, and so on. Then she licked her lips and let out a little innuendo, something like 'I'm willing to do whatever you want me to do.'

"It gets worse from there. I won't bore you with all the twists and turns, but the long and short of it is that she seduced me. She showed me how little she had on under the muskrat. I was such a damn fool. We did it right there in the office . . . and then she disappeared for a couple of weeks! I'm just about to cross off her name from the class list when she shows up with the three guys, the absentees. They marched into my office and accused me of sexually harassing poor little Gina. They demanded a B grade for the class, and when I told them to go to hell, they threatened to write a letter to the dean. I threw them out of my office, self-righteous as all hell."

"Wait a minute," Livia said. "Sex with a student was a dumb mistake, but it's 'he said, she said,' not fatal. And what they were trying to pull is extortion. I'll bet if you check the records, they are flunking most of their courses, so no one's going to believe the story concocted by a bunch of deadbeats."

"Yeah, but all of that is beside the point. The point is that one of those bastards taped the conversation when we talked, and I, dumb fuck that I am, never denied that I'd had sex with Gina, not once in the whole conversation. One of them—I forget which one—was carrying a Bible under his arm and I thought at the time something was phony about that. Must have hid the tape recorder under it, or in it. Anyway, I'm screwed. I'm going to lose my job."

"Well, let me know what you plan to do," she said, trying to project the same sort of tired resignation she was getting from him. "I've got a class in fifteen minutes." But she couldn't resist a parting shot. "You can always appeal to the ideals of Athena," Livia said, rising from the table and feeling the torn plastic cushion clawing at the back pocket of her slacks. "You've done everything the faculty handbook asks of us, and more. You know, 'collaboration with colleagues'—that's me, every Sunday afternoon—and 'close contact with the students'—that's the gorgeous Gina." She left him staring into his coffee cup.

长甲

CHAPTER 19

Long Nail

Old Stonebridge. 1973.

Bu’er was painfully aware that many of the FourOnes doubted her leadership abilities. Because she rarely went into trances, some said she had no connection with the spirits. Others were disturbed by the circumstances of her kidnapping, thinking that her foreign origin made her unfit to lead them. A few even criticized her for leaving them so frequently to work as a healer with Mingling. Heiyen and Guzhi gave her their unwavering support, but neither seemed capable of envisioning any sort of leadership role for her other than going into trances to contact the spirits. Bu’er said only that she had done all she could, nursing and healing members to the best of her ability. “Mingling has taught me that whatever I am called to do, the call must begin in my own heart and mind. Otherwise it is not from the spirits.”

It was then that Long Nail appeared, joining their gathering one evening as they chanted under the shed by the abandoned shrine of the tutelary god Tudigong. He looked from one face to another in the flickering candlelight. The chanting stopped and the FourOnes looked at the newcomer. His own facial features were unusual, his eyes, under a pronounced widow’s peak, were narrow, mere slits, as though in a perpetual squint. Finally, he located Heiyen and Bu’er, who happened to be sitting on the ground together. He mumbled a few words that neither understood, then fumbled in his cloth bag and took out a piece of paper, extending it toward them.

Heiyen unfolded the paper, read it carefully, then stood up and read it aloud to the assembled members. It was a letter of introduction from the FourOnes at Fuping, a county town larger than Old Stonebridge, about thirty miles distant. It stated that the bearer's name was Yang Boting and that he had come originally from Sichuan Province. He had joined their group and had quickly proved to be adept, capable of going into trances and bringing messages from the spirit world. They had given him the sect name Changjia, "Long Nail," and said that they wanted to share him with the believers at Old Stonebridge. Members welcomed him, and, because it was late, Mr. Hu, a friendly and faithful member of the sect, offered Long Nail a place to stay for the night.

For the next two weeks Long Nail attended every group meeting, listening to the messages from the spirits and the discussions about their plans, but he said nothing. He brushed aside the usual polite questions about his family and place of origin. Then, near the end of one of their evening meetings, he surprised everyone. Guzhi had not attended, and Bu'er, as usual, did not receive a message. Just as the members were rising to leave, they heard a rumble from the throat of Long Nail. His slit-like eyes opened wide, the irises rolled up in his head and his eyeballs were blank as orbs of white bone. Mr. Hu rushed over to him fearing that he was having a seizure.

Then the words poured out of him, clear and even elegant, completely unlike Long Nail's ordinary hesitant and mumbled speech. Someone grabbed a pencil and began scribbling down the words, and ten minutes later, when he returned to normal consciousness, the group was stunned to discover they had received a message from one of the Daoist Immortals, Zhang Daoling. He said that the FourOnes were his "seed people," chosen as a foundation for a new society.

"Who is Zhang Daoling?" someone asked. Most had never heard of him, but Heiyen answered, "He was one of the founders of the Zheng Yi sect. Of all religious sects, they are the closest to our beliefs." The others shook their head in wonderment. How could this dumb egg Long Nail have spoken so fluently unless the words were truly coming from the great immortal?

About a week later, following a meeting in which Long Nail had brought a second powerful message from Zhang Daoling, Heiyen spoke to Bu'er and Guzhi.

"I feel uneasy about him," Heiyen said. "He has been with us for only a short time and already has brought us strong messages from the Immortal Zhang."

"I have doubts as well," Guzhi said.

"I am trying to be fair, but I can say that it upsets me that he gets messages from the Immortal Zhang so easily," Bu'er said, "maybe too easily. Zhang Daoling has never taken an interest in us before. Why now? I think that many of our people respond to Long Nail because they are so discouraged, doubtful whether we will ever be able to publically establish our way. His messages are so clear about the future."

"That bothers me as well," Guzhi said. "What if Ma Jin hears of this? He would be forced to take action against us. And if we encourage Long Nail, it will be like making him one of our leaders. Would that be right? Should we let that happen? He is more aggressive than you, Heiyen, urging things you would never advocate." She put her hand on Bu'er's. "And daughter, you know our people seek reassurance from the spirits. I'm getting old, and this Long Nail has an ease with the spirits. It appears that they wish to communicate through him, not you."

"We must be guided by the spirits," Heiyen said, trying to conclude the discussion.

"But which spirits?" asked Guzhi, unwilling to drop the subject. "Zhang Daoling or our own spirits that I have contacted all these years? I will speak straightforwardly," the old lady continued. "How do we know Long Nail is really contacting Immortal Zhang, and moreover, if he is, how do we know that he is getting the message correctly?"

"In normal situations Long Nail is quiet," said Heiyen, "an inarticulate bumbler. But in trance he becomes full of the spirit. It must be the Immortal speaking through him."

Guzhi acknowledged his reasoning, but added: "There is another thing that disturbs me—that disgusting fingernail of his."

"Yes, his name." Heiyen looked at Bu'er and explained. "You are too young to know this, daughter, but in the old days, the imperial officials and the other mandarin classes kept all of their fingernails excessively long, to show that they were superior to the working classes, that their work was of a higher status, intellectual, not manual. Now, of course, our government officials glorify manual labor and the working classes."

"That is exactly why I am bothered by the long nail. The authorities may see it, think he is advocating a return to the old ways, and crack down hard on all of us. We should not call attention to ourselves like that. It is too dangerous."

"He has told me," said Heiyen, "that the nail means only that not everything about the old way was bad."

"That may be true, but now is not the time for that point to be made. We have just come through the misery of the Cultural Revolution and I think the Party leadership is correct, we should lift up the working people—they have been oppressed for the whole of Chinese history. The sight of that long fingernail, even if it is only on the baby finger of his left hand . . . it still makes me sick!"

As the weeks passed, Long Nail continued his stay at Old Stonebridge, showing no signs of wanting to return to Fuping. He had become the FourOnes' main source of information from the spirit world. The messages urged the FourOnes to take a stand and establish their community openly in Old Stonebridge. Bu'er began to worry as more and more FourOne people came from the countryside to hear this new phenomenon who delivered such clear visions of the future. She noticed, with irritation, that many of these new visitors were letting their left baby fingernail grow long.

Everything came to a head one Saturday evening. They doubled the size of the shelter at Tudigong's shrine, adding a tent-like extension to provide space for about eighty people. Long Nail had delivered a message that night from Guangong, the god of war, a clear call to reject Party control of Old Stonebridge and set up a FourOne tribunal to guide the city to a new social order. After Guangong's message was read aloud, Long Nail rose and said with great conviction: "Now is the time, let us heed the words of the god." The people cheered.

Guzhi was stunned, aware that Long Nail had seized the reigns of leadership. "This is a dangerous path," she said to Heiyen, imploring him to do something. Heiyen looked to Bu'er but she just shook her head sadly and remained silent. Heiyen got up and spoke, trying to slow the momentum that Long Nail had begun, suggesting that they could not make a move until more messages came to them from other spirits confirming the will of Guangong. But his words got a lukewarm response.

Then Long Nail got up and spoke again. Guangong, he pointed out, was the god of war who had guided the Chinese nation since the time of the Han dynasty, over two thousand years ago. Down through all the dynasties, from the Han to the Qing, his power had saved them from the attack of foreign enemies and helped them put down many internal rebellions. "He has spoken," Long Nail said, "now we must act."

Guzhi stood up to speak, holding her hand above her head. The cheering for Long Nail subsided. "We have been here in Old Stonebridge for many years, free to practice our way," said the old lady, "because of the forbearance of my nephew Ma Jin. But if you go ahead with this insane plan, he will have provincial troops here in twenty-four hours and all of us will be shot dead or thrown in jail. They will consider us rebels." In response there were voices of opposition raised, but above them the mumbling of a larger number of the group who were now doubtful.

Long Nail was not so easily turned aside. He found a wooden box and stood on it, elevating himself above the assembled crowd. "I do not speak for myself. I am nothing but an insignificant human being, as inarticulate as a young child. But Guangong has spoken and we must do his will." A good number of the crowd were nodding in agreement. "I am willing to submit to a test to prove that the god has spoken through me," continued Long Nail. "I vow to go into seclusion for one week in my room. Mr. Hu will lock the door from the outside. Just as the emperor fasted in days gone by, before the great sacrifices of the summer and winter solstices, I too will eat nothing and drink nothing for the whole week. When I come out, one week from tonight, I will go to the place of the spirits and bring back Guangong's final word . . . then we must obey him, whatever the consequences."

There were loud cheers as Long Nail stepped down from the box, but Heiyen shook his head and muttered, "He dares to compare himself to the emperor!"

During the week that followed, the rumor spread through the countryside that a holy man had immured himself in Mr. Hu's storage shed. There were no windows in the little hut and just one door, which at Long Nail's request Mr. Hu had locked from the outside. As the days went by, more and more people passed the hovel, standing respectfully near the door and bowing their heads. Hu assured visitors that Long Nail had not come out, and no food or water had been passed inside. The seer's reputation for sanctity increased, and, as the time approached for his emergence on the following Saturday evening, larger crowds gathered. Some were tying bright-red ribbons to the branches of an alder tree nearby, on each a prayer to Guangong and Zhang Daoling asking for their help and blessing.

When the time arrived, a large crowd assembled, many of them from out of town, to witness the seer's emergence. Deputy Xiaogong reported the gathering to Mayor Ma Jin, who had just returned from a week-long Party meeting in Taiyuan. When he was told the size of the crowd, the mayor came running. "Who set up this tent? What in the hell is going on here?" he shouted at the people as he arrived. He quickly spied Heiyen and Guzhi. "I know this must be your doing," he growled, "like every other problem I have had over the last twenty years!"

"Jin, I believe the Red Guards caused you far more trouble," Guzhi said.

"There are no Red Guards anymore, but I see that you two are still here, disturbing the minds of our people."

"This craziness is not our fault," explained Guzhi to her nephew. "We advised against it." She told him about Long Nail's vow and how when he came out he would seek the spirit of Guangong to guide the FourOnes. She carefully omitted the plan to take control of Old Stonebridge. "He should be coming out any time now."

Ma Jin rolled his eyes heavenward. "I can't believe you stupid cabbage heads believe all this shit. Thirty years of Party indoctrination and we still have imbeciles praying to a so-called immortal who died two thousand years ago. When this lunatic comes out of his doghouse, I'm going to throw his ass in prison."

The crowd waited, with respect and anticipation, but Long Nail did not emerge. Finally, after some murmured complaints, a man began to knock timidly on the door. Then more loudly. But there was no response. Others pressed toward the door and the knocks became pounding, but still there was no answer.

"Comrade Hu," shouted Ma Jin, "open the damn door."

Hu fumbled in his pocket, frantically searching for his keys. Once, then twice, through the same four empty pockets. "I guess I left them in the house," he said, turning to go search for them.

Ma Jin lost his patience and barked the order to Xiaogong, his hulking deputy: "Kick the door down," he ordered, "like they do in the American movies." Xiaogong bashed the door with his big foot. It fell backward into the hovel, ripped off its hinges. Ma Jin marched in, gagged on the smell, and found the decomposing body of Long Nail slumped in a chair.

Ma Jin quickly rose to the occasion, telling his deputy to dump the body into a pine box. He sent it back to Fuping as quickly as he could round up a donkey cart and hand deputy Xiaogong the reins. "Tell them that we have conducted an investigation and determined that this turtle head committed suicide."

千里之第一步

CHAPTER 20

On the Heels of Nixon

China. 1976.

China at last! Livia sat in the airport at Kuala Lumpur, gate three, waiting for her flight to Hong Kong. She watched a pair of Chinese toddlers, who appeared to be twins, playing on the floor at the feet of their mother. They hurled green and yellow foam-rubber squares at each other and the mother, who was making an effort to be patient. "From Malaysia?"

"No, the States. San Francisco," said the mother in perfect English. "Their granny and grampy live here."

"You were smart to bring cubes instead of balls. They'd be all over the lounge."

"I'm a kindergarten teacher. I get the geometry of toys."

Livia smiled, settled back, and closed her eyes. Marriage and children. Would that ever be her lot? Her biological clock was ticking. Would she ever have children? And the prior question—or find someone she wanted to marry? Her résumé of past mistakes was getting longer. A couple of brief encounters in college that went nowhere. Falling in love (she guessed that was the right word for it) with Henry, who was . . . gay? Bisexual? Asexual? Then the hapless Damian at Athena . . . Her thoughts were interrupted by a yellow cube that struck her in the left breast and landed in her lap. The mother apologized. Livia waved her hand. She threw the cube back to the child, and immediately two more came flying at her.

Poor Damian. Kept the moral high ground, flunking the four students, but had to leave Athena. They had denounced him with the tape as evidence, but the dean knew that the charges made in the letter were unprovable, and determining the authenticity of a tape recording was problematic. Since Damian made it clear he was leaving Athena, Webber decided not to pursue the issue. Damian landed a job teaching English at a new college in Saudi Arabia, about as far into oblivion as you could go, she thought, without falling off the edge of the earth.

A green cube came flying at her head. She snatched it midair and pitched it back at the naughty thrower. It struck him on the forehead. He broke into gales of laughter. "I'll watch these two for a few minutes if you want to get a snack or go to the bathroom." The mother smiled gratefully and walked off toward the restrooms. Livia got set for a volley of foam rubber.

They boarded the flight on time, and, as the flight crossed the South China Sea, Livia pondered her luck in getting to China so much sooner than she had thought possible. Dean Webber hadn't taken back his demand for publications but decided to help her get them. He gave her a year's leave, letting her work out an exchange with an anthropologist at the University of Malaysia. And part of the deal was a three-week study trip to the People's Republic, so although no Americans were yet able to visit China (except for Kissinger and Nixon), she could slip in as a faculty member from a Malaysian university. She had immediately telephoned a former teacher at Chicago, a Chinese archeologist named Zhang who had contacts in the PRC. From him she got a letter of introduction to a professor at Beijing Normal University, Xu Jingli. He had gotten his PhD in the States in the late '40s, knew English well, and might be willing to help her extend her research during a semester teaching in Beijing. If that worked, she could finally take the first steps toward fulfilling her dream to return to China. And the childish idea of looking for her sister.

The 737 throttled back, floating down through an urban canyon lined with high-rise apartments and office buildings, landing smoothly on the tarmac of Hong Kong's Kai Tak Airport. Livia's group of seventeen colleagues gathered their baggage, went through customs, and were met by a fat Chinese man wearing a Hawaiian shirt. He pumped a sign up and down that said *Welcome Malaysian Friendship Group.*

"I expected an emaciated man in a rumpled Mao jacket and baggy pants," said Irmgard Schelling to Livia. Schelling was the only other American in the delegation, a sociologist interested in the PRC's experiment with people's communes. Besides the two of them, there were three Australians, two Brits, and a New Zealander. The remaining nine were Malaysian citizens, five Malays and four Chinese, all of them speaking fluent English. After two days of orientation and sight-seeing in Hong Kong, the group would cross to Kowloon, take the train through the New Territories and into the People's Republic of China. Livia felt a shiver of anticipation—part excitement and part fear—as she thought about returning to the land where she had been born almost thirty-seven years before.

Their first stop was Canton—Westerners were now asked to call it Guangzhou. Her first impression of the city was dismal, a huge claustrophobic warren of shops, flats, businesses, and offices cut through by narrow congested streets crammed with every sort of vehicle: buses, trucks, autos, motorcycles, pedicabs, bicycles, even a few rickshaws. And mobs of pedestrians. When their bus finally reached its destination, things opened up a bit. They crossed over a small bridge onto Shamian Island, carved into the bank of the Pearl River. There was a vista: the pewter band of the water, the slate-gray sky, and the uneven outline of buildings across the river belching smoke into the atmosphere, grim variations on a dull palette. But at least there was a view. Built by the Brits and French in the nineteenth century, the island's architecture was now a shabby remnant of the colonial past.

They were taken to Expanding Virtue Hotel, Moscow modern, a more recent addition to the architectural mix on the island. Each visitor was assigned a room and a roommate and given a short time to unpack. Their first meeting, an official welcome, would take place immediately in one of the hotel's conference rooms, where they gathered an hour later. The room had a long table with hard-backed wooden chairs varnished with an oxblood stain, slightly sticky in the heat and humidity. There were two places at the head of the table, occupied by their tour guides, Mr. Li and Miss Hou. They were the representatives of China International Travel, which managed all groups of foreign visitors. Livia noted that there were exactly eight chairs on each side of the table, at each place a glass of lukewarm tea, with leaves floating in a greenish-yellow fluid. Next to each glass was a packet of information, a map of Guangzhou, a note pad, and a small gift box that contained a ballpoint pen and a sharpened pencil.

"You are welcomed to the People's Republic of China," said Mr. Li. His black hair was slicked to each side from a central part and he wore a neatly pressed, gray Mao suit. "We hope you will learn very much from your visit here," he continued. "We also eagerly desire to be learning from our friends from the respected nation of Malaysia. We hope that we will be able to give you some useful information about our young country as well." Some eyebrows lifted at this statement, and Mr. Li smiled knowingly. "Yes," he said, "we are an ancient country but also a new one, recently liberated from many old oppressions.

"The Provincial Governor of Guangdong, Comrade Wang Xuebing," he said, sweeping his hand backward to indicate a large photo on the wall behind him, "is full of regrets that he is not able to welcome you in person, but sends his greetings." Next to it was a bright-red banner reading *People's Republic of China—ten thousand years!* Mr. Li read a brief, generic message from the governor that echoed what he had already said about mutual learning and respect. Then he pointed to the second and larger portrait on the wall and added with a sly smile, "We are certain you recognize our Chairman Comrade Mao Zedong. We have this present also to give you." He opened a box and passed out copies of Mao's *Little Red Book*, bound in plastic and having a permanent place-marker ribbon, like a prayer book.

The session went on in a fashion that would be repeated many times during their three-week stay in China. A presentation as they reached each new city, followed by questions and answers. Most of the questions were respectfully asked and adequately answered. The Malaysians were unfailingly polite. Some questioners tried to challenge the views expressed, usually a member of the Western group.

"Miss Hou, are women really equal to men in the People's Republic?" asked one of the Australians.

"Women hold up half the sky," she responded, quoting Chairman Mao.

"Why are all the menial jobs held by women? How many women are in the higher positions of leadership? Why are there no men teaching in elementary schools?"

The Malaysians looked embarrassed at these aggressive questions, but Miss Hou and Mr. Li were ready with answers, even getting in a dig or two of their own. "How many men teach in your elementary schools?" they asked innocently. They admitted that their nation still had problems. They pointed to the baleful influence of the "evil trio" and their crafty plots: Liu Shaoqi, the "Confucian"; Lin Biao, the traitor to Mao; and Deng Xiaoping, the capitalist roader. Their insidious influence poisoned the pure well of the revolution. But Hou and Li were confident that their great nation would become prosperous and strong in the future, under the guidance of Mao Zedong's thought and the infallible leadership of the Communist Party. Through it all, Hou and Li exuded friendliness and good cheer, with occasional giggles that disarmed the group. It was hard not to like them.

Their tour had been carefully planned and tightly organized. They would visit and see schools in Guangzhou, industrial-production brigades at work in Wuhan, state-run businesses in Shanghai, hospitals and clinics in Nanjing practicing acupuncture and other techniques of traditional medicine. After visiting the people's commune in Dazhai, their tour would end with a glimpse of the former imperial splendor in Beijing. From there they'd return to Guangzhou, then back to Malaysia. Each day was fully scheduled, free time was squeezed into brief slots. They found out quickly that Li and Hou became nervous whenever they were in congested areas, encouraging them to stay together at all times.

Livia thought about her plans for Beijing, knowing she would need to escape from the group for a day at least. Maybe two. With the rigid schedule and the constant presence of Li and Hou, it would not be easy. If she were to return to China for research and a longer stay, she would have to see Dr. Xu Jingli. She toyed with the idea of just asking Hou and Li for a day off to visit someone at Beijing Normal, but immediately rejected it. Unless that someone was expecting her and had gotten permission for her visit, she would be out of luck. They wouldn't let her go there on a fishing expedition. She had to get there herself, find Dr. Xu, and hope he was friendly and disposed to help her, as her mentor Zhang thought he would be.

On their third morning in Guangzhou, with these plans in her mind, Livia had decided to see how carefully the group was being watched. She woke up at 5:00 a.m. and dressed quietly so as not to wake her roommate, an ethnically Chinese Australian political scientist with the improbable name of Cherry Bing. She left a note on her own pillow for Cherry to find, saying that she couldn't sleep and was taking a walk. She would return by eight. She found the lobby empty except for a clerk dozing behind the registration desk and a pudgy man sitting in an upholstered chair with an open newspaper draped over his stomach and chest. He too seemed to be asleep.

Livia slipped out the front door and into the darkness. The streets were wet from a rain during the night, but it would get to be a sunny, humid day as the sun sucked up the moisture from Guangzhou's streets. The sky was clear of clouds, and she could see a few remaining stars. People were already awake and going about their activities. She could see scattered lights on in apartment houses and smell the acrid smoke rising from small charcoal fires as all over the city women began to prepare breakfast. Livia followed a course she had memorized from her city map, hugging the shore of the Pearl River until she came to a bridge over one of its tributaries. She looked behind her but saw no one. She crossed over and headed toward the famous Western Market. There the booths had already been set up and hundreds of people were already shopping. She took one last look over her shoulder before entering, knowing that once she was in the crowd she would never be able to spot someone following her. Again, she saw nothing suspicious.

It was principally a food market, each booth having its own specialty.

Vegetables, pasta fresh and made on the spot, spices, bags of rice, millet, and other grains. But what was most intriguing and repulsive was the meat market. Chinese often joked that they ate everything that walked, crawled, swam, or flew—and, as she knew from Taiwan, slithered. Seeing the collection of creatures in the market, she could believe it. Hanging on an iron hook, she saw a dehaired brown dog, slick as a football. Next to it, two hairless white cats. The thought of eating such pale, sickly looking flesh almost caused her to retch, and left her feeling the nausea creeping up her esophagus. She saw Han pork butchers, Muslim beef butchers. A lamb shop with nine heads lined up on a board—she counted them—looking glassily at her through goatish eye-slits. *The Supreme Court*, she thought, then wondered if she were losing her sanity. Squirrels, rabbits, snakes, fish as long as her leg or small as a willow leaf, eel, shellfish, crustaceans, and a variety of small animals that Livia did not recognize or could not name. In fact, the whole place looked and smelled more like a zoo than a market. She saw Tibetans selling Buddhist bells and prayer wheels, bear paws and other dark and shriveled items whose identity she didn't care to know.

Other delicacies beckoned, but she did not have much time and hurried back to the hotel, where she found her colleagues having breakfast. Livia quickly dodged behind a partition that separated the dining area from registration and watched the front door. She peered through the perforated, carved screen, and a minute later, the pudgy man she had seen earlier entered the hotel, a newspaper folded under his arm. It was clear that her little cloak-and-dagger game would have to be played carefully.

When they reached Beijing, the group was housed at a hotel located in the southern sector, just to the east of the long north-south thoroughfare that ran through the center of the old city. Her roommate for this last stop was Irmgard Schelling. Standing at the window she could see the amazing symmetry of the Forbidden City in the near distance—all squares and rectangles. She looked to the area southeast of it and saw an indistinct cluster of gray buildings. Somewhere in that section, if it still existed, was the Presbyterian mission where she had spent the first years of her life: 42 Flower Market Street. She would have loved to go searching for it, but there was no time. They would leave Beijing in four days, and she had more important plans that would hopefully bring her back for a much longer stay with plenty of time to find the site of the old mission.

She devised a plan to slip Mr. Li and Miss Hou and whoever might be watching the group for the government. She went to breakfast the next morning with the others, but ate only a bit of congee, and told Miss Hou she felt sick and would spend the day resting in her room. "So sorry you miss the Ming Tombs and the Friendship Store today," said Miss Hou, exuding compassion. "Lots of good bargains." After breakfast when the group headed toward the tour bus, Livia walked to the elevator as though returning to her room. She pressed the button for both the second and ninth floors, but got off at the second. Then she walked across the mezzanine, staying close to the wall and away from the balustrade that overlooked the lobby. In case Li and Hou had reported her sickness, she didn't want anyone to see her leave the hotel. She located the stairway that led down to the restaurant and to a side exit. She took a soft felt hat from her bag that would cover her hair, put on sunglasses, and wrapped a scarf around her neck. Then she slipped out the side door.

She had memorized the city map and knew exactly how to get to Shida, the famous Beijing Normal University. The first bus took her north toward Tiananmen Square. She got off there, walked east along Changan Boulevard and boarded another northbound bus at Nanchizi Street. The street was tree lined, with spring buds beginning to break open. There were lots of old shops and businesses, many with the traditional tiled roofs curving upward at each corner. The bus proceeded north along the eastern moat of the Forbidden City, turned west then north again past the two towers where in the old days the sound of drums and bells marked the hours of the day. Livia got off at Anding Gate and walked the rest of the way.

She stood just across the street from the entry to Beijing Normal, stopping to observe students coming and going. Like almost all large institutions in China, the university was surrounded by walls, and the gates were always guarded. She saw the small guardhouse over on the right side. After some interior debate, she decided to stride forward with confidence, as though she belonged there. As she approached the gate, a uniformed man immediately burst from the guardhouse waving her off. She tried to explain in Chinese. "I am looking for Dr. Xu Jingli. I am a PhD," she added, hoping the academic credentials would impress the guard.

The guard was not impressed. He waved his hand again and shook his head vigorously. "Foreign visitors not allow to enter," he stated in broken English. She tried again, arguing in Chinese, but to no avail. So much for her prestigious PhD.

On the way back to the hotel she cursed her herself for her stupidity. She should have shown him the letter of introduction from Dr. Zhang. It was the way you got anywhere in China. She would try again tomorrow.

When Livia got back to the hotel, she entered by the front door and headed toward the elevator. "*Huilaile*!" shouted the woman at registration. "She's back!" Livia froze, turning to face the woman behind the desk. She saw a young man and woman in white jackets approaching her from the right. "Dr. Wayman," the receptionist said, "this is Dr. Han and Dr. Wei. They were sent here. Treat your illness. They not find you in your room."

"I felt a bit better," Livia explained, thinking quickly, "so I went out for a short walk. But I'm tired now and must go up to my room and rest."

"They will help you." Livia was worried as the pair followed her up to her room.

"We give you strenuous examination," they promised. Not a comforting prospect.

The two doctors spent a long time with her. First Dr. Han did a diagnosis of her various pulse beats, placing his fingers lightly on her wrist. Finally, he nodded at Dr. Wei, and she looked carefully at Livia's tongue. They conversed in hushed and rapid Chinese, which Livia could not understand. She was worried that they would declare her a fraud.

"Nothing serious," said Dr. Han finally, handing her some pills wrapped in a brown piece of paper. "Take before you go to sleep tonight and next three days. You pay the hotel," he said, handing her a white slip of paper, charging her the equivalent of $1.45 for their services. "Includes medicines." Livia marveled at the cost, socialized medicine looking better all the time. The pills were ugly black balls, the size of small marbles. "You overtired, fatigue. Now you lie down on bed." Livia followed their instructions, and Dr. Wei pressed various points on her body, on her feet, behind her knees and arms, and a place between her left shoulder and breast. She felt suddenly warm and a bit woozy.

"Now," said Dr. Wei, "I put you to sleep. You close your eyes, you do not try to see what I do." Livia closed her eyes. Dr. Wei sat behind her. She felt fingers gently touching her temples. Then Dr. Wei lifted her hands, and, although she could not see, Livia felt that the hands were moving just above her face. That quiet, warm feeling was her last memory until Irmgard's return wakened her.

"How are you?"

"Better. I've just been treated by two traditional doctors. It must have helped. I feel rested."

"Is that your medicine?" She pointed to the four pills resting on the night table. "Looks like four rabbit turds."

"I'm supposed to take those one a day and get rest." Livia realized that far from exposing her, the doctors had given her a perfect cover for tomorrow. She showed Irmgard the doctors' bill. "Look what they charged me for an hour-long exam by two doctors . . . How'd you like the Ming tombs?"

"I hated them. I'm claustrophobic. All those people crowded into dark rooms and narrow tunnels underground." She shuddered. "It was like rush hour in the London tube, but worse. But I did like the row of the animal sculptures outside the tomb."

"Well, I'll have to skip the Great Wall tomorrow, too."

The next day Livia tried a different gate, the east entrance to Beijing Normal. When the guard emerged waving his hand, she handed him the Chinese letter of introduction and this time spoke English. "I am here to see Dr. Xu Jingli. In Social Sciences." He didn't understand everything she had said, but was clearly impressed by the letter. He read it carefully, then refolded it and placed it back in the envelope.

"You wait a moment." He went into the booth and made a phone call. He returned and pointed to a building. "Over there. Room 204. Upstairs."

Xu Jingli was waiting for her the top of the steps. He was dressed in a gray Mao suit, a small-boned man with white hair, neatly combed. While he read the letter, she had a chance to observe him more closely. He had an angular face, sharp cheek bones, and a pointed chin. Overall, an air of composure and inner strength. Xu was definitely a survivor. When they returned to his office, he offered Livia a chair, then went to sit behind his desk. Finally, when they were both firmly in their proper places, he smiled faintly and said, "How good to hear from my old friend Dr. Zhang. And to meet you, Dr. Wayman, his bright student. Let us see what we can do."

"Let's drink some baijiu," said Livia. She and Irmgard were sitting in the hotel bar, ready for the group excursion to the Peking duck restaurant where they would be celebrating their last night in the city, trying to decide what to drink. Of all her roommates on the trip, she felt more at ease with Irmgard than any of the others.

"How about vodka? I hate baijiu," Irmgard said. "It tastes like lighter fluid, or rubbing alcohol."

"Lighter fluid? And I thought I had experimented in college!"

"OK, OK. The way I imagine it would taste. Beer, no, we can get that back home. Chinese wine is terrible." She sighed in resignation. "Let's go with the lighter fluid."

The next day they would be flying back to Guangzhou. Livia liked her roommate and felt the need to come clean. "Irmgard, I owe you an explanation. I want to tell you about what I did during those two days when I was pretending to be sick."

"Pretending?" Irmgard raised her eyebrows. "Well, I love a bit of intrigue."

Livia laughed. "Nothing that exciting," she said. "This trip has been a great opportunity for me. Didn't think I could ever get to China so soon. I had a personal project I wanted to pursue, and I didn't want you to get burned if I screwed it up." She explained to Irmgard how she'd gotten to see Professor Xu, how she desperately wanted to return on a teaching visa and continue her research on women's leadership in traditional religious groups. She meant to focus on the role of Buddhist nuns. She mentioned nothing about searching for her sister.

"How did it go? Can you come back?"

"A big disappointment," Livia said, signaling to the waitress to refill her baijiu. Irmgard pointed to her own glass. "Xu implied, without giving me any details, they had gone through hell during the Cultural Revolution. The professors were sent to the countryside to 'learn from the peasants.' It got so bad they had to shut down the university. It just reopened three years ago and they do only undergraduate work. There was no way he could invite me to come right now. But maybe in the future . . . we're going to keep in touch. What's your take on the communes?"

"A failure, I think," Irmgard said as the waitress brought them fresh drinks. "They've had a couple of decades to make the system work, and it doesn't. Of course they won't admit it. I thought that before I came and have seen nothing to change my opinion. I think the traditional family is so deeply embedded in the Chinese psyche, or gene pool, or whatever, that it will never go away completely."

Livia looked over at their group gathering near the main entrance. "Bottoms up. Looks like it's time to march off to eat Peking duck. That's another thing that's never going to go away." Now feeling its effects, she downed the rest of her baijiu, clinking glasses with Irmgard: "To the holy trinity that will never go away: family, ancestors, and Peking duck. Oh, I almost forgot baijiu! A quaternity . . . or is it a quadruped, . . . or quadriplegic . . . or whatever," she babbled, giddy with the liquor. "Ganbei!"

"Cheers." She hugged Irmgard as they got up to join the group and her roommate hugged her back, with more warmth than she had expected.

Chapter 21

Karmic Bonds

Fall 1976.

Irmgard, Henry, and Livia sat around a table in her favorite restaurant, the Crescent Moon. It was the day after Thanksgiving, and with the semester winding down, she suddenly found herself with unexpected visitors. Her mother had talked about coming for the holiday but had canceled a week earlier, explaining that she was tired and needed to rest instead. Livia felt uneasy, noticing that her mother was taking special care in choosing her words.

Two days later, Irmgard, her friend from the semester in Malaysia, called to see if she would like a visit over the Thanksgiving holiday. Livia was eager to have her, thinking fondly of her three weeks in China and the many evenings when they ended the day in a hotel bar, comparing notes on their adventures. Was there something magical about those evenings, or were the shared insights just a product of boozy wisdom? When they returned to the States, Livia to Athena, Irmgard to a women's college near Raleigh, they planned to keep in touch. Irmgard said she could come for three days.

Then Henry called. He was giving a paper to a conference at Ohio State and wondered if she was up for a visit. "Sure," she said without thinking, "great to see you. Oh, another friend will be here, someone I met on the China trip. But you'll like her."

"OK, see you Friday afternoon."

There were only a few customers at the Crescent Moon that evening. Most of the students had gone home for Thanksgiving break. Only some faculty and a few locals were present, so the noise level was reduced and it was easier to have a quiet conversation. All three of them started with Yuengling beer, on tap. "Is this some sort of Chinese beer I haven't heard about?" asked Henry.

Livia laughed. "Chinese beer, here in the hills of Ohio? First choice here is moonshine. Nope. It's an old German beer, been in business for maybe a hundred years. I think from somewhere around here, maybe over in western Pennsylvania. Anyway, I like it."

"I liked that Tsingtao stuff they had in China. It's a little lighter," said Irmgard.

"Which the Germans taught them to make—also about a hundred years ago," added Henry.

"I believe I read that in my Fodor's," said Irmgard, a bit tartly.

The waitress brought their plates. Livia was feeling on edge. She knew she would have felt entirely comfortable with either Irmgard or Henry alone. But there was a different chemistry with the two of them together. Some kind of competition was going on. Irmgard acknowledged that Livia and Henry were experts on Chinese culture while she was not, but she kept bringing up observations from the recent trip, relying on her personal experience of the current situation on the mainland.

"Cheers and bon voyage to Chairman Mao," said Henry, clinking glasses with his two companions. With Mao dead and new leadership in charge, Henry was making plans for his first trip to China. But for now, Irmgard had already been there and he had not. His experience was limited to Taiwan, and Irmgard's remarks implied that Taiwan was not the "real China."

When the food came, they got serious about eating and talked sporadically about life in their various academic situations, each quite different. Irmgard taught at a woman's college in North Carolina. Henry joked that he and Livia should switch places, since he would be at the small college he longed for and she would be closer to her mother in New York. They all ordered a second beer.

"The people's communes were an interesting sociological experiment," said Irmgard, returning to the China topic again, "dumping a family system that began over three thousand years ago. What chutzpah!"

"Chutzpah isn't the word for it. Madness would be more accurate," said Henry.

"Still, when you think of all the oppression and suffering caused by that old family system, the communes seem like an overdue attempt to set things right, equalize things, make women's work as important as men's. A noble experiment anyway."

"Noble experiment!" Henry exploded. "You can't just manipulate people that way, like rats in a laboratory. Millions died in Mao's 'noble experiments' in the early '60s."

"But without the communes, women would still be doing the slave work from morning to night, and getting nothing for it. At least they tried to put men and women on an equal footing."

"That's just propaganda! What the communes were really about was getting political control for the Communist party. You go to Taiwan and do one of your surveys of Chinese women—how many of them do you think would want to join a commune? . . . Lucky if you could find one in a hundred!"

Livia was stunned. It was an academic argument, but somehow charged with a lot of emotion. What was going on? "You two are oversimplifying," she said. "You both need to step back and look at it more objectively." She had never heard Henry get so upset before. She knew he had always felt a certain loyalty to Taiwan. And skeptical of the motives and methods of the PRC. But never so emotional about the issues. Livia felt herself in the mushy middle ground, between the two of them, unable to join in the argument.

"Really," Henry said, continuing his attack, "there's no comparison. Just look at the policies of the two governments on religion. Taiwan doesn't directly encourage it, but they allow the people to practice it without interference—except for a few secret societies they consider subversive. So you get a rich mix of all sorts of religious practice on the island. An anthropologist's paradise. It's what allowed Livia and me to do our research. In the PRC the Party has strangled religion. Centuries of culture lost."

"So you're against the PRC's policies because they make it hard for graduate students to do research!"

"That's trivializing what I said!"

"Well, there are much bigger issues involved. And, anyway, freedom of religion is one of the rights given in the constitution of the PRC."

"Surely you're not saying that makes any difference, are you?"

"That it's there, yes. And now that Mao is dead, I think things will change. New leadership, new policies. Anything can happen."

So it went, until Livia finally said: "Friends, let's call it a draw and go home. I'm bushed."

When they got back to her apartment, Livia found two sheets and a blanket, handing them to Henry. He didn't say anything, but didn't seem happy about the arrangements. Something about his mopey behavior and his silences prevented her from asking why.

Livia had been Irmgard's roommate for the last four days of the China trip, in Beijing. As they got ready for bed, she was surprised to see her friend strip down naked. "I can't sleep with anything on. I wore that nightie in China. I guess I was trying to be more proper with strangers. I hope you don't mind."

"Suit yourself . . . or maybe unsuit yourself," she punned. Irmgard just grinned.

They talked a while about a few of their companions from the trip. Livia turned over, as if to sleep, but couldn't. There was some kind of electricity in the room. Maybe it was the thought of the naked body sleeping, or not sleeping, next to her. It was a long time until Livia dozed off. Sometime closer to the early morning, and after some half sleep and a lot of tossing and turning, she was awake again and realized that Irmgard was, too. Irmgard said: "This is crazy. Would you mind if I gave you a massage?" Livia mumbled something affirmative, and soon she felt Irmgard's hands on her neck and shoulders, her fingers crawling down her spinal cord and lower back. The hands were small but strong and the fingers pressed hard, almost to the point of pain. She liked it, the overall effect was relaxing. "I'm learning a form of acupressure."

"You get an A. And I don't give out As easily. Ask my students."

"Mmm," said Irmgard, letting her fingers slip under the elastic of Livia's silk pajamas as she massaged her lower back. They then moved lower, and Livia felt the hands caressing her buttocks. As Livia's body began to respond, a flood of memories, of Mother Canisius and Hillesum, overpowered her.

"Irmgard, don't. I'm sorry. I'm just not ready for this."

"Your call."

An hour later, after both had finally fallen asleep, the phone rang. Livia groaned, lifted herself to press the light button on the alarm clock. It was five thirty. "God, who could this be?"

"Don't answer it . . . probably a crank," said Irmgard.

"I'd better," she said, reaching for the phone.

It was a call from Adele's hospital in Brooklyn. Her mother was there, as a patient, said the caller, who identified herself as Evelyn Schroeder, a nurse in oncology. Adele had not been feeling well for the last two weeks and had been unable to work. Last night she had taken a cab to the hospital and checked herself in. It was serious. Her mom had asked for her. Could Livia come right away?

Fear suddenly beat like a drum in her chest. She should have suspected that when Adele cancelled the visit something was seriously wrong. But her mother had seemed so healthy. Livia asked Mrs. Schroeder all the usual questions; the answers were noncommittal, except for one: yes, cancer a possibility.

Irmgard had gotten the drift of the conversation. "I know you've got to go. Don't worry. I'll be out of here as quickly as I can."

"I hate to ask you, but I'm just sick with worry. Know I can't sleep any more tonight."

Livia wrapped a green terry-cloth robe around herself, fumbled at the belt, and went to the living room to tell Henry. She found the sheets and blanket neatly folded on the couch. Henry was gone. She saw a scribbled note on the coffee table. "I'll be in touch later. Sorry."

An hour later, she was on I-70 heading east toward Pennsylvania and the turnpike. Her thoughts went around in circles, mostly fixing on her mother, but also confused with questions about Henry's leaving and about her relationship with Irmgard.

It was pancreatic cancer, and it had metastasized. The doctor, one of those shoot-from-the-hip types, had said that her liver looked like Swiss cheese on the X-ray. Livia sat by the bedside in shock, holding her mother's limp hand. She was at least quiet now, peaceful after the morphine injection. Earlier, as the pain of the cancer dug at her insides, she moaned. "I don't care if it is early," Livia said to the attending nurse. "She's in terrible pain. Give it to her. Now."

After three days at the hospital, Livia began to organize her time around the three phases that kept repeating themselves in the course of her mother's days and nights. The period of increasing pain leading up to the shot, the comatose time after the morphine, and the lucid intervals when she awoke from the sedative and before the worst of the pain began again.

"Thanks for coming, Livia. I'll be gone soon. I'm not afraid of dying. It just came on so suddenly."

Her mother was only sixty-four. The doctor and nurses were honest enough to not try to pacify her with false hopes. "It's gone too far. No treatment possible at this stage. We will do our best to minimize the pain."

Good and bad come together, thought Livia, *like twins in the womb. Cain and Abel.* Pancreatic cancer was cruel and painful, but it was swift. That thought was her only consolation in the days that followed, as she prayed for a quick end to her mom's ordeal.

"I try not to think about the past," Adele said during one of her lucid intervals, "but I loved the months we were together at my apartment here, when you were doing your writing. When we sat there after dinner, talking like friends instead of all the momma and daughter stuff . . . There are a couple of things that I want you to have. A diary that I kept for years, beginning with the trip to China. I wrote regularly in those years. You might find it interesting. There's not much recently—I guess I grew out of it. It's locked in a metal box on the shelf in my bedroom closet. The key is on the sill above the closet door."

Livia looked at her mother, wondering how well she really knew her. She thought about the deep and private places in her mother's life, and was grateful that the diary would open a door to them before it was too late. Her mother looked tired from all the talking, but added: "Besides the diaries . . . the locket, the talisman . . . belonged to your sister . . . Bailian gave it to her . . . and . . ." The last words, an unintelligible mumble, died on her lips as she drifted into a drugged sleep.

Back at the apartment Livia found the key without difficulty, opening the metal box that held the diary and a tarnished silver locket and chain. She was eager to read, but decided to slow things a bit by making herself a pot of tea. She let the leaves steep a while, then poured herself a cup and sat in the upholstered chair with the floor lamp behind it, sipping the strong tea. Taking a deep breath, she closed her eyes for a few minutes, aware of the scent of the flower tea and the way the vapors warmed her eyelids and clarified her vision. Then she switched on the lamp above her and read the first entry, written on the day that Harold and Adele had moved into the Presbyterian mission in 1935, near the legation quarter of Beijing. It began with the words: *Here we are, half way around the world, in a strange and frightening city . . .*

The words were written before she was born, the private thoughts of her mother in her early twenties. She read straight through to the entry which recorded her own conception and found herself laughing and crying at the same time. *"White as milk, healthy as an egg, nourishing like congealed blood! Now is time to buy." He yodels his nonsense in the hutong, and she is conceived. Don't the Muslims say man is created from a blood clot? Blame the clotted bean curd, blame the tofu man!*

She pulled herself out of the chair, poured another cup of tea, and continued to read until, near the end of the diary, she finally fell into an exhausted sleep sitting in the chair.

It was early the next morning when she woke up. She had somehow got to the couch, and the sun was coming in the window, just as she remembered it from the months she had lived here. It fell on the same window sill, struck the same moss-green couch as it rose, then gradually dropped onto the red and blue of the worn Persian rug with its rhomboid and floral patterns. The sunlight was a grid-work of light, divided into nine squares by the mullions of the casement window. All this was as it had been years ago, when she worked on her dissertation and she and her mother had become friends. But instead of the timeless tranquility she felt in those months, now the squares of sunlight and blurred mullions seemed to glide quickly across the carpet. How many days left? She had to get back to her mother.

When Livia arrived, Adele was in phase two. She kissed her mother's forehead, sat down to wait for the morphine to wear off.

"Mom, I loved reading your diary. I'm almost finished."

Adele winced as she turned to look at the diary in her hand. "I'm glad. After you've read it, I want you to destroy it." Seeing refusal in Livia's eyes, she added: "Please do that for me."

"Mom, how can I? It's precious. Your grandchildren, if I ever have any kids, might like to read it. Please don't make me do that."

"Some of the entries are so personal—I'd feel like I was hanging out my underwear on a clothesline . . . You know the old Chinese saying, 'The best traveler leaves no tracks'? I'm trying to be a good traveler. I think we better talk about the service, cremation and that sort of thing . . ."

About noon, after the nurse shot her mother with another dose of the drug, Livia went to the cafeteria to get a sandwich. She flipped through the diary as she ate, thinking about the things that had surprised her. One of them was the reason for the failure of her parents' marriage. She had always assumed it was a matter of her mother needing to escape from the domination of her father and the restrictions of being a minister's wife. There was that, but something much more positive. She was strongly drawn to Buddhism, trying to understand the lives of the women in the nunneries she visited. One entry was written a few months after she had recovered from her fall. The title was *chujia*, which meant leaving home to become a monk or nun. She could tell that her mother admired the Chinese women who could take that drastic step.

Livia saw that her own academic work had taken her to the same place as the personal quest had taken her mother. She had studied Buddhist women in positions of leadership and authority. She knew that the step of chujia was the only way women could follow their own spiritual path, escaping male authority in a traditional Chinese world. It was the only way they could live free of the "three dependencies"—obeying their father when young, deferring to their husband after marriage, and their eldest son in old age. She could see that Adele had "left home," too. She didn't have an official community to support her, other than the Zen center, but she had somehow worked it out on her own terms.

There was one other surprise that often appeared in the diary: Adele's clear belief, a sort of maternal instinct perhaps, that Victoria had not died. *Yuanfen,* she wrote, at the beginning of an entry where she first expressed a desire to return to China. It was a term she had learned from a nun. "If I can't find her, I can at least be closer to her. I know she is not dead." Livia was not sure she believed in such intuitions, but then, she was not a mother.

Livia was familiar with the term *yuanfen*. It was karma, the belief that every sentient creature was born into the universe in accordance with its acts in a previous lifetime, but Chinese Buddhists took the idea a step further. Yuanfen meant karmic bonds, destined personal encounters in life that were forged because of important relationships in a previous life. Parents and children, close relatives, husbands and wives, teachers and friends—all of these came together, not by chance, but out of a destiny woven in an earlier lifetime. For herself, thought Livia, that would include Harold and Adele, Henry, Damian, Naomi, Sister Canisius, Irmgard . . . And then the thought struck her: *Was Victoria on the list?* She wasn't sure she believed in the idea.

Livia left the cafeteria about noon. It was now filling up with staff and visitors looking for lunch. She returned to her mother's room and sat by the side of the bed. Her mother was unconscious, but the pain was evident in the strain that drew her face taut. Livia felt miserable in her inability to do anything, knowing that words could not help, only morphine.

It was late that afternoon, after the drug's effect had worn off, when Adele came back to a conscious state. "Thank you for coming," she said in a frail voice, fraught with pain.

"Oh Mom, you don't have to talk. Of course I would come. I love you," she said, taking her hand and holding it against her cheek. Adele nodded but then her eyes fluttered and she drifted off into a series of incoherent and unconnected phrases: "Late for work . . . tell Harold I signed the papers . . . the rent check . . . where are my keys?" Each phrase seemed an effort. Her eyes were squeezed shut, her head twisting this way and that, the tendons in her neck stretched tight. Livia felt miserable and helpless. More words tumbled out without any sense, stopped, started again. Then, suddenly, her mother's eyes opened and she looked straight at Livia. Instead of jumbled words and phrases, she uttered a perfectly clear statement, "I can't go to China. Will you go for me, Livia?"

Without thinking, Livia squeezed her hand and said: "Yes, Mother. I'll go for you. You can rest now." Those were her final words to her mother, and tears burned in her eyes as she said them. Livia watched her face and saw a sort of miracle. All the tension drained away and she relaxed as she slipped away from the world.

It was clear now that whether her work took her to China or not, she must go for the sake of her mother. And search for her sister, as she had promised.

CHAPTER 22

Out of the Red Dust

Livia chose a funeral home in Brooklyn, near her mom's apartment. It looked like they all do, the walls a soft pastel in the blue-green range, shiny white cornices and trim around the doors and windows, thick padded dark-blue carpets perfectly vacuumed, rooms with couches and tightly upholstered chairs, end tables with heavy lamps, and coffee tables with nothing on them but boxes of tissues. Copies of soothing landscape paintings hung on the walls. The staff in black suits and ties, their hands crossed in front of them, or linked behind their backs, nodding gravely, looking properly mournful and understanding.

The "chapel" was simply a large room with an altar that was bare except for a polished-brass cross standing on a plain linen runner—Christian belief at its lowest common denominator. If she had said that her mother was a Buddhist, she supposed, they would have been happy to remove the cross. They had asked Livia how many people she thought might come, and she gave them a number. Too few, as it turned out. There were many now standing behind the chairs in back of the room, with others still coming in the door. The solicitous staff were quietly moving in some extra chairs. Livia had thought of her mother as a loner, but now she realized that many, at both the hospital and the Zen center, were her friends.

"Dear friends, coworkers, and family of Adele Wayman," Livia began, then realized that the word *family* was inappropriate, since she was the only relative present. "I feel completely inadequate to do this, but I want to try to say a few words of appreciation about my mother's life. It seems as though, from my high school years at Hillesum Academy all the way up to the present year, I was mostly away from home—in high school, college, graduate school, doing research in Asia, and now teaching in Ohio. So I ask those of you who are friends and coworkers, and who knew her on a daily basis, in some respects better than I . . . I ask you to help me. After I have finished my brief remarks, I invite everyone present, if they feel so led, to contribute some remembrance of my mother that will help us all to understand her better, so that we may celebrate her life."

Livia took two folded sheets of paper out of her coat pocket. She had not trusted her emotions to allow her to do the eulogy from memory. She unfolded the papers and pressed them flat on the slanted surface of the small wooden podium. What to say? Her mother a sort of Buddhist, she a sort of Catholic, and the others perhaps mostly Christians of some kind, with some Buddhist practitioners from the Zen center, a scattering of Jews, and some unbelievers—the mélange of New York City.

She read the following remarks:

"I loved my mother. That statement may hardly sound remarkable, but for me, it was a discovery, and unfortunately, it came late in my life. On the other hand, I was fortunate that it came at all. As a young person I suppose that I merely assumed that I loved her, as I assumed that she loved me. We probably even said those words to each other. But not often, and then mostly at the end of letters and long distance phone calls. With so much time apart, it was not something I felt deeply, I am sorry to say, until recently. Nor was it something I thought about very often. Taking parents for granted is an old story and common among the young and thoughtless—a phrase which describes me, for much of my life, rather well.

"At the end of graduate school, however, my need to write a dissertation brought me an opportunity. Mom asked me to live with her while I worked on it. I would have access to New York's great libraries. The time together proved to be a blessing, or as she might have said, it was the workings of karma. We got to know each other as adults and learned to love each other as adults. Not that it was all harmony and bliss, but our few squabbles ended quickly because one of the things we both learned was how to respect the differences in each other.

"In retrospect it all seems so unremarkable—a mother and daughter learn to live together and to love each other. Yet it may be more rare than I think, and even if it is common I don't hesitate to say that it has been the most important thing to happen in my life up to this point."

As she finished reading these words, Livia looked up from her text. She glanced over the people gathered in the chapel and was surprised to see, standing near the back on the right side, a face she hadn't expected. It was Harold. And barely visible at his shoulder, Tillie. She had informed them of the funeral service, of course, but hadn't expected them to come. Livia looked down at her text. It blurred as she felt the sting of tears in her own eyes, as she realized that, after so many years, she and her mother and father were together again. She felt that she was about to choke up, so she stopped. In the silence that followed, she breathed deeply and slowly a few times before continuing.

"I will tell only one story. Not really a story, but something that happened just a week ago as I sat by Mom's bedside. I noticed that many people stopped by to see how she was doing, and she was very grateful for those visits. As I was. There were those who came from the Zen center. There were a few neighbors. And from the hospital, nurses, medical staff, doctors, and even some administrators.

"What surprised me most was the number of the hospital's housekeeping staff who came. I spoke to one such person at some length. I will call her Phyllis, a fictitious name so as not to embarrass her. She is here today. 'Your mom was a wonderful person. She knew us all and always had a word or two for us—asking a question about our families, making a remark about the weather—just ordinary things. But you could tell that she cared.' Then, Phyllis, you said something that I will never forget. You said 'We all liked her. Those of us on the cleaning staff of the hospital are used to being'—here you struggled to find the right word—'invisible.' For one like me, who also works in a large institution, those words were like an indictment. I thought to myself, what are the names of the cleaning staff at the college where I teach? I tried to picture one of those anonymous workers, and saw a couple of indistinct faces but could not remember a single name. I had never spoken to them. I realized that my mother had discovered something important about life that I had not. Thank you, Phyllis, for helping me to understand my mother better, and myself."

Livia folded up her prepared remarks and tucked them into the inside pocket of her dark-blue jacket.

"No one can know what happens after death. I will only say that Mom has left the realm of red dust. That is how the Chinese describe it when a person leaves this world of troubles. I know that she is now at peace because she found her peace many years before she died. What she did in her life may not be newsworthy, but she found contentment, and that is an accomplishment, I have come to realize, that many do not find. I could end with that thought, but I will add one other. Once, when I was living with her, she said to me: 'Buddhists should treasure little things.' I asked what she meant by that, and she pointed to the morning sun coming in the window as we sat at the kitchen table and held her hand over the steaming tea she had just made for me—'these things that seem so ordinary,' she said, 'but are wonderful if you give them your full attention.' She wanted to be cremated, not buried, but if she had, I would have written those words on her tombstone: she treasured the little things."

After Livia finished, others shared messages. They came tentatively at first, after a long silence, then tumbled out almost without pause, funny, poignant, and endearing things, more messages than she had expected. Finally, there was an extended silence, and just as Livia was about to stand and bring the service to a close, she heard the rumbling baritone of her father, offering a blessing she remembered from long years ago at the mission chapel: "May the Lord bless thee, may he turn his face toward thee, may the light of his countenance shine upon thee, and give thee peace. Amen."

Livia saw Harold and Tillie at the back of the room, heading for the door. She wanted to speak with him before he left, so she had to break away from the first cluster of guests who came up to her. "Sorry," she said as she pulled away from them. "Thanks so much for coming, thanks for sharing your thoughts about Mom. I'll be back in a few minutes."

She ran out into the parking lot and called after him as he and Tillie were heading toward their car. They both turned around.

Tillie took a few steps toward Livia and said, "Please, leave him alone. It was hard for him. We almost didn't come at all."

Harold held up his hand. "No, honey, I'm OK. You go get in the car. I'll be right there. I want to talk to Livia for a minute." Tillie frowned, then turned and walked toward the old Impala.

When the door had closed, he said softly, "Thanks for your message today. Your mom would have been pleased. I'm happy . . . that you got to know her . . . in the way you described." In contrast to the commanding tone of the blessing, his words were hesitant. She understood that he was struggling to talk about love but in his awkwardness, could not say the word. Still, Livia knew what he meant, and it made her both happy and sad: happy that he had tried to say them, yet sad as she realized that he had never said to her "I love you," nor had she to him. She couldn't make herself say the words now.

"Livia, about the cremation . . . what did she want done with her ashes?"

She hesitated. "Scattered in the ocean," she said, deciding that a half truth was better than the full truth. She couldn't tell him that Adele had asked her to keep a portion she wanted taken to China, writing a note, the day before she died: *China is the place where I first woke up, and . . . your sister is there. I want to be with her.*

"Dad, thanks for your words. That is such a wonderful blessing." And then, in an attempt to change the mood, she added, "Even if it wasn't in Latin."

Remembering the graduation at Hillesum, he smiled faintly, nodded, and slowly turned away. Then he stopped. "Livia, there's one other thing I want to say," he said, turning again to face her. "When you get as old as I am, you realize that it is time to finally say some things—things that are hard to say when you're younger. What I want to say is that at my age . . . I am beginning to realize how few people there are, in your entire life, whom you could say you . . . well, I mean I could say, I have been truly close, have shared real intimacy. Very few." His halting words did not include the word *love*, but that, she realized, is what they were all about. He said no more but kissed her cheek, then turned and walked back to the car.

CHAPTER 23

The Talisman

1979.

Three years had passed since her mother's death, the days rushing by "with the swiftness of a weaver's shuttle." She would be forty on her next birthday, and she suddenly remembered the first words of the *Divine Comedy*, the lines the nuns had made them memorize: "In the midpoint of our mortal life, I found me in a gloomy wood, astray . . ." At the time they meant nothing to her or her classmates. They were young then and felt their lives were just beginning. But the words now struck a chord that resonated . . . was she lost in a gloomy wood? Had she gone astray? She had told her mother that she would go to China. It was a solemn promise, really, but since then six semesters had gone by at Athena. She taught her classes, did her research, counseled students, and sat on committees. China was now open to tourists, scholars and business people from the United States, but she had not gone. Why?

She had plenty of excuses. At first there was the decision about whether to go all out for tenure at Athena. It seemed the logical thing to do and would give her a kind of insurance for the rest of her professional life. But she hesitated. Something about tenure suggested that life was closing in on her, a loss of the old youthful feeling that anything was possible. But Dean Webber had made it very clear: "Tenure is not going to fall into your lap. You have to desire it, work for it, or you won't get it, and a couple of years from now I'll be writing you a letter of termination."

So she put aside thoughts of freedom and adventure as juvenile, and went for security. Every bit of time and energy she could muster, over the next two years, she devoted to publishing her research material from Taiwan and Malaysia, revising her dissertation, turning it into a book manuscript, and finding a respectable press to publish it. Tenure accomplished, she began thinking about her personal issues, and if she were to be brutally honest with herself, her personal life was a big zero. Her brief affair with Damian was ancient history. She knew she was drawn to Irmgard, and that attraction made her question her own sexuality. But her feelings were not wholehearted and she couldn't square them with the morality of the Catholic Church. They had gotten together again, a few months after her mother's death, but when Livia had expressed her own doubts and begged for time, Irmgard lost her patience. She left with an ultimatum: "Call me if you ever figure it out!" The experience hadn't really clarified anything about her own sexuality, but after she was gone, Livia did realize that a sense of relief was stronger than her feelings of loss.

And then there was Henry. Thinking how often he had helped her, and of the long sweet letters he had written her from China, she couldn't doubt that he cared for her deeply. And she loved him in some way as well, but what did that mean? Though they had never made love, there was clearly some kind of intimacy between them. Her father had used that word after the funeral, and it seemed, in some strange way, to describe their relationship. Henry flitted in and out of her life like a butterfly, touching it for a time, and then he was gone again. But never for long. She had at first assumed that he was gay, but in the years that followed he never had a partner. Since he wasn't willing to talk about it, she didn't know if he had even tried to find one.

Then Dean Webber opened a door for her. "I want to get your input on who should be the next chairperson of Social Sciences."

"What's wrong with Waldschmidt? He's doing a good job."

"Yes, but Professor Waldschmidt's term will be up in a year and a half, and he doesn't want another. He might take a temporary appointment for a couple of years, but that's all."

"Well, there are plenty of others who would love to run the department."

"You really think so? Give me some names."

Livia imagined one of the Social Sciences department meetings, scanning the other nine or ten faces around the table. She mentioned a couple of names, but Webber shook his head. "Those two can write a good memo, but that's all. What we need is someone moderate, balanced, and political, in the best sense of the word. And if you hadn't noticed, that is you . . . Last year you chaired the committee that restructured the Social Sciences curriculum—a job full of more land mines than a highway in Vietnam! But you did it, and we got our new curriculum. A department chairman needs to be practical, needs to know how power works and isn't afraid of personal diplomacy—making all the phone calls, office visits, and personal contacts to get the work done. All that sounds like your job description. Memos! Who reads bloody memos? No, you're the one I want."

Livia knew that if tenure narrowed her future options, being department chairperson would narrow them even more. But Webber was right, she was the obvious choice, the *virtus in medio* choice, or in fairy-tale talk, the Goldilocks candidate—"not too hot, not too cold, not too hard, not too soft . . . but just right." She almost laughed out loud.

"Dr. Wayman, what is so funny?"

"Nothing. Just a private thought."

"So, Dr. Wayman, you should plan your research—I know that in your case it will require travel—and get on with it. I'll help make that possible. Then come back and do your duty."

Livia groaned. "I'll need some time to think it over," she said, but suddenly saw a way to China and knew that she would take his offer.

A few months later, they sat at the oak table in her tiny kitchen, each pulling on a Yuengling. "Henry, have a look at these photos. That's my father and mother at the Presbyterian mission in Beijing, standing in the courtyard in front of the house where we lived." The photo was yellowed with age, slightly faded and indistinct. But there was no mistaking Harold's and Adele's unsmiling faces.

"Is that you?" Henry asked, pointing to the little girl between them.

"What do you think?" she asked. "Let's see if you're a good detective."

Henry looked carefully at the photo, then examined Livia's face. "Well, your hair is darker. This little girl has light-colored hair, but hair color can change. Often does at puberty. And this little miss is quite skinny." He began to examine Livia's body. "Whereas you—"

"OK, stop right there. My recent weight gain is temporary." She snatched the photo and turned it over, holding it close to his face.

Henry grinned as he read the notation: *October, 1939, Peking mission.* "Well then, it's not you. That's a year or so before you were born, right?"

"How did you know?" Henry was always surprising her. He shrugged. "The little girl is my sister, Victoria. I've told you about what happened to her. It was a few months after this photo was taken, at the New Year festival in 1940, that she was kidnapped. Or disappeared. It's the last photo we have of her."

"Funny how looking at her in this photo makes her real, not just part of your past, but present."

Henry had gotten a Fulbright grant for a year's research in China. Livia had asked him if they could get together before he left. She wanted him to see Adele's diary, the locket, and the old photos she had discovered in her mother's closet. And to see if he would be willing to do a little groundwork for her while he was there. Her mind was full of plans, possibilities, and promises. She was trying desperately to sort them out, to figure out how to arrange her life for the next two years.

"I'm going to look for my sister."

"After forty-five years? Convince me that isn't just a wild goose chase."

"I know it sounds crazy, but I promised Mom and now I've got to at least try."

Henry put his hand on Adele's diary. "A firsthand account of China in the 1930s. Could I read it?"

"I wish I could let you. But Mom felt it should stay private and she asked me to destroy it after I was finished with it."

"D'you know why? Something shocking there?"

"I've read it a couple of times. Nothing shocking to me. But you've got to remember that she was the minister's wife. Supposed to believe in all the same religious teachings he preached about and support Dad in his work. So in that sense, yes, she probably thought that she needed to hide her true thoughts from everyone. To sum it up, I would say that she had a very open mind and a tolerant attitude. She learned a lot about Chinese culture and religions that she liked. Mainly, Buddhism. While Dad was losing his religious conviction, she was taking the first baby steps toward her own."

"Are you going to actually destroy the diary?"

"Yes. I promised that. But I wanted to talk with you about it first. And she didn't say anything about the photos, so I'll keep them. There are a couple of the head boy, Lin Kaiyuan. Somehow, when I look at the photos of him, I feel like I remember him. And there's one of Chen Bailian, the girl who cooked for us and was amah for my sister. I'm not sure what happened to either of them, but I think they are my only hope to find out what happened to my sister—if they, and she, are still alive. I was almost four in 1943 when we were marched off to the detention camp." Henry held up the locket, letting it catch the light from the ceiling fixture. It was mango shaped, badly tarnished. The delicate chain was broken.

"I'm going to get that fixed. Henry, open it and tell me what you think." Henry fumbled at the tiny latch, but finally was able to pop it open. Folded inside was a small piece of paper, now brownish, looking like old newsprint. He carefully unfolded it. He squinted, taking his reading glasses out of his shirt pocket. On it were written two tiny characters in a loop or oval. There were also some decorative calligraphic flourishes and a few indistinct markings on both sides of the oval shape. "What do you make of it?"

"It's a talisman. First character is easy: *bei*, north," he said, running his fingers through his hair. "You know that. But the other character is complicated. Lots of strokes and the ink has faded. I can't quite make it out . . . Could that be *yue*, mountain peaks? Yes, that's the character they use when they are referring to the five sacred mountains of China. This would be the northern mountains . . . Hengshan." He stopped as it dawned on him. "Oh my God. Do you remember the medium in Taiwan when you came to visit me at Ta Lou? She gave you the same talisman. Well, not exactly the same, but it was also a talisman of the god of the northern mountains. Of course, all the five directional mountains—north, south, east, west, and center—are great spirits in the Chinese pantheon, so they often show up on talismans. In case you're thinking this is spooky or something."

"Don't give me that agnostic crap, Henry. It *is* spooky, and you know it. I remember the medium's name. Deng Taitai, right? Damn! That was so long ago. About fifteen years, wasn't it?"

"Sixteen years . . ."

"Oh, right."

"Four months . . . and two days."

Livia looked at him. When she realized what he had just done, she was stunned. "Oh Henry, you're such a jerk. You were jealous of Irmgard, weren't you?" Without waiting for an answer she grabbed him, held her head against his chest, squeezing him tight. "Maybe you aren't good at this but you can at least let me hold you—if it bothers you, just pretend I'm your gramma. There's no one else in the world who has loved me that long, except for my parents." Gradually she felt his arms tighten around her.

找老师

CHAPTER 24

Finding a Teacher

Shanxi. Spring 1983.

Bu'er's day was taken up with visiting some of her patients in the vicinity of Old Stonebridge. Along with other techniques learned during her training as a Barefoot Doctor, she had become a skilled bonesetter. On a windy and warm day in late May, she borrowed Heiyen's rusty bicycle to go see a patient. Old Mrs. Chin's place was a farm on the eastern edge of town, north of the road which followed the course of the Dasha River. The old lady was almost eighty, still in good health, but had fallen on a stone path above the farm two weeks ago and broken her tibia. Bu'er had set the bone and promised to return to check it.

As her bicycle bumped along the dusty road, Bu'er was aware of certain public improvements in the town. Mayor Ma had managed to hire some rural laborers to scrape and level the main street, filling the ruts and potholes that had made bicycle travel nearly impossible. Now it was possible. She noticed the earthen walls of many of the homes had been recently repaired, bricks inserted, and new mud spread over the holes and gaps where the old ones had fallen out. The Jin family had opened a small noodle factory in the middle of town, and the Zheng family had started a knitting shop that produced multicolored hats and scarves. Some were kept for the local market, but most were boxed and shipped to Datong or Beijing for sale to tourists. As their business increased, the Zhengs had hired five elderly women from the village who were skilled knitters. There was talk that their increased production might allow them to expand to foreign markets, such as Japan. These were signs of a new prosperity under the "reform and opening" program of Deng Xiaoping.

Bu'er pedaled across the old bridge at the town center, glancing out at the muddy Dasha River that flowed by. A hazy sun was reflecting off its yellow waters. The location was now famous as the place where Mayor Ma had stood up to the rogue Red Guard brigade during the last days of the Cultural Revolution. Her own part in the event was conveniently forgotten. The Stonebridge Party Committee had proposed a modest plaque to commemorate the event, over the objections of Mayor Ma, who warned of the dangers of a "personality cult." She knew that he also hated being reminded of this ugly chapter in his life. In the end, there was a compromise and a small plaque placed there which said merely *Bridge of Courage*, without mentioning the event or any names.

Bu'er continued on the road past the bridge, following the course of the river toward the east, until she came to the last house where Mrs. Chin lived and raised her pigs with spectacular success. Bu'er stopped and leaned her bicycle against the shoulder-high earthen wall, peering over at an enormous sow lying on the ground with distended teats nurturing nine or ten eagerly sucking piglets. She had to smile at the sight.

"Ai!" cried Grandma Chin when Bu'er touched the bruised skin above her cast. "You need to help me get on my feet, not poke at my sore spots."

"I've been told that before . . . I have a lot of unruly patients. You are doing well, but you should not try to go back to work. Use your cane and you can get around, but no heavy lifting. You are old now, Grandma, and your bones are not so strong anymore. They will be slow to mend."

"I have my business to keep up," complained the old lady. "I've had to hire Erdong, my niece's son. He's a strong fellow but I can't afford to pay him much longer or he will eat up my profits, like the pigs gobble up their fodder."

"Your prospects are bright. From what I just saw, I can predict a nine- or tenfold increase in the near future." The old lady smiled proudly. Since old man Chin had died three years earlier, the pig business had got better, an unexpected improvement that puzzled her neighbors, who thought that Mrs. Chin, without a man's management skills, would have to sell her farm.

"Erdong," she shouted, "make some tea for the doctor and me. Bring the good cups." She turned her piercing eyes toward Bu'er and got back to the point. "How long till I'm up?"

"Perhaps six more weeks. I will come and check you every week. Maybe, if you have to let go of Erdong, I could find someone of the FourOnes to help you."

"Your people are kind, but I don't believe all that stuff about the gods and spirits speaking through old Granny Guzhi . . . have they started talking to you yet?"

Bu'er wasn't sure whether the old lady was being ironical, but she thought not. She sensed behind the question a sincere interest. "Grandma," she said, "that is a troublesome question." She paused briefly, swirling the tea leaves in her cup to make them sink. With her new prosperity, Granny Chin was now drinking a good grade of Iron Guanyin tea. "The FourOnes have expected me to become one of their leaders for many years, but I do not often hear the voices. I have some understanding of things, but I do not know if that knowledge would be helpful to the FourOnes. The one thing I can do well is to diagnose and heal. I understand herbs and methods of treatment, as I have been taught by my teacher, Mingling. You know her. She has treated your husband. Guzhi has tried to teach me how to go to the spirits, but unlike the art of healing, I do not believe that can be taught."

Mrs. Chin look at her intensely and Bu'er was reminded of the beady eyes of a crane looking for frogs at the river's edge. "Maybe you have not found the right teacher."

"What do you mean? Are you saying that you could be my teacher?"

"Ha!" cackled the old lady. "I could teach you only about pigs . . . but there are many sorts of teachers under heaven and they do not all walk on two feet! My teachers are right outside the door."

"Who do you mean? Your neighbors?"

"No, the neighbors are the ones my late husband listened to. The things he learned were useful but they are not enough. When the neighbors were our teachers, we survived, but just barely. Now with my new teachers, my pigs have truly flourished and I have prospered."

"I see you are being deliberately mysterious. You want me to ask you—who are these teachers?"

"It's the pigs themselves. They are my teachers." Bu'er looked at the old lady's face more carefully, expecting her to laugh at her own joke, but she didn't. Was she becoming senile? "After old Chin died and I knew the responsibility was mine, I went to the pigs and asked them: 'What do you want, what makes you happy and fertile pigs?'"

"So you don't believe that Guzhi can talk to the spirits but think you can talk to the pigs!" she observed.

"I'm not an idiot. Of course, the pigs don't speak our language, so I took my time and observed them carefully. I watched them for hours and days at a time, listening to the sounds they made, their oinks and grunts, watching them look for water, for food, and a place of protection from the sun. I listened to their every sound, watched their every movement, and slow though I am, I finally learned from them. If you doubt this, look for yourself. The pigs are happy and fat, with many piglets. And I no longer just survive. My purse is getting fatter. I'd get fatter myself if I didn't have to work so hard."

"A wonderful story, but how does it apply to my situation?"

"That part is not so easy," she said, her arthritic fingers clasped around the rustic tea cup. "You must find your own teachers. You must think about your own needs and observe things carefully. Then you will find them and you will learn something."

Bu'er left Mrs. Chin, having promised to return the following week. As she rode the bicycle back toward the western part of the village, thinking over what the old lady had said, she began to consider the possibility that there was some reason in her crazy ramblings. She began to see some similarities between her words and what Mingling had taught her, years ago, about the virtue that resides in every creature, if you observe it carefully. But you must look beyond the humans, she thought, who have so many conflicting points of view: Confucians, Daoists, Buddhists, Communists, and Capitalists. Instead of studying these, she thought, you must study the other creatures who are always there, always the same, the creatures with legs, wings, fins, and even those who live but do not move, like herbs, grasses, and trees.

Bu'er, Heiyen, and Guzhi had gone to a farmhouse on the southern edge of a small town called Zhongduzhuang, some twenty miles west of Old Stonebridge. Government agents had been investigating them, so they moved their meetings from one home to another in different towns near the northeastern border of Shanxi Province. Traveling was a hardship, but better a moving target than a sitting duck. The land around Zhongduzhuang was hilly and dry, the clay earth full of stones, very hard to farm successfully, so the enterprising townsfolk had taken up brickmaking, and stacks of crudely made bricks stood next to a kiln on the eastern edge of town. The first signs of prosperity had appeared, but the town was still too small to attract much attention and was a safe place for the FourOnes to meet. So they met in the home of one of the town's prosperous farmers.

A local member began by complaining to Heiyen. "The government has been harassing us, on and off, for many years, so we are always feeling anxiety. We do not receive clear directions from the spirits. You, our leaders, are getting old. You say that sister Bu'er will be our leader, but she brings us few messages from the spirits. Where do we go from here?"

Heiyen responded rather formally, intending to address the concerns of all those who had gathered. "Your questions are on the mark. I have given much thought to them myself, over the last years, especially since the death of Long Nail. I would summarize our situation as follows," he said, speaking in a voice loud enough to reach those crowded into the back of the room. "We have made gains. We have created a network of members in six or seven counties, some here in Shanxi, some in western Hebei. Many people have been drawn to the rules we live by," he said in a louder voice, fearing that some could not hear him. "We respect the mountains, the waters, the land, and all growing things. We acknowledge with gratitude the gifts of Heaven and Earth. We do not seek riches. We do not seek power over others. Both men and women can be leaders among us. We do not harm humans or animals. We see all religions as ways to the same goal. We respect our ancestors and the great spirits. We follow their instructions. All these beautiful ideals have been heard and accepted by the people who have joined with us.

"But there have been serious loses, too. Three years ago, the Long Nail incident almost destroyed us. If Mayor Ma had not quickly shipped his body back to Fuping and declared him a suicide, we would have had the Shanxi provincial police or the People's Liberation Army on our backs. And worse by far than that were the wounds to our own society. We don't keep exact numbers but I think we lost half of our members because of his death. Many lost faith in our leadership and in our ability to contact the spirits, and we have not yet regained the number of those lost." The heads of many of the listeners were nodding in agreement.

"Then there is the continuing problem that we cannot practice our principles openly. To speak the truth, we are like barren mules. We can pull our loads, but we are infertile and unable to reproduce ourselves. We exist only in the homes and hearts of our members. To obey the will of the spirits and to be really successful we must establish beautiful villages and towns that will create communities of harmony and peace."

Guzhi spoke up. "We have met so many obstacles over the years. First there were the war years, then there was the Great Leap Forward and the starvation, then the Cultural Revolution and the chaos. Then Long Nail. If the spirits want us to openly establish communities of peace," she asked Heiyen, "why have they not made it possible for us to do so?"

Heiyen answered in the simple way he usually did. "We must have faith."

Guzhi just shook her head. "We have been practicing faith and patience for a long time."

As the discussion continued, Bu'er listened carefully but did not speak, sensing that they were approaching a crisis.

"And now," Guzhi was saying, "the government is again seeking to destroy us."

"This has happened before. We must remain faithful through all the tribulation," suggested Heiyen, "leaving the time of our success to the decision of the spirits."

"Those are the sentiments of a young man," said Guzhi. "You may have years left to go through yet another affliction and strength to continue the work. But I do not. I am almost eighty." Some of the older leaders shook their heads in agreement, as though some general spirit of weariness had descended upon them all.

"Hardly a young man," Heiyen responded. "I am seventy years from my mother's womb. I too wonder when the time will come . . . But what are we to do now? We have asked the ancestors and the spirits and their answers have not been clear." A silence fell over the room.

Finally, Bu'er spoke. "Mingling," she began, "although she is not a member of our family, has taught me much."

"Mingling is not one of us," Guzhi said in her typically abrupt fashion. "She is a good person, but she does not understand our ways and has not joined our society. I do not think she has answers for us."

"She has been my teacher for so many years," said Bu'er, undeterred by the criticism, "as have you and Heiyen. But you are right, she does not see herself as belonging to any group. The nuns of Yindong An thought she would join them and she did not. We have hoped she would join us, but she has not. What I can say is that she is committed to the people and the cause of their health, and that is no small thing. It is just that now the Barefoot Doctors are no longer needed, so her service takes a different form."

"I sometimes think," sighed Guzhi, "that Mingling is the only true communist left in China!"

Heiyen gave a rare laugh. "You had better not let that opinion get back to the comrades in Beijing." There were general chuckles among those present.

"I will continue my thought," said Bu'er, bringing them back to the issue at hand. "Mingling is wise about the world. She has opened my eyes, and taught me to learn from the creatures around us . . . We live in a vast world, all of Heaven and Earth and everything they embrace. We humans are only one of the legions of creatures that dwell in them. We say that we follow the Way, but it was Mingling who taught me how to discern it. You look at a humble thing like a cicada, or a garlic plant, or any growing thing. Your eyes tend to pass over them so quickly, and you dismiss them as just an insect, just a clump of grass. But if you look closely, you see that each is a world in itself. You look carefully at the wings of that cicada and see a fabric translucent like glass, more delicate and more beautiful than any human embroidery. You look at a bird egg and you see a vessel more perfect than the finest Song dynasty porcelain. What I see most clearly, among all living things, is an order and a pattern." The members of FourOnes listed to Bu'er in wonder, for they had never heard her speak at such length and with such eloquence before.

"Cycles of yin and yang," she continued, "growth and decline. Our society has had its cycles, too. We must observe them carefully. We have grown and been diminished, and now begin to grow again. It would be all too human to assume that this growth is destined to continue without pause. But the law of life around us is one of cycles, of growth and decay, expansion and contraction, life and death. The recent changes in our nation are astonishing. Who knows how far they may go? Perhaps, for the good of the FourOnes, we must begin to think in longer spans of time. We must accept that now is not time for advance but retreat, to hide ourselves once again among the people until the time is right. A few years, one way or the other, is nothing. Larval insects dig their way under the ground, to rest, to wait, to gain strength, some for a year's time, some for many years. Like the cicada, when the time is right, they will emerge, with wings! The garlic plant withers and retreats into the bulb that is protected by the soil from the winter cold, so that it can grow more strongly in the spring. Is this not the message for our society as well? The cycles of increase and decrease, activity and rest, growth and decline, will continue all around us, each according to its own nature. Are we alone exempt from the Way?"

The FourOnes present were stunned. When Bu'er had ceased speaking, there was a respectful silence that held as the group looked at her with new eyes. In a way, she was affirming the advice of Heiyen, but she did it with eloquence and was able to relate it to realities all around them. "I do not mean to be so formal," she added, almost apologetically. "What I am trying to say applies to everything, even the humblest of things. It applies even to raising pigs, as I have recently learned from Granny Chin, but I will spare you the lecture on pigs." In her own heart Bu'er knew that although the spirits had not spoken to her directly, the words she had said came to her lips without any effort on her part. She did not have to think what to say.

Guzhi looked at her, and sensed a confidence that she had never seen before. She was moved, feeling a smarting in her eyes. Was she about to weep or was that just the pain of tired eyes? The older she got, the more easily she wept. She thought of the little foreign ghost they had taken from her parents many years ago, so fragile yet so strong. They had tried to protect her, to nourish her as a gift from the spirits, the one who was to be their leader. It was as if this long history, with all its ups and downs, was pointing to this very moment. The time of her leadership was near, and she would awaken something new in their hearts and minds. She could feel it. Bu'er had faced down the Red Guards at Old Stonebridge, and now she had begun to speak to the FourOnes with understanding and authority.

语言道断

CHAPTER 25

When the Way of Language Fails

Shanxi. Winter 1984.

It was sometime after midnight. The cold winter sky was illuminated by a half moon slipping downward toward the horizon, like a bright boat sinking toward the water. She had never seen the ocean, but wondered if it was like this, the light clouds like waves and the blue-black sky the dark waters beneath.

Bu'er followed the familiar path from Baita village south toward Old Stonebridge, skirting areas of human habitation as far as it was possible, and when it was not, walking through the empty streets by night. She hiked the mountain paths with heavy steps, saddened by her disagreement with Mingling. She was on her way back to join Heiyen and Guzhi, having chosen to be with them in their time of trouble.

She and Mingling had been walking back from a visit to the Zhao family's farm in a small village about two miles from Baita. Zhao's oldest son Lin had broken his forearm in two places as he and some other workers were struggling to rebuild a wall. A heavy stone became dislodged and it fell on Lin as he was bent over at the base of the wall. When the call for help came, Mingling had brought Bu'er with her because of her skills as a bone setter. The work had been difficult, and, as they were returning to Baita, Mingling said to her: "I am getting old. I can do the herbs, but I need your strength and skills for difficult cases like this one."

"I was going to talk with you this evening. That letter that came yesterday—it said that Heiyen has been taken to Taiyuan by provincial agents. He's now being held in jail. They were going to take Guzhi as well, but Mayor Ma intervened and said he would keep her under house arrest. He assured the agents that she was no danger to society."

"Well, that leaves you as the only leader left. You must be careful."

"I am sorry, Jiejie, but I feel that I must return to Old Stonebridge. The FourOnes there will need me."

"That would be a mistake. Under the present circumstances, you can do them no good. You should stay here where you are safe."

"I must go," said Bu'er stubbornly. "From the beginning my karma has placed me on a different path, and I must follow it."

"Your presence will injure, not help them. Leaderless they will be seen as harmless. But if you join them, the authorities will take not only you but perhaps some of the others as well. You should stay here where Grandma Ai and I can hide you—Baita is a village of no account. If you go to Old Stonebridge, they will find you and you will end up in prison, or worse."

"I will leave this evening. You are my elder sister, and I respect your advice as always, but I must do this."

Bu'er was about halfway back to Old Stonebridge. She found a familiar cave as the sky began to lighten, the one where a man had tried to rape her years before. Bu'er might have chosen another place to rest during daylight hours, but each time she made the journey between Baita and Old Stonebridge she deliberately chose to rest in this cave, to prove to herself that she was no longer afraid. She did not want to live in fear.

The cave was at the back of a narrow grotto, a short climb above the path. She sat on a stone at the mouth of the grotto, enjoying the first rays of the sun. She would soon seek a place to rest deep in the cave, but for now she chose to enjoy the sun on her face. She closed her eyes and felt her aloneness. It neither saddened her nor made her happy. She had long ago accepted it as her destiny, but she had also been chosen to be a leader with a task to perform. But what was the task? That had never been completely clear to her, or to those who had adopted her, for their work had been thwarted at every turn, and she heard few messages from the spirits. Last year she had spoken with eloquence to the FourOnes trying to convey the teachings of Mingling, but it was hard to see how that translated into the leadership role they expected her to play. They needed more than eloquence. What was the next step?

She thought of her American parents, dim memories of a family she usually refused to dwell upon. No, her responsibilities lay here, with her living family, the FourOnes. She struggled to accept her calling, as a foreigner, one who would never be fully accepted, here or there.

Who was she? In truth she did not even know the meaning of her name. The numbers *one* and *two* kept cycling through her brain. "Not two"—what did it signify? Oneness? But what did that mean? Mingling had once told her that her name had a deep meaning. And that she would know what it means at a later time, when she was ready. But that time had never come, though now she was fifty years old.

She thought over the whole of her life. The taking at White Cloud Temple, learning the Buddha Dharma at Yindong An, and later the gradual initiation into the FourOne Society. The wars, the disasters, the Cultural Revolution, the periodic ebb and flow of their movement. Chairman Mao's death and the great changes that followed, the beginnings of freedom and prosperity under Deng Xiaoping. What was her path and the way of the FourOnes under these new circumstances? If she could figure that out, she might be able to be the leader they needed. Whether she looked to the past or to the future, her mind was beset by doubts.

Beijing had once again sent investigators out into the countryside to enforce the government policy on religion. They were not a band of ruffians like the Red Guards, but highly trained professionals. They were looking at the Muslim groups in Xinjiang, searching for underground Catholics, and trying to monitor certain Protestant house churches. They also sought out unauthorized sectarian groups, and that brought their attention to the FourOnes . . .

Her mind still troubled, Bu'er slipped into Old Stonebridge late in the night, going directly to Guzhi's tiny quarters in the back room of an old woodworking shop, near the site of the demolished temple of the river god. The old lady, who did not sleep soundly, tottered to the door to answer Bu'er's knock.

"Is it you, Daughter?" she said, pinching the bridge of her nose and massaging her temples to clear her vision. "This is too dangerous. You shouldn't be here."

"You are my family. How could I not come?"

"Father Heiyen is in prison. He was taken away three weeks ago. I would be in prison too, but for my nephew. And they know that you, too, are one of the leaders. I hoped you would stay with Mingling. They will find you here."

"I couldn't stay, Grandmother. We've had a conflict. We argued, and I left."

Guzhi cast a worried look at her. "Sit down and tell me about it. I'll make us some tea."

"Things have changed, Grandma," Bu'er said as she cradled the teacup in both her hands and felt the warmth spread to her palms and fingers. "Since Western medicine has come to the countryside, the day of the Barefoot Doctors is over. Mingling is now quite old and has chosen to spend her final years as an herbalist, living at Baita with Grandma Ai. She is way past the official retirement age and of no interest to the government now. I told her that I had to come to be with you."

Guzhi listened to her account of their conversation. She shook her head sadly. "Mingling was right. You should have stayed in Baita. I said the same to Heiyen before his arrest, and now both of us are in prison. You are next."

"Is this the will of the spirits?"

Guzhi said: "I never know about that. But I do know that we can plan nothing right now. We are like cockroaches on the kitchen floor, our only hope is to remain unseen. The moment we move they are here to stomp on us."

"I told Mingling that you are my family. I told her I had to see if I could help you."

"You can't help Heiyen. I am all right, but I'm not supposed to leave these two rooms," said Guzhi, gesturing with a sweep of her hand. "Go to Mingling. She is your family, too, and she will conceal you. You should remember the old saying: 'The nail that sticks up is the one that gets hammered.'"

"She is my teacher and my elder sister. If I am captured, hiding with her, it will not go well for her. She will be thrown into prison as well. I am like the poison of the castor bean plant, dangerous for anyone to touch. And what of the other FourOnes? Mother, I can't abandon all the people who rely on us."

The old lady was quiet. Finally, she sighed. "All through the years I have urged caution. The messages have come through me. Heiyen and the others were always so certain about their meaning . . . but perhaps it is easier to believe in them when they come through someone else. It was hard for me to accept that I was chosen as the vehicle of the spirits. I don't know." She sighed again. "I just know that I am old now, and that there is nothing more I can do."

Tears came to Bu'er's eyes as the old lady spoke. She still clearly remembered the early morning after she had been kidnapped, bumping along in the big wooden box. When the lid came off the box and she looked up at the stars in the cold morning sky, it was Guzhi's hand that had first reached out to her and comforted her. They had now been together, off and on, for over forty years.

"Mother, what should I do?"

The old lady stared at her for a long while, without speaking. Then her eyes lost their focus, and her head began to swing from side to side, the movements slow and deliberate. Her concentration seemed to stop the passage of time, holding it motionless in the present. Bu'er knew that she had gone to the world of the spirits, so she closed her eyes and waited. Then finally the familiar low voice whispered. "Go to the mountains. You must go to Wutaishan."

Bu'er bowed her head and thought about the implications of the message. Wutaishan was the land of sacred mountains, to the southwest in Shanxi. It was a remote place with deep valleys and high mountains. Yet there were some FourOne members in the place, mostly poor farmers who worked the harsh land with endless toil. She could likely find a place of safety there, temporarily, but what of the future?

After a while, Guzhi came out of her trance. She asked Bu'er what she had said. Bu'er repeated her words.

"That does not seem like a good plan. Few of our people live in Wutaishan. They have to work so hard just to survive," she mused. "But what alternative is there?"

Bu'er had to smile. "As always, Grandmother, you are your own harshest critic! You are well named."

Guzhi agreed. "My fate is in my name. As is yours." Bu'er was about to ask her what she meant, but the old lady went on: "Now here is what you should do. Write a letter to Mingling and tell her you are going to Wutaishan. Send it through Grandma Ai. Don't sign your name. We can't mail the letter from here, but I will give it to someone I trust who can take it to the post office in another town. Mingling will know. She must choose her way, to join you or to remain in Baita village. But I know she will come. You must take care of your elder sister and she must take care of her meimei. Go now, Bu'er, before someone finds you here."

But someone had spotted Bu'er and reported her presence to the provincial agents. On the evening of the next day, as she was about to set out on her journey to Wutaishan, they seized her. They took her back to the municipal building at Old Stonebridge where they told Mayor Ma Jin to hold her in custody, waiting for the arrival of the interrogation team from Taiyuan, who would come in two days. There was no jail at the municipal center, but the little room where she was imprisoned could be locked and was guarded day and night by a deputy chosen by Ma Jin.

Guzhi was frightened for her, but had an idea, a way for her to set Bu'er free. But she had to do it right or it would be the end of the road for both of them. Even Ma Jin's patience with her had its limits. She knew that death was not so far away for her in any case, but did not wish to hasten it. She brewed tea and poured it into an old thermos, carefully following a recipe once given to her by Mingling, fortifying it with a good dash of baijiu and a few other special ingredients. As she aged, Guzhi had found it more and more difficult to get a good night's sleep. "Take these mushrooms," the healer had said to Guzhi, "and boil them with your tea leaves. Add mint leaves. They will make you tired and your mind foggy. You will be able to go to sleep. You might see strange things in your dreams but they are not real. Above all do not take this with any kind of alcoholic drink. The strange visions will become stronger and you might lose consciousness."

Late at night, Guzhi walked over to the municipal center with the thermos in her cloth bag. The night was cold, and the guard would appreciate a hot cup of tea. "The Mayor has told me that no one can see the prisoner," said Xiaogong, Ma Jin's deputy, when he answered Guzhi's knock at the door. The burly Xiaogong was a bit thick and had been assigned the night watch. As the old lady entered the room, he used the interruption to open the door of the iron stove, adding a few pieces of charcoal to keep the feeble heat alive. He knew Ma Jin would be angry if he used too much coal.

"Yes, I know about Jin's orders. I did not come to visit the prisoner. I made you some tea. It will warm your fingers," she said, holding up a hand toward him, "and your toes." She found his cup and poured the tea. He waved her to a chair and took a swallow of the brew as he sat down on a blue plastic couch.

"Do you like it?"

"It has a bit of fire in it," he said, grinning at her appreciatively. "Warms the guts." He was forbidden to drink alcoholic beverages on the job, but if someone else had slipped something into his tea, it was not his fault. He enjoyed the feeling of warmth spreading through his body. Guzhi asked him about his grandmother, whose name was Attending Phoenix. It was a rather grandiose name, but an inspired choice, for it had been predictive of her good fortune. She gave birth to three daughters and four sons, including the father of Xiaogong. He began to talk about Attending Phoenix and his father, complaining that the new one-child policy of the national government would not have permitted her to have so many children. "My father was the youngest. He wouldn't have been born and neither would I. I would be nothing!" he said indignantly. "Or I might have been born as something else, like a bird or a dog." His mind became fuddled as he tried to sort out the implications of the one-child policy and Buddhist teachings. Who would be the *I* who was nothing? It was all too confusing. He shifted to the subject of his brothers, and his words gradually became more slurred. Finally, he mumbled incoherently, then slumped to his side on the couch. Guzhi hoped that he was merely asleep, nothing worse. He was, after all, a good boy.

Guzhi got up, and walked over to the door to the other room. Xiaogong had locked it but left the key in the door. She turned the lock and opened it to find Bu'er standing ready to come out. "Oh Mother, thank you. I heard all that. What did you give him?"

"I gave him visions," smiled the old lady. Now hurry, you need to leave for Wutaishan. It's the middle of the night and you can go safely, first to the farm of Chen Da and his family. They will protect you. As you go on, stay with FourOnes you know along the way. Do not leave one home until you know the next will hide you. Travel at night. Leave no tracks. Mingling will find you there. May the spirits guide your steps."

Guzhi relocked the door to the cell, poured out the rest of Xiaogong's tea, rinsed the cup and placed it on the table. She took her thermos and returned to her house to see what would happen.

About three hours later, at first light, a groggy Xiaogong awoke to find his prisoner gone. He rushed to the home of Ma Jin, pounded on the door and woke the latter from a deep sleep.

"What do you want, turtle head? You're supposed to be watching the prisoner. Get back there and do your job."

"The prisoner is gone," he said sheepishly.

"What? Gone? Are you crazy? What happened?"

"A phoenix came and took her!"

"What do you mean, you idiot? There is no phoenix. That's an old lady's fable!"

"No, Mayor Ma, it was real. I locked the door last night and it was still locked this morning but the prisoner was gone. Is that not a miracle? I saw the glorious phoenix, with wings extended, reaching from one horizon to the other, its feathers flashing every color of the rainbow. It took the prisoner away. What could I, a mere mortal, do to stop a phoenix?"

"Dog farts! Why am I surrounded by . . . by . . ." He groaned, fearful that his tenure as mayor was over. *My town,* thought Ma Jin, *would be known not only as the place where fifty-year-old women escaped from his jail, but as the place inhabited by piss-brained morons, idiots who believed that a giant phoenix comes to liberate prisoners.* On the other hand . . . Ma Jin was never one to be bound by the tenets of orthodoxy, state sponsored or otherwise. His supple mind began to consider how he might turn the visit of the phoenix to his own advantage and that of his beloved town, Old Stonebridge.

Once again Bu'er was on the road, heading southwest by night, stumbling and tentative as she followed an unfamiliar path toward the small farm of Chen Da and his family, still miles away. As she walked, Bu'er's mind slipped into the worries of the previous night. The past was full of ambiguities and when she tried to imagine the future, her mind was clouded with doubts. Yes, she had found a niche of leadership. She could speak words that helped the FourOnes understand the Way. But was that enough? What more could she offer them?

Then the thought dawned on her that such musings about past and future were useless, and not just useless, but harmful. She decided to focus instead on the present, as she had been taught to do long ago by the nuns at Yindong An. Her anxious stumbling ceased then, and she walked more slowly and surely, realizing that the way to reach Chen Da's farm sooner was to walk more slowly. She felt the pressure of her feet on the ground, sensing the different textures she could feel through her sandals: soft grass, loose dirt, sharp-edged pebbles, and smooth stones. One foot ahead of the other, step by step, one foot ahead of the other, each one different yet all the same, just a part of the way. None better, none worse. She became aware of her breath, moving in and out as she walked along the path. Thoughts fell away like the flower petals from a tree in the spring. As her mind was emptied of discriminations, the words of a poem by an ancient sage came to her. Bolai had taught them to her. Although she did not fully understand them at the time, the poetry was strong and she had repeated them to herself many times over the years, loving their music. Now, as her mind cleared, she had, at last, understood their deeper meaning.

With one mind, in harmony with the Way,
All self-centered striving ceases.
Doubts and uncertainties vanish
And life in true faith is possible.
To come directly into harmony with this reality,
Just simply say, when doubt arises, "Not two."

There it was. *Bu'er*, her name. And now she understood what it meant—not with her mind but with her body. *Not two* had nothing to do with *one* or *two*, or with any numbers at all. It was in fact the opposite of numbers. She did not need Bolai, Mingling, or Guzhi or anyone else to tell her the meaning of her name. She had known that something like this could happen, but had never dared let herself think about it, and those times when she did, she had imagined it would happen at some deep place in her mind or spirit. Now that it was happening, she felt it all over her body, a kind of lightness that filled every part of it. But in truth there was no mind, no spirit, and no body. She knew . . .

Her feet felt like they had grown wings. They barely touched the ground as she continued on her way, toward Wutaishan, and her body sang as she repeated again and again the last two lines of the poem: *Yu yen dao duan. Fei qu lai jin.*

When the way of language fails,
there is no yesterday
no tomorrow
no today.

CHAPTER 26

Letters from China

Dear Livia,

Sorry for the delay, but I wanted to wait until I had made some progress on your project before I wrote. Now I do have some info for you—see below.

My own bibliographical work at Capital Library is almost complete and I'll be returning to south China for field work, then back to BU in late spring. I figured I'd better get my own project done before I went off on what I called your "wild goose chase."

Reading those words, Livia remembered what a shock it had been to hear from Professor Xu Jingli. Not a word from him since they'd talked at Beijing Normal in 1976, then last summer, a letter from him urging her to apply for a one-semester appointment for the spring semester of 1985, teaching an intro class in anthropology and giving a weekly lecture to the faculty on the past fifty years of social science development in Europe and the United States. Trying to fill up the black hole in Chinese education, she thought.

It was a godsend. Dean Webber had let her off the hook a few years ago, but now it was clear that she would be the next chair of the department. The letter answered both issues. With such light teaching responsibilities, she could collect materials for her own research and give the dean a firm date for taking the chair position. And best of all, she could finally do something about the promise to her mother.

Naturally, she said nothing to Webber about the personal project. It was almost too embarrassing to say the words *search for my sister*, even to herself, much less to anyone else. When she looked at it rationally, the project seemed completely quixotic. Going to China was the easy part, but finding a sister who had disappeared over forty years ago—that seemed impossible, even ridiculous, so she had mentioned that part of her project to no one but Henry.

I know I promised to be your eyes and ears in Beijing, but it's only in the last two weeks I've been able to follow up on the leads you gave me. Some good news: I found 42 Flower Market Street where you said the mission was located, southeast of the Chongwen metro stop. It's both there and not there. The address is now a middle school. The only old building left from the mission is the residence house where you must have lived, but it now houses administrative offices for the principal, vice-principal, and some of the faculty. The chapel and other buildings have been torn down to make way for two-story classroom buildings along the east side of the compound.

Livia felt her heart jump when she read these words. She had gotten her visa and would be leaving for China just after Chinese New Year, and Henry's letter allowed her to imagine herself walking into the compound, touching the doors and walls of the old mission residence, hoping it might evoke some early memory of her family.

I asked around the neighborhood and finally found an old lady, Granny Wang, who admitted knowing something about the old mission. She is now in her eighties, and has lived in the neighborhood since she was a child. She knew the Chen family well, I think. She said that the "Old Mister," Deacon Chen, died during the Cultural Revolution. She thought it was in 1967. A group of Red Guards saw his neatly tended courtyard and became suspicious. They forced their way through his front gate and ransacked his house. They found some of his Christian books, denounced him in a public meeting, and demanded he write a self-confession. Seems he was a stubborn old bird, so he stood up to them and refused. One of the young men struck him in the face, not very hard she said, but he fell to the ground senseless. Apparently died of heart failure a few days later.

At this point Granny stopped and told me that she had never spoken to a stranger about such things, but now that Comrade Deng Xiaoping was in charge, it was possible to say that Chairman Mao was not perfect and his cultural revolution had some bad things about it. Deng says Mao was seventy percent right and thirty percent wrong. I shouldn't have teased the old woman, but said that no doubt among the thirty percent were the two times that Mao had sacked Deng himself. She ignored that but went on to tell me what she knew of the amah and the houseboy. It seems the Old Mister's daughter, Chen Bailian, had left home right after the war and became a Buddhist nun, but she said that was a long time ago and she didn't know where she was, if she was still a nun, or even if she was still alive. Granny did know something about Lin Kaiyuan. He worked as a public security officer for many years, is now retired, and no longer living in the area, although she had seen him a few times over the years. You might be able to find him.

Henry then went on describing his experience of Beijing. The old city was rapidly disappearing, he wrote, new buildings everywhere, lots of private cars and expressways to accommodate them. Fascinating to watch this experiment in modernization, which he described in some detail. Then he added a final bit of advice.

Granny Wang seemed to know a lot about the mission, and as I was about to leave I asked her if she had been a member of your dad's congregation. I think the question surprised her because she shook her head "no" right away, almost reflexively. But I could see the tension in her face. Things are opening up, Livia, but there is still a lot of fear. I would definitely look her up when you get here, but go carefully when you talk to her.

She had to tell him, so she made the phone call. It would be nice if, just once, her father would answer the phone, but as usual, it was the voice she expected. "Hello, Livia, how good to hear from you . . . You must want to speak with your father." Right. Livia tried, but could not bring herself to like the woman. At the same time, she had to be grateful to her. Without Tillie, Harold might be . . . she didn't even want to think about it.

"Yes, I would like to speak with him."

"I'm afraid that won't be possible right now. He is napping. He needs his rest, you know."

"Could I call back a bit later? Or ask him to call me. I'm leaving for China in a few days and I have so much to do. He isn't sick, is he?"

"I don't know. He just seems so tired all the time. I try to let him rest when he can. He did tell you that we were making a trip to Taiwan in April, didn't he? If his health is good, of course. You could call back . . . no wait, I think I hear him getting up. He must have heard the phone ring." After a long pause, Livia heard Harold mumble a congested greeting.

"Dad, how are you doing?"

He cleared his throat. "Well, I'm fine. For an old graybeard."

"What do you mean, you don't have a gray hair in your head," she teased him.

"That's between me and my hairdresser . . . I don't know why I've gotten so vain. I think it is one of the seven deadly sins your church is always preaching against. But when Tillie Grace and I go out in public I don't want people thinking I'm her father." *If she didn't dye her hair,* thought Livia, *that wouldn't be a problem.*

"Anyway, how are your plans coming along for the China trip?"

"I'm leaving Sunday afternoon. Listen, there's something I need to tell you. My friend Henry was in China for a couple of months this winter. While he was in Beijing he did some searching for me. He found the site of the old mission on Flower Market Street. The old house where we lived is still there but the church was torn down. The compound is being used as a middle school now."

There was a silence. "I know what you're doing and I think you are making a mistake, leaving yourself open for a big disappointment. I would do your teaching and research and forget about the past."

She tried to control her feelings but couldn't. "Dad, why do you have to be so damn negative every time I bring up the mission?"

There was a long pause. "Because it brings up so many bad memories—the disappearance of your sister, the war, the detention camp, the end of my work in China, the end of . . ." She knew why he had paused. He didn't want to talk about his first marriage with Tillie listening. "Why can't you just leave it alone?"

She forced herself to be calm, finally saying, "It's part of my history, I've got to do it. My sister . . . ," she began, but couldn't bring herself to finish the sentence.

There was another long silence at his end. Finally, he dredged up an old Chinese phrase, *"Yilu pingan."* Safe trip.

PART III

THE SEARCH

鬼

CHAPTER 27

Ghosts

Beijing. Spring 1985.

Livia's arrival in China was followed by two weeks of frantic activity—getting oriented at Beijing Normal, setting up housekeeping, beginning classes, and getting to know fellow faculty members. Now it was time for a break. Livia and two friends, all three "foreign experts" at the university, were out to eat at Youyi Binguan, the Friendship Hotel. As the only English-speaking professors currently teaching at the university, they had become instant friends.

"The name of this place makes me feel all warm and fuzzy inside, but look around," said Rachel. "It's dismal." The Youyi was located at the northern edge of the old city, the dining room where they sat a gloomy place with inadequate lighting—not romantic, just bad—high ceilings, heavy drapes, and no windows.

"Yeah, don't hug your teddy bear yet. That 'friendship' wasn't meant for us to begin with. It was between the Chinese and the Soviets," pointed out Livia, "back when all the Chinese children were learning Russian in school. Now they're studying English. The place was built to house Soviet diplomats, aid workers, and advisers here in the '50s and early '60s . . . But look," she said, "still some Russian dishes on the menu."

"Livia," said Terri, "how in the world did you find out about this old dump?"

"*Lonely Planet* says it's where all the diplomats and foreign correspondents hang out." She shifted to a conspiratorial whisper: "And MI-6, the CIA, and the KGB. Just look around at them. Half of the people here must be spies, the other half moles and counterspies."

Rachael looked around skeptically at the assembled diners. "I think you're bullshiting us. Most of them look like tourists to me." Rachael Gresham was from the United Kingdom, teaching English to the undergrads at Beijing Normal and lecturing the faculty on the British novel since 1945.

"Spies or no, I love this place," Terri said. "It might be ugly, but it has atmosphere—a lot more interesting than anything in north central Indiana. The major architectural form in my neck of the woods is the silo." Terri Phelan was from Ball State, the Indiana teachers' college, in Beijing to lecture on Western educational theories.

Livia sipped her Tsingtao beer. "How are your students," she asked looking at Rachel, "fun to teach?"

"So far I'd say they're sweet, disciplined, eager to learn, but I can't get them to have a real discussion. They don't want to express their own opinions. They feel more comfortable if I do all the talking and they take notes."

"They have been told what to think for so long, you're not going to get an open discussion without a lot of preparation. Getting their trust won't be easy," said Livia. "I'm finding the same thing."

Terri nodded. "They seem so completely innocent, maybe like American high school students before the '60s happened." Livia and Rachel looked doubtful. "Well, at least in the cornfields where I come from . . . Remember that student party they invited us to last Friday night? They were jumping around doing what they called 'break dancing,' trying to show us they were up on the latest thing in American culture. It was so pathetic it brought tears to my eyes. What is that? Nostalgia for a lost innocence? I didn't think I was such a romantic."

The next day was Saturday and Livia was finally ready to go in search of Granny Wang and the Presbyterian mission. Following Henry's directions, she got off at the Chongwen Gate metro station, walked south and east, stopping occasionally to ask, "Please, could you tell me, where is Flower Market Street?" Once there, she followed Henry's written directions and found Weaver's hutong, where Granny Wang lived.

They sat in her lean-to, attached like a barnacle to a wall in the shabby courtyard of the house where her nephew lived, a space shared with three other families. She offered Livia the only chair in the tiny room, sitting herself on a plastic five-gallon bucket. Remembering Henry's warning, she began with general pleasantries, then gradually led her toward the past and her own childhood. The old lady looked uncomfortable and gave vague answers to her questions, pleading her advanced age and defective memory. Then she offered Livia tea and went outside to make it, on a tiny stove just outside her door.

"Jasmine, my favorite kind," she said to her host as she returned. "The scent is so wonderful. I used to drink it in Taiwan all the time." The old lady told Livia that her own family had originally came from the province of Fujian, where the local teas were similar to those grown across the straits in Taiwan.

Granny began to warm to her, and finally posed her own question to Livia "Do you remember me at all?"

"No," she said, being careful with her words. "I suppose I was too young. Did you belong to the mission congregation?"

The vagueness of Livia's own memory seemed to relieve Granny Wang. "I was there a few times. I think I may have seen you once or twice. You were just a toddler." Her fears relieved, the old lady gave her two pieces of information beyond what Henry had already discovered. "Your friend told me that you are looking for Lin Kaiyuan and Chen Bailian. I've been asking around and have found that Bailian, who was your sister's amah, entered the Buddhist order at Guangji Monastery on the other side of Beijing, so you could try asking about her there. It's on Fuchengnei Street, west of the Three Seas area. Do you know that place?"

Livia nodded. "I'll find it." She thought of how easy it was to get around Beijing. All the streets ran north-south or east-west. Just follow the numbers. Impossible to get lost.

"I have seen Lin Kaiyuan a few times, but not recently."

"Well, thank you for asking after him," Livia said, mentioning to the old lady that she wanted to stop by at 42 Flower Market Street to see what was left of the Presbyterian mission.

"You may be too late," Granny said. "They are tearing it down to add new classrooms for the middle school. Today. You'd better go right now if you want to see anything."

Thanking her profusely, Livia left Granny Wang immediately, following the street numbers eastward. Why the hell had she put this off so long? Sure, she was busy the first weeks, but she should have come right away. She followed the numbers down Flower Market Street until she came to 42. On the pillar opposite a sign said *Middle School 27*. She entered the gate and saw the new classroom building off to the right as Henry had described it; to the left a demolition was in progress, clouds of dust rising above piles of splintered wood and broken plaster. Her heart sank as she saw her desire to reconnect with childhood memories crushed by the bulldozer that had destroyed the house before she had arrived. There would be no running her hand on a wooden door frame, or walking on the same courtyard paving stones where she had played as a child. The old mission house was rubble.

And then she saw a man she had not noticed before, sitting on a low wall to the left and behind her, watching the demolition. She could not see his face, but something about the angle of his shoulders and the tilt of his head suggested dejection. She walked over to the wall and sat next to him. He glanced at her, then looked away quickly. The two of them sat there, together, watching as the last wall of the building collapsed into the dust. One group of workers pushed bricks, plaster, and shattered wood, left by the bulldozer, into heaps. Another crew was pitching them onto the bed of an ancient truck.

Livia was curious about the man but wasn't sure how to begin a conversation. Finally, she said, "Building a home takes so long. Destroying it is so fast," and when he failed to respond she decided to ask him a direct question: "Did you come here to watch them tear it down?"

He nodded. "An old friend told me they were tearing it down. So I came. I used to work here . . . Are you an American?" Another silence followed as she looked at him more closely. The man was wearing a threadbare blue Mao jacket and could have used a shave, so she thought he meant he had worked at the middle school, perhaps as a janitor or grounds keeper. He was elderly, his hair gray and short. Roundish face, large ears, and crow's-feet at the corners of his eyes gave him a fixed, pleasant look, though he was not actually smiling.

"Yes, I am," she answered. She introduced herself, using her Chinese name. "My name is Wei Liya."

"Wei Liya," he repeated. "That's strange. These buildings they are now destroying were once part of a Christian mission. It was built long ago, before the Japanese came. The surname of the last pastor and his family was also Wei, and their second daughter was named Liya. But that was a long time ago."

Livia was speechless, knowing then who he was. Instead of saying his name or asking him directly, she fumbled inside her backpack and took out a small album of photos, flipping pages to a photo of the staff of the Beijing mission taken in 1939: Harold and Adele with Victoria between them. To Adele's left stood Bailian, to Harold's right Kaiyuan. She held it over for the man to look at. He studied it carefully. He looked back at Livia, looked again at the photograph, seemingly speechless, too. She saw that his eyes were shining. "I think you are truly a Western ghost," he said finally. "Where did you get this photo?"

"They are my parents. And that is Jiejie, my elder sister . . . the one who was lost."

"I know who they are," he said, looking away to hide the tears that came to his eyes. "All of that happened when I was a young man . . . and you are Meimei," he said finally, looking at her again, and using the term of endearment that he had called her so long ago. Then, grinning through his tears and tugging on his earlobe, he pointed to his own image: "You see that young fellow with the big ears. That's me."

"Yes, I know. And that means you are a Buddhist holy man, for all his statues show Gautama Buddha with big ears." Livia was stunned. Was this karmic destiny? She had found Lin Kaiyuan, without even trying.

He laughed and shook his head. "Forty years! Wars, revolutions, years of reviling your country. And now we are friends again. Who can know what is next!"

She took his gnarled hand and held it. He did not pull away. "Do you remember the poem about Cixi Taihou that you taught me . . . and climbing the mountain? I used to sing it in the detention camp. '*Wo wo shou . . .*'" She recited it for him, a childish singsong, and she could see his lips saying the same words with her as she spoke. "Where did you get that song?"

"I can't believe you still remember it. I have not heard those words for forty years! I learned the tune in elementary school but made up the words myself."

"Why did you choose those words?"

"Because I could tell your spirit was strong. You would do big things in your life."

"You were wrong about that," she said, thinking of the procrastination, the excuses, and how long it had taken her to get here. "I am a very ordinary person."

They talked for an hour. She asked him about his life. He had been for many years, beginning right after the Revolution, an officer with the public-safety bureau. Then, when he turned forty-five, he was made an inspector. Ten years later he retired and now lived with his wife in the Chaoyang district just east of where the old gate had been, near the Temple of the Eastern Peak. He knew nothing of Bailian's whereabouts, although he had heard that she had become a Buddhist nun. He wagged his head. "That really pissed off her old man!" He also knew of Old Chen's death. "I am sorry that we could not protect him. At that time gangs of Red Guards controlled most of the city. When they weren't fighting the counterrevolutionaries or each other, they attacked us, the police. Can you believe that?"

"I've heard it was a terrible time." Livia told him of her mother's death and that her father was still working for the Presbyterian missions, now intending to go to Taiwan. She skipped the account of her father's downward spiral and his second marriage. And then, finally, she could hold the question no longer. "My sister, Victoria . . . Do you think she could still be alive?"

Kaiyuan shook his head sadly. "I don't know. We hoped so, for so long. Probably not, or she would have turned up by now. A little

Western ghost would be hard to hide all these years among the people of the yellow earth." The old man put his fingertips to his temples as though trying to remember something. "Old Zhang and I drove them to the temple that night. But we waited in a tea shop on the opposite side of the square, so we saw nothing. Only afterward, your father called us, and I remember us pushing through the crowds calling her name and trying to find her. Your mother wouldn't give up . . . And then, finally, driving back to the mission that night without her. It was terrible. The police searched for days but without success. When I became an inspector, I remembered that night and went to public-security headquarters in the Xuanwu District trying to find her case file, but she disappeared at the time of Japanese occupation. The war followed, then the revolution. Everything was confused, many records scattered or destroyed. I could find nothing about a little foreign ghost who had disappeared at White Cloud Temple."

He handed her his card, which said, *Lin Kaiyuan, Inspector, Public Security. Retired.* "You must come to visit me and my wife this Sunday. The address is on the card. We will teach you how to make dumplings. We started making them every Sunday when our two daughters were young and we carry on the tradition still. The best dumplings in Beijing!" Then his mood shifted. "That we met today, is *ming*," he said, pointing upward. Destiny. "What happens in life is determined by Heaven, not by chance."

"My mother would have called it yuanfen."

"That, too."

The next day Livia found Guangji Monastery, on Fuchengnei Street, just west of The Forbidden City. The sign to the right of the gate indicated that Guangji was the national headquarters of the China Buddhist Association, which gave Livia hope they would have records. When the office clerk found that she was an American, he went to find a monk who spoke some English. She and the new monk spoke in the quiet central courtyard of the monastery, sitting on some stone steps on the west side of the enclosure. There were many trees, and the stones of the shaded courtyard were covered with moss. It was hard to say whether her Chinese or his English was more fluent. They used both languages as they tried to converse.

First she told him about her research, and he obliged by helping her to locate some of the most important nunneries in North China. They spoke of the secularization of Buddhist institutions during the Cultural Revolution and the current improved situation since Deng Xiaoping's opening and liberalization program. Now some monks and nuns had gotten permission to return to their communities. "Like myself," he said, smiling. His religious name was Fuyun, Floating Cloud.

Then she asked about Chen Bailian. "I think she must have entered the order sometime after the end of the war and before the establishment of the People's Republic. Chen Bailian, of course, was her family name," Livia explained needlessly.

"That was a long time ago. She would have been given a new name when she entered the path, and she'd be known by that name now for very many years. She might not be a nun anymore. Who knows? Many have left, you know, and many have died in the chaos. Do you know her Buddhist name?"

"No. But she was my amah. I was born here in China, too, in 1940." Livia asked Fuyun if the monastery kept records of when a person left home, and if so, wouldn't they indicate the person's previous name, before they took the three refuges and joined the Buddhist community. "I take refuge in the Buddha, the Dharma, and the Sangha," she said, repeating the sacred formula.

The monk seemed moved that she would say those familiar words, ones that he himself would have recited as he left the world to follow the Buddha's path. His attitude changed slightly. "It is possible that such information exists. But so much has been lost—our records, our sutras, our images—during the years of the Cultural Revolution. The records are a mess here, some lost forever. But I will speak with the archivist. You come back next week. I will tell you if we have any information for you." Livia left with a flicker of hope in her heart.

大同

CHAPTER 28

Datong

April 1985.

She had taught her courses, done her research. But still no progress in the quest to find her sister, and now a sense of urgency seized her, almost panic, as she realized she had only six weeks left in China before her visa expired. It had taken longer than expected, but she had finally got word from Fuyun that he had information for her. "Wei Liya, I have good news," he had said as he slid into the visitors' room where she was waiting. "Our librarian has found the record of Chen Bailian's entry into the Dharma path. It was on Guanyin's birthday, in 1950, here at Guangji. Her religious name is Shanghui. She lived for ten years nearby, in a nunnery affiliated with us, then transferred to Huayan Temple in Datong. You must begin your search there, but be prepared for disappointment. That was about twenty-five years ago."

"Thank you so much!" burst out Livia, reaching out to seize his hand in her excitement. He jerked his hand free and stepped backward, as though she had seared him with a hot poker. "Oh, I'm so sorry. I know that monks are not supposed to touch women." She backed up to a respectful distance.

Fuyun forced a tight smile, bowed, and left quickly, like a man fleeing a sudden occasion of sin. "I hope that you find her," he said over his shoulder.

Coincidentally, as she began to make plans to go to Huayan Temple, she discovered that her university had organized a short trip to Datong the following weekend for foreign experts and graduate students. Led by Professor Tang, head of International Studies, they would visit the famous Yungang Caves at Datong on Saturday, stay overnight, visit Longxian, a twelve-hundred-year-old pagoda on Sunday morning, then return to Beijing. Livia, Rachel, and Terri had signed up for the trip. Suddenly it felt like some providence was clearing a path for her.

It was about ten at night in Datong. She was standing on a raised terrace outside the East is Red Hotel, escaping from the Western pop music blaring from amplifiers in the ball room. She walked over to the balustrade, placing her hands on the railing. Below her, the city spread out toward the horizon, the lights mostly dim and the buildings indistinct, though a few hotels with their neon signs popped out of the murky nightscape. In this smoggy city, somewhere about a mile to the west, was Huayan Monastery. If she was lucky, Bailian might still be there. The night was warm and the city was quiet, except for the blare of karaoke from the ballroom Livia had just escaped. Terri came out to join her on the terrace, sitting on the balustrade and looking out at the city. "God that music's awful. They think it is the coolest thing, but it's at least ten years old—even in the corn belt."

"What we heard this morning, outside the caves, was fifteen hundred years old. And I liked it better—so uncool," confessed Livia. "I feel like some relic of the past!"

"Just say you're classical, like the music," Terri said.

"I'm still trying to process what happened today. I'm trying to find a Buddhist nun, so I wanted to fill myself with the feeling of the place, but now I just feel disoriented, like I've been marched through three entirely different human ages in the space of five hours: the Buddhist, the Socialist, and now the Western. It's scary. Did you ever feel like you should have been born in some other age or in some other place?"

"Nope. I'm twentieth-century America all the way."

"I guess most normal people are. This morning I looked at those Buddhas and bodhisattvas and felt something like a kinship, some kind of connection with them. Maybe I'm imagining it. Then I walk out here tonight and look at this ugly coal city and think about the grimness of socialist planning. I asked our guide this afternoon if he didn't think it was dangerous living in a city like this, in the midst of polluted air and coal dust. You know what he said? 'I think we who live in Datong are bodhisattvas for the people of China. We will all die young, but it will be for the welfare of the rest of China.' You have to be young to talk like that! Buddhist Datong lasted over a millennium, the socialist city lasted only thirty or forty years. And now the Western city of neon signs, flashing lights, and karaoke crooners. How long will it last?"

"That's not all. D'you know what's going on in the hotel basement?" Terri asked. Livia shook her head. "You've got to see it. There's a sign at the top of the steps: *Dancing lessons downstairs.* I must be getting desperate, but I went down to check it out. At the bottom of the steps was a long corridor with a lot of doors on both sides. There was a red light bulb outside each room! Five lights were on, I counted them. They can put up signs for dance classes, but everyone knows they're selling sex. I asked the attendant, just to needle him a bit, if the rooms were big enough for two people to tango. He said, 'Big enough. But dancing lessons for men. We have no teachers for women.' He said all of this with a straight face. So that's part of your new world, too. And guess what? I heard Professor Tang say the People's Liberation Army runs this hotel and its various enterprises. Mao would roll over in his grave!"

"I doubt it. I think he'd be down there learning how to dance. Or more likely, order an instructor to come up to visit his penthouse suite. Come on. Let's try again," she said, taking Terri's hand as they returned to the ballroom.

The morning after the karaoke party, Livia left the group. She informed Tang that she had a research project to pursue and would not be returning to Beijing on the bus with them. "Sorry to miss the Longxian pagoda, but I'll come by train the next day, in time for my Monday afternoon class." That would allow her to explore Datong on her own.

She found Huayan Monastery with no trouble, on Xida Street in the southwestern corner of the city. It was quite large, with a temple of five golden Buddhas on a terrace above and below a building that housed a library of some eighteen thousand sutras, one of the most important collections of Buddhist writings in China. Other records were carefully preserved as well, and the archivist was able to help her navigate them. Shanghui, she discovered, had come here from Guangji Temple in Beijing in 1960, as Fuyun had told her. She had then disappeared from the rolls, like so many others, during the Cultural Revolution. But unlike the majority, she had returned to Huayan twelve years later, in 1972. She had then left for Wutaishan, where she had joined a small community of nuns housed near the famous Xiantong Temple in Taihuai City. There is a chance that she may still be there, said the archivist.

As Livia left the temple and headed toward the train station, she was almost overcome with excitement. She would have to get to Wutaishan as soon as possible. Time was running out, and maybe Rachel or Terri would cover a few of her classes. She would have to make up some excuse for the trip, some bit of research she still had to do. She couldn't face telling them about the search for her sister, which now seemed totally impossible given the short time that remained. But it was her only chance.

五台山：朝拜

CHAPTER 29

Sacred Mountains

Wutaishan. May 1985.

Livia had taken the train from Beijing, returning to Datong, then headed south by bus on a two-lane road, up the steep ascent to Wutaishan, a mountainous landscape and pilgrimage destination sacred to Chinese Buddhists for the past fifteen hundred years. According to her travel guide, some of the peaks reached an altitude of more than twelve thousand feet, the rugged land revered by pilgrims as the earthly dwelling place of Wenshu, the Bodhisattva of Wisdom. It had been for centuries a meeting place for Tibetan and Chinese Buddhism. *My God,* she thought, *a millennium and a half!*

It was May, but a cold front had blown through during the night, dusting the landscape with a light coat of white, powdery snow. The north sides and higher elevations of the mountains were still covered with a heavier blanket of winter snows. Her bus, with its dozing passengers, crossed a high pass, then began a descent, maybe a thousand feet, to the central town of the region, Taihuai City. According to the guidebook, it was a monastery town with great religious significance and now was the county administrative center as well. As it happened, Bailian's Xiantong monastery, awkwardly translated by her guidebook as "Monastery of the Numinous Made Manifest," stood in the middle of town, just north of the signature icon of the place, the Ta Yuan Pagoda.

Livia stepped off the bus and looked around. It was like standing at the bottom of a gigantic bowl, with the white-topped mountains rising around the perimeter. Dusk had fallen, and she felt light-headed, shivering in the cold thin air. The shops in the town were closing. She found a small hotel. First thing tomorrow morning she would go to Xiantong monastery.

She had found Kaiyuan so easily, but he had not been present when Victoria disappeared into the crowd at White Cloud Temple. He and his wife had been friendly, teaching her how to make stuffed dumplings, but she got no help in her search. She approached the large gate of Xiantong, realizing that Bailian was her last hope. Her guidebook noted that the monastery had been first built about fifteen hundred years ago, about the same time as the barbarians were sacking Rome. She caught the implication: While this great cultural monument was being established, the West was locked in bloody barbaric battles, making it clear which culture was superior. Guidebook authors were shameless.

But a feeling of exhilaration swept over her as she walked under the pailou and entered the main gate. She stopped for a moment to enjoy the feeling, wondering how many thousands of Buddhist monks, nuns, and layfolk had passed through the gate over the millennia. The thought caused a sudden shift of perspective, as her own life and its purposes suddenly seemed very small and unimportant, set off against the vastness of these cold, unchanging mountains and the passage of so many years of human history.

Livia had found Xiantong quite easily, but the porter became suspicious when she asked how to find a nun named Shanghui. "Why do you wish to see Shanghui?"

"She is a family friend of many years ago," she said guardedly. "I have been teaching at Shida this year and thought I would try to see her before I returned to America." The man seemed unconvinced, but nodded and asked her to sit down and wait for him to return. "I will bring her here."

Livia paced nervously back and forth in the waiting room of the nunnery, overwhelmed that she had actually found Chen Bailian. When the nun entered the waiting room, Livia immediately seized her hand in greeting. "Bailian! I have searched for you for so long. I am Wei Liya. You worked for my parents at the Beijing mission . . . on Flower Market Street . . . many years ago . . . you were my sister's amah . . . you remember, don't you?"—words randomly tumbling out of her mouth. She was forgetting decorum, not thinking clearly.

The nun withdrew her hand and pulled back, suspicious and distrustful. "My name is Shanghui."

"Yes, of course, I am sorry. I will remember to call you Shanghui. But you were Bailian when you worked for my parents and took care of my sister."

"That was many years ago, and I am no longer that person. I try not to think about things that happened so long ago."

"I understand. So much has changed since then."

"Why have you come here to see me?" the nun said, after an awkward period of silence.

Livia took a deep breath, then said to her more calmly: "Shanghui, I want to show you a photograph." She dug into her backpack and found the same photo she had shown to Kaiyuan. The nun seemed reluctant, but she did look at it carefully, and then said, "Yes, that is I, when I was a young girl, many years ago." She backed away from the photo, distant and cool, as though from a sordid episode in her life, showing no enthusiasm for the sudden reconnection with her past.

Her coldness flustered Livia. She could not think of what to say next. Finally, Shanghui said, "When we leave home to follow the Dharma, we leave everything—mother, father, sisters and brothers, our money, property, and status. We leave the old family, the old life, and we find a new one. That is what I did. There is no point in thinking about the past. In truth, such thoughts are harmful."

"I came here hoping you could tell me something about my sister." Livia told the nun some things about her own life, her Chinese studies, her teaching, her mother's death and her father's remarriage. "As she lay dying," she explained, "Mother asked me to come to China to search for my sister. That is why I am here." She paused, hoping for some expression of interest. "I think that my mother died a Buddhist. She was content in life and showed compassion toward the sick, like Buddha did toward all those who suffered." But as she said these words, Livia felt her hope sinking. The words sounded contrived and pretentious, even in her own ears.

"I am happy for her," said the nun coolly. "May I ask if you follow the Dharma?"

"I have studied the Dharma for many years. I have learned much from the teachings of the Buddha, and they have influenced my life in many ways."

"Knowing the teachings is not enough. Practice is what is important."

"I know that," said Livia, feeling some irritation at the nun's didactic tone. "May I ask why you decided to become a Buddhist?"

"I think that I was always a Buddhist, even when I worked at the mission. But I did not know it. Enlightenment is awakening, you know, becoming aware of what is already within you. After your father told me to leave the mission, I realized that it was my destiny to follow a different path."

"I have read my mother's diaries, and I know that she and my father did not blame you for what happened."

"Perhaps they did not blame me, but my own father did. He was very angry, not at your father, but at me. He was a Chinese father, and a Christian. I disappointed him in both respects. I did not follow the path he laid out for me. I never wanted to be married and have a family. When the Christian path closed for me, the Dharma way opened. I followed it, and I have never regretted my decision."

Despite her growing irritation, Livia thought of what a remarkable woman she was. She had made her own life, and avoided the three dependencies. She thought of the male figures in her own life—her father, the priests, her professors, Dean Webber—and knew that she herself had not escaped so cleanly. That Bailian, as a young Chinese girl, had been able to follow her own leadings, seemed a wonder.

"Reverend Mother, I will ask the question I have come to ask. Do you think that my sister could still be alive?"

"She disappeared so long ago. I am surprised you would ask after someone dead to both you and your parents, after forty-five years."

Livia felt annoyed at the answer. She could understand the nun's negative view of family, but why couldn't she give her a straight answer to the question she had asked? "I don't know how to respond, except to say that she was alive in my mother's heart and mind."

"Your mother is dead, your father is quite old, you are middle-aged and established in your profession. What can be gained by looking for your sister? Isn't it better to let go of the past and live in the present?"

"You sound like my father."

"You should listen to him. After all, the police and other authorities have searched for her and failed. How can you, a foreign woman, have any hope of finding her, especially after so long a time?"

"When my mother was dying, she suggested it was destiny, hers and mine, yuanfen as she called it, to search for Victoria. I think she would have come herself if she had lived."

"She offered no other reason for wanting you to come to China? Yuanfen. I myself think that term is used too often, too loosely. Every time some coincidence happens between people, it is said to be yuanfen."

"I have a strong leading within myself to do this. It is not just my mother's wish." It occurred to her that the nun had not directly denied that Victoria might be alive, allowing her a small shred of hope that she knew something. Perhaps the nun's elusive way of talking was her way of hiding what she knew. But why?

"Have you thought of the possibility that, even if your sister were alive, she might not wish to see you?"

"That's impossible. If she is alive, she would surely want to see me."

The nun shook her head. "I have not wished to see my father, mother, or my sisters, not for many years."

"She would want to know. I'm sure of it. I could tell her who she is and where she came from. I could offer her the chance of returning to America."

"If your sister is alive," said the nun drily, "she must, by this time, already know who she is. Where she came from may not be an important question. And as for going to America, why would she want to do that?"

"I don't know why you are arguing with me," said Livia, beginning to lose her patience. "If you know something, you must tell me. If she is alive, it is not up to you to decide. It is up to my sister."

"You do not understand our situation here." A bell rang in the distance, and Livia could see that the nun took note of it. She paused. "I will just say this: she may be alive or dead. I do not know. And if she is alive, I do not know how to find her."

That was the most straightforward thing the nun had said, yet it was still not entirely clear. The statement was placed in present tense. Had she known of her at some time in the past? But just as she was about to pursue that possibility, the nun said: "You must excuse me. It is time for evening service. I am one of the chant leaders and must be present." She rose from her seat. "And talking is not permitted after the service. I hope that you have a safe return to Beijing."

No, no, thought Livia, suddenly panicky, *it can't end like this. I can't allow her to get away so easily.* "May I return tomorrow? Could you ask some of the other nuns if they know of her?"

The nun looked displeased, but finally said: "If you must. Come late in the morning, to the monastery guesthouse. I must go now."

As Livia walked up the stone steps to the main gate of Xiantong Monastery the next day, she thought that even if she were never able to find her sister, it was already miraculous that she had found both Kaiyuan and Bailian. Perhaps it was hubris to expect another miracle in a single lifetime. Had the nun been living at one of Wutaishan's more remote locations, she would never have found her at all. She walked along the terrace on the left side of the main courtyard just outside the wall. Here, looking west, she could see groves of tall evergreens. Above them, the pines became smaller as the mountains rose in sweeps of vegetation and rocky outcroppings to the barren snow-covered peaks. She rang a small bell outside the entry to the guesthouse. Her anticipation ran high, but she could not get rid of the thought that Bailian had become her antagonist. Why wouldn't she give her a straightforward answer?

"Wei Liya, are you well today?" said the nun, as they sat down on a wall in the courtyard of the guesthouse. There was a slight note of friendliness in her voice.

"Yes, Reverend Mother. And are you well?"

"Yes."

"Have you spoken to some of the older nuns about my sister? Have any of them heard of her? It is hard for me to believe that if she is still alive and living here in China that she could have gone unnoticed. With her Western features and her red hair."

"There are hundreds of millions of Chinese people. Many faces, many appearances. Brown eyes of every shade, even a few blue and green eyes, especially here in the northwest. What chance is there to find a single person of no importance among all these millions?" The nun paused then, following these hard words with others that contained a note of compassion: "I understand that you have come a long way to seek your sister. So I ask you this. If I tell you that I have asked, and no one here has ever seen or heard of her, would you be satisfied that you have done all that is possible?"

Livia was not sure she had understood the nun. Her words seemed like another evasion, an answer to a question she had not asked. So she posed a straightforward question: "Shanghui, I will ask you: Do you yourself think my sister is dead?" Livia felt that she had come to a turning point. She wanted the nun to answer, without equivocation. She even found herself hoping that the nun would say, *Yes, neither I nor any of my sisters knows anything of her. She must have died.* Then Livia could be satisfied that she had done everything possible to carry out her mother's wishes.

Time was running out. She had found Kaiyuan and Bailian and neither could help her. There were no records of her disappearance in police files, and there was nowhere else to turn. She could go home with a clear conscience, become a department chair and live contentedly in her small college town. And try to figure out her relationship to Henry. But the nun continued to perplex her. Perhaps, she thought, her own Chinese was sometimes not equal to the task of asking questions in the right way nor understanding the nun's ambiguous answers.

"I am certain that she is dead, one way or another," said the nun after a period of silence. Livia heaved a sigh of disgust. Was the woman incapable of a straight answer? Was that answer the closing of the door, or had she once again left it open a crack? "Moreover," said the nun, "as some of the sisters have said to me last night, we do not even know who you are. You have shown me a photograph of myself and some others I have known in a previous life. But you are not in it."

"How could I be? I was not yet born!"

"You spoke of meeting Lin Kaiyuan. You could have gotten the photo from him." The nun dropped her eyes and began to count her beads, perhaps a sign that she was becoming impatient with the conversation and wished to end it. Livia could think of nothing else to say. Maybe it was time to give up and go back to Beijing.

Reluctantly, Livia rose to leave. It was then that she thought of the locket and talisman. "Before I leave, I want to show you something." She reached into her backpack and pulled out a small embroidered bag. She opened it and then turned it upside down. The locket fell into her hand. "My mother said that you gave this to Victoria," she said, handing the locket to the nun.

The nun looked at it carefully, then shuddered. Livia saw a startled look break her mask of severity. Emotion rose and colored her pallid face. "Now I believe you," she said finally. "I gave this talisman to your sister . . . so long ago. I told her that if she wore it, the god of the northern mountains would always protect her. The night we went to White Cloud Temple for the Lantern Festival, the night she disappeared, she forgot to wear it—it was why she was so upset that night. Is the talisman still inside? I would like to see it again."

"It is. Did you write it yourself?"

"I had it written."

"I've wondered why you chose the northern-mountain talisman."

Shanghui looked at her, as though baffled. "Because here in the north we live under the protection of the god of Hengshan, the northern mountains. And of Bodhisattva Wenshu."

The nun then looked carefully at the faded piece of paper and the blurred characters. She shook her head, returning the paper and locket to Livia. "I have not detached myself from the past as completely as I had hoped. I may be able to get some information for you. I am not certain, and it might take some days, but I will try. Give me your name card. I will write to you in Beijing if I am successful. Then, if you are able, you may return and we will talk again."

Two days later she was back in Beijing, her mind now alive with possibilities, waiting at the US consulate on Xiushui East Road. It was one of the most attractive neighborhoods of Beijing, the tree-lined streets quiet and breathing an air of secrecy, with the grand embassies and consulates of many nations hidden behind high walls. She had walked passed fifty or sixty Chinese people standing in a line that wrapped around the corner, feeling privileged to go ahead of this long queue of supplicants. She was admitted at the main gate by an American soldier with a buzz cut, who checked her passport before allowing her to enter. He showed her to a waiting room full of people where she sat for an hour until an attaché, a young man in a dress shirt and slacks, called her name. "Miss Wayman?" His name was Carl Reed. He didn't seem to know much about citizenship issues.

"Your sister disappeared?"

"Yes, perhaps kidnapped, long ago. I don't know if she is alive, but if she is, and I can find her, I need to know some things. I've got to know what to do if I find her and she wants to return with me to the States."

"Miss Wayman, I didn't hear that. If your sister is alive, an attempt to get her out of China would cause an international incident. The Chinese would be enraged."

"Could she be a Chinese citizen? By this time, she would have somehow lived here for over forty years."

"I don't see how she could be a Chinese citizen. She would have no national identity. She is not an American citizen, and frankly, Miss Wayman, without citizenship she has no identity at all."

"She was born to parents who were both American citizens."

"But she was born in China. They would have to have applied to get citizenship for her."

"I know they didn't."

"Did you say she might have been kidnapped? If so, the case could be made that she was kept here unwillingly. That might open a door to something."

Livia sighed, aware that they were talking hypothetically. Mr. Reed did not know the rules that would apply to such an unusual case, but he promised to talk to one of their consular experts. He asked her to return in a week. A feeling of extreme frustration grasped her heart. Always "come back later," but she was running out of time!

One thing was clear. If Livia wanted to take her sister to the United States, she would have to first get her back here to safety in the US embassy until her case could be adjudicated. That could be extremely difficult.

地坛

CHAPTER 30

At the Altar of Earth

Back at Shida she was in the mail room picking up a couple of letters, one from her dad, one from her dean.

"Livia!"

She turned and there was Henry. She hugged him, which seemed to unnerve him less than usual, but when she tried to kiss him on the cheek, he pulled away.

"OK, sorry," she said as she watched him run his fingers nervously through his hair. "So your visa finally came through. How long will you be here?"

"A couple of months in China, mostly in Fujian. Same dialect as Taiwan so I'll hit the ground running. And there's much more religious activity going on down there than there is here. It seems like the farther you get from Beijing, the more things loosen up religiously." Henry had to leave for an appointment, but they agreed to spend the next day together.

She tore open the letter from Webber, which was just a bit of cheerleading, reminding her to gather her research materials so that she would have lots to work on when she returned to her administrative responsibilities. Harold's letter was brief, a note inviting her to visit them in Taipei—if she had the time. His letter could not be mailed directly from Taiwan to China but had to be routed to her via Presbyterian headquarters in Tokyo. More disturbing, in the same envelope, was a page from Tillie, urging her to come. *It's typical of him to say, "If you have time." He's having some heart problems. Started a week after we arrived. The doctor can't say for certain, but there is a chance that if you don't come now you might not see him again.* Since Tillie would normally not be eager for her to visit, Livia was alarmed. She called JAL immediately and booked her ticket for the following weekend.

The next day, late in the morning, Livia and Henry met at the Altar of Earth. They were sitting on the southeast corner of the platform, enjoying the sun on their faces. They let their feet swing rhythmically.

"Takes me back to my childhood, Henry."

Henry nodded and smiled, but said nothing. It was a brilliant day, the yellow tiles that lined the walls of the square compound gleamed brightly in the sun. The green grass, the clear blue sky, the lipstick red of the pillars and doors of the temple buildings completed the bright palette. The Chinese emperor used to come here, north of the Forbidden City, to worship the spirits of the earth at the summer solstice—the gods of various mountains, the rivers, the seas, and the spirit of Sovereign Earth. Now it was just a park, but unlike the popular Altar of Heaven to the south, rarely visited by tourists. So they mostly had the place to themselves.

"Henry, you could have flown straight to Shanghai. Is this detour because of me?"

Before he could answer there was a loud clatter as two young skateboarders rolled into the compound through the east gate. While waiting for the noise to abate, she looked over her left shoulder and saw a young man wearing a cowboy hat with a guitar strapped over his shoulder. He sat down and began to tune it.

"Skateboards and cowboys. What next? Ever since Deng went to the US and wore that ten-gallon hat, cowboy music has been hot in China," commented Livia. Henry did not respond.

"What?" he said finally. "I know you got me here because you want to say something." As she was about to speak, the man with the guitar began playing "The Yellow Rose of Texas." So she said nothing, thinking the music not a suitable background for what she wanted to say. The man went on with "Home on the Range," followed by "The Old Chisholm Trail," his technique not bad.

"Henry, it's time for us to talk," she said when the music finally stopped.

"About what?"

"About us, our relationship. We keep tiptoeing around the subject. I mean, we go back a long way. You keep coming in and out of my life. And I've noticed lately that you don't get so nervous when I hug you—although kisses are still out of bounds. Is that a warming trend? We're good friends and you've helped me tremendously, so many times. But I want to know if there's something more . . . I think *intimacy* is the word I'm looking for. That's what I want to talk about."

She looked aside at Henry, sitting on the edge of the altar, his long legs dangling over the side. His eyes were fixed on something below them. He looked uncomfortable. "My dad once remarked how few people there are," she continued, "even in the course of a long life, with whom we can claim intimacy. That really hit me. I guess I'm feeling my age. My mom is dead and now Dad may be dying too—I'm flying to see him in Taiwan next week. I can't keep putting off things. Are we something more than friends? And if we are, is this something we should acknowledge? Or even celebrate?" Circling around, the two boys on skateboards clattered by, giving Henry time to think. He stared straight ahead but said nothing.

"Talk to me Henry. What do you think?"

His discomfort was obvious. She had the sense that he would respond vaguely, that some kind of evasion, some kind of weasel words would follow, allowing him as usual to avoid the subject. So it was a complete surprise when he said: "Well, Livia, I'll just say it. I love you. I always have." It was her turn to be speechless.

After a long pause, she finally said: "I want to say the same words back to you, but I can't, at least not just now. I love you in some way. There's no doubt about that. It's saying the words that puts me off. I think because that word *love* is so muddled in my mind with all the conventional understandings of what it is supposed to mean. I mean, if we had jumped in the sack and had fantastic sex, plus all the other stuff we do have, well, I guess I wouldn't hesitate. Oh shit . . . what I'm asking is, do we have something special between us, something strong enough to . . . evolve into some kind of commitment?"

Livia looked at him, and she saw, behind his glasses, a helpless look in his eyes. "It's hell, isn't it?" he said. "Here we are, professors . . . we make our living standing in front of audiences fluently expounding all sorts of complex ideas . . . but we stumble and bumble around trying to express the simplest feelings."

"Yeah, the most important things. It's pitiful," she said, intuiting his thought but also unable to put it into words.

"Are you saying we should try living together?"

"I think you might be a tolerable roommate," she said, after a pause, trying to lighten the mood a bit. "And I'm not aiming at sex . . . really, no expectations. Friends, living together. Why not take the step and see what happens?"

"Livia, this is so hard for me," he said, his voice choking slightly. "I'm just scared to death that I won't . . . that I will disappoint you. I'm afraid I could never . . . be the partner you deserve."

"There's only one way to find out—except that I'm not sure how we could do it. You're in Boston, I'm in Ohio. Neither one of us is going to just quit our jobs and move to the other city. I know that."

"Well, that part might not be so hard. There are two or three couples at my university that have these long-distance relationships. One flies to St. Louis, then two weeks later the other flies to Boston. So for each one, it's just once a month you have to make the trip. It can be done."

"Maybe something like that could work . . . You know when I first had to face my feelings for you? When you came to visit and got jealous of Irmgard that night the three of us were together. Until then I would never have thought we were more than good buddies."

"Yeah. That's when it hit me, too. I hated myself that night. Inside I knew it was always more than just friendship, at least on my side, but I couldn't let myself admit it. I didn't know how to express my feelings for you. Especially the physical part. And if I couldn't express it physically, why try to put it into words? Even now I don't know what to say. Have you ever heard of Klinefelter's? I've been talking to an MD about it. It's possible that there is a physiological basis for my . . . uh, sexual apathy, and it might be treatable. It goes back a long way. In high school I had to pretend to have the same feelings as the other guys, you know, horny for the girls, talking about who puts out and who doesn't—all that teenage boy crap. Then when I got to college I began to face the fact that I might be gay, but honestly, I couldn't think of a single male that I ever felt attracted to. Sexually I mean." Henry stopped speaking and put his face into his hands.

She let his confession hang in the air for a while. "I had a really bad experience in high school, too," she said finally. "A nun made a sexual advance to me." Livia searched for words to express what had happened. "She touched me. At first I didn't feel repelled by it . . . no, I want to be honest. I was excited by it. But then I ran. I can't say exactly what happened—maybe I've blocked it—but it was a terrible experience. It went against the morals I had been taught to believe. It was a vulnerable time for me, and I was just overwhelmed with shame. I had just become a Catholic, I was so idealistic about things. It affected me for years, and in some ways I don't think I'm over it yet. I tried to have a male-female relationship a few times since, but they never quite worked out. And I never knew whether it was because I was really a lesbian or whether I just hadn't found the right guy. Or maybe I am both . . . Why is life so damn complicated?"

They had gotten to a place of shared discomfort, if that was an achievement. Where to go from there? Finally, Henry shook his head and laughed gently: "A heap o' problems . . . maybe we should completely shift gears here and do it the old fashioned way."

"Like what?"

"The old leap of faith. Publish the banns. Get married . . . I could get on my knees with a ring in a little velvet box and profess my hopes and expectations."

"What?" said Livia, in feigned shock. "You didn't bring the damn diamond? But I *like* the part where you get down on your knees. And, by the way, if you want to go traditional, you should think about flying to

Taiwan with me and asking Dad for my hand in holy wedlock. I want four bridesmaids, a flower girl, a ring bearer . . ."

It all ended in farce, Livia wondering if they had accomplished anything. But as they walked companionably from the old imperial altar toward the Anding Metro station, holding hands, she realized that if they had not solved everything, they had at least made a start.

The flight from Beijing to Taipei was roundabout—no direct air connections between the two Chinas. She landed at Tokyo-Narita on time, the connection with China Airlines was prompt and her 737 to Taipei landed on schedule. When she walked through the outer doors at arrival and left the terminal air conditioning, Livia was hit by the heat and humidity like a blast from the door of an industrial oven. What a contrast to the clear and cold weather at Wutaishan, just a week earlier. She took a train from the airport to Taipei central, then found a taxi to take her to the Presbyterian church where Harold and Tillie were staying. It was on Aikuo Road, not far from the university where she had done language studies in 1964, over twenty years ago.

As the taxi headed south, she marveled at the changes in the city. Highrise buildings everywhere, broad boulevards with green medians planted with palms, lavender bougainvillea, red and white oleander, and well-tended flower beds. When she first lived here, the only private cars belonged to Chiang K'ai-shek's generals—old Fords, Chryslers, Buicks, all black and shiny. The generals went to a lot of meetings. She remembered passing hotels and seeing fleets of the gloomy cars outside being groomed by their drivers with soft rags and feather dusters, like mahouts pampering their elephants. And inside the hotel, around a conference table, she imagined the generals presenting their fantastic plans for retaking the mainland. Plans! Livia wondered if her own thoughts about a life with Henry and her hopes for finding her sister were any more realistic than the ridiculous schemes of those aging generals of Chiang K'ai-shek.

As her taxi moved along through neighborhoods, the memories came back. They passed within blocks of Snake Street on the east, and on the west she strained to see the Japanese restaurant where Henry and she had recovered after their adventure. And touched for the first time. They drove past the central plaza, and there was the same ugly presidential palace and the balcony from which Chiang K'ai-shek and his son used to wave to the crowds. It was a different country now. Peanut was long dead, and Froggy, the former secret service chieftain, a budding democrat.

The door to their apartment opened and Livia read a bit of optimism in Tillie's face, even before she spoke. "I'm glad you could come. It will mean a lot to him," she said.

Livia made an effort at congeniality. "Tillie, thank you for the letter. And for all you've done for Dad." Tillie nodded and offered her hand. "What do the doctors say?"

"The doctor thinks it is some early stage of congestive heart trouble. It might be temporary. It might not."

"Are you going to return to the States?"

"When he gets better. Right now the trip would be too hard on him."

"How are his spirits?"

"They could be better. You'll see. Just don't expect too much of him. He needs his rest."

Livia entered the bedroom. Her father was propped up on his pillows, appearing to be asleep. She took his hand in hers and leaned down to kiss his forehead. His eyes opened. "My little Papist." He smiled faintly. "Thanks for coming. And for all the letters you've sent." His hair was rumpled from sleeping, and though it was mostly still black, at his part she could see the gray roots. The sight touched her.

"Living in China has been great," she managed. "Sometimes it feels like I've come home."

"I'm sure I wouldn't recognize it," he said, shifting from his slump into a more upright position. "Hard for me to imagine how much it must have changed since the '40s. Here in Taiwan they consider it the devil's workshop."

"Well, then the devil must be a crane operator. There's so much new construction—roads, banks, office buildings, hotels, high-rises going up all over Beijing. You wouldn't believe it. Half of the cranes in the world must be there!"

"It used to feel so flat to me. The highest structure was the Drum Tower. Of course it wasn't the capital then . . . What's it like teaching at Beijing Normal? And how's your research coming? And the other search?" He didn't want to say Victoria's name.

"I've never taught such earnest students. They write down everything I say like it's straight from Mount Sinai. I've been interviewing lots of Buddhist nuns. Fascinating stories. I'll have lots of work to do putting them in order, for articles or maybe a book. With the search for Victoria, I don't know if I'm getting anywhere. I wrote you about running into Kaiyuan at the old mission site. And of meeting Old Wang Taitai. You do remember her, don't you?"

"Oh yes, she was one of the faithful. Maybe she was afraid to say it, but she never missed a day at worship. The righteous Wang Taitai. Say hello for me if you see her or Kaiyuan again."

"Neither of them could help me much. But just last week I finally found Bailian, living in a nunnery at Wutaishan. She had joined the order right after the revolution. She was not very welcoming or cooperative."

"I'm not surprised. I felt I had to let her go after Victoria disappeared. I felt badly about that, but if she hadn't let Victoria get away from her . . . I can see why Bailian didn't want to help you. Meeting you would have dredged up a lot of unhappy memories."

"I really don't think it's that. She's a Buddhist nun—wouldn't be clinging to old disappointments from so long ago. I have the feeling that she knows something that she can't or won't tell me."

"Where do you go from here? How much longer are you going to continue looking?"

"I've only got two weeks of teaching left, then exams, then back to the States. So it would be a miracle if I got anywhere with this."

"I warned you," he said.

Tillie appeared at the door. "Would you two like a cup of tea?" Getting an affirmative nod from both, she headed back toward the kitchen.

"Dad, I know you think your mission to China was a failure—"

"Let me count the ways."

"I can remember you saying that after four hundred years of missionary work, there were so few Christians in China . . ."

"And probably a lot fewer now—after forty years of Communist propaganda and the Cultural Revolution."

"Just the opposite. Way more."

"Really? That's hard to believe."

"Seems that after all the missionaries got kicked out, the Chinese made Christianity their own—now the emphasis is on healing and Jesus as a healer of the sick. Groups all over China are meeting in homes. Some of the young ministers go flying around the countryside every Sunday on their motorcycles, stopping for gatherings at five or six different homes. I've seen estimates of thirty or forty million Chinese Christians."

Harold shook his head in disbelief. "Well, that's just somebody's guess. You can't believe such numbers."

"Yeah, they're not census figures. But whatever the number, there are way more than there used to be. So smile and take some credit for this growth. And think of the individuals. Mrs. Wang is still a Christian, I'll bet, and Old Chen died as a Christian. A martyr, really. I'm sure his faith gave him the strength to face up to the Red Guards."

Tillie came back with a tray. Teapot, three cups, and cookies on a plate. She poured a cup for each of them.

"How are the Papists doing? I presume you're still of that persuasion."

"Growing, too, but not as fast as your Protestants. Half the Catholics are loyalists, accepting the Party control, ordination of bishops, and that sort of thing. The other half is underground, loyal to the Vatican. It's a touchy situation. And yes, I'm still a Catholic, though not a very good one. I've started thinking of myself as a sort of pilgrim—like it's not an accident that the place I'm searching for Victoria is Wutaishan, where the Buddhists have gone on pilgrimage for over a thousand years."

"Pilgrimage," he said, a bit of mockery in his voice. "So you're what . . . a Buddho-Catholic?"

"I'd rather not use a label. I could say I look out at the world as a Christian but sometimes through Buddhist spectacles . . . Anyway, the famous *Pilgrim's Progress* was written by a good Protestant, wasn't it? And the practice of pilgrimage is a universal among the world's religions."

"What do you mean by the Buddhist spectacles?"

Livia thought about that for a while. "Well, one example: I think more now about the huge silence of Catholicism, which is usually forgotten amid all the sermons, encyclicals, pronouncements, and creedal statements . . . I think of the centuries of silence of the monks, nuns, and priests, meditating in monasteries and religious communities all over the world . . . just an example."

"I like that," he said, closing his eyes. "The older I get the less useful I find words."

Tillie, holding up a plate of cookies, gave Livia a quick signal that pointed at the obvious—Harold was getting tired.

"Let's eat our cookies and drink our tea," Tillie said.

His eyes blinked open. "I can always rally for a good cookie," he said, taking a bite of the shortbread and sipping his tea. "The best confection of Scotland," he added, "next to the Presbyterian faith. How you managed to make these cookies in Taiwan, I'll never know . . . They don't have the right ingredients here," he explained, looking at Livia. "Tillie Grace is a wonder."

Tillie shook her head at his silliness as she stood up to leave, making a sign to Livia. "Sorry I can't stay longer, Dad. My teaching duties in China call. Let's continue the discussion next visit—back in the States. Glad to see you're still in the game."

He smiled at her in wonder, still holding on to her hand. "Thanks for coming. Never thought I would have a daughter teaching at the famous Beijing Normal University! Where did you come from, Livia?"

"The tofu man, Dad," she said impishly, and was gratified to see the look of astonishment on his face. "See you soon and we'll talk more about it."

不二

CHAPTER 31

Not Two

June 1985.

It was the final week of classes at Beijing Normal, the following week free, allowing the students to prepare for final exams. In the States this would be called the "Grand Cram," but in China there was no comparable pejorative term for it. The students called it "Earnestly Study Week." On Wednesday, before her final class, Livia found in her mailbox a brief letter postmarked from Taihuai City. *I have some information that might be useful to you. Come as soon as possible.* The Chinese characters were neat and easy to read, but the nun had signed it English style, using her secular initials *CBL.*

"Rachel," asked Livia, "can you cover for me exam week? I hope to be back here by next weekend, but if I'm not, would you mind proctoring my exam? I'll work out the test questions and leave them with you before I go."

"More intrigue! I love your exciting life. It's not a fling with a guy, is it? A full week in a five-star hotel in Shanghai, with a rich and handsome businessman? My life is such a bore. Are you making any progress with your research?"

"I'm not sure, but this trip to Wutaishan is crucial. Either I find what I'm looking for, or I'm done with it. My visa expires a week after the semester ends. And the dean is threatening to throw me under the bus—make me chair of social studies. I'll need to get back to Athena."

"Good luck, friend." She gave Livia a hug.

Livia finally reached the top of the 108 steps leading to Pusading, Bodhisattva's Peak. It was a monastery complex on a hillock that rose above the town of Taihuai, just north of Xiantong Temple where she had first inquired about Shanghui. She was breathless, and her legs ached. *Damn,* she thought, vowing to get back to regular jogging when she returned to the States. At the top of the steps was an ornate pailou, marking the entry to the temple area. She walked under the structure and sensed the feeling of crossing a threshold, the transition from a secular to a sacred place. It reinforced the odd sense that had taken hold of her, that her search was in some way a pilgrimage. Once inside, Livia turned to the left and sat down on a gently scalloped wall to catch her breath, looking down on the clusters of pine trees below her.

She had reached Datong late on Thursday, found a hotel, and took the bus to Taihuai the next morning. The porter at the nunnery had told her that the nuns were attending special services at Pusading, and would be there until late afternoon the same day. He suggested that she might wish to go there and wait for them to finish.

The gentle murmur of chanting ceased, and a bell tolled. The nuns, perhaps twenty or thirty of them, began streaming out of the front door of the temple. They crossed the courtyard and began to walk down the steps that Livia had just climbed. She watched them carefully, looking for Bailian's familiar face. The last stragglers emerged, two together, then one, then no one. Disappointed, she waited for a minute or two, then walked toward the screened walls of the temple. From inside, behind the window screen, came the nun's familiar voice in a whisper: "Wei Liya. Inside."

"I will go first," the nun said, after they had spoken briefly. "Wait a few minutes and then come to the bell tower in the first courtyard."

When she got there, Shanghui was sitting at the top of the flight of steps in front of the main door. Livia sat on the step below, facing her. It was late afternoon, but the day was clear and cool, and the sun felt good, striking them at a comfortable angle from the west. "This monastery is often visited by pilgrims. It is a good place for us to talk. We will not attract attention here."

Livia wondered at the secrecy. She noticed a number of visitors walking around the courtyard, most clustered around the large bronze incense burner near the entry to the main temple. They held the incense sticks between their folded hands, bowed toward the main image inside, then inserted the incense into the sand tray inside the burner.

"When we first talked, you asked me what happened that night at White Cloud Temple. I was reluctant to talk about it, since those who follow the Dharma should not dwell on the past. But my progress on the Buddha's way is not as great as I had hoped. I will tell you what I still remember about that night, so long ago.

"As you know, my name at that time was Chen Bailian. I was only sixteen years old, amah and cook at the mission . . ."

After she finished her account, the nun was silent. Livia thought about the power of the old Chinese belief in fate and karma, sensing something of the helplessness that her parents must have felt over forty years ago at the sudden loss of Victoria and the futility of the search for her.

"I must now tell you what I have found out about your sister. I was not certain of this when we last spoke, but now I know that she is not dead. She is in hiding. It is possible that she may be at a place not far from here." She stopped, giving Livia a chance to digest the information.

Livia felt a surge of excitement. "Will I be able to see her?"

The nun smoothed her robes over her knees and folded her hands in her lap. "I will get to that. I do not know all the facts about her, and what I do know is mostly learned from some of my older sisters, one of whom had taught her as a child. Her name is Bolai. Soon after the kidnapping they took her to a nunnery to hide and train her. She stayed there for some years. She learned how to work in the fields, to cook, to chant, to read the sutras, to meditate. She learned about medicinal herbs. Above all, she learned how to live a disciplined life."

"Did you yourself ever see her or speak to her?"

"Not in those early years. I encountered her just once, about five years ago."

"Did she know who you were?"

"Yes. I told her that I had once been her amah at the Beijing mission. She remembered. That one is very smart. She asked if I knew anything about her father and mother, but of course, I did not. All we knew was that they were taken off by the Japanese to a detention camp."

"Why didn't you tell me all this right away?"

"I had to make sure who you were. Telling the wrong person could be very dangerous—to her, to me, and even to you."

"What do you mean? How could it be dangerous?"

"Be patient. I will get to that."

Livia nodded calmly, but inside her feelings churned. Secrecy, danger? What had she stumbled into?

"So to continue. After some years, those who had taken her returned and took her away from the nunnery. Over the next years they introduced her to their own religious beliefs. It is complicated, but they were members of a secret sectarian group. They call themselves Siyishe, the FourOne Society. The *four* represents the four main religions that are approved by the Chinese government: Buddhism, Daoism, Islam, and Christianity. The *one* symbolizes that all religions are ways to the same truth, just as the four great rivers of China all flow to the eastern sea. In their communities, men and women are equal. Both can be ministers. They believe that their mission is to establish a new society in China, neither the old imperial one nor the current socialist one. And they believe in revelations brought from the spirits, messages given to mediums for the people."

"I studied a group like that in Taiwan."

"Such groups are not uncommon in China. This one has many more beliefs and practices. I am not familiar with them all. Now, Wei Liya, do you see how great the danger? The government fears and hates secret societies. They hate the idea of mediums whom they cannot control and whose words they cannot censor. They hate the talk of changing Chinese society. And they hate the existence of a person like your sister,

Bu'er. That is her name now. The authorities know that she is a revered leader, and because they cannot control her they will try to silence her, one way or another."

"Can I see her? Where can I find her?"

"That is a problem. I can tell you where to look for Bu'er, but it will be up to her to decide whether she is willing to risk meeting you or not. Knowing the danger, both to you and to her, you must decide whether you want to go on with your search. If you wish to seek her, you must begin your journey immediately. I know that your time in China is almost over."

"Shanghui, thank you for your help."

The nun took a piece of paper from inside her robe, folded in half, and gave it to her. "I have one more thing for you. It is for those who wish to go on pilgrimage to Wutaishan. Keep it until you get there. Then you will understand it."

"But I am already here," she said, puzzled.

"Not yet, but you will know when you reach the real Wutaishan."

The next day, following Bailian's instructions, Livia walked from Taihuai City on the main highway south and found the small road going off to the east. She found herself among a company of pilgrims walking from the city toward three bodhisattva shrines. No one spoke as they walked along the road, but she felt a comfort walking in their midst as they went to fulfill their sacred purpose. She wore a large pilgrim's hat she had purchased in Taihuai. It covered most of her face and made her feel almost invisible, anonymous, just one ordinary pilgrim among others.

As she walked along, she thought about her sister's name. Bu'er, "Not two." It was not an ordinary Chinese name, but she did recall encountering the name once before, in a Daoist tale. It was the name of the only woman in a group of eight whose members were seeking to become immortals. Strangely, one of the men was Qiu Chuji, the man who founded White Cloud Temple in Beijing, where Victoria had disappeared. He was the Immortal people believed came to join the crowds the day after the Lantern Festival. Of the eight students, the woman was the most intelligent and the most zealous, and their teacher predicted that she would be the first of the group to reach immortality. Livia remembered that this Bu'er, in her zeal for immortality, had harshly defaced herself to destroy her physical beauty so that she could avoid the unwanted attention of men.

Livia and her fellow pilgrims followed the road to three caves—really natural grottoes that had been transformed into places of worship. The first and most elaborate of them was Guanyindong, the Cave of the Bodhisattva Guanyin, about two miles from the main road. It was decorated in the Tibetan style, the original stone entrance almost invisible in the buoyant and colorful architecture that had been added as a façade. Destroyed by the Red Guards, the temple was now almost completely restored with fresh paint and new images. It was the goal of most of her fellow pilgrims, but she spent little time there, leaving for her intended destination, the wilderness area east of the caves.

The next cave temple was smaller, and still badly damaged. She walked to it alone, and found no one there but two monks of the Pure Land sect, cleaning up the place as best they could. After introducing herself, she asked the monks if they knew of a hermit living in the area called Bu'er. They merely smiled, shook their heads and continued to work. She asked a few more simple questions but received no answer, so she decided to move on. She wondered whether they simply didn't understand her Chinese or perhaps were unwilling to speak. An hour's walk farther on brought Livia to the last of the three caves, dedicated to the Bodhisattva of Wisdom, Wenshu. It was a wreck, filled with piles of shattered wood and apparently abandoned, but Livia thought it would offer her a good shelter for the night.

She was now at the end of the pilgrims' trail. Beyond Wenshu's cave, to the east, was wilderness. There would be many caves in the rock-walled valley, Bailian had said, some of them empty, others inhabited by solitary monks or nuns. It was in this rugged territory that she might find her sister.

Livia reached into her backpack and took out the paper Bailian had given her the previous afternoon. She looked at it again and decided to read it.

It told of a famous monk named Wu Zhuo who came to Wutaishan seeking a vision of Wenshu—the bodhisattva in whose cave she was now resting. He had not been successful, but he persisted in the search anyway, and one day, after months of looking, he saw an unearthly white light in a grove of pine trees. An old man, leading an ox, emerged from the trees. "In this world of red dust," said Wu Zhuo to the man, "where shall I find Wenshu?"

The old man answered: "One moment in deep meditation and you can build the seven jewel-studded pagodas of the Ganges—though even they will finally turn to dust. Yet if you still your mind, just one time, that is true awakening . . . This whole world is a sacred place, and every grain of sand, every blade of grass, is Wenshu."

Livia refolded the paper. Why did Bailian give her that story? It seemed to say that it was not necessary to come to Wutaishan, that the sacred mountain was everywhere, in every grain of sand. But perhaps you had to discover that for yourself. It was an intriguing idea, but she was here now and too tired to think much about it. Not two minutes after zipping herself into her sleeping bag she fell asleep, exhausted.

When she awoke the second morning, it was chilly. The oval gap of the cave mouth looked out into a sea of mist. She thought of what she would give for a cup of hot tea—then realized that she could actually make one. She had brought along a thermos with a metal cap, some loose tea leaves, and matches. She found plenty of splintered wood inside the cave shrine and built a pyramid of it at the cave mouth but just inside, protected from the damp air. The dry kindling flamed up quickly, and she warmed her hands over the small fire. She dropped a pinch of tea leaves into the metal cup and poured water over them. When her fire had burned to coals she placed the cup on a flat stone among the ashes. Then she waited patiently while the water warmed and steeped the tea leaves. When the liquid turned amber, she removed the cup from the fire, letting the metal cool until she could hold it in her two hands. She reached into her backpack and pulled out a bag of sweet biscuits she had bought on the street in Taihuai. As she drank the warm tea and ate a biscuit, the phrase *zhizu* came into her mind, "knowing what was enough."

As she sipped her tea, she thought of her meeting with the official at the US consulate and realized that the problem was greater than she had imagined. Not just finding her sister, which she still had not succeeded in doing, but how to get her back to Beijing and the embassy if she did. She now knew that Victoria was wanted by the authorities. One false move by Livia could land her in jail. But first she must find her. Reluctantly she got up, packed her bag, and continued on her way. After two hours of groping about in the mist, the fog lifted. The rays of the sun began to melt patches of the light snow where it had fallen.

The way had been hard. Late in the afternoon, after hours of rugged hiking, she found herself a cave, and decided to stop for the night. This one had no religious purpose. It was a natural cave. She had covered perhaps five or six miles during the day. The path had been rugged but discernible, making its way through rocky terrain up the valley toward the east. She had found seven caves along the way. Four were empty, natural fissures in the hillsides. Three were inhabited by recluses, two of them men and one an old woman. Livia thought how difficult it would be to live in such a remote place, even if you were young. This woman looked seventy or eighty, had short, unkempt white hair, and an obvious vigor unusual in a person so old. The hair was not as short as Buddhists wore it, but the old woman wore a threadbare black robe that made her look like a postulant nun. At each place she asked if they knew of a Bu'er who lived in the vicinity. All three shook their heads, but offered no further explanation. Livia also came upon two subsistence farmhouses, both made of piled stones without mortar. She asked them also about Bu'er and received the same answer.

As she lay in her sleeping bag that night, she thought she might be able to continue the search for another day. Two at the most, giving herself three more to return to Taihuai and on to Beijing. Her food was running low, and she was not certain how long her body could run on biscuits anyway. She could probably get food at one of the farmhouses, if there were any more ahead, but their poverty bothered her. She would be embarrassed to ask them to share what little they might have.

It was late in the morning of the next day when they came. Two young men wearing uniforms. She had stopped her trek to enjoy a vista that looked forward up the valley. They had come silently up the rocky path behind her, and just as she became aware of their presence they had seized her arms in tight, bruising grips.

"You come with us."

"Who are you?"

"You must come with us. Back to Taihuai."

"Why?"

"You come now. Or we drag you back." They were not accustomed to being resisted. One of them looped a rope tightly around her waist and began walking back in the direction from which they had come.

"Hey, I am an American. I'm not a dog on a leash," she said, stumbling in the effort to keep pace with them. "I have a valid passport and visa. It's right here in my backpack. You can look for yourselves."

"We know who you are. You come quickly."

Livia learned the meaning of *forced march*. They covered the same distance she had walked in half the time. Her feet were blistered and her legs ached. Below Wenshu cave, all three climbed into a waiting jeep and headed back to Taihuai.

黑猫白猫

CHAPTER 32

Black Cat, White Cat

She stood before Captain Xi Guiting, chief of Public Security for Taihuai City and county. He glared at the guard. "Take off the rope." He dismissed the man and lit a cigarette, exhaling through his nose and teeth, motioning her toward a chair. The teeth were stained brown.

She sat down, waiting for him to explain. The Captain said nothing. Two minutes passed and Livia finally burst out in frustration: "Why have I been arrested? I have done nothing wrong. I demand that you allow me to call the US consulate."

Again, silence. Finally, he said: "That is not possible. There was a windstorm in the Datong area and telephone lines are down. You may write a letter if you like." He drew deeply and slowly on his cigarette, and continued to gaze at her with unblinking eyes. There was a kind of feline strength and latent energy to the man. Was it sexual? She shuddered inwardly, waiting for his eyes to do the "stripping stare" as they moved down to the rest of her body, but they remained fixed on her face. "Would you like a cigarette, Miss Wei Liya?" They had confiscated her backpack and would know who she was by searching through her things, including her passport and Shida identity papers.

"I don't smoke."

"One of life's few pleasures," he said. "Are you too busy to smoke, Miss Wei? I've heard that Americans are always busy."

"Cultural comparisons are tricky. Could we get to the point? Why am I here?"

"Ah, yes, that *is* getting to the point. Why *are* you here?"

"I was invited to teach at Shida. They will soon be missing me. I must return right away."

"I think not. I have called the university, inquiring about you. They tell me you made arrangements to be gone until next weekend. So what is the hurry?"

"How did you call them if the lines are down?" The captain's face was chiseled, a mask devoid of expression, but she saw a flicker of emotion at her words. His hair was black, cut short military style, the skin taut and shining over his forehead. The man was thin to gaunt, yet he projected a tensile strength. He was an ascetic, she decided, the cigarettes smoked not for pleasure as he had implied, but as a source of energy that fueled habitual self-discipline.

Livia thought of Bailian's words, that her sister had learned a disciplined life in the nunnery. Captain Xi, she thought, was one like her, yet her opposite, a man not disciplined out of compassion for others but for the success of his own purposes, and presumably, the Party he served.

"I ask you again. Why are you here? By here I mean Wutaishan. I know why you are in Beijing."

"I am here on a kind of pilgrimage. Wutaishan is the most sacred mountain in northern China."

"I do not need a lecture about my country's geography, Miss Wei. A 'kind of' pilgrimage, you say? Are you a Buddhist?"

"I greatly admire Buddhism." He sneered at this equivocation. "Your Constitution," continued Livia, "guarantees the freedom of religion."

"And the approved religions are also stipulated: Daoism, Buddhism, Islam, Catholic and Protestant Christianity."

"Yes, and so in coming to Wutaishan I am walking with other pilgrims to the sacred places. Exercising my right to practice an approved religion."

"A religion you do not profess. And if you are here on pilgrimage, why were you apprehended so far off the normal route, miles beyond the usual pilgrim destinations?"

She could see that he was angry, struggling to keep a tight control over his feelings. "I may have gotten confused and strayed from the path."

"I completely agree with you, Miss Wei. You have definitely strayed from the correct path." He mashed his cigarette butt on a small ashtray, letting the charge sink in. Then he tapped on his cigarette pack, extracted another, lit it, and drew the smoke slowly into his mouth, then blew a circle of smoke that drifted above his head. Livia watched in amazement. Does anyone in the United States do that anymore? She had seen it done in an old movie. James Cagney? Now the Chinese were the cigarette virtuosos, the cancer statistics of tomorrow. After his display of nonchalance, he asked a pointed question: "What do you know about a person called Bu'er?"

"I do not know anything about her."

The Captain struck the desk top with the palm of his hand, momentarily losing control. "You *do* know something about her. You know that Bu'er, a nongendered name, is a woman! I do not accept lies, Miss Wayman. Again, why were you asking about her?"

Livia realized that the interrogation had moved into dangerous territory. She remembered the risks mentioned by Bailian and decide not to answer the question. Instead she repeated her demand to call the US consulate.

The Captain merely stared at her. Finally, he rapped loudly on his desk, and a guard appeared. "Take her back to her cell."

Shit! she thought. Was this the end of the road? She had been excited by the chance of finding her sister, and energized by the idea that she was a pilgrim . . . but now she was in prison! It was late in the afternoon, and her only human contact since the morning interview with Xi was the guard silently bringing her a bowl of watery soup for lunch. She wondered about the captain, a man taut as a metal spring. She had to admit to herself that she was afraid of him. He could be a cruel sadist. Or was he, after his own lights, a dedicated public servant and a loyal member of the Party? That was not clear, but there was definitely something frightening about his intensity.

Surely she would soon be released. If she did not return to Beijing Normal, they would notify the consulate. But that might take time, possibly another week. She had foolishly not given Rachel or Terri a clear idea of where she would be at Wutaishan, but at the time she had no inkling of danger.

An hour later Captain Xi had her summoned again. After another long silence, he said: "My patience is limited. I ask you again, Miss Wei, how do you know of the woman who is called Bu'er?"

"I am not going to say anything further. I want to talk to the US consulate."

"Yes," he said, "you may do that. The telephones lines may be reconnected in a week or two. Do you know that your visa expires in nine days? After that you will no longer be a welcome guest in the People's Republic. You will be here illegally." Livia again said nothing.

"Once again: How do you know of Bu'er?" Livia did not reply. "It is time, then, for you to return to your room. Being a rich American, it must be difficult for you to live in such humble quarters. But I will tell you half the families in China live in places smaller than that room."

The next day, the Captain summoned her again, morning and evening, doggedly repeating some version of the same questions. "How did you learn about Bu'er? Why do you wish to see her? Where is she?" Each time she refused to answer, vowing inwardly never to say anything that would lead them to her sister or Bailian. Finally, the Captain said, "If it were to be proven that you had come here to make contact with a seditious group, rebels who advocate overthrowing the present government, you would be tried by a court, jailed, and never again leave China. That would not be the purpose of your visit, would it? To meet with such a group?"

She said nothing.

"No, I didn't think so," he said sarcastically.

That night she sat on the edge of her cot, elbows on her knees, face in her hands, frightened as she had ever been in her life. She imagined all the dreadful things Captain Xi might do, realizing that he had plenty of time to break her. As she thought about the trajectory of her life, Livia became more and more depressed. From early on, she had been aware of the inner prompting that had pointed her to China. Yet despite her promise to her mother, she had delayed coming, distracted by her job, tenure, and other matters that had seemed important at the time. If her life had a meaning, she had played fast and loose with it.

And now, finally in China, she had put off the hard work of the real search for weeks. She had fun with her friends, ate dumplings and steamed buns, drank beer and baijiu, did some sight-seeing and acted as though the search for her sister was a personal adventure, more like a lark than a solemn obligation. She was ashamed of herself. Her notion that she was on a pilgrimage now seemed utterly pretentious, and the words she had spoken to Lin Kaiyuan came back to mock her: "I am just an ordinary person." That, at least, was true. She was physically at Wutaishan . . . but, as Bailian warned her, her spirit had not yet reached the real place. She had read the story too soon.

She tried to think what options remained. She had bungled everything, blundering into this situation and endangering her sister's safety. The best she could hope for would be to convince Captain Xi that she knew nothing about Bu'er's whereabouts, gain her freedom, and return home as soon as possible. She lay down on her cot, exhausted, and drifted off into a sleep disturbed by fearful dreams full of threats her legs were too paralyzed to flee.

Early the next morning, Livia heard a click as the door knob to her room turned. The guard, face as hard as ever, told her to follow him. They walked down the familiar corridor, but did not turn right into the office of Xi Guiting but left to another door which led to a reception area. As she entered the room, she saw a man standing with his back to her, looking out the window. He wore a gray Mao jacket, and had a round balding head fringed with wisps of white hair. He held her backpack in his right hand.

The man turned around and she saw his disarming smile, the first friendly expression she had seen in three days. He held out his hand. "I am Tang Zhigou. Are you Professor Wayman? Wei Liya? Is that correct?" Livia nodded, suddenly aware that Xi Guiting had never once addressed her as *professor*. She extended her hand to shake his. Tang then nodded for the guard to leave them. "We are returning this to you," he said, handing her the backpack. It has been examined carefully but Captain Xi assures me that nothing has been taken from it. You may wish to check." Livia looked through the backpack and found nothing missing.

Tang Zhigou motioned toward the door. "If you will, please come with me. I will explain." As she walked out the front door of the office, she fervently hoped never to see the face of Captain Xi again. They walked down the street, then turned left at the next corner, walked another block, and came to what looked like an old temple, with two stone lions guarding each side of the main gate. Green tiles covered the top of the wall, which had been painted white. "This is the Party headquarters for Taihuai county. It used to be the temple of the city god. I think we are now the gods of the city!" He chuckled.

The interior courtyard was pleasant and spacious, the eaves, brackets, pillars, and walls of the buildings bright hues of blue, green, and red. Large urns of bonsai pines and cedars stood ranged around the perimeter of the courtyard, each placed directly in front of a pillar. The sun fell cheerfully on the bright colors of the buildings and the smooth stones of the pavement.

"Come into my office, Professor Wei." She followed him into a large room furnished in a comfortable Western style. Photos of Deng Xiaoping, the governor of Shanxi, and other Party leaders were hung on the walls, along with a couple of traditional-style landscape paintings. Tang placed a pinch of tea leaves in each of two cups. He poured steaming water from a thermos into each glass, then covered each with a lid. "This is a local Guanyin tea. I hope Wenshu Bodhisattva will not be insulted."

A clever man, thought Livia, with a gentle wit. Quite a relief after humorless Captain Xi. "I am sorry that you have been so badly treated.

It was a regrettable mistake. Chinese and Americans are now friends. Sometimes it takes a while to get the message through the ranks. The ideas of the leadership are not immediately welcome at the lower levels of command."

"Thank you, Tang . . . a . . .may I ask the office you hold?"

"I am party head for Taihuai county."The highest ranking official in the locality.

"Then, thank you, Chairman Tang." She said no more, waiting for him to make the first move. She sipped her tea. "This is very good."

Tang smiled again, his round, pleasant face and engaging smile hard to resist. "Professor Wayman, please tell me what I can do for you. I would like to make amends for your treatment."

"You have no questions to ask me? Am I free to leave?"

"Yes, of course. You may return to Beijing. Or continue your travels here in Wutaishan. Whatever you wish—although I had hoped to discuss a few things with you before you leave, just to get to know you better. It is not often that we provincials get the opportunity to talk to an international visitor." Livia began to relax.

"I would be glad to do that."

"My first concern is to make sure that you did not suffer any physical violence during your detention."

"Captain Xi was harsh in his questioning. I think he was trying to frighten me. But the bullying was mental. He did not harm me physically."

"That is good to hear."

"To tell you the truth," she said, thinking, *Good cop, bad cop*, "I do not understand what this is all about. It makes me suspicious—why one official was so intimidating while the other, yourself, is so friendly and accommodating."

Tang held a pen between his thumb and forefinger. He tapped it on the desk absently, as though struggling for the right words. "Professor Wayman, I think you Americans have not yet understood what a disastrous period the Cultural Revolution was for us. The violence let loose during that period was terrible. Much suffering and many deaths. It has set us back for decades and divided the current leadership into two groups. The first group was well educated, dedicated to implementing practical policies that would help China enter the modern world. Many of these men and women had suffered through the war with Japan and the Civil War between us and the Guomindang. And the Great Leap Forward. By the early 1960s, the desire of this group was to bring an end to all the turmoil and create a period of peace and prosperity for the Chinese people.

"The second group of today's leaders are of the younger generation. They were the ones who became Red Guards during the Cultural Revolution. The schools were all closed at that time, so the only education they had was the ideology of continuing revolution and class warfare. They were judged not by their knowledge but by the zeal they displayed to preserve the ideological purity favored by Chairman Mao and the Gang of Four. I was part of the first group, Captain Xi was of the second." He paused in his account, then said in a lowered voice. "I trust you, Professor Wayman. I want to show you something." Tang reached down and pulled up his gray trouser. His brown leg was streaked with angry white scars. "The other leg is the same. I won't bother to show it to you."

Livia was horrified by the sight and moved by his small confidence. "How did that happen?"

"I was denounced by the Red Guards and beaten with bamboo rods for my so-called bourgeois counterrevolutionary views. At that time, the possession of paintings like these," he said, indicating the landscapes on his walls, "was enough to condemn a person. I was made to march through town in disgrace. Little children ran along ridiculing me and a few other unfortunates. They pushed us along with cattle prods. But I was one of the lucky ones. I did not die."

"Did Captain Xi do that?"

"Oh no. I did not know him at that time. I met him for the first time a few years ago. I am only saying that he is of that generation, a former Red Guard. He is a good officer, just a bit overzealous."

"I see. It is hard to imagine how terrible that period must have been. You may know this already, but some American leftists actually idolized Chairman Mao for his efforts, as they saw it, to preserve the pure ideals of the revolution."

"Premier Zhou Enlai used to say that the Americans were naïvely idealistic, about a number of things. You think, for example, that your democratic ideals are so compelling that they only need to be proclaimed and people will desire to follow them. We never had that illusion about our socialist principles. Comrade Deng Xiaoping has said that the color of the cat doesn't matter, black or white, as long as it can catch the mouse. Those are the words of a practical man. They describe a selective use of democracy and capitalism to achieve our overall socialist goals."

"Chairman Tang, your government may be wrong in thinking you can adopt capitalism's economic principles, and not, in the end, lose your socialist identity."

Tang raised his eyebrows. His face darkened. "An interesting thought, Professor Wayman. But I believe that you may be deceived if you think that socialism could disappear so easily."

"Perhaps. In any case, I have to be grateful to your nation that I was invited to teach here. You are paying my salary."

"I'm sure it's a good investment," Tang responded graciously. "And whether communist or capitalist, we both must deal with uncertainties and follow our principles. Professor Wayman, you do not hesitate to speak your mind. I admire that. I have enjoyed talking to you but we have detained you too long. I have reserved a room for you at the Gueike Guesthouse. I think you'll find it very comfortable. Tomorrow you may return to Beijing or stay here for a few more days. As you wish. But I know that you have only a few days left on your visa, so you need to be on your way home before it expires."

That night Livia sat in the small bar of the Gueike, sipping an Old Turkey bourbon straight up, expensive as hell, imported all the way from Kentucky. She was the only foreigner. The few others in the bar, mostly Chinese business types, were drinking baijiu. She was thinking of the incongruity of swigging whiskey in this holy land of Buddhism, but felt she owed herself a little indulgence after having emerged from what seemed like a medieval Chinese dungeon into the modern world, all in a single day.

Emotionally exhausted by her ordeal, she felt the impulse to return to Beijing the next day, read her students' exams, and fly to the States as soon as possible. But words rose in her mind, the jingle that Kaiyuan had taught her: *Wo pa shan. I will climb the mountain.* And in the place of the adolescent zest for her pilgrimage, a more sober and fierce determination took hold of her: to fulfill the solemn promise she had made to her mother. She would return to the desolate valley where Captain Xi's men had taken her and in the short time that remained continue the search for her sister.

姐妹

Chapter 33

Sisters

Livia began her trip by hiring a local taxi to take her as far as Wenshudong, saving herself a full day's walk. She paid the driver and began by bowing to the Bodhisattva Wenshu, even though there was no statue of him in the rubble of the empty cave, then headed east toward the wilderness area. If the nun's little story meant anything at all, and the bodhisattva was in every blade of grass, then he was also in the empty space left by the destruction of his image and in the trackless area where she was headed as well.

She hiked east on the same trail she had followed four days earlier. In her backpack she had water, some crackers, a small jar of unsweetened peanut butter, some tea leaves, and three bananas. She had read somewhere that the fruit was a perfect food and you could survive on bananas for a full month without suffering any nutritional deficiency.

She had decided to wear the talisman for the search. She wasn't sure she believed it could help her, but it couldn't hurt. She walked quickly past some of the caves passed previously, but did not stop until late in the afternoon when she reached the last of the seven. It was time to find shelter for the night, and there she found the same old woman in the tattered black robe she had questioned on the first trip. This time she was hoeing her garden of greens, a tiny plot on a small area of good soil to the left of the cave entrance, where a trickle of water fell into a small catch basin. The woman was small and wizened, her skin brown and wrinkled by years of exposure to the sun. She looked more like a peasant than a nun. She nodded to Livia as she came up the path.

Without much hope of a different response Livia asked the old lady the same question she had asked three days ago: Did she know of a person named Bu'er?

Instead of a denial, this time the woman said, "Have you eaten yet?" It was the standard Chinese greeting, but Livia noticed that the woman was studying her features very carefully.

"Yes, Grandmother, but I need to find shelter for the night."

The old lady examined her carefully. "You are tired and thirsty . . . You risk dehydration," she added, and Livia was surprised at her use of the rather technical term. She fetched a wooden ladle to the catch basin and scooped up a cup for Livia. The word *zhizu* again came to mind. *Last night bourbon in a bar,* she thought, *and tonight cold clear water in a gourd, certainly more appropriate for a pilgrim.* After she drank the water, the nun took the ladle from her and returned it to a narrow ledge just inside the cave mouth, where Livia could see a few simple kitchen utensils.

"Do you follow the Dao?" Livia asked. The old woman nodded. "Do you follow the Buddha's path?" Again the nun nodded. Then a torrent of barely intelligible words followed, with quick and lively gestures and a wave of her hand toward the heights of the mountain above them.

When it became clear to her that Livia understood little of what she had just said, she shrugged, gave her a gummy smile, and spoke slowly. "No teeth. Hard to talk about important things. Hard to talk about anything!"

Livia nodded, and the woman motioned for Livia to follow her. They walked along a faint path to the right of the cave, entering a craggy ravine where some pine trees had established themselves in the few pockets of earth that had collected in crevices between the rocks. They came to a narrow cave entrance. The nun used the universal symbol of sleep, her cheek against her folded hands, to indicate that this was her place for the night. Livia thanked her profusely, and, turning her body sideways, she slipped into the welcoming space as the woman walked back toward the larger cave. Livia took a deep breath. The air was full of the most beautiful smells, which she traced to a row of small cloth bags standing on a ledge at the left side of the cave. She opened one to see what they contained and found dried herbs inside.

It was just after dusk, but Livia fell asleep immediately, then awakened early the next morning at first light. She enjoyed the warmth for a while, feeling an immense attraction to the thought of living as a hermit in a place such as this: the perfectly clear air, the pure water, the eternal stones, the green of the pine trees, and the blue sky. It was the sense of living close to the most elemental forms of nature. *Just as it came from the hand of God on the first day of creation*—the words recalled from her days at Hillesum, but she could not remember who had written them.

She decided to find the old lady and see if it was possible to get hot water for her tea. She was not there, but Livia found a primitive stove of stones just inside the cave. Two glowing coals burned inside, and a primitive kettle stood next to it, still hot to the touch. The woman had anticipated her need, and on another stone was a chipped ceramic cup with a small pinch of dried leaves in it, obviously meant for her. She poured hot water over the leaves and sniffed. It was not regular tea, but something in the mint family, pleasant to smell. So she sat on a stone, ate her peanut butter and crackers, a banana, and drank the welcome tea. Because this time the recluse had not denied knowing of Bu'er, and because the tea was clearly left for her to enjoy, Livia decided to stay. She would wait for the woman to return from wherever she had gone, and ask her some further questions before moving on toward the unknown terrain to the east.

Time dragged on and the woman did not return. But just as Livia was filling her canteen at the catch basin in preparation for moving on, the recluse reappeared. Without any explanation for her absence, she quickly placed a few dry sticks on the coals in the stone oven. When the flames leapt up she placed a kettle of water to heat over the fire. "I am sorry," Livia said, "I was so tired last night that I did not introduce myself. "I am Wei Liya, an American pilgrim to Wutaishan."

"I am called Mingling," the old woman said. She placed some more mint leaves in Livia's cup and in her own. Then she reached inside the pocket of her robe and took out a piece of paper that had been folded twice, and, almost thoughtlessly, as if it were the most ordinary gesture in the world, she handed it to her. Livia's heart began to race as she unfolded it. There were three Chinese characters written on it: *Who are you?* It was unsigned. Now her heart was beating wildly. She found a pen in her backpack and with her hand trembling, she wrote under the question: *meimei.* Then she refolded the note and returned it to the nun, looking at her quizzically. The woman said: "Do not worry. I will take care of it. You sit here and wait."

She swallowed her tea and made preparations to leave again. Livia took the talisman from around her neck and said: "Take this with you also and give it to her." Mingling took the locket, turned away, and disappeared up the mountain path. Livia realized that the nun had never once mentioned her name, but who else could it be? It was Bu'er. Against enormous odds and on the verge of giving up, she had found her sister.

The nun returned in midafternoon with two pieces of paper that she handed to Livia. One was the original note. At the bottom, underneath the word *meimei*, was the single Chinese character *lai*, "come." The other note was a simple map meant to guide her up the path, crossing a stream, walking through a steep ravine and across a large fallen tree. Some distance beyond the tree, the path jogged to the left and rose to a large cave, then continued on and upward to a second smaller cave entrance. That was where the path stopped. The whole map reminded Livia of a child's treasure hunt map, or a pirate's map that led to the X-marked spot where the treasure was buried. Livia was ready to leave immediately, but the nun said no. It was too late in the day. "She will be expecting you tomorrow morning."

She did not sleep at all, but spent the night thinking about what she would say to her sister, the right Chinese words and phrases to express all the things she wanted to ask and tell her. She went over them again and again in her mind, but for some reason they did not form a natural progression, and she was afraid she would forget them. After tea the next morning, the nun announced that she would take Livia part of the way. "No, Grandmother, please, you have already been up and down twice. I will find it myself."

"Too difficult. Bu'er is wise but not so good at making maps. I will go part of the way." As it was, Livia could barely keep up with the old lady. She recognized the stream, the ravine and the fallen tree, but would have easily gotten lost when the path disappeared among fallen rocks in stone-clogged crevices. At least the map, together with her careful observations on the way up, would help her return. When they reached the fallen pine that had apparently died of old age and been blown down by the wind, the nun pointed Livia in the right direction and said: "The first cave large, the second small. Go to the second cave. Fifteen minutes' walk above the big one."

Livia sat waiting at the entrance of the upper cave, grateful to rest after the difficult ascent. She waited nervously for a few minutes, hardly able to believe that she would actually meet her sister.

And then she came, soundlessly, appearing just outside the entry to the cave, opposite Livia. She wore a cloth wrapped around her head, which she immediately removed. Livia could see that her hair had been shaved, even the hair on her eyebrows. She did not have the marks of incense burning that would have identified her as a Buddhist nun. Her complexion was dark, the skin rough, apparently badly aged by a life outdoors in the sun and wind. She noticed the pale marks on her face as though she had had small pox as a child. But neither the dark complexion nor the facial marks could hide the fact that she had her mother's nose and jaw, a definiteness of feature that gave strength to her face. Her body was mostly hidden under loose-fitting peasant clothes, but she was clearly slender, as her mother had been.

"Jiejie," Livia said. "Elder sister."

"Meimei," she replied, her face serious and alert. She paused. "I did not know that I had an American sister, one who speaks Chinese. Mingling said that you resembled me and I can see that is true."

"I have been looking for you for so long . . . I . . ." Livia felt the tears coming and stopped. Bu'er nodded, and they said nothing else for a few moments, both perhaps overwhelmed by the unlikelihood of this meeting. Livia was familiar enough with Chinese customs to know that she should not try to touch or embrace her sister.

Then Bu'er said, matter-of-factly, "If you had not sent the talisman, I might not have believed who you are. Let us go inside where we can sit down."

They sat on stones, facing each other, their knees just a few feet apart. Unlike the larger cave below, this one showed no evidence that anyone had ever used it as a place to live. Livia looked out at the wide panorama of mountains and felt a sense of security in the shelter of the cave.

"You must be tired. You have come a long way to see me. And suffered many difficulties."

"How do you know about my difficulties?"

"My people have told me. There are members of our group here in the eastern part of Wutaishan, some live in Taihuai, some on farms. You and the two officers were seen."

Then a flood of words poured from Livia, telling Bu'er of their parents—the divorce, the death of Adele, Harold's sickness. Of how she herself had studied about China for many years, of her teaching. She told her sister of the quest to find her, of finding Kaiyuan and Bailian—she was careful to call her Shanghui—and of how the latter had finally told her to come up into this valley.

"I had to make certain that you were really my sister. The government wants to destroy our society. Our two leaders, Heiyen and Guzhi, are already imprisoned."

"Jiejie, do you still have red hair? And was it curly? You get that from our grandmother, you know. Hers turned gray when she was very young." Why did she ask a silly question like that? Livia knew that was a bad start, but now that she had finally found her sister, her mind churned with excitement, and the important questions she had formulated during the night slipped from her mind.

"Mine became gray when I was about forty," Bu'er said. "I was happy because it removed one sign of my Western origin."

"You got that from Granny Manigault. She liked her gray hair, too. But she called it silver. Thought it made her look attractive." Bu'er smiled, as though amused by their grandmother's small vanity. "You don't speak English any longer, do you?"

"I remember only a few words. *Mama, Papa, please, bye-bye.* But the English would come back quickly if I tried to relearn it."

"I think we both have a talent for language. Jiejie, do you remember Mother and Father?" She was suddenly aware of a sort of formality in their exchange.

"I have a few memories, but nothing very clear. I remember sleeping between Father and Mother as a child. I remember the warm feeling. I remember that Father liked to carry me on his shoulders. It was wonderful to look at people from such a great height."

"He is tall. He did that with me, too."

"But it is Mother that I know, not Father."

The words struck her as odd, and Livia wondered briefly if she had misunderstood what Bu'er had just said, but instead of pursuing the point she nervously hurried on to another question. "Do you remember being kidnapped?"

"I do."

"Are you angry with them—I mean, the ones who kidnapped you?"

"I was frightened of them at first, but they were always kind to me. But that was a long time ago and now I am not angry about anything. For forty years they have been my family—they and Mingling whom you have met down below. She is my jiejie. Heiyen and Guzhi, our leaders, are like my father and mother. They took care of me and raised me. I am still part of that larger family."

"What do you mean—your larger family?"

"We call ourselves Siyishe, the FourOne Society."

"Why did they kidnap you?"

"We believe that the spirits sometimes send revelations to the world through mediums. One of the messages they had received before they found me said that a foreign ghost child with red hair would come from across the ocean to be their leader. The child would be under the protection of the god of the northern mountains. And so it happened. When they discovered me, it was their duty to bring me into their community and raise me."

"Do you believe that?" said Livia, thinking of the spirit-writing sects she had studied in Taiwan.

Bu'er looked at Livia curiously. Finally, she answered. "Of course."

"How can you be certain what they told you is true?" she said and immediately regretted it, realizing that she sounded like a lawyer cross-examining her sister.

Bu'er frowned, but eventually said: "Because they are good and honest people. And because I was a white-skinned child with red hair, who came from across the sea. And the god of the northern mountains has protected me. The nunnery where I learned the Dharma and was sheltered for so many years was in the Hengshan mountains." She reached into her pocket and pulled out the talisman, as if to emphasize her point. Then she added: "I have become one of their leaders."

Livia stood up. "Excuse me for a moment," she said, standing suddenly and walking over to the mouth of the cave, to regroup and try to recall the important questions she had planned to ask. She took a deep breath, trying to calm herself. Bu'er's responses suddenly awakened in her a realization that should have been obvious, even before they had met. The two of them would be so utterly different. They shared the same blood, and might even resemble each other a little physically. But now she recognized that there was an immense gulf between them, far wider than the valley between the mountain where she stood and the one she could see in the distance. You could conceivably hike from this mountain to that one, but she wasn't sure there was a way to bridge the gulf between her and her sister. Bu'er had lived in rural China her whole life, and she in urban America. Bu'er was completely Chinese, and she herself was completely American. Despite their shared DNA . . . It would take months, if not years . . . Bu'er's being was shaped by the thoughts of Confucius, Laozi, the Buddha, Zhuangzi, Sima Qian, Han Wudi, Da Mo, and many more of the creators of Chinese culture. They were part of her being, as real as blood.

Livia's own ancestors were a different cast of characters: the Jewish prophets, Socrates, Jesus, Augustine, Aquinas, Dante, Luther, Descartes, Darwin, Freud, and the rest. And, yes, Marx.

She walked back to the stone where she had been sitting, uncertain of how to proceed. Some of her previously formulated questions remained tantalizingly beyond her reach, others she did remember no longer seemed appropriate. Yet despite their clear differences, Livia felt at least one strong bond between them—the sense that both shared the common destiny of all human beings in every culture, shaped by so many inner and outer forces beyond reckoning.

"Jiejie, does this mountain have a name?" she asked, then wondered why such an irrelevant question had popped into her mind.

"It is called Recluse Mountain."

"Because hermits have lived here?"

"Not that so much, but because it is surpassed in size by the mountains that surround it, yet is more important than they are. Just like the five platform mountains of Wutaishan, north, east, south, west, and central, though overshadowed by the peaks around them, are yet the ones with power. Below the earth of some mountains, like this one where we sit, is a network of underground caves, numinous realms, if you know how to find your way in."

Mountains of power? Numinous realms? Livia wondered if she spoke metaphorically or, more likely, referred to actual caverns under the ground where they sat. Or, was it like Bu'er's understanding of the reason for her kidnapping, magical thinking? If so, sadly, Livia could not share the magic. Maybe the holy places of Wutaishan were territories forever forbidden to her profane feet. However beautiful or even sublime they might be, her Western tradition could never rank mountains according to their levels of spiritual power. We can level the mountaintops to get at coal, she thought, carry off the dirt to make roads, and bulldoze them to fill valleys. They are just heaps of geologically shaped chemicals. How can you reverence a heap of chemicals? That, she supposed, was her koan: How can a heap of matter be sacred? Could she and her sister . . . Livia sat down on the stone again, facing her sister, trying to think if there was some way to cross the divide.

Then Bu'er did it for her, in her own way, seemingly without thought or reflection. She stood, walked over to Livia, and placed her hand on Livia's shoulder. It was not the cool distance Chinese tradition might have dictated, nor the warm hug Livia might have wished. But it was something.

"Meimei, I had a strange feeling just now, as you walked away from me . . . that your spirit was leaving me as well."

"Yes, I was thinking how different we are."

"Yet in some ways the same. I think both of us, in our own way, have been searching for our lost family."

"I suppose you're right," she admitted. "When I was young, I hoped that our parents would get back together, but it never happened. Now Mother is dead. Our father is still alive but we do not live together. I think that when I became a Catholic, it was a way too of looking for a family."

"We both have our spiritual families, which are very different . . . But there is something else. Look out there," Bu'er said, pointing toward the entrance of the cave. Livia turned her eyes toward the sky and the mountains outside. "One of our great sages said that 'Heaven is our Father, Earth is our Mother, and even you and I, small beings, have a place in their embrace. And all creatures, great and small, are our brothers and sisters.' Though it is not visible to the eye, there is something that unites us, I believe, and makes us all a family. Perhaps that sort of family," she said, looking gently at her sister, "will have to be enough for us."

It struck Livia that her sister's words were said with great formality and precision. Bu'er seemed so still, so composed, so accepting of things the way they were, as though, having found and affirmed the link between the two of them, she was now ready to move on. Livia's mind raced as she thought what she still needed to say before that happened. "Jiejie, would you ever want to leave China? Come with me back to America, where you would be safe? Getting you to the US consulate would be difficult, but if . . ."

"Physically, it might be possible. I am a nightwalker, I know how to move undetected. I have done so my whole life. But no. My karma has placed me here, just as yours has placed you in America, to be a daughter to our parents in my place . . . to study, to teach . . . and given you courage to come here to find me. I do not know why. The dispensations of Heaven and the results of karma are beyond understanding. I think you want to change things, to make things better. But already, nothing is lacking."

"Jiejie, you are in danger," said Livia, feeling her own courage to be minimal compared to that of her sister. "The authorities could imprison you or even kill you."

"I doubt that they would kill me, but even if they did, my life, while it lasts, is meant to be here, not in America. Mingling is with me. Heiyen and Guzhi are still alive, and so many others who depend on me. My purpose is not to add years to my life. One can run for a thousand miles but never escape karma."

"I am sorry Mom died before she was able to meet you. She understood about karma and would have been able to understand you, probably better than I."

"I have already met her." The words were so common that Livia almost let them slip by again, thinking that she must be referring to her early childhood at the mission. She was just about to hurry on to her next point, that their father was still alive and how wonderful it would be if he could meet her before he died. But suddenly the other possibility dawned on her.

"What you just said . . . you have already met Mother. What did you mean?"

"Many years ago, Heiyen and Guzhi asked me to contact my ancestral spirits. I told them I did not know my grandparents, so I could not contact them. And that my parents were probably still alive. So there was no one in the spirit world to contact . . . But then, about four or five years ago, she came. I was not sure, then, but from what you have told me, I now know it was her."

Livia did not believe what she was hearing. But she could not bring herself to say the words of skepticism that arose in her mind. So she said nothing.

Finally, Bu'er spoke again, "You said before that she asked you to come find me?"

"Yes. She had a feeling that you were still alive."

"Now she knows . . . There must have been some unfinished karma between Mother and me, as there is between you and me, that led us to come together. Now our time is too short to do more than acknowledge it . . . I must keep moving. But if we do not have the opportunity to work it out in this lifetime, there will be another. There is always time." The gap again. Then her sister added: "Karma has caused many meetings and separations in my lifetime, including this one. I do not want to create the need for any more."

Livia suddenly felt that she should go, leaving her sister to the destiny that had chosen her. They talked for a while longer, yet there was a tentative quality to their words, as though each was conscious of their inability to accomplish very much. They sat then without words for a while, in a communion of silence, and it did not seem awkward. Livia could not believe that her mother's spirit had come to talk with her sister. And yet . . . in her own heart, ridiculously, she felt a pang of jealousy. Swallowing her skepticism, she took a timid step to cross the divide again: "Jiejie, when Mother came, what did she say to you?"

Just then there was a loud sound that rose in intensity, fell, then stopped. "Did you hear that noise?" asked Bu'er.

"I think I did. Could it be the wind playing tricks in the cave?"

"I do not think it was a natural sound."

"I'll go and see."

"Wait. May I keep this?" asked Bu'er, holding up the *Beiyue* talisman in her right hand and taking Livia's hand once more with her left. She squeezed it, and feeling the strong and hardened hand, Livia thought of how different their lives had been, and yes, would continue to be.

"Of course. The talisman is yours. I think Mother kept it for the time when she could give it to you."

"So she did," said Bu'er, letting go of Livia's hand. She made a slight bow toward her and said with an odd look on her face, almost mischievous, "Tell Shanghui that I will never again forget to keep it with me."

Livia walked outside the cave mouth to see if she could discover the source of the noise. There was silence. The colors of the mountainscape had become more vivid, as they do toward the late afternoon. She had just enough time for a momentary appreciation of the rich blue, green, and ochre panorama of the sky and earth when she heard a sound to her left and saw three men, uniformed and armed, come around the crest of the hill. They were followed by a man wearing a neatly pressed gray Mao jacket. It was Chairman Tang. Her momentary feeling of relief died suddenly, and the words of greeting choked in her throat when she realized what he had done. She thought of Bu'er, trapped in the cave like a cornered animal. The hunters stopped.

"You bastard. God damn you to hell," she screamed at him in English, meaning every word of the ancient curse. She trembled with frustration, knowing it was too late to rush into the cave and warn her sister.

Tang did not understand most of her words but got the import. "I assume that was not a compliment," he said. He made a quick gesture with his hand, ordering the three soldiers into the cave. Livia made a futile attempt to block them, the first man shoving her roughly aside as they strode past.

"As Comrade Deng Xiaoping so wisely said, Miss Wei, whether it is a black cat or a white cat doesn't matter, as long as it catches the mouse. Captain Xi was the black cat, I am the white cat, and I have caught the mouse."

"I wouldn't be so sure," said Livia hopefully, remembering the look on Bu'er's face. "You may be the gods of the city, but these mountains are not in your jurisdiction." He looked at her strangely, searching for the irony.

One of the men ran outside. "Chairman, she is not here. The cave goes on."

"You have flashlights," he said angrily, pointing his finger at him. "You and Han follow the cave. Tell Jin to come out here and search around the back in case there is another exit." He looked back at her. "Go back to America, Miss Wei, you are no longer useful to us. We would be pleased to return you to Taihuai by jeep, but that would be against regulations. You will have to get back there yourself."

Livia was free. As she turned to leave she could not resist saying, over her shoulder: "Chairman Tang, as one of your wise men said long ago, the best traveler leaves no tracks." She left them to their search and walked quickly away, retracing her way down the mountain, intending to warn Mingling of their coming. But the old lady was also an excellent traveler, and Livia found no trace of her in the cave at the bottom of the path. Could her sister have gotten here so quickly? Livia checked the smaller cave, around back where she had slept the night before. The only evidence there of the old woman's presence was the faint smell of herbs that still lingered in the air like the wake of a ghost.

Livia had kept her promise and now it was time to go home. But before leaving she had one final duty to her mother. She reached into her backpack for the small blue silk bag, then emptied the contents on the ledge where the sweet-smelling herbs had been. Why Captain Xi had not questioned her about the small bag, she could not say. Perhaps a little bag of ashes had seemed to him like nothing at all. Or maybe it explained everything.

The next morning, Livia stood at the Taihuai station waiting for the nine o'clock bus to Datong. She had dropped a plain postcard in the mail at the local post office, addressed to Shanghui. Without a signature, it said only, *The talisman has been returned to its owner. Thank you.*

It was a few minutes before the hour, and the bus stood ready to go, the engine running. The door opened, and passengers began to board. She was the last of five people in line, but as she was about to get on, she looked to her right and saw Captain Xi Guiting coming toward her, alone. He walked in front of the bus and signaled the driver to wait. He extended his hand toward Livia, likely complying with what he understood to be the Western custom. "Professor Wayman," he said, pronouncing her English name with accuracy. "You may like to know. They have not found her . . . yet. I came to say good-bye." There was sincerity, not malice in his face. The black cat, too, had been playing his role.

She took his hand and looked closely into his eyes. There was a question there, something still unresolved. She knew what it was.

"As you may have guessed, it was a matter of family." She did not elaborate, and although there was no smile, something in his face changed and she knew that he now understood at least part of the puzzle. "Do you think that family is as important in China today as it was in the past?"

"More important," he answered without hesitation, "now that it is no longer taken for granted . . . The ashes, yes?" She only nodded, and he seemed to understand that he would get no further explanation. He turned and walked slowly back toward his office as she boarded the bus.

And in her mind as she took her seat, like a mantra: *Every grain of sand, every blade of grass . . .*

Book Club Discussion Questions

1. Among the novel's themes, family is central. How is family broken for both Livia and Bu'er, and how do they try to mend it?
2. Rudyard Kipling once famously wrote: "East is East and West is West, and never the twain shall meet." Do they, in fact, meet in *A Call to China*? In what ways? Have you experienced the meeting of East and West?
3. The climax of the novel in the final chapter takes place at Wutaishan, the famous and ancient pilgrimage site of North China. Is Livia's quest a pilgrimage?
4. Each sister has a kind of religious awakening. What are the circumstances surrounding each experience? How is the inadequacy of words and language to express religious experience described in the novel?
5. Christianity and Buddhism are the religions most prominent in the novel. As ancient traditions with many followers, they are perhaps easy to accept as important. What about the small sectarian religion of the FourOnes? Can the reader take it seriously?
6. Choose one of the secondary and supporting characters, such as Mingling, Heiyen, Guzhi, Mayor Ma Jin, Bailian, Long Nail, Henry, or Naomi. Show how this character contributes to one of the themes of the novel.
7. How does the novel deal with the position of women in society, in China and the U.S.?
8. There are some parallel experiences in the lives of Livia and Bu'er, among them sexual trauma, struggle with leadership figures, success and failure. Discuss how these parallel experiences are both similar and different for the two sisters.

About the Author

Jeffrey Meyer has always felt a connection to China. He felt his "call to China" as a young boy, after reading Pearl Buck's *The Good Earth* and Lin Yutang's *The Importance of Living*. He would go on to devote his life and career to learning the Chinese culture.

Jeffrey earned a degree in History of Religions with a focus on Chinese religions from the University of Chicago. He has lived in Taiwan and China, researching symbolic architecture, sectarian spirit-writing, and moral education. While abroad, he was also a student learning the language and a Chinese history teacher to American students. He has traveled extensively throughout the region.

A professor at the University of North Carolina at Charlotte for thirty-five years, Jeffrey taught Asian religions in the Religious Studies department, with a focus on Buddhism and Daoism. He is married with three grown children, currently living in Davidson, North Carolina. *A Call to China* is his first novel.

CPSIA information can be obtained
at www.ICGtesting.com
Printed in the USA
LVHW091543120619
621000LV00004B/63/P

9 780996 686471